A Silver Moon for Rose
a novel

Ruth Bass

A Silver Moon for Rose
by Ruth Bass

E.P.I.C. Publishing Services, LLC
www.epicpublish.com

Printed in the United States of America
ISBN: 978-0-9913270-7-2

For Miltie,

a/k/a H. P.

Acknowledgements

It says, up front, that these characters have nothing to do with the living or the dead in real life. But what is actually true is that the Rose Hibbard trilogy is based on several kernels of truth about the life of my grandmother, Rosa Adelaide Warner Haskins, to whom I am grateful – not only for providing the inspiration for my fictionalizing her life, but also because she was dear friend and role model for me. Her mother died young, and she took over the household and coped with my increasingly difficult great-grandfather – and she went to school across the street at the age of three, all of which are part of "Sarah's Daughter." I owe her a great deal because thinking about her teen years pushed me into fiction after a career of minding the facts in the newspaper world.

Again, for this final chapter in Rose's life, I thank Cia Elkin for her meticulous work in editing me once more and going over the manuscript page by page with me. Granddaughter Summer Wojtas gets credit for the cover design of "A Silver Moon," and was extraordinarily patient while I changed my mind, changed the title and asked for detailed fixes. Michael, Elissa and Amy Bass continued to encourage me, especially after my major editor and partner, Milton, died before the book was finished. His critiques of my writing were always the most valuable.

I also thank people who have contributed in some way to the emergence of this new novel, including Charlotte Finn, Judith Viorst, Robb Forman Dew, Kimberly Cooney, Jackie Harmon Moffatt, Alan Wallach, Dan Greengold, Jayne Church and publisher Wendy Vincent. Now it's a trilogy, and the Hibbard family and friends can get on with their lives without me.

A Silver Moon for Rose

A Silver Moon for Rose is the third book of the Sarah's Daughter Trilogy. Other books in the series are:

Sarah's Daughter (Gadd & Company Publishers, Inc., 2007)
Rose (Gadd & Company Publishers, Inc., 2010)

For additional information on these titles, as well as other books by Ruth Bass, visit www.ruthbass.com

CHAPTER ONE
Hattie's Secret

Hattie Munson rummaged through the top drawer of the chest in her bedroom, pushing aside her best black leather gloves and two silk scarves in her search for the well-worn white gloves that she knew had to be in there. She sighed, thinking that it would be easier to find things if she sorted everything once or twice a year the way she had been taught. But she did hate sorting.

Ah, there they were, fingers still intact but palms a little stained and the wrist edges frayed. They would suit perfectly for blacking the stove, another task she found odious. She might not organize gloves and scarves regularly, but she always tended properly to caring for the big stove in the kitchen. It was her life, really, when you thought about it. Heat, food and the comfort of warmth.

She took a small white cap out of the drawer, put it on and tied it under her chin. She had a habit of smoothing her hair back from her face, and she didn't need any of that blacking getting into her hair. In the house, no one would see her in the cap, and it actually felt good. She had always liked the caps and bonnets they made her wear at the village, so she'd taken them with her.

Next she pulled out the oversized man's shirt she kept just for this task and put it on over her house dress. Mr. Munson had been a sizable man, and this was far better than an apron. Now she was ready for the behemoth in the kitchen. It was amazing, she thought, how that stove consumed time as well as firewood. What with getting it going in the morning, seeing to the dampers to make the fire hotter or not so hot, emptying the ashes and keeping the wood box filled, she spent more time on that stove than nearly anything else in her life.

She opened the black wax and daubed some on the rag of toweling she had saved for just that purpose. She began to rub the wax on the cast-iron stove, starting with the curlicue shelves at the top, the hardest part really, since she had to keep the wax from clumping up in the openwork. She wondered how often the housewives of Eastborough blacked their stoves – with their children and chickens and husbands to see to, they had less time for this chore than she did. Still, from what she'd seen in a house or two, they were quite meticulous housekeepers. She had to hand them that. Anyway, she did the stove once a month, and it had not one iota of rust anywhere.

Her white-gloved hands, getting darker by the minute, moved across the lids and stove top, then the oven door and the shelf on the side where she dried her scarves and mittens in the winter. She had risen early, kindled only the smallest fire to make her oatmeal and coffee for breakfast and then let it die out. The kitchen was cooling down, but never mind. She was quick, and she'd soon be done with it and start a new fire. Besides, this was a task to keep a body pretty warm. Elbow grease her father had called it. She didn't know where that phrase came from and thought it likely her elbows had no muscles at all, never mind grease. Her whole arm would be a trifle sore by nightfall.

As she bent over to wax under the oven door, she wondered if Abby Hibbard might know how to wax a stove. Rose had taught her sister many things, and Miss Abby might be just the one she could get to take over this job next time around. She smiled, thinking about not ever polishing the stove again, then straightened slowly, putting one hand behind her back where it tended to kink up. Come to think of it, Rose Hibbard could probably tell her where "elbow grease" originated. Rose seemed to know every word there was. But she wasn't of a mind to ask her.

"Thunderation," she said aloud, enjoying the forbidden word. "Now I reckon I've smeared some blacking on my shirt." She pulled off the soiled gloves, tossed them into the stove and unbuttoned the big shirt. Well, she had smudged that but spared the dress, she found to her relief. Just as she laid the shirt over the rocking chair arm in the kitchen, she heard a sharp rap at the door. As she pulled the curtain aside to see who was there she remembered, too late, that her Shaker cap was still on her head. Jason Harris was on her doorstep.

"Thunderation," she muttered again, under her breath this time but still enjoying the feel of the phrase. She moved the bolt and pulled open the door, watching Jason's face to see whether his eyes would spot the cap. He gave no sign but instead pointed to the sheet-covered object behind him on the porch.

"It's your table, Hattie. Finished at last, I reckon. Ready for you to run your hand over it and see if it's smooth enough to suit your fancy. Shall I bring it in?"

She brightened, forgetting that she was hardly dressed to receive visitors, even one who was doing some work for her. She invited him in, and he picked up the covered table and set it in her kitchen.

"Shall I whisk off the cover the way magicians do?" he asked.

"However you please," Hattie answered. "I confess I'm anxious to see it."

Jason whipped the old sheet aside, and in spite of herself, Hattie gasped softly. It was truly beautiful. He had taken part of a tree and turned it into a piece of art. A useful piece of art, she reminded herself. The small table gleamed, the warm tones of the cherry wood coming through the coats of varnish he had put on. This would be pricey, she knew, but she had a place for it in her parlor, and she would get her money's worth just admiring it.

"You like it," Jason said, grinning. "Better run your hand over it, make sure it's like glass, or whatever it was you said."

Such a handsome man, Hattie thought, this widower every unmarried woman in town, no matter her age, was looking at. It had amused her to watch them shift their customary seats in church so they would be certain of at least greeting Jason Harris when he left on Sunday mornings. Sometimes his aisle looked as crowded as a pig sty after the feed is poured into the trough. She'd had a few thoughts about him herself, but she was of no mind to get married. She'd done that and paid dearly for it. Well, she thought, trying to be a little more honest about it, she'd also been paid dearly, hadn't she.

She focused on the table again. "It looks sturdy as well as handsome," she allowed. "You must have found a well-behaved tree in that woodlot of yours." Her eyes narrowed briefly. "Worth waiting for, I do believe."

12

Jason nodded. "Better try out those hinges on the leaves," he said, adding quietly, "my apologies for the long delay, but it took some time before I was ready to get at this kind of work again."

Hattie nodded in her turn but decided not to say anything sympathetic about Nell's death. She lifted one of the leaves and heard not the slightest creak or squeak. She lowered it again and smiled. It was more beautiful than she had expected, but she resolved not to ooh and aah until the bill was in her hand. As if he had heard her thought, Jason fetched a small slip of paper from his pocket, folded it and handed it to Hattie. "If it satisfies, that would be the freight," he said. "I did warn you that it wouldn't be cheap."

She tucked the slip in the pocket of her skirt without looking at it. Time enough for that later on. "Would you set it in the parlor, Jason?" she asked. "And then you'd better skedaddle or people will begin to wonder why your horse is outside this house for more than a half minute."

Jason chuckled. "Oh, no, Hattie. They won't consider it for a tick. You're the one who would ponder such a thing if you saw my horse outside a farmhouse while the farmer was in the barn or throwing wood or tapping trees."

That made Hattie laugh, too. She did love a juicy bit of gossip, and she knew she had a talent for hearing things and seeing things that other people walked right past. And all the church-going in the world wouldn't keep her from passing on what she learned and maybe adding a touch of embroidery as she did so. It was, actually, one of the reasons she went to church. She certainly didn't go because of the Rev. Lockhead and his pious sermons. Ah, someday she'd learn something truly interesting about him. She was certain of that. She was looking forward to it.

She stepped into the parlor and saw that Jason had placed the small table next to her Boston rocker. It truly was beautiful. She thanked him again and saw him out, grateful that he had not inquired about the small cap on her head. She'd wager he saw it, though, and was glad he had a reputation for being tight-mouthed. She took off the cap and fingered its thin netting. Eldress Miriam had never called it a cap, she remembered. She called it a "neat." No wonder. Hattie knew every hair on her head was in place because of the "neat."

Her thoughts returned to Jason. He really would pretend he hadn't seen her odd head wear. In all her visits to his workshop while the table was being built, she'd never heard him say a word about his brother-in-law, Miss Abby's father. And he could have, she was certain. Silas Hibbard had stirred up a lot of talk by carrying on with that hotel woman several years back, and Hattie still wondered about the way that woodpile had fallen on Silas' wife and crushed her to death. But this town protected its own, and she had only lived here fifteen years, give or take, so she was "from away," as they liked to say. Why, that Nessie Brown over near the tracks had lived in Eastborough close to thirty-five years, and she wasn't a local yet.

She tucked the ties inside her cap and removed the paper from her pocket. Seventy-five dollars. She knew it would be costly, but she could afford it. She would go by there tomorrow, perhaps even later today, with the full payment in cash. She smiled, thinking that would place her horse and buggy outside the widower's house. Perhaps she would stay for a cup of tea. She smiled again. He really is quite a handsome man – and

14

charming, she thought. A lot more charming than Silas Hibbard, who so often seemed gruff and whose black eyebrows often pulled together in a frown. But she supposed some of those unmarried women had their eye on him, too. Men hereabouts didn't stay single for long. They all needed wives to tend the fire, cook the food, empty the chamber pots and ... she didn't even want to think about it. Perhaps she really could get Miss Abby to do some of those things for her. The child had certainly been well-trained by her mother and then by Rose, and she must be twelve or so by now. High time she found a way to earn part of her keep. It was hard to imagine that Silas Hibbard's fancy chickens were any way to make a proper living. She shuddered at the thought of chickens running around pecking at things in the dirt. She did hate chickens, at least the live ones.

Hattie tapped the stove with her finger. It felt cool to the touch, but she opened the firewood door and poked in the ashes to see if any coals remained. She grabbed a handful of the slivers of wood she kept for just this situation and carefully fed them into the gray mass. Amazingly, a spark flew, and she blew on it, pleased to see the shreds of wood catch. She fetched some small sticks from the wood box and placed them in a row above the kindling. She closed the door and figured the fire would blaze up by the time she had changed out of her house dress. It was time to harness Annabelle and take a trip to Mr. Goodnow's . She did hope Henry Goodnow would have replenished his supply of tea by now. She put great store by a cup of tea made properly, and his offerings had been meager for the past fortnight.

Upstairs, Hattie hung her house dress on a hook on the closet door and put on a long, gray and cream plaid dress with a high collar and a tight waist. She had put on her corset first thing

15

that day, knowing that she'd be going out. She glanced at herself in the glass and nodded. She still had her shape, she thought. She was of no mind to let herself go the way some of these women in Eastborough did. Still, she knew it was partly because they had all borne children, and she was grateful that she had managed to escape that. She often aimed a critical eye at the way they brought up their offspring, but in her secret heart she knew she would not have been what was called "a good mother." Before she left the room, she went to her desk, opened the small middle drawer and counted out $75. She tucked the money in her pocket.

Back downstairs, Hattie threw a thick blue shawl over her shoulders and headed for her barn, harnessed her horse and backed her out of the stall. Annabelle was tossing her head, eager to set out, and backed right into the bars on the buggy. Minutes later, they were on their way to town, bouncing a bit as the wheels went in and out of the slightly frozen ruts in the road. It would be more like mud by the time she headed home, Hattie thought. Spring may be the best time of the year, but it's hard on roads. And one's back, she sighed, as the wheels hit a sharp dip.

CHAPTER TWO
Of Caps and Chickens

On his way to take care of his Chinese chickens, Jason Harris pondered the morning visit to Hattie's place. He was quietly pleased that she had been taken with the table, a piece he had made with great care and, if the truth be known, had hated to part with. But what was that odd cap she was wearing? Some idea was niggling around in his head, but he couldn't think where he had seen such before. He'd wager no one else in Eastborough had anything like that. And certainly Hattie had never worn it to church. She had seemed a bit fussed when she opened the door, so he wondered if it had something to do with the cap. Or mebbe just the fact that she'd been caught waxing her stove.

No one in town knew much about her, except that she had high-falutin' tastes and the means to serve them, apparently. She had moved in, mebbe a dozen years ago now, without telling anyone anything about where she came from or why she had decided to live in their town.

Her reticence to talk about herself made him chuckle. She made up for it by talking about everyone else constantly, to the point where most of the women folk were wary of being in her presence. But he'd noticed that the men liked to talk to her, if they could manage a chat without upsetting their wives. He enjoyed a conversation with her himself. And now, he chuckled again, she's going to make trouble by coming around here to pay for the table, hitching her horse to my post and setting the neighbors' tongues wagging.

He didn't care. He wasn't even slightly interested in gossip or in any relationship with Hattie other than what they already had. His heart still ached over the loss of Nell, gone now for only three years and leaving a space a hundred times her size in his house and his days. He felt his eyes start to water and shook himself hard. No time for that, he told himself. The chickens need feeding, they need new litter on the floor and new straw in their nests, and then I'll have to see to the rest of the animals.

He lengthened his stride and had almost reached the barn when he heard the sound of a buggy on the road above the house. Ah, she had already set out on her day's rounds, he thought, as Hattie Munson and her little horse Annabelle whirled by. He went into the barn, scooped out a pail of grain from the big open barrel and yelped with surprise as a large rat scrambled out of the bucket, dropped to the floor and scurried out of sight.

"Gol dang it," he said aloud. A man should know better than to dip into a grain barrel without looking, he chided himself. This was the third time Jason had seen the rat, and he was hoping it was the same one, not part of a clan. He'd tried several different covers for the barrel, but the rat figured them out as if he were a person and had gnawed his way right through one slab of wood. Jason dipped a second pail into the water trough outside the barn door and walked along behind his three cows to the small door that led into the chicken house. As he lifted the latch, the commotion began, which made him smile. These ladies – and the roosters – were always glad to see him and he them. He understood why Abby always wanted to see his chickens. The Bantam Cochins were so soft.

Silas feels the same way about the chickens, he thought. It had been a surprise when his brother-in-law announced that he was spending his hard-earned cash on fancy chickens. But he could see that Silas had taken a shine to the Cochins, and against Jason's advice, he'd introduced them into the same space where the Rhode Island Reds had been for years. "Working fine," Silas had said after a week or so. "They don't seem to give a dang about each other's looks." So Jason had retreated, oddly pleased that his prickly brother-in-law had been right for once.

It didn't happen often, Jason thought, thinking back to when a poorly piled stack of wood had crushed Sarah Hibbard and left Silas with three children and no notion of how to carry on. He had dealt badly with Rose, with the schoolteacher who wanted to help her, with the two young ones and, to top it all off, with the cat. Rose never mentioned her father kicking Sarah's cat, but Abby had told him all about it when she was staying with him and Nell for a spell. Jason didn't think anyone kicked cats, and it bothered him for some time, although he never said a word to Silas. No need to stir up trouble for Abby, and the cat was fine. He'd checked on that.

He picked up the galvanized trough and banged it against the wall to get rid of remnants of grain and whatever chicken droppings might have been in it. It was strange how these supposedly domesticated birds fouled their nests and their food. Their wild counterparts were so careful not to do that. After the birds had flown, he'd taken a look at a finch nest tucked into a piece of gingerbread trim on his porch and noticed that it was ringed with tiny gray beads. Turned out they weren't decoration but just the adult birds' way of moving baby bird droppings out of the soft center of the nest. Chickens, Chinese or not, weren't that neat. He filled the trough with fresh grain, and the chickens, waiting at his feet, lined up on both sides and began to eat. Then he took the round container that held their water, opened the window and dumped it outside. He put a small amount of water from his pail into the pan and swirled it, tossing that out the window as well. By and large, he thought, these Cochins were pretty clean, but they drank with grain on their beaks, and it tended to harden up in the pan.

He kept their dishes about as good as the ones in the kitchen, Jason thought to himself. Well, why not. They couldn't do for themselves, and he'd invited them here, hadn't he. And he had to admit, those long days after Nell's passing he had spent extra time down here with the chickens. He had found it comforting that they just went on with their lives, today the same as yesterday and tomorrow promising to be the same again. Mebbe they were dumb, he thought, but they dealt with their days a minute at a time, and he was learning to do that, too.

Shakers, he realized suddenly. Hattie had talked about furniture she'd seen at that village where the Shakers lived, back when she'd asked him to make the table. That cap, he'd wager a fresh egg, was Shaker headgear, and Mrs. Harriet Munson had more than a stopping-in connection to the people she'd taken her design idea from. No wonder she'd been so flustered when she answered the door – she'd realized too late that she was wearing the cap, and he was prob'bly the one person in Eastborough who would find it interesting.

Jason left the chicken house, made certain of the latch and then dropped the hook in place as well. You'd think a hen could lift a latch for all my precautions, he told himself. But he always double-closed this door. The Cochins had been pricey, and he wasn't about to lose them to a careless moment. In the main part of the barn, he put away his buckets, checked the grain barrel to see if the rat had returned and then hunted up a sheet of metal to cover it. He'll find his way in, he told himself, shaking his head. And he's not just getting a share of the grain. He's a filthy creature. At least that's what Rose said.

Thinking about Rose calmed Jason as he made his way back to the house. That girl had such a soothing effect on everyone, including her difficult father. She couldn't be all sunny inside all the time, but she didn't set her worries out in front of the rest of the world very often. He grinned. When she did, he thought, people sat up and took notice, including Silas Hibbard and any children who misbehaved in that one-room schoolhouse where she was teaching.

His grin faded. High time she left the teacher's chair and married Newton Barnes, wasn't it? Three years since Nell's death and a little more than that since the night Rose and Newton had come to say they were engaged to be married. He'd bet two eggs Newton expected that ceremony to be a past event by now. Silas, of course, wouldn't ask her – he was just grateful she was back home for the time being, and he wasn't about to knock over full milk pails. Jason wondered if an uncle had any rights of interference. He'd think on it.

CHAPTER THREE
Endlessly Engaged

As it happened, Rose was thinking on it, too. Looking out over her class of beginning pupils, she felt as if her head were coming apart. These little ones had learned so much this year, and she was proud of that. She could teach, she really could. From the first day she herself had been a pupil here, just three years old, she had thought the teacher a supreme being. Now there's something, she considered, that the Rev. Lockhead wouldn't approve of a-tall. No supreme beings among us sinners, just the one – was that a capital O? – we can't see and mostly can't hear even if we try.

She pulled her thoughts back to the class. It was her third year, and she knew it was even more successful than the other two, even though Mr. Clyde Hawkes had praised her for the way all "her" children performed when they moved on to his classroom at age nine or so. But she was being pulled in two directions, as hard as folks yanked on taffy at the square dances. She loved it here where she could open up new worlds for the ten or twelve little minds in front of her. And she had to admit, as she'd confessed to Alice and Emily, that she enjoyed primping for school each day instead of putting on a house dress and scrubbing the floor. And then she nearly bit her tongue in two, realizing that, married to Peter Granger for the past year, Emily had worn many a house dress and mopped many a floor. But her friend had just laughed and, with a glint of mischief in her eye, had remarked that marriage wasn't just about calico dresses and mops and that she primped every evening before she went to bed. Rose, who was accustomed to falling into bed to sleep as long as possible, could not imagine "primping" for the occasion, but still, she couldn't imagine wearing her nearly threadbare nightgowns in front of a man. It really was time to marry Newton. The teaching, she had promised him, was just an intermission, a space between two parts of her life. And she should have moved along to the next act.

He had been patient, but she knew he had expected to be married long since. She was nearly twenty, and she reckoned the whole town was talking about her endless engagement by now. Even Mr. Goodnow had raised an eyebrow when she went last August to order some new supplies for her class.

"Figured you'd be buying fabric for a long white gown by now, Rose," he'd said in his kindly way.

"It's not quite time," Rose had answered. "I don't seem to be quite ready."

He had put his hand on her arm and asked her if she was afraid getting married meant being wedded to a stove and a chicken house, and she had looked at the floor without answering. It did seem a little like that. Mr. Goodnow often put his finger right on her difficulties, which was most distracting at times. She loved Newton, but she loved her pupils, too. And she'd be exchanging all this for long days of washing clothes, keeping the fire going and cooking the meals. She wished she could have it all, but she knew that was plain impossible. Against the law in this state to have married women teaching. It didn't make sense. It wasn't as if a body lost her brain when she said "I do." But it was the law, and that was that. It was the very thing that had taken Ruthann Harty out of the classroom and put her in it, so she ought to be a tad grateful for the rule.

She went back to thinking about the debate going on in her head. She knew she loved Newton far more than she loved this classroom. Sometimes she woke in the morning aching to be with him instead of in her old bed at her father's house. But the shadow of her mother hung over her when it came to being a housewife. Sarah Hibbard had always looked so tired by nightfall. Rose remembered her mother's morning smile, but she had an even clearer picture of how Sarah's mouth became a thin line by the time they turned down the wicks on the lamps. She remembered even more clearly how she had to take over all those daily duties when her mother was gone – and how she had thought almost every day that she did not want to become her mother, much as she loved her.

"Excuse me, Miss Hibbard," a small voice said.

"Yes, Hope?"

"I need to go out, ma'am," the child said anxiously.

"You may go, Hope," Rose said, not envying anyone the need to use the school outhouse, which badly needed repair work and was therefore quite cold and drafty. At least, while things were still thawing out, it didn't smell too bad.

She turned back to the class. They were fidgeting today. This was the fifth or sixth child who had asked to go to the outhouse, which was most unusual. After the third one, she'd gone out to make sure they didn't have a puppy or a kitten in there. But no, it was just the empty privy, and if you had permission, it gave you a way to leave your chair. She sighed. An hour of the day stretched out in front of her, and she needed to do something special. Turning to the blackboard, she erased all the numbers and letters they had worked on earlier and drew a large circle and then two smaller ones next to it.

"You will take turns," she said, "adding one line to this until we have a picture of something. If the chalk pauses, your turn is over." The children perked up almost immediately. "Your line can be straight, curved or angled, but you must not hesitate. Who knows what hesitate means?"

Jared's hand shot up, and she nodded to him.

"It's when there's a space, Miss Hibbard," he said, standing in his place as they had all been taught to do. "When the chalk stops to take a rest."

"Exactly," Rose said. "You may go first, and then you may choose the next person."

She heard a shuffle as all the children moved eagerly to the edge of their seats. They were intrigued with this new thing, and she hoped it wouldn't disappoint them. She watched as Jared carefully drew a swooping line that connected the large circle with one of the smaller ones. He handed the chalk back to Rose and chose Allen to follow him.

The game went on, and Rose watched as the drawing seemed to be some odd thing on wheels with smoke coming out of the top and eyes in the middle of the large circle. The children were laughing now, but not when they were at the board. As they took the chalk, they became very intent on pulling a line without stopping. Once in a while, the chalk squeaked, making Rose

25

shiver, but most of the time it went smoothly. Watching, she hoped no adults would appear in the doorway for any reason and see this ridiculous project. She smiled to herself. She would tell them it was chalk practice, that these little ones needed to learn how to use chalk better. As the last child added a line, Rose asked if anyone knew what the picture was. Jared raised his hand again.

"Yes, Jared?"

"I believe it's just a Thing, Miss Hibbard," he said. "And I like it, ma'am," he added.

"I like it, too," Rose said. "And now you may go, row by row as usual, to get your wraps. You are dismissed, and I will see you all in the morning."

"Good afternoon, Miss Hibbard," they said in such perfect unison that it was hard to believe no one had given them a signal.

"Good afternoon to all of you," she answered. As they trooped out in an orderly fashion, she sat down at her desk and began to neaten up the papers and books that had been scattered during the day.

Three minutes later, the little building was quiet. She could see her father's house across the street, and all was quiet there, too. She smoothed a few stray hairs away from her face, then took a fresh sheet of paper and drew a line down the middle. She would make a list of whys and wherefores and sort out her thinking. She wrote "Wife" at the top of the left-hand column and "Teacher" at the top of the other. Then, suddenly, she laughed out loud. What on earth was she thinking? She was going to be married. She was going to stop saying "goodnight" and "safe home" to Newton whenever it was time for them to go their separate ways. She was going to cook his meals, wash his

26

clothes, mop the floor, keep the fire burning, sew on his buttons and make the bed they would sleep in together. Whatever they did all day, they would end up in that bed, and she had to admit – only to herself – that she was looking forward to it mightily. She liked being close to Newton, she liked the shivery feeling that sometimes ran from her neck to her ankles when he touched her. She sometimes felt downright sinful about her wish to be closer and closer to him.

The Rev. Lockhead would be shocked, she thought, twirling her pen. It was a good thing the preacher had no idea what was going on deep inside the heads of his parishioners – she was certain plenty of them had wandering thoughts while he shouted his messages from the pulpit. Once, a little worried about her thoughts, she had told Ruthann how guilty she felt, and the teacher had laughed at her.

"I'd be a sight more worried if you had no thoughts about any of that," Ruthann had said. "Your only real problem is that you are split in two – wanting to be in two places at once and teetering around as if you were on a raft trying to keep your balance. I say, 'Jump in, young lady,' while you're still young enough to swim."

That had made Rose laugh out loud. Sometimes Ruthann seemed to teeter, too, but she wasn't going to tell her that. She remembered how the teacher had waited a long time before she wore her engagement ring where the town could see it. Maybe, Rose thought, maybe Ruthann had some reservations about getting married before she said I do. Perhaps she ought to go visiting on Saturday and see about that.

Rose crumpled the list and tossed it into the stove where the embers were dying down. Her desk cleared, she wiped down the blackboard, threw her shawl around her shoulders, checked the stove once more and went to check out the privy, lifting her skirt a little to keep the hem out of the mud. It's merely a precaution, she told herself, as she lifted the rusted latch and slowly opened the door. Nothing was amiss, so she shut the door and went on her way, wondering how best to get word to Newton that she wanted to see him tonight. It was, she reckoned, nearly warm enough to sit on her rock. Well, perhaps not. But perhaps Newton would think to bring his buffalo robe. It was where she did all her best thinking, although it was much harder to keep her mind in order when he was beside her. But, she thought, blushing a little, it was where she could be truly alone with him.

She thought it might be quite forward of her, despite the engagement, to go directly to Eliva Barnes with her message. But Abby could go. That was it. She'd send a message with Abby, who was always itching to get out of the house and away from any possible chores these days.

Rose pulled her shawl closer. Spring might be coming, but that was a bone-chilling wind coming at her. And the robins were not back from their wintering in the south.

CHAPTER FOUR
Invitation to the Rock

The object of all this thinking was working along the trough behind his five Jersey heifers with a square, long-handled shovel, scraping up manure and flinging it into the wooden wheelbarrow. When it was full, he trundled it up the ramp outside the barn door and dumped it on top of the pile that had been accumulating all winter. Feed one end and it comes out the other, he grumbled to himself. But he didn't really dislike the task. It was one of those chores where he could see his progress clearly, and he'd never minded the smell – would Rose say aroma, he wondered? – of manure. Hen manure, now, that was a different thing. No one would call that stench an aroma.

He chuckled to himself. The more time he spent with Rose, the more his brain seemed to work like hers. A few years back, he'd never have thought of comparing cow and hen manure. Mr. Chandler slurred it all together, which took a little getting used to the first time he said it. Hemanure. In any case, it always smelled awful, and Newton knew his nose was probably just reflecting the way he felt about chickens in general. He didn't like them. They ate dirt, they pecked fingers and sometimes they left their droppings in their nests. He didn't know of another bird that did that.

Rose's way of thinking amused him most of the time. He was never sure what tack her brain would take, so her comments often took him by surprise. Even now. After more than enough years of being promised to each other. He'd thought they'd be married by now, but she was bound she was going to teach. He'd heard enough about young men needing to sow their wild oats before they got hitched. It seemed as if Rose had to sow her serious ones. But sure as the reverend would preach on Sunday, she was taking her time about it.

The last time he'd been out to the Chittenden place, Joshua had ribbed him about the delay. "She said she'd need an intermission," Newton had said, "between school and getting married."

"Seems like Act Two, Three and Four must have passed by now," Joshua had commented, muttering something about a Shakespearean play. His wife, holding their second baby on her hip, had bitten her lip, Newton noticed, and said not a word. He gathered they both thought it was high time Rose left the classroom and took her vows. At that very moment, he'd resolved that he'd talk to her about it – and then they'd gone square dancing and he'd stolen several kisses out behind the town hall, hugged her as tight as he could – and decided to wait until a better time. He had a real dislike for touchy subjects, and he knew this was very touchy.

He finished cleaning up behind the heifers and walked around the barn to the manger side so he could admire the heifers' fawn-colored faces and soft ears. They were eating, but they all stopped and looked at him. In another month or two, if all went well, he'd have five calves and five milking cows. He was quietly excited about that, doubling his little herd in such a short time, but it was nothing compared to his thoughts about marrying Rose and having a place of their own and, he had to admit, babies. More than one or two, he hoped.

Whoa, there, Newton, he said to himself. Not so fast. You and Rose haven't had a word between you about babies, although she does take to Ruthann's little ones. What if she turns out to be shy about being with a man in that way. What if she wants another one of her intermissions between saying "I do" and having a romp in bed. He chuckled a little. Rose was forever reminding him of the "rules," what they could and what they could not – would not – do before they were married. But he knew she found it hard to resist. Every once in a while he let his hands slip down her back so he could pull her even closer, and she always yielded so easily that he would have a moment of wondering if some of the rules were going to be broken. Then she would come to and pull away. Despite who knew how many layers of fabric were between his hands and her skin, he thought about the day when the cloth would be gone. He wondered what people called a lady's backside. He knew he should say "limbs," not "legs," but what were the buttocks politely called? Or perhaps they were totally unmentionable. In any case, even clothed, they were quite inviting. He reckoned most young fellows like him prob'ly thought the same.

Newton wasn't much for praying, but he prayed every Sunday these days that Rose was about done with intermissions. He sighed and then, pumping a bucket full of water, he sluiced out the channel behind the heifers and pushed away the thought of being in bed with Rose. It would just make him "all hot and

31

bothered" as Joshua put it. He went back for a second bucket of water and threw it into the trough. Pretty clean now, he told himself, thinking it might be good idea to dump a pailful over his head.

He took a last look at the Jerseys, slid the barn door into place and headed for his parents' house. It was nearly suppertime, and he wished he could somehow see Rose and try to settle things now. Just as he reached the door, it opened and Rose's little sister – not so little these days – came out.

She grinned when she saw him. "I brought a message," she said, tilting her head to one side and looking at him expectantly.

"And you have delivered it?" Newton asked.

"Indeed," she said in a teasing voice.

"Was it for my mother?" he asked, unwilling to knuckle under to this nonsense.

"No."

"For who?"

"For whom?" Abby countered.

"For _whom_?" he said, gritting his teeth.

"For you." Then, relenting, she added quickly, "Rose hopes you will meet her at the rock this evening. She will be there after the seven o'clock train whistle."

Newton nodded. "I'll be there. You can take that message back since we were fortunate enough to meet. And do not tease her, Abby. It's just not fair."

Abby laughed, turned away and, holding her skirt so high that he could see her knees, ran off so fast that her braids bounced on her back. Newton smiled and bounced a little himself as he shook off a long day in anticipation of the evening. He could never quite believe how he could so crave sleep every night and then, when he had a chance to be with Rose, stay wide awake and get up early a few hours later ready for a new day. The nights he was in bed soon after sundown and up long before the sun rose, he often felt sluggish for the first hour. He wondered if the special strength she gave him would go right on after they were married. Now that was something they could talk about this evening before he tiptoed into the touchy subject of a wedding ceremony.

Newton pushed open the door to the cellar and found his father just finishing up in the milk room. He joined him at the sink and helped wash out the strainer and the pails that had come from the barn.

"Didn't intend to leave you with all the chores, Father," Newton said apologetically.

"I reckon you had plenty to do with those heifers," Elmer Barnes answered. "No need to worry yourself with my barn. Been doing it for so many years, I begin to think I could do it in my sleep."

"It's going to be even harder when those five calve," Newton said. "You'd better start collecting board from me. I hardly earn my keep these days."

"Ben Chandler takes money from his boys who live home, and Peter Granger, before he was married, never had a dollar to call his own, but I reckon I'll go on feeding you and your brothers until you're set up with a wife and a place." He looked sideways at Newton and added, "Which ought to be right soon, unless you want to send Hattie Munson into the asylum."

Newton had started to frown at the start of that last sentence but burst out laughing at the idea that he and Rose could be the cause of Mrs. Munson's losing her mind.

"Rose says gossips never lose their minds because they're too busy to get lost," he answered, going right past the comment about his postponed wedding. "I reckon it's time we washed up for supper, sir."

His father sighed and shook his head but said nothing more. The two men turned all the milking equipment upside down to drain and then scrubbed to the elbows at the set tub. As they took turns drying their hands on the roller towel, Newton muttered that he expected he and Rose were about ready to set a date.

"I don't concern myself with these things much," his father said. "But your mother is quite taken by Rose and cannot understand why she doesn't seem to want to become part of this family."

"That's not it a-tall," Newton replied quickly. "I made a promise that she could teach for a while and I'm keeping that promise until she tells me it's time." His father nodded, and the two went up the stairs to the kitchen, where Eliva Barnes had started dishing up the supper as soon as she heard their footsteps on the stairs.

"Abigail Hibbard was by and said Rose would meet you at the usual place this evening, Newton," she said as she ladled beef stew into a soup plate for him. "I expect you know what that means."

"Yes, ma'am," Newton answered. "And I saw Abby when she came out, so the message has been delivered twice." He took the plate and went into the dining room, sat down where he always sat and took a spoon from the tall glass jar that was always on the table.

"I gather it's not an emergency," Eliva persisted, hoping she could pry at least a small nugget of information from this son who never talked about his personal affairs.

"Neither death nor taxes," Newton answered, smiling at her and then going back to the stew. He pushed two carrots aside and took a large spoonful of meat, potatoes and broth, thinking the subject was now closed.

"Spooning," his younger brother said. "That's what … ow! What you kicking me for?"

"Keeping you from saying anything stupid, that's all," Newton said, pulling his stockinged foot back to his own place.

Eliva frowned at them both and decided to let it go. She felt Newton must be in something of a dither about the wedding that wasn't happening. She certainly was at times, no matter how hard she tried to stifle her worrying. When she and Elmer were courting, she counted the days until they would tie the knot. She had hoped that would end everyone's interest in them, and she had been pure worn out with knowing that half the town was watching their every move. She sighed, thinking that the ceremony hadn't ended the watching, and she could not fathom why until she asked her mother.

"They're wondering if you're with child, Eliva. The widows and storekeepers and clergy have this insatiable need to be the first to know. You take notice. Are they looking you in the eye when you meet them at Mr. Goodnow's? Or do they glance first at your midsection? They are not trying to see if your shirtwaist has been properly ironed, believe you me."

Eliva sighed again. Her mother had been right. From then on, she had been totally aware that a fair number of people she met were stealing looks at her waistline, and she took to wearing voluminous shawls and carrying large baskets with both arms laced through the handle just to thwart them. That experience stopped her from prying into Newton's seemingly stalled wedding, but it didn't keep the anxiety from spinning around in her head like a thread on a bobbin.

"More stew?" she asked, coming back to the present. Everyone at the table nodded, and she fetched the pot from the stove and ladled out second portions. Then she refilled the bread tray with biscuits.

"Wonderful aroma," Newton said, spooning up the stew.

"Aroma?" his younger brother said. "What happened to smell?"

Newton started to laugh. "If you were betrothed to Rose, you wouldn't have to ask a question like that," he said. "Smell is for manure and rotten eggs. Aroma is for things that smell good, like flowers and stew."

"And perfume and girls?" his brother asked, pushing his luck. Newton didn't answer, but he planted another kick under the table and his brother grunted, "All right, all right."

They finished their meal in near silence, and Newton excused himself, carrying some dishes to the kitchen as he left the table. Eliva smiled – he never walked by an undone task without doing something about it, she thought. Rose is a fortunate young woman.

Minutes later, he came to the dining room door wearing a fresh shirt and told his family there'd be no need to leave a lamp on for him because he could find his way in, night or day. And then he was gone, clattering down the stairs and out the cellar door.

36

When Eliva sighed for the first time, Elmer Barnes looked up, eyebrows raised, but said nothing. She was happy not to explain that she wanted Newton to get married but didn't want him to. She would miss him so at this table. So many good things have contradictions, she thought. When she sighed the second time, he said quietly, "It's all goin' to come right, Eliva. Just wait."

The pestering from his younger brother had set Newton to thinking about Rose's aroma, how sweet she always smelled and how clean she would be after a day in the classroom, especially compared to him. He had no illusions about having an aroma after a day at the farm, but the best he could do was put on the clean shirt. Taking a bath in the middle of the week was unheard of, and besides, he could only do it in the kitchen when his mother was finished in that space for the time being. He couldn't even imagine the ribbing his brother would dish up if he started taking baths on Tuesdays or Wednesdays.

Rose would say she didn't care, and he hoped it was true. He broke into a trot, wanting to be with her as soon as possible and hoping she was already at her rock, the place where she went to think and where they had been meeting, day or night, for three years now. A thousand days, he thought, a thousand days of thinking about her and trying to get her out of my head and thinking about her some more because she never seemed to go away. He began to wonder if he was demented, so he'd asked her how many times a week she thought of him, and she had erupted in the laughter he loved to hear.

"A week?" she said when she had stopped. "A week?"

"Well, a month, then," he had said, starting to wish he hadn't asked.

"A day, Newton, a day. An hour, even. How many times in an hour?"

"An hour?" he had said, disbelieving.

"Twelve times an hour," she had answered. "Every five minutes. More than that on occasion. And you persist in planting yourself in the back of my mind when you're not right up at the front. You, of course, have cows and hay and the horse to consider, so you ..."

He had interrupted by kissing her on the mouth, and that had ended the discussion about who was thinking about whom. He hoped he was still there, at least every half hour, but she'd been so wrapped up in teaching of late that he was uncertain. He was certain she loved him, though, by the hour at least.

He slowed to a walk and switched the buffalo robe to his other arm. Going to be dang cold on that rock of hers. Certainly no peepers singing. That thought made him grin. It had been on this very rock that Rose had explained to him that the peepers weren't birds and couldn't sing. Just little frogs rubbing their legs together, she had said. Well, if those frogs hadn't emerged yet, it would be cold. He reckoned he'd have to try hard to keep her from getting a chill. The very idea warmed him instantly, and he broke into a trot again, his feet landing almost without a sound on the leafy path. In a few minutes, he arrived at the huge flat rock, and Rose was there, standing, looking off to the east. He stopped and looked at her for a minute. She looked so beautiful there, silhouetted against a not-quite-dark sky, her hair pulled back into a bun suitable for a teacher and her skirt moving slightly in the breeze. He saw her shiver and pull her shawl tighter. He grinned again. Yep, he'd be needing to keep her warm, all right, a task he was already looking forward to.

As if he had spoken aloud, Rose turned, saw him and jumped off the rock, running until she ran right into him, nearly knocking him backward.

"Whoa, there," Newton said, putting his arms around her and letting the buffalo robe drop to the ground. "No sense killing the person who has arrived to shield you against the cold."

"I have been here five minutes, I reckon," Rose mumbled into his chest. "And it seemed like five hours. I haven't laid eyes on you in four days."

He pushed her head back, gave her a peck on the cheek and said, "Lay the eyes on, lady, lay 'em on. They are ready for you. But I must point out that you won't have them anymore if you lay them on me."

Rose laughed. "It's a figure of speech, you ninny. I'm retaining my eyes."

"I know what a figure of speech is. Learned it from the pigtail person who sat in front of me at school. I never see those pigtails anymore, but I figure the hair is there somewhere." And with that, Newton pulled two large tortoise hairpins out of the bun on the back of her head and let her hair fall over her shoulders.

"That's better," he said. "I am unable to sit on a rock with a schoolmarm. It makes me squirm inside the way I did when I was afraid Miss Harty would call on me." Holding the hairpins in his mouth, he started running his hands through her hair, over and over, the calluses on his fingers catching on strands now and then.

"It would be shameful for you to experience the slightest discomfort," she answered, startled to think Newton had ever had a squirmy moment. She took the pins from him and thought about flicking his hat off and running her hands through his hair. She wondered if it would make him feel the way she did at that very moment, her stomach flip-flopping a bit at his gentle touch. But he stopped, and the moment flew away. She tried to visualize what a moment might look like, certain at least that if she could see it, it would have wings. She turned toward Newton, staring at his face, her hands flat against his shoulders, thinking that a moment on the wing would be like a hummingbird, hovering until you reached for it and then gone. You are being idiotic, she told herself, and stood on tiptoe to kiss him on the mouth. He kissed her back and for what seemed like a long time, they stayed like that, gently kissing and moving slightly from side to side. She decided that for once she would not be the one to break away, so she went on kissing him until he pulled back and looked at her in surprise.

"I was afraid you had sewed us together," he said, smiling down at her.

"Would if I could," she answered, wondering if that was bold and unseemly of her.

"Let's," he said, forgetting his resolve to talk about all sorts of other less enticing subjects first.

"Yes," she said. "Let's. But it's not sewing."

"Close," Newton said, hoping he was following this curious line properly. Sometimes Rose's mind switched back and forth more than the road up the mountain, and he was afraid he might plunge off the track. "You often tie a knot after you thread up one of your needles."

"Let's," she said again, her voice now only a shade above a whisper.

"Let's what?" he said, keeping his voice steady and certain now that they were on widely different trains of thought. Rose dropped her head on his chest. She didn't move for a minute. Then she looked up at him again, her eyes very blue even in the fading light, the black centers large. Her fingers tightened on his shoulders, and he responded by trying to pull her even closer.

"Tie the knot," she said softly. "Tie the knot."

He heard her. But he was afraid he really hadn't. He opened his mouth to give a saucy answer, then closed it, realizing that somewhere in the midst of what had begun lightheartedly, they had turned serious. With some trepidation, he tried again, and his voice croaked, but he managed to get out a gravelly, "When?"

"As soon as school's out," she answered quickly. "Unless that's haying time," she said and instantly wished she hadn't mentioned anything about farm work. But he said nothing, just dropped his arms, picked up the blanket, took her hand and led her back to the rock. He spread the buffalo robe and swept his hand dramatically between her and the rock.

"Have a seat," he said, his voice finally working. "Tying knots comes way ahead of haymaking." He sat down facing Rose, who had pulled her knees up to her chest. He crossed his legs Indian style and reached for her hands. "Way ahead," he added.

Rose took his hands, a little puzzled by his response. She had expected him to whirl her off her feet, as he had sometimes done in the past, kiss her until she was breathless and then hold her close for the rest of the evening. She watched as his fingers played with the ring he had given her the day she agreed to marry him, and they sat for several minutes in a silence she was afraid to break.

Finally, she let go of his hands and turned up the wick on the lantern she had brought with her, then reached out to him again. As his long fingers stroked hers, she felt the familiar warm shiver trace its way along her spine. Still, she said nothing.

At last he spoke. "I have dreamed of this moment, Rose," he said. "At least I think I have. Is intermission over?"

At that, she smiled. All those months ago, she had promised him she wouldn't run away after he told her about his nightmares, in which she was always running away from him. But she had also told him that she needed intermissions, that whenever she ran away, she would come back. Now she was having trouble speaking.

"Over," she said.

With a yank on her arms, he toppled backward and pulled her over on top of him, kissing her and lacing his fingers through her hair so she could not pull away. It occurred to him, as she kissed him back that he had nothing to worry about. She wasn't going anywhere. Intermission was over.

He rolled her off and turned on his side to face her. She shivered slightly, and he reached across her to pull up the robe. She snuggled close to his chest and could hear his heart pounding and wondered if hers was making that kind of racket, too. Two clocks ticking. Then he shifted his body so her face was opposite his. As if she were made of porcelain, he carefully traced around her eyes, down her nose and along her lips. She closed her eyes, worried that she might burst into tears like some flighty thing and spoil it all. She could not remember being happier than this.

"What day is that?" he asked.

"What day?" she said without opening her eyes.

"The last day of school," he said.

"Sometime in early June. The little boys will be gone by mid-May, but the girls will keep on till prob'ly the first week of June."

"And then we'll get married."

"Yes."

"I like it when you say 'yes'. It's become my favorite word."

"It's a tiny word."

"Yes."

Rose could not think why she had seen a need to start that ridiculous list earlier today. With her eyes still closed, she raised herself on one elbow and ran her finger around his eyes and down his nose. When her feather-like touch traced the curves of his ears, she felt him tremble and realized she had never touched him there before. She did it again, then moved on to the chin, then across his lips, back and forth. She heard his breath quicken and knew she should stop, but she kissed him instead, and they were soon lost in the most intense kiss of their courtship, rocking back and forth, shifting from lips to necks, necks to ears, ears to eyes and back to lips. Rose opened her eyes and found that his were on her, and they each pulled back at the same time.

"Whew," Newton said.

"Yes," Rose answered. And they both started to laugh, holding each other and rolling around on the rock like two wrestling youngsters, laughing so hard they could not speak. Gasping, Newton suddenly sat up, and Rose followed.

"Will we always laugh like that?" Rose asked in as even a tone as she could manage. She prayed it would not occur to him that it was a serious question. She should have saved her prayers for another day. Newton had realized long ago that Rose would not ever get over being her mother's daughter, which was both good and not so good.

He decided it was time to get rid of the cobwebs if he could. "Forever," he answered solemnly. "I intend to make you laugh at least once a day, and I expect you'll do the same for me." He paused and decided to take the bull by the horns, as he knew people were fond of saying. Foolish idea, he told himself, given the bad temper of bulls, but he said aloud, "You are not Sarah, and I am not Silas, and I am going to kiss you and laugh with you every day until we are a hundred. Then we'll make our way to this rock and think it over again."

He knew, Rose thought. He's always known. And I'm a flibbertigibbet for not knowing he knew. She smiled. She was all tangled up in "knew" and "known" and it was really "unknown" she was trying to deal with. She would be cooking and cleaning and hanging out the wash when it was freezing cold and taking care of the chickens, but she would not become her mother. She so loved all the things her mother had done for and with her, but she hated the way Sarah Hibbard's mouth had gone from a smile in the morning to a thin line by suppertime. She was plumb worn out, Rose realized. She'd learned a little bit about that in the months that she had taken her mother's place, seen to her brother and sister and tried to do everything her mother had done. Those had been hard days, especially with Father at the drink and like a wounded bear half the time.

"I love you, Newton Barnes, I do," was all she said, her face so serious that he wanted to kiss it until she stopped looking as if she were in church. But he knew more spooning was dangerous territory if they were to live by all the rules Rose had made. So he answered lightly, "And I you. More than I can tell you. More than hay or Jersey heifers or even my little brother."

Rose began to laugh again, and he stood, grinning, and jumped off the rock. She followed, jumping right toward him so he had to catch her, but he dropped a kiss on her cheek and released her immediately.

"We need to go now," he said.

"Need to?"

"Your rules, Rose. My heart wants to stay, and my head knows better and I'm listening to my head."

"I told Ruthann, all those years ago, that you weren't one of those young men who take advantage," Rose said.

"It ain't easy," he said in a low voice.

"Isn't," she said, but she took his hand, and they started down the trail with Newton carrying the blanket, and Rose swinging the lantern. She wanted to stay and lie close to him and talk about getting married and about where they would live and all those things. But she knew he was right.

CHAPTER FIVE
Abby's Mixed Feelings

Rose tiptoed up the stairs at her father's house – she never thought of it as hers anymore – and undressed as quietly as she could. She slipped on her nightgown, again noticing that even in the dim light of her candle the sleeves were quite frayed. Not suitable for a wife, she thought again. She started to slip into bed and saw that Abby's eyes were wide open and watching her.

"Nice and quiet, Rose," her sister said. "But I always wait up for you."

"You'll have to outgrow that habit," Rose answered in a soft voice, deciding to give Abby the news first.

"Why?" Abby asked, a little resentment in her voice. "Why do I have to outgrow everything that's fun?"

Rose gave her a hug and said, "You'll find new things that are fun, and then you won't care about the other things."

"Maybe."

"You have to outgrow the habit of watching me undress and come to bed because I am going to marry Newton and move away."

"I know that."

"But you didn't know until this very moment (was this one of the winged moments, Rose wondered) that it will be this year – June, in fact. As soon as school is out."

"Won't he be haying then?"

Rose laughed. "He said it comes in way ahead of haying. Said it twice. So I am disposed to believe him."

Abby sat up and clapped her hands just the way she had done for years when she was excited about something. "Will that make Newton my brother?" she asked. "I'd like that."

"Brother-in-law is what they call it," Rose said, smiling. "He'll be Charles's brother-in-law, too, and Father's son-in-law."

"Complicated," Abby said, frowning a little. But she quickly skipped on to other things, questions tumbling out faster than peas from a pod. "Where will you live? Are you still going to be a teacher? Does not even Father know? Will you have a beautiful dress like Miss Harty?" She paused and then said, suspicion in her voice, "But Charles knows, doesn't he?"

"Whoa," Rose interrupted. "I don't know, no, yes, probably not two times."

A grin replaced Abby's frown. "You know I'll remember the questions in the right order, but I'm not sure about 'not even Father.' Does a yes mean he knows or he doesn't?"

"He doesn't. You did have a negative in there, you know."

"And the 'probably not two times?' So Charles may know?"

"Only if he was putting his eavesdropping ear against a rock," Rose laughed. "But I wouldn't put it past him. You know how he listens at keyholes and under windowsills and most anywhere else when it suits him."

"Sometimes, Rose," Abby said, remembering a few important times in the past, "it's been real handy, Charles being so nosy."

"Indeed, and sometimes it's a plain nuisance. Now go to sleep. The sun will be up at the usual time in the morning, and we'll be loath to answer her summons." And with that, Rose rolled over on her side, started to think about wedding dresses and was asleep just as she was trying to see herself in her mind's eye, all decked out in yards of fabric. Abby lay awake for a long time, thinking about what home would be like without Rose. After awhile, she said aloud, "You are a piggish person, Abigail Hibbard," and then clapped her hand over her mouth and hoped she hadn't roused Rose. But her sister slept on, and Abby managed a smile as she thought how happy Rose was these days. But at the same time, a tear spilled out of her eye and left a damp spot on her pillow. "I'm not a pig," she whispered to herself, "I'm not. I won't be." And she, too, dropped off.

Across town, Newton was having a much harder time falling asleep. He would be up before the sun, and he knew he'd have to push himself to avoid dragging through the day's work. But it had been an evening worth remembering, and he was not too tired to savor all the details. The day after school was out. He'd have to get a move on or he and his wife would have no place to hang their hats (or share their bed, he thought, grinning), and he was dang sure he didn't want to bunk in Silas Hibbard's house, or even with his own parents for that matter. He wondered how Rose would feel about the small cottage at Ruthann and Joshua's farm. It was miles from Eastborough, and he didn't know if being near Ruthann would compensate for not seeing Charles and Abby on a daily basis. She was so close to them, ever since her mother had been killed, but they were much older now, so mebbe it would work out. He could move his heifers, of course, and he knew Joshua would make room in his barns, in exchange for Newton's help on the farm. Perhaps it would be the best thing, getting a fresh start away from all the things that Rose had spent the past few years worrying her head over. He reckoned they would be needing another session at her rock to talk about this prospect. Warming to that idea, he too rolled over, gave a long sigh that relaxed his body and slept.

But not everyone in Eastborough was asleep. The Reverend Lockhead, who often had nightmares so violent that he would wake up in a sweat, was having such a night. He had come bolt upright in the bed he shared with Mrs. Lockhead, his flailing arms sending the quilts flying and leaving his wife almost entirely uncovered.

"What, what?" she said incoherently, reaching out for blankets that were no longer within reach. "What is it?" she said more crossly, as she became more awake. "What now?"

"Another of my torturous dreams, my dear, and I apologize to you for interrupting your slumber," the minister said, pulling the quilts over her again. He could not imagine why God was sending such dreadful thoughts into his sleeping brain, but the nightmares came more and more often these days, and they often were filled with people he knew, folks who lived in Eastborough now or had recently died. And they were so angry, calling his name and yelling at him. He had never been able to decipher what they were saying and had begun to think they were speaking a foreign language. Or, and he shuddered at the very idea, in the language of the devil. He believed in the devil, and he hoped Satan was not in his bedroom, but he was no longer certain. He wished his heart would stop pounding.

Fully awake now, his wife reached out her hand and took his. "You are overworked," she said in a soft voice. "We must arrange a day or two away, perhaps three, and find ourselves a quiet place, perhaps in the mountains, where we are free of all your parishioners and their troubles."

"You are a great comfort to me," Calvin Lockhead replied. He rolled over, gently pushed her on her side and put his arms around her, fitting his body against her back. "A very great comfort," he added, wondering at the same time whether it was right for him to enjoy such comforts. Still, he was a man and a clergyman, and surely God himself would understand that.

"It is my duty, Mr. Lockhead," she answered with a hint of mischief in her voice. "Just my duty to you, like all my other duties. Washing, ironing, adding the starch, stoking the fires." And then, he was quite certain, he heard a small giggle, and she went back to sleep. He, too, closed his eyes, hoping that would not set off the bad dreams again.

Hattie Munson was still awake, too. And still dressed in her street clothes. She had done all her errands and then stopped at Jason Harris's place to pay him the $75 for the new table. He had met her at the door and to her great regret had stepped outside to talk with her on his porch. She had hoped to be invited in, just to set folks talking about why her buggy was outside the widower's house. But Jason was having none of that. Sometimes she felt he was seeing right into her mind.

He had taken the cash from her, his eyebrows raised a little, but he hadn't made any comment. Then he'd inquired whether she'd like to see his Chinese chickens, and much as she disliked clucking poultry, she had accepted the invitation. At least she figured on getting inside the chicken house with this man who had begun to really intrigue her. It turned out he was quite proud of those hens, wanted her to hold one and was perturbed when it pecked her gloved finger and she let it go. Well, the darned thing hadn't broken its leg or anything, had it? But it put a damper on the visit. She'd left then, a little mortified that she had appeared to be afraid of a chicken. She did have to admit they were better looking than most she'd seen, even at the Shakers.

She picked up her newspaper, which came every week in the mail. Turning up the wick on her kerosene lamp, she read until her eyes closed and the paper slipped onto the floor. Then she rose, put out the light and made her way up the stairs in the dark. She undressed, put on her nightdress and climbed into the big spool bed that had been her grandmother's. She had no shades or curtains on her upstairs windows, so she never brought a light to this room and had made a habit of dressing and undressing in the dark. It must be on towards midnight, she thought, and the night train will be going through soon. She tried to wait for the whistle but her eyes were done for the day. She was asleep a half hour before the engineer went through the Eastborough station without stopping.

She would have been less inclined to sleep had she known that both Jason Harris and Silas Hibbard had her in mind. With a sigh directed at the empty half of his bed, Jason tossed and turned for an hour before he could settle in. He missed Nell so, never more than at bedtime when they would often have a chat in the dark about their day. It was always an easy talk, and he wondered now why it was so much simpler to speak one's mind

51

without rancor or argument when it was dark. Even without Nell there, he had fallen into revisiting his day once he was in bed.

He grinned as he thought about Hattie Munson being obviously terrified of a chicken and then terrified that she'd broken it when she dropped it. It would take more than a three-foot drop to damage one of those birds, Jason knew, but he'd pretended to examine the creature as if it might have been hurt. It would be good for Hattie's gossiping soul to worry a bit, he reckoned. She was what his mother would have called "a piece of work." He wasn't sure where that came from, but he knew what it meant. It meant Hattie. And he'd nearly slipped and asked if she had never tended the Shaker chickens. He'd best keep that idea to himself for the present.

Feeling a little more lighthearted than usual, he turned onto his stomach, faced away from the empty side of the bed and was asleep long before midnight. But several roads away, Silas Hibbard had already slept, wakened, used the chamber pot that he still kept under the bed, heard Rose come in and tried his darndest to catch what the girls were saying in their room. But their voices were too low, and he wasn't Charles – wouldn't be tiptoeing over to the door to listen. He smiled. That boy, now close to being a young man, was still such a rascal at times. Imagine his naming a calf Ruthann, naming a barn animal for a teacher. Silas still couldn't believe the impudence of that, but the calf had turned into a cow, and he'd overheard Charles call her by name when he thought no one was listening.

Sarah would have laughed three days over that, he thought. Sarah. He still missed her something fierce, but the family had gotten through the worst of it, and he had not touched a drink in years now, so they were managing. But he missed her. Missed the drink, too, if the truth be told. He wondered if the town had forgotten his fling with Miss Jennie, a page in his life that he wasn't proud of. Still, he smiled a little, she had provided him with considerable pleasure, even if it was sinful of him. Someday, mebbe, he'd find someone else, but single ladies didn't exist in abundance in Eastborough. There was Hattie, of course. The very idea of courting her favors stretched his mouth and his moustache into a broad smile. He'd be staying on the sidelines for the present, he decided, still wishing he'd made his admiration for Sarah plainer to her as they went along, but he couldn't do it over. If Rose ever made up her mind to marry Newton, that was what he'd tell him, his new son-in-law. He'd tell him to say something besides "Isn't my breakfast ready yet?" or "I can't find my Sunday shoes." Something appreciative every day. If only he had known to do that when there was still time.

The next time he woke, Silas heard the train whistle and knew he'd better get into some real sleep or he'd be a dunderhead around the place in the morning. And Charles would be thinking he'd gone back to the hard cider. He drifted off and was soon snoring.

CHAPTER SIX
Dreams and Nightmares

Rose knew her friend Emily threw off the covers every morning and practically jumped out of bed. But she and Alice didn't feel that way. If they had their druthers, they'd snuggle in and wish someone else would see to the chores required at break of day. At least the sun was getting up earlier these days, Rose thought, as she slowly pushed her way out of the bed she shared with Abby. Spring was here or nearly so. It was much harder when people had to get up long before the sun got around to it.

She felt particularly poky this morning and wondered why. And then remembered that she'd had a lot less sleep than usual, what with all that time on the rock with Newton, and it had been a restless night with strange dreams. She shivered, not liking what she could remember of the dreams. More like nightmares, she thought, as she started to dress. She had been wearing a white dress with a long, long train, and she was in a church and her train caught on the doorstep and then snagged at every pew as she tried to walk down the aisle. It was horrid, and she couldn't remember how it ended. She hoped it wasn't a bad omen, just when she and Newton had set a date for getting married.

Only a bad dream, she told herself, pulling on her stockings and using her special button hook for the closing on her shoes. How many shoes had this button hook seen, she wondered. Her mother's, as well as hers. She quickly brushed her hair and twisted it into a bun at the back of her head, fastening it with the large hairpins Newton had pulled out the night before. He did like to set her hair loose, didn't he? She wondered if he'd want it flowing over her back for their wedding. She was quite certain it wasn't proper, but Newton didn't always cotton to what other people thought was proper. She headed for the stairs and, in the kitchen, added kindling to the embers in the stove and started fixing breakfast. Father, she figured, was already in the barn.

As she stirred oatmeal and set up the toaster rack, she went back to thinking about her bad dreams. Why on earth would she see herself in a gown with a long train? She didn't want anything fancy like that, and all that extra fabric would be too dear anyway. Perhaps she could wear the dress she'd worn for Miss Harty's wedding. It was so pretty, and it had been hanging in the closet all this time, never used again. It wasn't suited to square dances or church – inappropriate, her mother would have said – and those events were pretty much the extent of her socializing. All those people in the church had stared at her in the dream, she remembered now – Mrs. Munson and Mr. Goodnow and Peter Granger and so many others. And her face was as red as a full-grown beet. Ugh, she thought. They do all stare at a wedding, and she was bound to blush to the roots of her hair. Being a teacher and getting older hadn't taken away her tendency to turn red whenever she was the center of attention. Except in the classroom. The children for some reason didn't make her flush. Suddenly she recalled another part of the dream. Charles was taking her down the aisle, not Father. What did that mean? Would she want Father anyway? She'd already given him her Declaration of Independence, so he couldn't give her away, could he? Not like giving away an egg or a potted plant. Land sakes, she didn't want to think about any of this.

The oatmeal was bubbling, and she realized she'd better pay attention, or it would stick to the pan forever. She stirred harder and heard her father's heavy footstep on the stairs. He stopped to take his boots off in the hallway but didn't come through the door. Must have gone to the bathroom, she thought, and at that very moment heard the toilet flush. She smiled, thinking what a blessing it was to have the privy gone and smiled again when she thought about Charles regaling them all with the tales of cleaning it out. Where was that boy, anyway? He should have been coming in from the barn, but it was possible he hadn't managed to get out of bed. She knew he stayed up late many a night, sketching one building after another by the light of a kerosene lantern. She had even threatened him with having to pay for the kerosene because he used so much.

"Morning, Rose," came a gruff voice from the door. "Charles is seeing to that heifer of his and then he'll be along."

Rose nodded and took a warmed bowl off the back shelf of the stove. She filled it with oatmeal and took it to the dining room table where a pitcher of top milk and the smaller pitcher of maple syrup were set beside her father's place. He tucked his napkin into his shirt collar and began to eat. Rose went back to the kitchen and toasted two slices of bread for him. She set that beside his place with a pot of the strawberry rhubarb jam she'd

56

made the summer before. When she took off the paraffin layer, she'd noticed two or three spots of mold on the jam and had skimmed them off. A little worried about whether that was the right thing to do, she had tasted the jam and thought it quite fine. It would seem wasteful to discard what appeared to be perfectly edible. For the thousandth, more likely the ten-thousandth time in her life, she wondered what her mother would have done. She needed to stop counting things, like buttoning shoes and wearing dresses and worrying about what Sarah might have done.

"Charles can serve himself, Father," she called into the dining room. "I need to get to the school." She heard a low grunt in return and took it for her answer, so she used the bathroom, rinsed her hands, threw a shawl around her shoulders and headed out the door, calling over her shoulder, "Oh, and Abby needs to get up before Charles takes his breakfast." Another grunt came from the dining room, and she was on her way.

While she walked quickly across the road to the one-room school, she started thinking about that dream again. It was like something that would have happened to Alice – not *her* Alice, but the wonderland Alice, she thought, like meeting queens who kept shouting, "Off with her head!" Sometimes when the front of her head was burning up with color, she wished she could take it off, but Emily always laughed at that idea and reminded her that body parts could not be unhitched and put back again so easily. She would tell Emily about the dream or nightmare or whatever it was. She needed to see her today in any case because Emily should be one of the first to know about the wedding. And, other than Miss Harty's, Emily's was the only wedding Rose had ever been to. She pushed the dream into the back of her head, unlocked the schoolhouse door and found that Emily's husband, the unpredictable Peter Granger, had been in ahead of her and started a nice fire in the wood stove at the front of the room.

The room was warm and cozy, and Peter's work had given her a few minutes to spare, so Rose took several sheets of paper, tore them into four-inch squares and wrote the numbers one through five on them. She made three sets, piled them on the desk, took out her pincushion and set it on top of the slips of paper. That, she thought, will get us going on arithmetic in a new way. It would be a simpler version of what she had done with the older children in her very first class, and she hoped it would work. Then she wrote the date on the big slate at the front of the room and, under that, her quote for the day. This time it was:

"True, I talk of dreams
Which are the children of an idle brain,
Begot of nothing but vain fantasy."

--William Shakespeare

So much for dreams, she thought, wondering how she would go about explaining this one to these young ones. She hoped that fantasy thing explained hers, at least. The children seemed to like the quotations, and they were beginning to realize, she knew, that many things existed outside their Eastborough world. She so wanted them to know that. She so wanted to see what was farther outside her own Eastborough world than she had been able to see so far. Oh, dear, she thought. Once I'm married, will we get outside? Ever again? But before she could start thinking about all the marriage questions again, she heard children on the steps. Some walked a considerable distance, but they all seemed

58

to arrive at the same time and on time. She went to let them in, giving a pull on the bell rope as she walked past to open the door.

Nine, no ten, eager faces looked up at her and waited for her to step back and let them in. She had decided from the beginning that a headlong rush to the cloak room was not the worst thing in the world. They were full of beans, as her mother used to say, and letting off a little steam right now might make a quieter classroom later. She was certain other teachers would be aghast at her form of welcome in the morning, but she was the only teacher there, so no one really knew.

Once they had hung their jackets and other wraps, they took their seats, but the buzz went on, a roomful of little bees communicating with each other. It always made her smile – they had parted less than twenty-four hours earlier and yet they had so much to say to each other. Actually, she figured, what she'd done in the time since the class was dismissed yesterday was quite momentous, too – and she wished she had Emily and Alice there right now so they, too, could buzz.

She went to her desk, clapped her hands twice, and the sound lowered itself to nothing in seconds. As usual, they all sat looking straight at her, waiting to see what would happen next. And she never did the subjects in the same order from day to day because she had thought that one of the boring things about school in her day.

"You may all stand, and we will sing "My Country 'Tis of Thee," she said, pulling a small pitch pipe out of her desk drawer. She gave them the starting note and a signal, and chirpy young voices joined in the song, which they had learned the week before. When they finished, she asked them to be seated, and she went around the room pinning a slip of paper on each child.

"Be careful," she cautioned. "These are common pins, which means they have a safe end and a sharp end, and we don't need any scratched or punctured fingers." The children were busy looking at their own numbers and those of the youngsters near them, but they didn't say anything. They had learned that Miss Hibbard's games turned lessons into fun, and they would wait for the explanation.

"I need someone with a number one to come forward," she said as she pinned the last child.

Three hands went up, and Rose chose Jared because he wasn't very good at arithmetic. She needed success on the first example, so it was better for him to be part of the puzzle. "Now I need another number one," she said, and another hand went up. She told Melvin to come forward and handed each boy a pencil. "You, Jared, must hold your pencil horizontally – do you know what that means?"

"Yes, Miss Hibbard. It means flat across, like the horizon."

"Perfect. And you, Melvin, will hold your pencil vertically, centered on Jared's." Melvin immediately put his pencil in place. "Now, class, what have we here? Think about the pinned notes and the pencils."

At first, they all looked puzzled, and then Hope's hand flew up.

"Yes, Hope?"

"It's arithmetic, Miss Hibbard. They are an arithmetic problem."

"Exactly. So what do we need now," she asked, taking two more pencils and holding them parallel next to Melvin.

Hope's hand waved wildly, and two others went up more hesitantly.

"Go ahead, Hope," Rose said.

"You need me because I am a number two," Hope burst out in a rush.

"Precisely. Come forward, Hope and take your place. Does everyone now see what we have? One – that's Jared – plus – that's the crossed pencils -- and then Melvin's one equals two, which is Hope's number. Now, supposing Hope takes Melvin's place – you may take your seat, Melvin. What happens now?"

Emma's hand shot up, and when Rose called on her, she said, "I think you need me, now." Sure enough, she was a three and was invited to come forward and complete the problem. As she turned to face the class, several of the children started to giggle. It had taken less time than Rose could have imagined for them to absorb her new idea.

The next half hour flew by, with children creating new problems and answers moving into place. Then, suddenly, two threes were up front, and no one could answer. Rose had only gone as far as five with her labels. Quickly, she penciled a six on a slip and pinned it to her lapel and took her place. The children laughed and clapped, and their first human arithmetic lesson was done.

She turned now to the quotation on the blackboard, something that ordinarily started the day in her room. She read it aloud and, really not expecting an answer, asked if anyone knew who William Shakespeare was. But Rebecca knew and announced that he wrote plays a long time ago. "I believe he is dead, ma'am," she added, and the class giggled.

"Quite right on both counts," Rose said, nodding her approval. She moved on to the subject of the quote, asking if any of them had dreams when they were sleeping. Several children raised their hands and one by one told about things that they'd dreamed while asleep and how sometimes they were scary.

"And what about dreams when you are awake?" Rose asked. "What about the things you wish might happen, your dreams about nice things you'd like to do next week or next year or sometime when you are older? We'll start with you, Hope, and go around the room clockwise. Does everyone know what clockwise is?"

Seeing almost everyone nod, Rose told Hope to go ahead, and so the children talked about their dreams, about going to California some day, about getting a new dress, about taking a train ride, about swimming in an ocean. Rose was pleased to find they could think about things that might come true or might not, but that they wanted to think about anyway. It was what she had always done, and now she knew that some dreams at least came true, even if bad things might be mixed in as well.

The day passed quickly, from recess to more lessons, to lunch and more lessons, and Rose dismissed them promptly at three o'clock, reminding them not to run down the stairs outside the door. She heard their feet clatter quickly despite her warning, but she heard no outcries, so she figured they had all made it without falling. It was a worry. They were always in such a hurry and she had learned that while these little ones were very agile, they were also quite foolhardy.

She put away everything on her desk, put on her shawl and headed for the door. As she turned the key in the lock, it occurred to her that a visit to Grandmother Jane would be a grand idea. She could tell her grandmother about the nightmare and see what she had to say. One thing Rose knew. Grandmother Jane always said what she thought. She didn't mince words. The idea made Rose smile. She had minced onions, and that made her cry, all those little bits giving off their onion smell. Or aroma. Does the brain use a knife to mince words, she wondered? Stop it, Rose, she told herself. Just stop it and get on your way. She would see Emily on the way back.

She stopped first at her father's house to get a jar of blueberry jam to take to her grandmother. Just a regular Red Riding Hood, she thought, as she put the jam in a small basket, along with her knitting and a book she had just finished. Grandmother didn't get to the library often, and she might like something different to read, although this Ambrose Bierce person certainly didn't write anything cheery. Clara had left the book behind when she moved west again, and Rose found it hard not to read any book that was available. But Mr. Bierce's view of the Civil War was so dismal that it made her wonder about the men from Eastborough and Ripton who had fought in places a long way from here. None of them talked about it. And that made her wonder even more. She could not even imagine a writer inventing a boy like the one in "Chicamauga," and she considered it a miracle that the story hadn't given her nightmares. Only weddings, she thought, as she changed her shoes and set off to her grandmother's house.

CHAPTER SEVEN
Grandmother Jane Speaks Up

The walk to Grandmother Jane's was always a pleasure and never more than in the spring. Rose moved quickly but had time to take note of the bright yellow colts foot that seemed to relish growing in or near gravel and the grass-green skunk cabbage that was quite tall near the small stream that ran near the road. It took her nearly a half hour to get to what everyone in town called Hibbard's Hill, a farm high enough to have a pleasant outlook over the valley. Rose turned to look when she reached the gate to her grandfather's far pasture, the only place where the undergrowth didn't block the view.

When she reached the small house, she climbed the two big stones that led to the open porch and the kitchen door. "Grandmother?" she called. "Are you home?"

"And where else would I be, young lady? Where else? I'm not much for gallivanting," her grandmother said, reaching the door just as Rose pulled it open. "And you, Rose, are a sight for sore eyes, not here in so long that it's a wonder the soreness hasn't rotted them away."

But she smiled as she spoke and reached out both hands to her granddaughter. "Come in, come in, don't let the dratted flies in. They are hatching as if there were no tomorrow, and I am swatting them regular. Your grandfather can sweep one right off the table with his hand, qui cker than you can say 'get it,' but my fingers and hands just don't work that way."

Rose started to laugh. Grandmother was bubbling like hot fat in a big kettle, she thought. She knew she hadn't been here for a while, and every time she came she wondered why she hadn't made the effort sooner. And every time she came, Grandmother said she was a sight for sore eyes. After the climb, more than likely she was just a sight. And while she talked a blue streak – oh, dear, why was the streak blue, Rose thought – she was wise as well. And that, never mind streaks, was why she had come.

"It's nice to see you looking so well, Grandmother," Rose said, setting her basket on the table.

"And what else would I be?"

"I didn't mean ..."

"Of course you didn't. I'm an old woman who doesn't have enough people to talk to, most days, and I tend to run on as if I had to use all the words I know in a minute or two. Come, sit, have a glass of lemonade. I made some this morning, thinking perhaps the day would warm up enough so your grandfather would like a glass with his supper. Don't know as it has."

Rose sat on a kitchen chair while her grandmother fetched a tumbler and filled it with the fresh lemonade. She looked around at the room she loved, the sheen of the table pockmarked with years of use – including children banging a spoon now and then – the huge sink with the set tub beside it, the thick slab of maple where Grandmother rolled pie crust and chopped cabbage or

65

onions, the black wood stove, fancier than Sarah Hibbard's but not quite as large. It was a room that in Rose's memory had so often smelled of freshly baked cookies or thick beef stew or slow-baked beans.

Interrupting Rose's thoughts, Grandmother Jane set the glass of lemonade on the table and Rose took a sip. She took the book and jam out of the basket and set them on the table. Jane Hibbard lowered herself slowly onto the chair kitty-corner from Rose's.

"So, to what do I owe this visit on a mid-week day? I don't suppose you walked all the way up here to bring me a pot of jam and some reading matter, did you?" She reached for Rose's left hand and glanced at the ring she was wearing. "It's a relief to see that you haven't thrown over that nice young man of yours – and that he hasn't lost patience and walked away from you."

Rose couldn't help herself. She laughed again, patted her grandmother's hand and said, "If I can get ten or twelve words in edgewise, Grandmother, I'll tell you why I'm here on a mid-week day. You are right, of course, I have a reason. But it's nice just to see you, too."

"Have you set a wedding date then?"

"Yes."

"Well, that's another relief. Is it ten years from now, or will I live to see it?"

"That's the question, Grandmother. Not ten years – right after school closes this year for the summer. So it's June. This year. No ifs, ands or buts."

"And the question?"

Rose twisted the engagement ring on her finger before she answered. When she looked up, she said with a rush, "I had this dreadful dream last night, a nightmare it was, me all tangled in a lot of white satin fabric and my face red and people staring at me and Charles taking me down the aisle of the church."

"Aren't you the one for complicated happenings in your sleep, young lady!"

"What do you mean?"

"P'raps I shouldn't say, but you had that horrendous nightmare when you were ill all those years ago, when you nearly froze to death and lay there all those days without speaking or opening your eyes. The dream about jumping over gravestones? Do you recall?"

"I had nearly forgotten – or mebbe just tried to forget," Rose said, not looking up and twisting the ring again. "Somberstones, I remember. Instead of gravestones."

"I'm not one to put much stock in what goes on in people's heads when they're asleep," Jane Hibbard said. "But I do think nightmares come when a body is troubled about something, even if what happens in the dream has nothing to do with the worry. Are you certain you want to get married?"

"Yes."

"Absolutely? You promised your Aunt Nell, which has been a puzzle for Jason, that you'd be married a year from the night of your engagement. Isn't that right?"

"Absolutely. On both counts. And I've felt guilty about Aunt Nell for the past two years." Rose paused, and then choked out, "But she would have understood, I know she would. And uncle never said a word," she added.

"Of course he didn't," her grandmother answered. "They have a soft spot for you, whatever you do. This 'absolutely' could be fifty years of your life, you know."

"I know."

"Then I think – and I'm no wizard – I think you are worried about the wedding itself."

Rose felt tears rising in her eyes and wished she could say a magic word to stop them. Perhaps that was exactly it, but what was wrong with her? Everyone else had weddings. Emily's had been very nice, people all dressed up and smiling, music playing and, once the church part was over, a big feed at her parents' house with everyone dancing while Thaddeus Clapp played his fiddle. Miss Harty's had been beautiful from start to finish, very elegant. Their weddings, so different, suited them perfectly, she realized suddenly.

"I don't know what suits me," she said a little shakily.

"I don't know precisely what that means, Rose, but we'll get at it, never fear. And if any of that water spills over, we'll mop it up. You ever walk across that rail trestle to take the short cut?"

Bewildered now, Rose nodded her head, wiped her eyes with her handkerchief and sipped more lemonade, hoping the cold, tart liquid would settle her down.

"Getting ready to get married has apparently put you on that trestle, a little worried that you might have figured wrong and are facing a train wreck. No doubt you still gnaw on fear of hard cider now and then as well."

Rose didn't answer, and her grandmother insisted, "Am I right?"

"Yes, Grandmother," Rose said. "But Father hasn't touched the drink in years now, and it can't be a sensible worry anymore. And we get along. We get along all of the time."

"Only since you laid down the law, young lady, and turned the tables on him. He's a good man, but even though he's my son and I think highly of him most of the time, I know he has faults. Everyone does."

"Everyone knows or everyone has faults?" Rose asked.

"Faults," the old lady said crisply.

"Even you, Grandmother?" Rose said, a hint of mischief in her voice.

"Well, perhaps not me," Grandmother Jane said, pleased to see that Rose was regaining her composure. "At least, not often. But you are the question here, not me. I suggest you consider abandoning the wedding entirely – no tangled fabric, no red faces, no staring neighbors, no Reverend Lockhead with his infernal preaching. I have a notion that even at a wedding he'd be moved to prescribe how everyone ought to behave."

"Abandon? But I said I want to get married."

"So run off and get married. Come back and tell us all about your adventure. Or," she added with something close to a grin, "nearly all about. The more I think about it, the more I like it. But what would Mr. and Mrs. Barnes say?"

"They'd be mighty disappointed at not being there, but they are so wonderful, Grandmother. You can't even imagine."

"Humph. Hard to figure on a wonderful mother-in-law, but one can always hope."

"But what are you saying, Grandmother? We should elope, the way people do in books? Just disappear and not tell anyone what we were up to? And then show up at church or something like Tom Sawyer and Huckleberry Finn?"

"That would add a priceless flair to the whole thing," Jane Hibbard said, her smile spreading across her papery face, deepening the wrinkles beside her eyes. "But the real world is a little different from the mischief Mr. Twain – or whatever his name is – conjures up. I think you would leave a note, perhaps with me, perhaps with Mr. Goodnow. You could – you must know this -- trust him with your life and all else. He wouldn't repeat a thing you ever said, even if all the town fathers were threatening him." She paused and added a little wistfully, "He's never even told me about your meetings with Silas in the store and how you took your stand with your father. And I reckon he heard the whole thing – and some other things at other times as well. He's as far from gossip as I am, come to think about it."

"Not even Emily?" Rose said, going back to the business of telling no one.

"Especially not Emily," her grandmother answered, keeping right up with her granddaughter's flying thoughts. "Some busybody would pump it out of her faster than you can get water from the well."

"We don't have a well," Rose started to say and then laughed. "I ought to know a figure of speech when I hear one, but I think you've put my mind in a muddle and in the clear at the same time."

The old lady pushed her chair back a few inches and smoothed the fabric on her cotton dress. "Puzzles get finished if you put your mind to it," she said. She stood, paused a minute and then went to the icebox to get a large blue enamel pot. She put it on the back of the stove, fetched two small sticks from the wood box and poked up the fire in the stove. Then she turned to Rose, her face serious. "But you must tell someone what your plan is, me or Henry Goodnow perhaps, because townspeople have long memories and you did disappear once before."

"I know," Rose said. "I know." She also stood and leaned down to plant a light kiss on her grandmother's cheek.

"I recall when I was considerably taller than you," Jane Hibbard said. "It's not so long ago. I'll be sorry not to be at your wedding if you run off, but mostly I want you and that nice young man to be happy."

"We are," Rose said. "And we will be. You have cleared away considerable clutter, Grandmother, and I appreciate it. The reading matter, by the way, is a book you may not like, but it seems almost like necessary reading. Clara left it at our house."

"That sounds ominous, but I thank you anyway. And now get on with you – I have supper to get."

Rose turned back at the doorway and said softly, "I had to disappear that last time, I really did. And I hope your eyes are better before my next visit."

Spunky, Jane Hibbard thought, even when she's worrying a bone. She chuckled as she pulled the stew onto the hottest part of the stove. And a little saucy, too. Not a bad thing in a young woman about to get married. Marriage was not easy hereabouts, and Jane sighed as she lifted the lid on the pot and stirred the contents. Not easy a-tall.

As for Rose, as soon as she was out of sight of the house, she picked up her skirt and ran down the hill. She so loved to run, but she knew she was too old for such things. About the only time any female past fifteen ran anywhere had to do with an escaped cow or calf, and then all hands were on the move. Running off, now, that was a whole different kettle of fish. She could not quite believe Grandmother Jane had advised her to just leave a note and take off with Newton to tie the knot. But the more she thought about it, the better it sounded. They would have to go somewhere, and she so wanted to be somewhere besides Eastborough, even if it was just a day or two. Where would they go, she wondered, and who would perform the ceremony? It was delightful to think of saying "I do," or whatever you had to say, without being prompted by the Reverend Lockhead. He was so proper and prissy. Proper, prissy preacher, she said to herself, slowing to a walk and popping her lips as she said the words. Proper, prissy, praying preacher. Proper, prissy, praying, presumptuous preacher. She laughed aloud at her own silliness and continued toward town at a fast walk.

When she reached the turn-off to Emily's house, she hesitated. She needed to tell Emily she was getting married but not tell her about running off. She could do that, she knew she could. But it was hard to tell Emily only part of a story. She had a way of knowing something else was there, and she knew how to dig for it. Rose told herself she had to steel herself against Emily's prying. Oooh, proper, prissy, praying, presumptuous, prying preacher.

"I'll start by telling her that," she said half aloud. And then she was at the door of the small house where Emily and Peter Granger were making their home. It was a cottage really, small but quite charming. It was hard to remember the days when Emily and the still slightly awkward Peter Granger – his feet had never quite fit with his body --seemed as unlikely a pair as a peacock and a donkey, but here they were, apparently as happy as larks.

How, Rose asked herself, does one know when or if a lark is happy? Not because they're singing. Singers sing when they're happy and when they're sad. Singers . . . oh, never mind, she thought. I'm off on a tangent again. She tapped the door three times and waited.

CHAPTER EIGHT
Abby Hires Out

Bull by the horns was Hattie Munson's favorite way of going at things. Hiring Abby Hibbard to do her bidding – and do the things she didn't like or want to do herself – was a good idea, she reckoned, and she was about to act on it. She pulled her horse and buggy in at the upper school, the one everyone in Eastborough referred to as the "big school," which was a misnomer, she felt, because it was the children who were big, not so much the school itself.

But never mind. She'd find Abby here when the youngsters came out, and she would pursue her idea. It did not occur to her that Abby might not be interested. She could not imagine a Hibbard who didn't need cash money, and she proposed to make her a good offer. She would pay a dollar for every Saturday morning that Abby worked at her house – starting at seven thirty and ending at the noon hour. Quite generous by any standards, Hattie decided.

Her small horse snickered and nodded her head up and down as the children spilled out of the school, girls from one door and boys from another. They were not allowed to shout until they were off school grounds, but their feet clattered on the wooden steps and they came in a rush that made the horse nervous.

"Calm down, Annabelle, calm down," Hattie said in a soothing voice that few townspeople had ever heard. "It's only the village hooligans, harmless as ripe apples, but I agree, they're noisier than the blackbirds that came out of the pie." Ah, she thought, there she is, an attractive mite and smiling as if she has just won a prize.

"Abigail!" she called. "Abigail Hibbard!"

Abby heard her name called and looked around to see who might have spoken, but the only person in sight was Mrs. Munson. She stopped and did a complete circle, still seeing no other adult.

"Over here!" Hattie Munson called . "I would like a word with you."

"Lordy, lordy, what can she want with you?" asked Abby's friend Eunice, who was planning to walk home with her.

"Have to see," Abby answered, trying to be calm but feeling a little knot in her stomach. If there was bad news, would anyone send Mrs. Munson to fetch her? It did not seem so. She walked quickly over to the buggy.

"I have a proposition for you, Abigail," Mrs. Munson began. "I wonder if we might discuss it while I drive you home."

"Certainly, Mrs. Munson," Abby said, thinking this was about the oddest thing that had happened to her since Rose had packed her off to Aunt Nell's all those years ago. "Shall I come up?"

Hattie nodded, stretched out her hand, and in three seconds, Abby was sitting beside her. Mrs. Munson certainly smelled nice, she thought, and then lurched as Hattie flicked her whip and the horse moved forward. The whip didn't touch the horse at all, Abby saw, to her relief. She could barely stand it when people hit animals or weren't nice to them in other ways. The way Mrs. Munson used it, the whip made a little cracking sound, and the horse knew it was time to go.

"How was your school day, Abigail?" Hattie Munson asked.

"It was fine, ma'am," Abby answered, wondering if that was why this lady had come for her.

"You are now thirteen, is that right?"

"Yes, ma'am," Abby answered, starting to feel uncomfortable and wishing Rose were here. Or Eunice. Or even Charles. She giggled, thinking that if Charles were here, he'd be hiding under the seat or something, listening but invisible.

"Is that amusing? Your age, I mean?"

"Oh, no, ma'am. I just had a funny – an amusing – thought as we were riding along."

"I believe Rose has trained you well in the household arts, Abigail. Is that true?"

"What would those be, Mrs. Munson?" Abby said, turning to the older woman. "I am not of much account when it comes to arts."

"Making beds, doing laundry, cooking, scrubbing the floor, blacking the stove – those kinds of arts, Abigail. Not all art is painting and playing the clarinet."

"Oh, yes, ma'am. I do all those things. Not every day, ma'am, and not all of them well, but I know how. Every girl, Rose says, has to know these things so she won't be a dunce when she gets married. Ma'am."

Abby saw that they were close to her house, and she hoped the questions would end when they reached the path to the door. She certainly wasn't going to ask Hattie Munson to stop in. Rose would be horrified by the very idea of "that woman," as she often called her, looking around the Hibbard kitchen and parlor. She was so absorbed in worrying about what to do next that Mrs. Munson's next question didn't register at all. She snapped to attention again.

"Abigail?" Mrs. Munson said. "Can you hear me? I asked if you would like to be my hired girl a few hours a week."

Abby gasped. It was the last thing she had expected, and for a minute she was speechless. But she recovered quickly and said in her calmest voice, "I would have to speak with Rose about anything like that." And then, just to be certain she had heard correctly, she added, "I presume I would be paid?"

"Did I not say hired, Abigail? Indeed, you would be paid," Hattie Munson said, smiling for the first time. "I have no idea what Eastborough pays for such work, but I would pay fairly, providing you turned out to be satisfactory."

Abby was thinking she could get money of her own this way, buy a dress or two, go to Ripton once in a while for real shopping and, oh, my, get a wedding present for Newton and Rose. But she kept her excitement inside, hoping Mrs. Munson wouldn't see how much she wanted to do this. When she answered, her voice was still even and quiet. "I am interested, Mrs. Munson. How many hours a week would this be? I have many chores at home, and more than a little school work each evening."

"You speak with Rose and your father, and I will come up with a proposal for hours and pay, Abigail."

"Only Rose, Mrs. Munson. Father has no say about what Charles and I do." She stopped abruptly, remembering suddenly that Rose had once said it was important never to give information to Mrs. Munson – either directly or by speaking to someone else in her presence. Abby had no idea why Mrs. Munson was not to be trusted, but she began to feel as if this new hired girl idea might be out of the question in the Hibbard house.

"What do you mean about your father, Abigail?"

"Oh, it's nothing. It's just that Rose takes care of us, and he takes care of the barn things," Abby said, hoping she had covered up her mistake.

"Perhaps you and Rose could come around on Saturday and let me know what your thinking is," Hattie said, realizing that this girl might be a mere child, but she was very bright and already, at thirteen, very protective of her family. But what *did* that mean, that Silas Hibbard had no say over his own kinder? Hmm. She would have to think on that.

"I'll ask her," Abby said, climbing down from the buggy. "And thank you very much for the pleasant ride, ma'am."

Good manners as well, Hattie thought as she flicked the whip again and moved on toward Henry Goodnow's store. She needed vanilla, and she might just mention that Silas Hibbard apparently had no say about his children's upbringing since Rose moved back to the house three years ago. Henry was so tight-lipped that he probably wouldn't let on a thing, but she planned to tell him about possibly hiring Abigail and maybe that would loosen his tongue.

She was still pleased with her idea for getting Abigail's help. The girl was mannerly, and considering that it was already Thursday, five days away from Saturday bath time, she seemed quite clean. Her stockings had several mended places, but Hattie knew the Hibbards were very frugal – of necessity, she reckoned. That man was attractive to look at, but she didn't figure he was much for making what she would consider a decent living. Chinese chickens and a small production of milk – it was hard to see how they managed to keep Mehitabel on. Still, she'd heard inklings now and then that indicated Rose would never have gone back to her father's house unless hired help was part of the picture.

Hattie sighed. She knew a great deal about Silas Hibbard and his drinking and, now, his not drinking, but she'd never been able to ferret out much information about Rose moving out, then moving back. Sometimes, she thought, no matter how hard you listened, you couldn't get past the fact that you weren't a borner. Borners ruled in this town. Their parents were born here, then they were born here, and they'd all die and get buried here. She brightened, thinking how much more interesting her life had been, not being a borner in Eastborough. She'd had that long stay with the Shakers where she'd learned to admire perfection and hate celibacy and then … but her little horse interrupted her train of thought by pulling up to a hitching post at the store. Sometimes, she thought, the animal read her mind. She stepped down, tied the reins through the ring on the post and went up the steps to talk to Henry Goodnow about Abby Hibbard. Even if he wouldn't tell her anything she considered real news, she reckoned she'd pick up a tidbit of gossip or two.

Eliva Barnes was at the counter getting her mail and chatting with Henry Goodnow, so Hattie slipped around to the glass cases that held buttons and thread and needles. She would poke around here a little and see if she could hear what they were saying. She hoped they were talking about Rose and Newton, who should have been married long ago and would be a disgrace to the community if it weren't for the fact that they were apparently just goody-goody about everything.

Hattie chuckled to herself. Their hats would fall off their heads if they knew how *she* felt about goody-goody. She sighed, thinking those days, those wild days of doing whatever she pleased, were all in the past. If she kicked up her heels now, Eastborough would probably run her out of town the way Jason Harris had gotten rid of that woman Silas Hibbard had taken a liking to. She reckoned it was the woman who had caused Rose to pack up Abby and leave Silas's house, but no one around here ever talked about that, either.

While Hattie busied herself among the buttons, Rose was sharing a cup of tea with Emily at her friend's somewhat cluttered kitchen table. Emily apologized for the utensils that were scattered over the table and explained that she had been trying to tidy up one of the kitchen drawers where she had a habit of dropping everything from measuring spoons to the potato masher.

Rose laughed, thinking this was a long way from the days when she and Emily and Alice tried to figure out the best way to get out of doing kitchen chores. It would be much harder, right now, to tell Emily the news and not tell her all of it. They had shared a lot since they first met as very little girls.

"We are getting married," she finally said, abruptly.

"Everyone knows that," Emily retorted. "But will I still be alive?"

"Right after the last day of school," Rose said, a little note of triumph in her voice.

Emily jumped up from her chair and leaned over to hug her friend. "I am so happy to hear you say that," she said. "Tell. Tell me all about it."

"There's little to tell. I've been wrong to procrastinate so long, but excuses kept popping up, and I made them. No more excuses. We'll be married before the Fourth of July."

"That's not much time for planning, but I reckon you have five lists in your head already," Emily answered, taking her seat again. "Is Newton actually taking time off from haying?"

"Mebbe it will rain," Rose said.

"Even you can't plan on that," Emily said, laughing. "So, apparently he's so relieved that you are not going to be engaged for thirty years that he's willing to risk the crop."

"He said I come ahead of haying," Rose said. "I'd like to, every year," she added a little wistfully.

"He's so sappy about you that he'll do whatever you want forever," Emily answered. "Peter's almost that sappy, and I like it."

"Did you ever have a doubt?" Rose asked, thinking about how anxious she had made herself only a few days ago and remembering at the same time that Aunt Nell had once used that very word about Father, saying he was so sappy about Sarah Sherman that they didn't dare let him use the saw at the mill.

"The night before the wedding," Emily answered quickly. "I sat in the privy for an hour, crying my eyes out and trying to stop and finally stopping when my mother knocked on the door and asked if I had decided to live in a toilet. When I came out, she put her arms around me and told me all brides who have a mind of their own go through this and I shouldn't worry, as long as I loved Peter." She stopped suddenly and looked at Rose's

80

frowning face. "Oh, Rose, I know you don't have a mother to do that for you, but I could, if you want. I really could."

"It's all right, Emily. I've been to see Grandmother Jane, and we pretty much made our way through the hopes and fears things. She's a wonder to talk to, even though her idea of a conversation is something with many twists and turns. If you can keep up, it all comes right in the end."

"You should talk," Emily scoffed. "Perhaps that's where your twisting, turning, seven-track mind came from. In the old days, it sometimes took Alice and I a half hour or more after we left you to figure out all the things you had in mind."

"Me," Rose said and laughed.

"Me," Emily agreed.

"More another time," Rose said, thinking she needed to leave before she said too much. She pushed her chair back and stood, and Emily jumped up and hurried over to throw her arms around her friend and hug her. "There," she said. "Did Grandmother Jane do that?"

"Something like," Rose said in a voice muffled by the hug. "But much frailer." She paused and added, "Her arms feel like ropes instead of arms." Then she pulled away and was out the door before Emily could see the tears that had welled up again. Everyone cried at weddings, Rose thought, but who knew that people cried ahead of time as well?

One more detour surely would do little harm at this point of the day, Rose thought, and she turned off on the lane that led to her Uncle Jason's house. He'd be with the chickens now, and she wanted to let him know the wedding would happen in June. Until her grandmother had mentioned it, she hadn't really considered how her uncle might feel about the delay. She had just felt guilty about the items Aunt Nell had given her for something old, something borrowed, something blue. She only needed the "new" part now, but if she was to wear the dress from Miss Harty's wedding, she'd have to think about what the new thing would be.

Sure enough, as she approached the door to the chicken house, she heard Jason talking to the birds. For her, it seemed like the most ordinary thing to be doing, but she knew people shook their heads over the old men and women who sometimes chatted to themselves as they walked along in town. Rose had spent enough time alone to know that hearing your own voice now and then was better than silence. She tapped on the chicken house door and waited for Jason to lift the hook from the eye. Oooo … hook and eye sounded dreadful even though she hadn't said it aloud. But she had no time to think about that because the door opened, and Jason asked her to step in.

"Greetings, Rose," he said. "To what do the chickens and I owe the honor of this visit?"

"Oh, Uncle, sometimes you are so silly. I'm not an honor. I'm just a niece."

"And a teacher, and a sister and a friend," Jason answered, closing the door behind her and hooking it again.

"You always do the hook," she said. "Even when you're right here."

"You never know when a breeze will set that door swinging and one of these fool chickens will take a notion to flap right out of here," he said solemnly.

"So it's a serious reason."

"Ayuh. And you came here to talk about the wind and the doors and the stupidity of chickens?"

"How do you know whether I just wanted to say hello," she countered in a teasing voice.

"Too busy for that, I reckon."

Rose was instantly contrite. "I'm sorry, Uncle. I've been less than thoughtful lately, but …"

He interrupted. "Just ribbing you, Rose, just ribbing. You know you're welcome here or even in the house if you prefer, anytime, day or night."

"I did come for a reason," Rose said, without acknowledging his little joke. "I wanted you to be one of the first to know that Newton and I are getting married right after the last day of school."

"This year?"

"Uncle!"

"Sorry, Rose. You left the door unhooked for that one." He crossed over to her and gave her what could only be called a bear hug. "I am delighted. You know that. And Nell would be, too, although if she's watching from heaven, she's probably begun to think you'd decided to be an old maid school teacher."

"I will miss it," Rose confessed, her voice so wistful that Jason gave her another hug, smaller this time.

"Course you will. But you'll have other things to do and, if you're lucky, youngsters of your own to teach so they'll be the best in the room when they start school."

Rose started to laugh. "You never rushed me about the wedding, so don't start on offspring before we even get to the altar." She paused, thinking it was quite unfair to leave this wonderful uncle in the dark about her plans, which might not include an altar a-tall. Still, she must talk to Newton first. It was all right that Grandmother Jane knew, but no one else could.

"Knew?" Rose almost said aloud. "She brought it up!" Rose still couldn't believe that someone in that generation was so forward about things. But she admired it.

"Little mud on your hem, Rose," Jason said, interrupting her thoughts. "Been on somebody's bad road?"

"I visited Hibbard Hill," Rose said, reining in her thoughts. "I've neglected Grandmother Jane, too, Uncle. Not just you."

Jason Harris laughed then. "Land sakes, Rose, you have to do whatever you've a mind to and forget the rest of us. You've earned the privilege times over. So stop fretting. And clean off that skirt before you start school tomorrow."

"Yes, sir," Rose said, grateful that they were talking about mud now, rather than weddings.

Jason saw the relief on her face and reckoned he'd veered away from the thin ice. He had always taken a liking to women, something Nell had teased him about on occasion, and he knew one of the reasons was that he liked trying to puzzle them out. They weren't like men, that he knew, had known for years. Men were easy to understand. But this woman, his niece Rose, was about as complicated as he'd ever encountered. Strong-minded, soft-hearted, able to make soap and raspberry jam and at the same time put a mountain of knowledge into youngsters' heads. He knew the men in charge of the school were dumbfounded by her, had been ever since Ben Chandler sat in on her class when she was a mere girl who put her hair up to look older.

Shaking his head, he gestured toward the door. "Perhaps you'd like to get out of this dusty place and step up to the house for a cup of tea?"

Rose's face fell. "Sorry, Uncle. I can't today. Abby will be waiting for me as it is, and I hope she has poked through the ice box and gotten a start on supper or Father will think the world is coming to an end."

"Still wants his women waiting on him, eh?" Jason said. But he grinned as he said it, and Rose gave him a small smile. "Reckon he'll have mixed feelings about you tying the knot. He's been a mite spoiled since you moved back home."

"He's kept his promises," Rose said. "And I've kept mine."

"He's never brought any of that up to me, Rose. Just want you to know. He's been as tight-lipped as a coyote with a live rabbit in its jaw, keeping his own counsel."

"I know," Rose answered softly. "And Mr. Goodnow never said a word, either."

"Henry? He's the town's most unsatisfactory source of news or gossip, as far from Hattie Munson's way of doing as a person could get. Now you get along home and tell Newton how pleased I am about your news."

Rose gave him a hug and was on her way. Jason watched her go and, not for the first time, wished she were his daughter. He loved Clara, but she'd gone off again, and he had no idea when she'd be back in these parts. He hoped Silas had some appreciation for what he had there. He sighed and headed for the house and his lonely supper. He didn't feel much like cooking now, so he thought he'd settle for crackers and milk. Too bad it wasn't quite time for blueberries to go with that.

As for Rose, she found Abby stirring a pot of leftover chicken fricassee on the stove. How pretty she is, Rose thought, with the steam from the food making her hair curl across her forehead. Fourteen already. Fourteen? And she'd been worried about whether supper would be on the way. 'Course, when she was fourteen, she'd taken over the kitchen, the chickens and the children, hadn't she?

Abby turned from the stove and said, "Biscuits are in the oven. I figured we could have new biscuits if we were having old chicken." Rose had no idea what the reasoning behind that was, but she nodded and glanced into the dining room, which was all set up for supper. What a relief.

"Am I allowed to become an employee?" Abby asked, still stirring.

"What?" Rose said. "Land sakes, child, what do you mean by that?"

"Mrs. Munson asked me," Abby said. "She said she thought I'd be well trained in 'household arts,' she called them."

"A hired girl," Rose said under her breath. A little louder, she asked, "Where would you live?"

"Live? Right here, Rose. What do you mean? You wouldn't make me move out, would you? I need to take care of things here, too."

"Of course you do," Rose said quickly, realizing she had spoken without really understanding all of this. "What exactly did Mrs. Munson propose?"

"Household arts," Abby said, "whatever she means by that. I reckon it includes mopping her floor, dusting, mending mebbe, ironing. She didn't say how many hours a day or a week, but I wouldn't want to work there on Saturday or Sunday."

"Did she exclude Saturday and Sunday?"

"No, but I'm not sure I want to work those days. And she didn't say what the pay would be, but I have time for an hour after school, and I am quick, so I would get a lot done in an hour if I put my mind to it."

"I suggest you stop at her house after school one day and tell her exactly that – an hour on school days. And ask what the pay will be and whether she will pay you every Friday or each day."

Abby clapped her hands. "Then I can do it?"

"I know you can do it, Abby, 'well-trained in the household arts' as you are known to be," Rose said, laughing now. "And yes, you have my permission to try it for a month."

"And I don't have to ask Father, do I?"

"No. I'll speak with him about the arrangement," Rose said. "You do know that it's important not to talk to Mrs. Munson about your family or what we do and say from day to day, don't you?"

"I will speak only of the weather," Abby said, nodding solemnly.

CHAPTER NINE
A Calf Named Ruthann

"Have a date yet?" Charles asked at breakfast two mornings later and, when Rose didn't answer, he pushed his foot against hers under the table and asked, "Date, Rose, date? Some of us have busy lives, and we need to know the date of your nuptials."

Rose looked up then and frowned at him. "Nuptials? Where did you find that word?"

"Perfectly decent word as far as I know," Charles answered. "Why is it that I answer your questions, and you pretend mine were never uttered?"

"Now it's *uttered*," Rose said. "Your vocabulary is expanding exponentially."

"Whatever that means," Charles muttered, plunging his spoon to the bottom of his dish of cereal.

"Not an unreasonable question, Rose," Silas said, hoping he wasn't going to start a prairie fire by intervening.

"No," Rose said and got up from the table.

"Not unreasonable or no date?" asked Abby.

"Oh, for land's sake," Rose said, her voice rising. "I haven't seen Newton in four days, and I, we, well, yes and no. It's not unreasonable, and we have no date as yet." She left the room, carrying her breakfast dishes to the kitchen, and pretty soon they heard her light step on the stairs.

The three still at the table looked at each other. "What's got into her?" Charles demanded.

"Case of the jitters, prob'ly," Silas Hibbard said. "She knows when, but she doesn't know exactly when, and Newton's out at Chittendens' place, so she can't nail it down, and it's making her jumpy."

"More like grumpy," Charles answered. "Sir."

"Lay low, young man, lay low. It'll come right soon," Silas told him, stacking his dishes and pushing back his chair to leave the table. The two children followed him, and Abby started putting things away in the kitchen and washing up the breakfast dishes. She was nearly finished when Rose came down and without a word picked up her wrap and went out the door.

"Grumpy," Charles said. "Definitely grumpy."

"Charles," Silas said in an even but stern tone.

"Yes, sir, I know, sir. I will be the last to plague her," Charles answered. He gestured to Abby, who picked up her wrap and her books and was at the door before he was.

As they walked toward the road, Abby started to tell him about her new position as a helper for Mrs. Munson, but Charles didn't even let her finish. Fresh from his failure to get information at the breakfast table, he hooted at her news.

"You can't, you can't," he insisted. "I don't want her to know about me and what I ask Rose and how I take care of my cow and whether my underthings are clean or not."

89

Abby began to laugh. "I'll tell her about all those drawings you have on the chest in your room," she said. "And that you call the cow Ruthann."

Charles stopped walking. "How did you know that? And you can't talk about drawings. Those are mine."

"We all know about Ruthann," Abby teased, stopping beside him. "Father and Rose think it's very funny. I took a lesson from you and hid in the parlor once when they were talking, so I found out. And if you are not nice to me, I'll tell Mrs. Munson." Abby smiled, thinking she had spent many a long year looking for something to hold over Charles's head and suddenly she had it. The cow named for the teacher.

"You won't, will you, Abby?"

"Reckon you'll have to treat me with respect from now on," she said, starting to walk again. Right now, I will only talk to Mrs. Munson about the weather."

"What will you do there?"

"Earn some money of my own," Abby said. "All my own."

"While my pockets remain empty," Charles sighed. "Just a scrap of twine, some hay dust, a half-melted piece of penny candy … little to make a fellow really happy."

"You'll get over it," Abby said, unrelenting. She had no intention of telling him she would share her pay with him, even though she was already thinking she might buy him a new shirt at Mr. Goodnow's. The sleeves were so short on his shirts that they ended well before his wrists, and when he buttoned the cuffs, the buttons strained to get loose.

When they neared the school, Charles took off at a run, not wanting his friends to see him walking with a girl, even though it was his sister. Abby smiled. Rose had long ago explained this to her, one day when she came home crying because Charles had acted as if he didn't even know her. She was in no hurry today. She needed time to think about what Mrs. Munson might want her to do on the very first day. Today. It would be today.

She was also thinking about Rose and the wedding date. Rose had been very short with them that morning, and Abby was certain sure that Rose was keeping some kind of secret. It was never easy to worm anything out of Rose, but she would have to try. It had something to do with Newton and the wedding. Abby smiled again. Well, if she couldn't make Rose talk, she would take it up with Newton. He was much easier.

Several girls were waiting at the fence for Abby when she reached the school, and the bell was ringing. "Thought you were going to be late, the way you were strolling along," Flora said. "Is everything all right?"

"Right as rain," Abby answered with a giggle. "That's what my Grandmother Jane would say, and she sniffs and snorts if you say rain is wrong if the hay's out, or if you have on your new shoes or it's your wedding day."

"Sniffs and snorts? You can't talk about your grandmother like that," Flora said. "It's not respectful."

"She doesn't mind," Abby said, knowing that, indeed, Grandmother Jane did not seem to mind anything she did, which made it right as rain to visit there. "But we need to hurry," she added. "The bell is on its last dings."

That made the whole group laugh, and they ran into the building, slowing to a walk as soon as they crossed the threshold. The school day was about to begin.

Across town at the one-room school, Rose was having trouble concentrating on the rows of pupils in front of her. Can't keep my pupils on my pupils, she said to herself. Now she knew what Grandmother Jane meant when she fussed about being at sixes and sevens. More like thirteens and fourteens, she thought, and every number dressed like a porcupine. She smiled in spite of herself. She didn't want questions from her family right now, and she hated being rude to them. She sighed, thinking even a short time was too long for her to wait for Newton to get back to Eastborough. And the long time was too short to send him a letter about her new plan.

It wasn't even a real plan, just bare bones. Now there's an ugly phrase. Who would want to see the bare bones of anything? She had better figure on how to add flesh and feathers before she had to talk about it with Newton.

A low buzzing broke into her thoughts, and she saw that her charges had started to whisper among themselves, so quietly that the sound was little more than that of a single honey bee making its forays into a snapdragon. Time to concentrate on what you get paid for, she told herself in her sternest inner voice. After the success of the human arithmetic problems, she had given each student a number between one and twelve, just as she had done in her first classroom when Mr. Chandler came every day to keep an eye on her. They could have a lesson right now with those numbers.

"Class," she said aloud, and the buzz stopped as if she had cut it with a knife. They are so good, she thought, prob'bly better than at home. "We are going to honor spring today and make a special spelling list with words that make you think of spring. We will start with number twelve, and as soon as Will gives a word, number eleven should speak up without being called on.

No need to stand, either. I will write the words on the board. You may begin."

"Garden," said number twelve, halfway out of his seat before he remembered the instructions. He sat down quickly, quite grateful to be first.

"Peas," said Number 11.

"Mayflowers," said Number 10.

"Rain."

"Seeds."

"Weeds." Everyone laughed at that, liking the rime.

"Skunks," said Number 6 with a grin, pleased to get another laugh.

"Woodchuck."

"Swimming."

"Pasture."

"Baseball."

"Easter," said Number 1, with a huge sigh.

"Why did you sigh, Mary?" Rose asked.

"I was afraid all the words would be used up," Mary said. "I watched some of mine go, and I had to keep thinking of another one, and I knew Easter always comes in the spring."

"You did well," Rose said. "It's hard to be last. But it's impossible to use up all the words, even if we had thirty children in this room. Now, each of you must copy these words in your best handwriting. Do it in a list down the page, please, and then we will work on learning to spell them. While you are doing that, I will add two more: bluebirds and housecleaning."

The pupils bent to their task, including the smallest of them, and Rose let her thoughts go back to the possibility of running off with Newton instead of getting married in the Reverend

Lockhead's church. She glanced at the list on the board and it came to her so suddenly that she nearly spoke aloud. "Swimming." They could go to the shore where she had visited with Miss Harty and get married and walk on the beach, and she could show Newton the sand dollars and the sea gulls and the lighthouse. They could go by train, which would be quite fast, and perhaps Newton would stay away from the hay for three days. She was so excited that she clapped her hands together and was startled when twelve pairs of eyes were suddenly focused on her.

"Never you mind," she said quickly. "I was just figuring on other ways to go from one to twelve or twelve to one." Someone in the second row giggled, and Rose knew that this number experiment of hers was turning out well. Oh, my, how I will miss these little ones, she thought, and then pushed that idea aside, replacing it with a mental picture of Newton's face coming closer and closer to hers.

While Rose's face flushed in response to her inner thoughts, Silas Hibbard's was nearly purple from plain old exertion as he bent beneath the sapling roosts in his chicken house, scraping out the litter and replacing it with fresh sawdust and a few handfuls of crushed oyster shells. But he was also thinking about Newton and wondering what Rose had up her sleeve. She rarely spoke the way she had that morning, and he reckoned something was up.

At least they had decided on a time to get married, and he'd begun to wonder if that would ever happen. He smiled as he remembered how he was so anxious to marry Sarah that he had snitched an end of chalk from the schoolhouse to make a row of circles on the barn wall, then crossed them out as the days before the wedding passed. Still, even if Newton was half as anxious as he had been, it was surprising that the lad would consent to a wedding just when haying season was getting under way. Silas knew it was none of his business. He had an idea that his only role in all this would be to buy Rose a dress and put on some kind of affair after the ceremony, but he could not for the life of him imagine the ceremony itself.

She'd given him her Declaration of Independence way back before she moved back home, and he knew he had no right to expect he would accompany her down the aisle of the church. She had made it terribly clear that he had no hold on her, and he had honored that outwardly, much as it chafed in his heart. So even if the reverend considered it proper for a father to give away his daughter, Silas wasn't going to do that. She was her own person. He didn't own her anymore.

"Never did, truth be known," he said aloud. He'd as much as lost her when he tried to stop her schooling, and even though he didn't succeed, he had not forgiven himself for that. Never had "owned" Sarah, either, come to think of it, although they'd rarely had a falling out.

He'd come to see Sarah and Rose as peas in a pod. The good thing was that he could ask Rose right out what she wanted to do, and she'd tell him, certain sure. He sighed, wishing he'd asked Sarah more often what her druthers were. He'd been something of a fool when it came to that. He finished spreading the new litter in the chicken house, checked the water trough and went out, latching the door. He'd ask Rose today, he told himself as he trundled the wheelbarrow of old litter through the main part of the barn and then outdoors. His chores done for the moment, he decided to see if she had come straight home from school.

As it turned out, he didn't get a chance. When he reached the kitchen, Newton was there, sitting in the rocker by the stove and, Silas could hardly believe it, twiddling his thumbs. The young man jumped up as Silas came through the door and greeted him.

"I'm waiting for Rose," he said. "She is changing out of her schoolmarm clothes and into something more suitable for walking in the woods."

"Walking in the woods, is it?" Silas said, grinning. "Stick to walking, young man, stick to walking."

Newton laughed. "Have you met Rose?" he asked. "When she says 'walking,' she means exactly that. After a long day's work and a long ride here, I'll be walking."

"She does mean what she says," Silas answered, suddenly solemn. "It's well that you know that from the outset." He started to say more but stopped when Rose appeared in the doorway wearing an old skirt and shirtwaist. She had Sarah's blue knit shawl over her shoulder and boots on her feet.

"We're going on a hunt for mayflowers," she said. "If it's not already too late."

"Your mother went every spring," Silas answered. "She called them trailing arbutus, I believe."

"Right," Rose said, her voice a touch crisp. She had so many things on her mind that she really didn't want to talk about wildflowers. Nor did she intend to actually look for any. But she'd tell Newton that as soon as they were out of this house. "Abby's in charge of supper," she added. "I don't know precisely when I will return."

"Abby is becoming quite capable," Silas said. "Charles and I have come to depend on her."

"Father," Rose began. "Father," she began again, thinking this was as good a time as any to tell him, what with Newton standing there and all. "Abby is going to earn some money for herself by helping Mrs. Munson with some household chores perhaps two afternoons a week after school."

"Hired her out, have you?" Silas said, his voice rising. "Without consulting me? And to that busybody?"

Rose sighed. "We agreed, Father, that I would see to Abby and Charles and make decisions about their upbringing. Abby is old enough to do some kind of work outside the house, and Mrs. Munson for some reason was interested in her in particular. She and I have discussed at some length that she is not to impart any news of any kind to Mrs. Munson. If she forgets that caveat, the employment will be over."

Newton watched this exchange as if he were at a play, his eyes moving from one speaker to the other and back again. Other than his eyes, no part of his body moved. Rose, he thought, was a wonder and rather fierce. He reckoned he'd try not to cross her, now or in the future. Still, he knew all too well how important it was for her to stand up to her father.

"A caveat, is it," Silas said, reaching out his hand and squeezing Rose's shoulder. "It's your decision, Rose," he said, his voice lower and softer. "It certainly is. And you prob'ly know as well as any of us what Mrs. Munson thrives on. It may be a good experience for Abby. I should have known you would see the forest and the trees."

"Thank you, Father. I trust her to be discreet."

Newton decided he'd had quite enough of all this politeness, so he cleared his throat a little loudly and said, "Shall we go now, Rose?"

She smiled at him and linked her arm through his. "Indeed," she said. And they went out the door. Silas watched as they made their way toward the road, Newton looking down at Rose and her face close to his shoulder. High time they were married, he thought, realizing that he really didn't want to think about Rose moving away. He felt his eyes start to water and shook his head. If he didn't watch out, he'd be as soft as a half-boiled egg. He'd better have a look at what might be turned into supper, in case Abby hadn't any idea where to start on that. He shook his head again. Hard to imagine that child hired out. His thoughts went back to Rose. She'd been more than a little short with them that morning, and he was certain sure she had more on her mind this afternoon than mayflowers. Well, he reckoned he'd find out sooner or later what was going on. He lifted the latch on the icebox and saw that a sizable piece of pot roast was right in front. That would do nicely, he thought, and took it out so it would start to warm up.

He was right about the mayflowers. As soon as they reached the road, Newton asked Rose where the best place was for trailing arbutus, and she had started to laugh. "I would like to go to the rock," she had answered. "The walking and the flowers were just a way to get out of the house."

"Thought so," Newton said, chuckling. "Your father knew that, too," he added. "So, let's get to the rock and mebbe you'll let me in on what's going on in your beautiful head."

"Why do you suppose there's anything there?" Rose teased, suddenly feeling more relaxed than she had all day and pleased no end that Newton considered her head beautiful.

98

"You are a half mile from being like yourself, so I reckon something is kicking up a storm in your brain, or some part of your brain."

"Oooh, what will happen if it goes up to a mile? Or two or three?"

"I will be beside myself, without doubt," Newton answered, putting his arm around her waist and pulling her closer.

Beside himself, Rose thought, one Newton next to another Newton. What a funny idea. But aloud, she said, "What will the neighbors think?"

"They'll think I still plan to marry you," he said, "which is true."

"That, Newton, is what we have to talk about."

He stopped right in the road, put his hands on her shoulders and turned her toward him. "What does that mean? Have you changed your mind?"

"Newton! How could you even think that? But I want to wait until we're at the rock, please."

He nodded. He knew – and now he knew that Silas knew – that it was dang near impossible to get around Rose or distract her when she was on a mission. As she appeared to be at this very moment. With his hands still on her shoulders, he turned her again and said, "Then let's put our minds on getting there."

"And our feet," she answered. When he released her shoulders, he took her hand in his and they went on, with Newton occasionally twirling the engagement ring on her finger. His grip tightened as he thought about school ending and a wedding band joining that small opal ring.

In a few minutes, they turned off the road onto the small path that led to Rose's rock. Once there, she opened the satchel she was carrying and spread out a small blanket for them to sit on.

"Grandmother Emma says you get piles if you sit on cold stone," Rose said. "It may or may not be so, but why risk it – whatever it is."

"Right," Newton said, thinking about taking her in his arms and warming that rock as it had never been warmed before.

"Right?" Rose said. "What do you mean? Do you even know what piles is?"

"I reckon if there's more than one of them, it would have to be piles *are*," he said, sitting down abruptly and pulling her down beside him.

"Is, I think," Rose said. "And I don't want to talk about them anymore."

In one quick move, Newton put his right arm across Rose's body and pushed her down, stretching out on the rock beside her. "Fine with me," he said, propping himself on his left elbow and kissing her, beginning at her forehead and gently touching her eyes, her nose, her cheeks and her ears with his lips. When she tried to kiss him on the mouth, he ducked his head, tweaked open the top button on her shirtwaist and kissed her neck on both sides and then under her chin.

After her first attempt to respond, Rose lay very still, not quite knowing what to do. Every time his mouth grazed any part of her skin, it felt so incredibly good that she knew it must be forbidden fruit, at least in the eyes of the Reverend Lockhead. She wondered, for the thousandth time, what these fruits were in the eyes of God, if he was paying attention. She shivered and Newton, thinking she was cold, moved closer, covering more than half of her body with his. She caught her breath, then pulled her arms free, grabbed him by the hair, lifted his head and kissed him for a long time, a sweet kiss that made her shiver again.

Newton drew away then, looked down at her and smiled. Rose hoped he was going to kiss her some more. But he reached for the bun on the back of her head, pulled out the tortoise hairpins and let her hair fall. The sun, slanting through the trees, caught some of the highlights in her light brown hair, and he ran his hands through the strands, over and over.

Then he paused suddenly, dropped down and said, "What did you want to talk about?"

Rose turned on her side to face him and said in a rather shaky voice, "I love you, and I have a plan for the wedding, and I hope you won't hate it." Her words came out in such a rush that it took Newton a second or two to get it straight in his mind. Then he said, incredulous, "Hate it? How could I hate any idea that included our getting married? What I want more than anything on this earth, more than six Jerseys, three Chinese hens and two weeks of perfect weather for haying?"

"How about seven Jerseys?" Rose teased. "Or haying done by magic?" But she saw how his face suddenly set in an almost-but-not-quite sad look that she relented and added quickly, "I think we should run away."

Startled and picturing the two of them going west like Clara, he snorted. But she put her finger over his mouth and went on, "Run away just to get married. It's called eloping. We wouldn't have to talk to the reverend – and I just know I'd never get through that without saying something sinful to him – we wouldn't have to listen to everyone's advice about what to do and what not to do, and we'd be by ourselves for the whole time, which is what I would like the most."

Newton was clearly astonished. He had pictured, for quite some time now, a church scene where all the relatives and townspeople were gathered, where Rose came down the aisle in a frilly white gown of some sort and where they would say "I do" or "I will" or whatever was required when asked to do so. At first, he had seen Rose on her father's arm, as Ruthann Harty had been on her father's, but had later figured that wasn't going to happen and had spent quite some time wondering how that seemingly entrenched tradition would be circumvented. He had a notion Rose would take care of it, and now it appeared she was planning on it.

"How would this eloping work?" he asked cautiously.

"We would make arrangements to be married somewhere else and then we'd take the train there, get married and stay in an inn for mebbe two nights, mebbe three, and then we'd reappear, married with no Eastborough fuss."

"I dunno," Newton said. "My mother prob'bly has her heart set on seeing her eldest get hitched. And I think your grandmothers would be as mad as wet hens."

Ignoring her impulse to ponder damp chickens, Rose said in a pleading tone, "Think about it, please, my dearest Newton. It would take care of the problem of my father doing the so-called 'giving away,' which I cannot have him do. And it would be lovely to surprise everyone after all this time." She stopped, took a deep breath and plunged on. "If you must know, I had a terrible dream about going down the aisle with my face beet red and my gown getting tangled on the ends of the pews and people laughing at me and ..." She stopped again, feeling tears popping up in her eyes and blurring her vision enough to make her feel they were about to overflow and ruin everything. She looked away and went on in a near whisper, "Sarah and Aunt Nell were there, in my dream, the only people who weren't laughing as I tried to free my dress, and they can't – they can't come."

And then the tears spilled out, first drop by drop and then in a torrent. Newton held her close and whispered whatever he could think of in her ear and finally took her face in his hands and pushed her back so he could look right at her. In his most serious tone he said, "So we'll elope." He kissed her gently on the lips and then drew her close again, waiting for her sobs to quiet. "But believe you me, Eastborough will make a fuss all right. Just not the one you're worried about."

In a minute or so, she mumbled something into his chest, and he pushed her away again. "I have no ears in my chest," he said softly, "so repeat that for the hearing parts, if you please."

That, he noticed with satisfaction, brought a tiny smile to her face. "I said," she said, trying to sound calm but failing, "you are close to perfect."

"That falls a little short," he drawled in that way he had when he was ribbing her. "I had assumed you considered me absolute perfection. Now, I expect, we'll elope and you'll start making a list of the things I must do to move toward that goal."

"And you're also very amusing," Rose said, actually laughing. She groped in her pocket for a handkerchief, discovered she had none, sat up and leaned forward to wipe her face with the hem of her skirt.

"Ever practical if not delicate," Newton said, hoping he wasn't pushing his luck. But Rose was already herself again, ready to launch into more details about her plan if he was of a mind to listen.

"Shall I go on?" she asked.

"Indeed," he said, turning and dropping his head into her lap. Rose traced a line around his eyes and down his nose with her thumb and then placed her hand on his face. She drew a deep breath and said, "I wondered if we could go to the sea. It is so beautiful near where the Hartys live, and I know my way around there a little, and there's an inn where you can sit on the porch and watch the gulls drop clams and crabs on the rocks to break their shells and ..."

"That's romantic, I must say. The killing of crabs and clams while we hold hands on a porch," Newton interrupted.

But Rose did not rise to the bait. "We can walk on the beach in our bare feet, stick our toes in the cold Atlantic and, oh, Newton, you can't even imagine how that air wipes out whatever cobwebs are in your head."

"No spiders in my cranium, Rose. I should tell you that before we are married ... no spiders. Occasional louse in my locks but nary a spider."

"Newton!" she exclaimed, now the one to interrupt. "You know what I mean."

"Hmm," he said. "And I think we should do it. So you need to tell me more." She started to squeal with delight, but he sat up quickly and covered her mouth with his, kissing her until she pulled away. Newton was well aware that it was time to stop. He drew back a few inches and lay on his side looking at her, and, as he had hoped, she stretched out on her side so their faces were just inches apart. He had just reached the point where he was wondering how any plan like this could be executed without the whole town finding out in advance when Rose spoke.

"Grandmother Jane – she is the one who suggested this, by the by, so that's one grandmother who won't have a conniption – said we could tell her or Mr. Goodnow, and neither of them would tattle. But when people found out we were missing, one or the other of them could explain where we were. Well, not exactly where we were, but what we were about. She said I had run away before and was obligated to the whole town not to panic anyone again. The best part, Newton, the very best part was that she is the one who suggested running away after I told her about the dream."

"Nightmare, sounds like," Newton commented. "And you did, of course, I wish to remind you, pledge that you were done with running."

"Nightmare," Rose agreed. "And that promise was only not to run away from you, had nothing to do with running away *with* you. I can see that your noteworthy memory is likely to plague me for all of my married life."

"A-yuh," he nodded. "But *with* is good. Quite good. I expect I could consult with Henry Goodnow about how we secretly get a license. And I cannot believe you would do this without telling Ruthann. On second thought, Joshua is the best person, being a lawyer underneath his overalls, to look into the preliminaries." Rose started to answer, but Newton could take no more of being just inches away from her. He pushed her onto her back again, raised up on his left elbow and leaned down to kiss her very gently. As the kiss went on, his right hand moved to the soft roundness above her waist, and when Rose did not stir, Newton cautiously started to move his hand in a small circle, startled by the rip of excitement that plunged from his throat to parts of his body that he figured might explode. Then Rose broke away and with an enormous sigh, tears in her eyes again, picked up his calloused hand and moved it to her waistline.

"Please," she said, with a catch in her voice. "Please."

"One day," he answered, rolling onto his back, "I want that word to mean 'do it,' and 'do it more.'"

"I know it's considered unseemly of me," she answered, her voice much stronger, "but I can barely wait for that day. And will it just be one?"

It was Newton's turn to laugh. "Not only unseemly are you, but a forward girl, possibly not even a lady, making such remarks. But I look forward to forward and unseemly and a thousand days, if it pleases you."

"Forever, Newton, my dear one. Forever. When you touch me on my scrawny neck, for land's sakes, it is like fire, and that's not even forbidden."

"Then why have we waited so long?" he sighed. "Why have you been there like a tempting dessert never letting me have a taste? You could have become stale, moldy or just plain crumbled into a heap in all this time. Or, come to think of it, it is I – you hear me not saying 'me', I trust – who should be in a heap."

Now it was Rose who laughed aloud. "Crumbled in a heap is my favorite picture of you," she said. Then she sobered and in one of her lightning changes of subject said, "Emily told me it might hurt."

"Are you worried, Rose?" Newton asked anxiously. "I don't know whether making real love will hurt you, but I don't want to do that. Are you afraid?"

"A little – but I trust you," she said, looking up at him with so much love all over her face that he wondered why they didn't leave that very night. He wasn't at all certain how it would go, but he had a feeling he'd be happier when they had gone past the wedding night. Perhaps he should try to clear the air now.

"Joshua says …" But he could say no more because Rose sat up quickly and in another swift change of mood said, "You discussed our, our, our …" Then she could not finish because Newton put his big hand over her mouth and said, rather sternly, "I discussed nothing except whether wedding nights were sheer bliss or a bit of trouble, having heard that virgin brides do not always take to the ultimate act immediately."

Rose pulled his hand off her mouth and gasped for air, snorting and laughing in such a way that Newton thought she might be choking to death. He gave her a little shake and she collapsed against him, shaking with giggles. He held her there, figuring this might be a time to just wait it out and see what happened. He had known for a long time that being married to Rose Hibbard would be a continuing adventure.

When she was still, he said, "Perhaps Ruthann's father would be the person to get us a license or make it possible for us to get one."

She sat up again. "Then you like the idea of the sea and the inn and the seagulls?"

"Especially the murdered clams," he answered. "But yes, I like it all. And in a year or two, my mother will get over not being there."

"Will she really mind so much?" Rose asked anxiously. "I respect her and like her, and I don't want to get off on the wrong foot with her."

"You couldn't," he answered. "I sometimes worry that she likes you more than she likes me."

"I'm sure I'll take to it quickly," Rose said, shifting the conversation again.

But Newton knew her well. "Indeed," he said, pulling her back down to the rock and stroking her left arm with his thumb. "Any lady who kisses the way you do and gives all those little shivers shows clear signs of being a quick learner."

"Will we be teaching each other?" she asked slyly, suddenly wondering if Newton had already tried this thing he called the "ultimate act."

"I reckon so," Newton answered, his voice very solemn. "Just as we've been doing for years on end now. It's taken a few dives into cold river waters, but I've not strayed from you. You know, for a girl without a mother, you know a lot of things."

"I've had to. And Ruthann has helped."

Newton stood, stretched his arms over his head and looked down at her. "It's high time we went back to where other people are watching us," he said. "Or I'll be into ultimate things now. Shall we look for those flowers?"

CHAPTER TEN
Abby's Tricks Fail

Before Rose even opened the door Abby could tell that her sister was no longer upset or whatever it was that had made her so strange the morning before. Rose's step was light on the outside stairs, and she breezed into the kitchen, a smile on her face. Her hair was down and flying in all directions, Abby noticed, but she reckoned she'd better not ask if Rose had lost her hairpins. She also saw that her sister had a bunch of mayflowers clutched in one hand, and that made her smile. Father had said Rose and Newton were going on a mayflower search, and then he had raised one eyebrow and laughed. But she could see that they had done exactly that. She couldn't imagine why taking out hairpins was involved, but never mind.

"What's left for supper, Abby?" Rose asked cheerfully as she tossed her shawl on the rocking chair and filled a small vase with water for the flowers.

"I saved you a whole plate in the oven," Abby answered. "I was afraid to put everything on the table for fear Charles would devour it all. He's so hungry all the time, Rose, and I sometimes look at him and see a pig with his feet in the trough."

That made Rose laugh. "Abby," she said in a mock scolding tone, "you cannot think of your brother as swine. It's inappropriate."

Feeling much braver about this unpredictable sister, Abby replied saucily, "Is flying hair appropriate?" And then immediately regretted this sally, thinking she was going to be in great trouble for being fresh.

Rose just gave her one of those adult smiles that are so annoying to children. "Hair is hair," she said, producing hairpins from her pocket and swiftly tucking hers up in a bun again. "And I am almost as hungry as Charles."

Abby pulled the warm plate from the oven and set it at Rose's usual place at the table. Then she sat down and watched while Rose ate. Even if Rose didn't tell her a thing about what she and Newton were up to, Abby was pleased Rose was no longer what Charles called "grumpy." She would not, however, repeat Charles' mistake in asking if a date for the wedding had been set. Her guess was everything had been settled in the past two or three hours. She went back to the kitchen to get Rose a tumbler of water and when she returned to the table saw that Rose was twirling her engagement ring on her finger while she ate.

"It's such a pretty ring, Rose," Abby said, suddenly thinking she might find a way to worm something out of her sister.

"I think so, too," Rose answered. "I look at it often because the colors change in the light." Abby sighed and decided she might as well report on her day with Mrs. Munson. Maybe when they went to bed Rose would talk about Newton. Sometimes she did that when the room was dark and they were almost asleep. She remembered that Uncle Jason had told her how people often said things in the dark that they wouldn't say when the sun was up.

"I polished Mrs. Munson's silver teapot today," she said, "and scrubbed her toilet and filled her wood box with the nicest split ash and the best kindling I've ever seen. She has a separate bin for the kindling."

"I wonder who chops wood for her," Rose said. "The kindling, you know, might come from Uncle Jason. He has all those well-dried scraps from his workshop, and he does cut them up in such neat pieces that you'd think he was going to make something with them. I know Aunt Nell set great store by them. And I reckon he'd have enough to supply Hattie as well. But who could imagine that?"

"All I know is she wants the kindling laying the same way in a special box," Abby sighed. "She has to be the most orderly person I've ever met."

"Lying," Rose said and then paused. "Or maybe it is laying. I can't put my finger on the right or wrong of that." Abby giggled at the very idea that a word stumped Rose, and then Rose said, "What else?" intrigued in spite of herself. Mrs. Munson had so often tried to delve into their lives and now she realized she might enjoy a peep into hers. But Abby was having none of it.

"It's all very well for me to complain about the kindling," she said, "but it would be quite inappropriate, as you are fond of saying, for me to gossip about my employer." To her relief, Rose grinned and patted Abby's hand.

"How right you are," she said. "And curious as I am, I will not ask such a question again. People are entitled to whatever privacy they can get."

"You too, I suppose?" Abby asked, her hopes roused again.

"Me, too," Rose agreed, refusing to rise to a bait as obvious as a worm wriggling on one of Father's fishhooks. The, seeing the disappointment on Abby's face, she relented. This was the little sister who had always defended her, and she must give her something.

"We did gather mayflowers, Abby, as you can see, but we mostly went to my rock to talk about wedding plans, and we settled almost everything."

"Oh, Rose, I'm so glad," Abby cried, adding with an impish look, "And was there kissing?"

"Not that you could see," Rose said, "since we weren't on a porch or outside a window where you were spying."

Abby sighed again. She reckoned she'd learned as much as she could, so she went back to describing her work day. She had been sent to the store for Hattie Munson's mail and learned that she had a post office box, just as Rose once had. "And quite a pile of mail," Abby said, "including the new shopping catalogue and a newspaper from Albany, New York."

"Hmmm," Rose said, returning her attention to her dinner and resolving not to even think about what that meant. Then she grinned. That Abby. She was putting out a tease as long as her braids to see if Rose could be tricked. It was hard not sharing her news with this wonderful sister, but she knew how easy it was for secrets to slip out and how tempting it was to tell just one person.

"Do you have homework?" she asked, figuring a change of subject ought to help a little.

"Only some reading," Abby said. "I do love that part of school the most, Rose."

"Mother would be proud of that," Rose answered and once again concentrated on what was left on her plate. In less than two minutes, she had finished and cleared her place. She told Abby she would take care of the rest of the washing up so the homework reading could get done as quickly as possible. She intended to turn down the wicks on the lamps early and get to bed where she hoped she would have a more peaceful sleep than she'd had in several days. At least, she thought, we must have blotted out the church nightmare. Unless, she realized with a sigh, dreams and nightmares lived in a world of their own and paid reality no mind a'tall.

CHAPTER ELEVEN
Abby Doesn't Tell

Almost the minute Abby stepped inside Hattie Munson's kitchen the next day, she knew she was going to have a hard time. After greeting her quite properly and presenting her with a written list of things to be done, Hattie immediately asked if all was well with Rose and her beau.

"Oh, yes," Abby answered instantly, wondering right away if her answer gave away any family secrets. She decided it didn't and added quickly, "Did you want me to start with the bathroom or the ironing?"

But Hattie was not to be put off. She waved her hand and said the ironing was a good place to begin and, in fact, she had already set two flatirons on the stove to heat. So Abby set up the ironing board and went to fetch the shirtwaists that Mrs. Munson wanted ironed.

"I put out two skirts to be pressed as well," her employer said. "They are over the back of a dining room chair and should be hung in the closet when you have finished."

Abby picked up one of the irons, splashed a drop of water on it to test the heat and was satisfied when it sizzled and disappeared. She started on one of the shirtwaists, carefully ironing the lace at the cuffs first, then the sleeves. She hoped Mrs. Munson had something to do, but Hattie seated herself in the kitchen rocker and watched as Abby worked.

"I saw them having a quarrel right in the middle of the road the other day," Hattie persisted. "Perhaps it was, in fact, just yesterday. They were walking along and then, suddenly, they stopped and, I do believe, had a serious disagreement." She paused, but when Abby said nothing, she went on. "It would be such a shame after all this time if your sister were to change her mind about that wonderful young man, wouldn't it?"

"I'm certain she hasn't," Abby said, again measuring her words carefully and saying them a second time in her head to see if they were out of bounds or not. She decided not. She couldn't let Mrs. Munson think Newton and Rose had a falling out. The truth was quite the opposite, but she would bite her tongue before she went into detail about that.

"Humph," Hattie said. "I reckon she thinks you're too young to be her confidant. You girls have done well since you lost your mother, but it's easy to see it's left a space in your lives."

"Our mother taught us many things before she was killed, Mrs. Munson," Abby said softly, thinking it could do no harm to defend a mother who had been dead all these years. "We have managed. And besides," she added defensively, "Rose always says you can't lose your mother, that she's with you forever, for better or worse. Ours, ma'am, would be for better."

Hattie chuckled. "And she taught you to keep your mouths shut about family matters, I do believe. Well, that's a quality to be admired." She sat forward and got up from the rocker. "I will be in the barn currying my horse if you need anything or have a question about the list of duties I've set out for you."

"Yes, ma'am," Abby answered with relief. She had finished the first shirtwaist and started on one that had a great deal of lace trim along the buttons, so she dampened the whole front and bent over her work. She did not look up again until she heard the door close.

This, she told herself, is something like those circus folks I've heard about, the ones who walk on a little wire. Except, she thought, if they slip they probably die. I would just be mortified. Now there, she giggled, is a word Rose would like. It even sounds terrible. She finished the fancy lace garment and carefully laid it on the back of the sofa. Mrs. Munson had said to hang it in the closet, but Abby knew it needed to dry a bit first.

Across town, Emily Granger was ironing, too, and thinking that more was going on with Rose and Newton than her friend had let on the other day. Time will tell, she decided, even though waiting was most unsatisfactory. They would get married and then Rose would have children and their children could be best friends, and it would be wonderful. She was sorry Alice was too far away to add her children to the group. In the meantime, she knew Rose would tell her the whole story when she was ready. And not until then. Rose never spilled beans accidentally. Never.

She frowned. If Rose and Newton lived out at the Chittenden place, she might not see them very often. And she had a feeling that was part of the plan. The cottage there, with some fixing, would work just fine for a couple. And Newton already had his precious Jerseys there. It always amused her that

116

Rose called them "precious Jerseys" most of the time. She seemed, Emily thought, to be a bit put out that the four-legged creatures took up space in Newton's heart. No need, Emily knew – Newton had been besotted about Rose almost from the first moment they had talked to him, when they were still just schoolgirls.

Newton, on his way back to the Chittenden farm, was thinking he'd better get at that little house. It needed better plumbing and a new sink in the kitchen. He smiled suddenly. He reckoned a chat with Charles would be an excellent idea. Rose had told him about the stacks of drawings Charles had, all kinds of barns and houses and even a church or two. It was hard to think of Charles as anything but a mischievous younger brother, but he knew the boy had talents way beyond shoveling manure and taking care of a cow of his own. A cow named Ruthann, of all things.

They'd be renting the cottage from Joshua, who had promised to supply some of the lumber and fixtures for the renovation. Someday, Newton hoped, they would have a place of their own, with plenty of space, a good heating system and a huge porch. Rose put great store by a porch, he knew, and perhaps Charles could figure a way to put a small one on this first house.

He did hope Ben Chandler's boys would take on his haying while he was walking on a beach with his bride. Newton laughed out loud at the absurdity of the long engagement ending with elopement, and his little horse nearly lost a step as he turned his head to see what set off his master in this unaccustomed way.

"She's a caution, Tommy, that's what," he told the horse. "I jes think I got her figured out down to the last button, and she turns me upside down again. Prob'bly going to do it for the next forty years, my pleasure, my pain. And worth it, all worth it." He flicked the reins, and Tommy picked up the pace. "Time's a-wasting," Newton said, still speaking to Tommy. "We have a lot to do while the school year plays out." He was still smiling and as the horse trotted along, he leaned back, yawned, wondered if he'd be less tired once they were married and he wasn't making these trips between Chittendens' and Eastborough. He let his thoughts wander into all sorts of times he and Rose had gone through. And then, thinking about being at her rock so many of those times, he dozed off and let the horse find the way.

Rose, however, was wide awake. Teaching had become second nature to her, so her two-track mind was running fast on this day. While the children read aloud, did their numbers on the big slate at the front of the room and spelled their vocabulary words aloud, she nodded and corrected and at the same time ran through the list of things she would need in what her mother called a hope chest. It was, she supposed, quite hopeful, actually, since it was supposed to contain what a young woman would need when she married. Pillow slips and bureau scarves. She didn't suppose she'd need any antimacassars, although she loved the word. Her grandmothers still used them on their wing chairs and sofas, but Rose thought they were considerable trouble – to make and to keep clean. Men always leaned their heads on them and apparently didn't have totally clean heads because the delicate pieces of linen were often a bit soiled. The idea of men with dirty heads made her chuckle, and she was instantly aware that the sound had stopped the whole class. They were all looking at her, wondering which of them had done something funny.

"It's not you," she said quickly, worrying that any one of them might think she was laughing at him or her. "It was just a thought that ran through my mind. They do that sometimes." Some of these children were so shy that she knew they took things personally and were quite sensitive. She wondered if their parents were so strict that they were always nervous about making a mistake or being laughed at. But she had no idea how to help them. She had grown up with many days of fearing her father and wondering if Charles and Abby would be all right. Several of the children nodded at her, and when they all bent their heads to their work again, she went back to her private thoughts.

She would need some kind of swimming outfit if they were to be at the shore in June. And a hat to shade her face when they walked on the beach. And shoes. She really had shorted herself constantly on shoes. She squelched another chuckle, thinking that shorting herself was hardly applicable to her shoe situation, not with her size nine feet. More like longing herself. She sighed. She had often longed for smaller feet, but it was only in China, she understood, that women actually did anything about it. And their treatment, apparently a lot like folding the feet, sounded too painful to think about.

She focused on the children again and decided it was time to change the mood in the room, hers and theirs. "Please put your pencils down," she said, "and stand at your place. Whoever has Number Twelve should step out and start to march clockwise around the room, followed by Number Nine and so forth."

The children practically jumped to their feet. They loved this kind of thing and never knew what Miss Hibbard would think of next. Rose, on the other hand, was hoping she wouldn't have to explain clockwise this time and, sure enough, Number Nine was heading in the right direction. The rest were following quickly as they moved away from their places and began to circle the room.

"Faster," Rose said, "but no running."

They began to really move and to laugh, one or two stumbling on the turns because they were all keeping their eyes on the teacher, waiting for the next instruction.

"Stop and stoop," Rose said. They all halted and hunkered down, the girls giggling and making sure their skirts weren't caught. She let them stay down for nearly a minute, then said, "Up and march, please. Eyes on the flag as you come toward the front of the room."

When they had circled the room four times, she told them to stop and return to their seats. That, she thought, should get out some of the extra energy and keep them from squirming until at least after the noon hour. She handed out paper and began the arithmetic lessons, telling the littlest ones to write their numbers from one to as far as they could go and beginning some problems in addition and subtraction with the older pupils. It was not easy to keep everyone busy with at least four levels of children in the room, and she did hate giving out what she thought of as busy work. But doing the numbers was better than that, since they all knew they had to write them carefully, not running a race to get down the most.

With her mind mostly on eloping with Newton, she was finding it hard to get through this school day. And it was going to be nigh impossible to keep their secret. She'd always been good at that, sometimes infuriating Alice and Emily with her unwillingness to share secrets with them. They could cross their hearts six times, and she wouldn't tell. And now, she wanted to tell them both. She was not only getting married but running away to get married. They would be so excited. But she mustn't tell. A secret was a secret, and she'd always said nothing a-tall could worm one out of her. Today she wasn't so sure. Ah, that was it. She'd discuss secrets with the children until it was time to ring the final bell. They would love that. She was quite certain no one would ask to go to the privy while they talked about secrets. And when school was out, she would go right up Hibbard's Hill and share her new one with Grandmother Jane. At least it would give her a chance to talk about the plan, a plan that made her stomach flip about the way it had when she was a 15-year-old sitting in front of Newton Barnes at school.

An hour later, the children were gone, and she gathered up her things and her wrap and headed out the door, locking it behind her and putting the big key in her skirt pocket. She felt a little sad about giving up that key and quickly replaced that thought with the fact that perhaps she and Newton would have a key for their little house. Although she couldn't imagine why they would need to lock the door out there in the country.

CHAPTER TWELVE
Newton Turns Carpenter

At that very moment, Newton was setting down his tool box in the kitchen of the little house on the Chittenden property. He aimed to get at what would be Rose's pantry today. Right now it was more like a closet with lots of shelves. He figured on knocking out a section of shelves, putting in a window and giving her a wide smooth space in front of the window to roll pastry and knead bread. He recalled Charles saying kitchens should have windows at the sink because people needed light to wash dishes and, the little rascal had added with a grin, "something to look at while dealing with people's grubby plates." This kitchen had no window by the sink, but perhaps light would help with pie and bread as well. He hadn't asked Rose, mainly because he reckoned she'd say a new piece of glass was too dear to bother with just for her. He had set aside money for this very thing, he had made the window, and he had the makings of the rest of the room.

As he pounded and measured and sawed, half his mind was on Rose. He liked to picture her sitting on her rock with her hair down, or with her skirt swishing from side to side when she walked in front of him or with her stockings off and her skirt pulled up on the rare occasions when she would go wading in the river with him. And more often these days, he imagined what she would look like with her head on a pillow, her eyes closed, her dreams coming and going. Now, with the wedding day coming soon, he had started to allow himself to think how she would look with the bed covers thrown off and her nightgown in disarray – and even without any clothes at all. Sometimes in the long weeks of waiting for her he had wondered what would happen if he undid any of the many buttons that kept her so wrapped in fabric. But whenever his hand slipped past the boundaries she had set, she rebuffed him, and he had put those thoughts on a top shelf again.

But with no clothes at all, he wondered? When the hammer hit his forefinger, he yelled "Judas priest!" and dropped the nail. Good thing I wasn't holding a saw, he thought ruefully, deciding that Rose and construction might not dovetail too well. He looked down at his hands then, calloused from shoveling manure and chapped from working out-of-doors in frigid weather and wondered if he should touch her a-tall with such rough skin. Still, he wouldn't mind if she took a notion to touch him, and her hands were not exactly smooth. She had complained, in fact, that the yarn sometimes caught in one badly cracked finger when she was knitting. With an effort, he put her out of his mind and concentrated on the pantry. He was so absorbed that he didn't hear Joshua come into the little house through the kitchen door. So he jumped again when Joshua spoke right behind him and said, "Coming along with alacrity, I see."

"Judas priest!" Newton said for the second time that day.

"Not like you to take even a traitor's name in vain," Joshua said. "Are you in over your head here?"

"Not a-tall," Newton answered. "But I pounded my finger an hour or so ago, and now it's a bit swollen and bruising."

"Not like you to do that, either."

"I was daydreaming and pounding nails at the same time," Newton laughed.

"Thinking about Rose," Joshua nodded. "It's hazardous. May not ease off even after you're married. You are getting married, I trust?"

"Soon as school's out," Newton said without thinking. He clapped his hand over his mouth and shook his head. "I'm as bad as a schoolgirl. Didn't keep the secret for even two days."

But Joshua was grabbing him and whirling him around the tiny room. "Thank God," he shouted. "Thanks be to God. The girl is setting a date!"

"But it's a secret," Newton said. "Although I think we will need help from you and Ruthann, so Rose would probably tell you anyway. I can't believe it just popped out of my mouth like that. She would be quite unhappy about not giving the news herself."

"So we'll pretend we don't know," Joshua said. "But how can we help? You'd better keep on now that you've let the cat out of the bag. Didn't cross your heart and hope to die, I trust."

"Some cat," Newton muttered. They were both standing still now, and Newton explained about Rose's plan to elope and get married near the seashore where she had visited with Ruthann. "She doesn't want the Reverend Lockhead, and it's a trifle awkward with her father even now, and she's afraid her face will be pink the whole time! She has been thinking about walking down the aisle to the point where it's given her nightmares. The astonishing thing is that her grandmother suggested we just run away."

"Had to be Grandmother Jane. Emma hasn't had a thought even half that wild in half a century," Joshua commented. "I must say, it sounds quite perfect, even though we won't be able to watch, and Ruthann's father can assist with arrangements at that end, I'm certain."

"Appreciate that," Newton said, already pleased that the secret was out. He would bring Rose here on Saturday, and the four of them could figure everything out. And he would have the pantry pretty much done by then, so she could admire it. He hoped she'd admire it.

"I can give you a hand tomorrow," Joshua offered. "You have a long way to go before this hut is habitable. Right now I have to see to a heifer that is not going to calve this spring but is ready to breed now and give us a calf soon after Christmas. I had a feeling it didn't take with her in the fall, and I was right. But she's the only one."

"Well, take my advice and don't be dreaming about Ruthann when you're dealing with Lord Coopersmith or you'll have worse than a swollen finger," Newton said.

"If he were a judge, I could not treat him with more respect," Joshua said, heading for the door.

Newton shook his head as he returned to his work. Jersey bulls had a reputation for being difficult, and the Chittenden bull was no exception. But his offspring were so perfect in build, color and milk production that they had learned to deal with his moodiness. And Newton could not believe how many farmers had brought a heifer or two here from a number of miles away, paying Joshua for the privilege of spending time with his lordship. At least, and Newton chuckled at the thought, the bull was nice enough to the heifers and did his job without stomping about and roaring. He saved those antics for times when he was alone in his iron-barred yard and pen.

Only a little sorry that the secret of the elopement had slipped out, Newton realized that sometimes things were clearer when talked over with friends. He would see if Rose could come out here at week's end and look over the little house and figure out how to do the running away. He looked with satisfaction at what he had finished in the pantry and muttered, "Hut, indeed. This is a house."

Rose was thinking about the house also as she headed for Hibbard's Hill and Grandmother Jane's kitchen. As she came into the yard, she thought about all the times she had spent here as a child, stacking wood and weeding asparagus and helping her grandmother strip fresh ears of sweet corn. She ran up the steps, scraped her shoes on the iron boot scraper – now that was something she wanted at her door – and tapped lightly. Without waiting, she lifted the latch and was surprised to see her Uncle Cal sitting in her grandmother's rocker by the wood stove.

"Well, good afternoon, Uncle," she said. "I did not expect to see you here today. It's been a long time. I trust you are well?"

"Well as can be expected, Rose," he answered. "Plenty of joints that snarl and creak regular. You've turned into a young lady since I last saw you. Hair up and lace trim on your shirtwaist."

"I've come straight from the schoolroom," Rose said, thinking it might turn out to be a wasted trip. She could not speak about the elopement plans in front of Uncle Cal, and he didn't look as if he were going to move.

"Your grandmother is out with the chickens. She fusses with them a good deal, it seems to me," Cal said. "You want to set and wait for her or risk getting pecked out there?"

Rose laughed. This crusty man had always been her favorite among the great uncles because of the way he talked and because she had heard any number of stories about how independent he was, how he paid fishing and hunting seasons no mind and, she'd heard, had even come home illegally in the midst of the Civil War. She'd like to take a chair and ask him about all of that, but she knew she'd better get on with her real mission, so she nodded and said she'd take a chance on the feisty chickens.

"Feisty is a good word. Small wonder you're a teacher," Cal said. He opened the door to the oven and put his stockinged feet on the ledge of the stove. "I'll steal a little warmth here while Jane is out of sight. She has some idea that the heat is leaking out when I open the door. I shouldn't think she'd give a fig if nuthin' was cooking, but women don't think same as men. Anyhow, I can see you have business on your mind, girl, but once you're done, come back and set with me a bit. Your grandmother would say you're a sight for sore eyes. Mine ain't sore, but you are a pleasure to look at. Just as well you don't have the older boys in that classroom, I reckon."

Rose felt the blush start at the roots of her hair and come over her face like a curtain, so she quickly nodded to Cal Chandler and left in a great hurry for the hen house. Her color was back to normal by the time she found her grandmother chattering away to the chickens gathered anxiously near their feeding trough. Rose saw the egg basket near the door and started around, gathering eggs while the hens were occupied with their food.

"Land sakes, child, you here again? Must be trouble in paradise," Jane Hibbard said, looking over her shoulder. She sounds surprised, Rose thought, but she looks as if she were expecting me. She retrieved a warm egg from beneath a hen who had not left her nest and received a sharp peck on the back of her hand for her trouble.

"Ouch," she said, withdrawing quickly but hanging onto the egg.

"She's a grouch, that one," Grandmother Jane said. "Thinks every egg she lays belongs to her and her alone."

"She'd end up on the Sunday table at our house," Rose commented. "Abby always talks Father into killing any chicken that takes a chunk out of her fingers."

"Not a bad idea. What's that child up to, anyway? Mr. Hibbard was down to the store the other day and heard Hattie Munson talking about how her shirtwaists had never looked better, now that Abigail was ironing them. Is that our Abigail? Working for Hattie?"

"Not the end of the world, Grandmother," Rose said, starting to laugh. "Abby's good at all the housework things, Mrs. Munson needed help, and now Abby is learning to work and not add a word to the gossip mill. She's learning discretion. It's quite refreshing. And amusing some of the time."

"Can't trust Hattie Munson even while you are standing in front of her, Rose, and I thought you knew that. She's not a bad woman, not sinful in the ways that the reverend seeks to weed out, but she does damage. damage to people."

"We know, Grandmother, how well we know. And Abby is being very careful. It's light work for the most part, so she's putting aside her pay each week for a new skirt or some other thing we can't afford. I am keeping track, Grandmother, I really am."

"I'm sure," Jane Hibbard muttered. "But Hattie can worm things out of people when they have no idea it's happening. And then she spins a tale that satisfies her. But you didn't come here to be told Hattie Munson is a gossip. What brings you?"

"Good news, Grandmother. We're taking your suggestion and are going to run off to get married. But Newton agrees that a few people have to know so the town doesn't think I've lost my mind again. He does think no one will miss him."

Jane Hibbard nearly knocked the egg basket off Rose's arm as she turned suddenly and put her arms around her tall granddaughter. They hugged for a second or two, and then Jane let go and stared at Rose.

"I didn't think you had it in you," she said. "What can I do, besides calm the waters when the news breaks that you are nowhere to be found?"

"That's about it. We'll have to tell the Chittendens because we'll need Ruthann's father to set up the licensing and someone to marry us, and I must tell Mr. Goodnow because he'll be taking me to the train in Ripton so no one will see me at the station here. Newton and I will meet there and go on to the Hartys' place where I may be able to stay overnight. Newton is going to arrange for a room at the inn overlooking the ocean and the beach where I so loved walking when I went there with Ruthann.

"Land sakes, child, you do move things right along when you've a mind to, don't you? Suppose there's not much sense to letting the grass grow under your feet after all these years, though. I am pleased as punch."

129

Rose's smile turned into a laugh as she listened to her grandmother's familiar use of yet another cliché. "But you won't tell Father or Uncle Cal or anyone, will you?" she asked.

"My lips are sealed," Grandmother Jane said. "Bursting to tell but sealed. Have you time to visit awhile? I want to talk to you about that book you brought last time. Too dreadful for words, really, and too dreadful to not talk about."

Rose nodded, and the two women left the chickens and headed back to the house. As they passed the woodshed, Jane asked Rose to pick up a couple of sticks for the stove, so Rose went into the three-sided building, unable to get near a woodpile without thinking about her mother. Still, these logs were neatly and firmly stacked, so she gritted her teeth and took four from the top of the stack. As she turned, she heard Jane say, "Oh, dear, oh, deary me. I didn't mean ... I didn't think ..."

Rose gave her a wan smile and said, "Never you mind. I have to do this often. I'm still a baby about it."

"Not a-tall, child," Grandmother Jane said quietly. "Some things in life never fade away. But every cloud has a silver lining if you study on it."

That did make Rose smile and then they were at the door, in time to hear the oven door slam shut. "That Cal has had his feet in my oven again," Jane muttered. "Prob'bly hasn't washed them in a fortnight." She opened the door and glared at her brother, whose eyes were closed, his feet on the floor teetering back and forth slowly to rock the chair.

"I know you're not sleeping, Cal Chandler," Jane said. "You've been warming your feet in the oven where I put custard pies and leg of lamb."

"Today, I hope," Cal said, pretending to rouse himself from a nap. "But it appears the oven is quite empty. By the by, not even my toes passed the threshold of that oven – just set them on the ledge, that's all. No need to get all riled up."

Jane sighed and took her basket of eggs into the pantry where it was much cooler. Rose drew up the step stool and sat near the questionable feet, looking up expectantly at this favorite great uncle.

"Your grandmother cannot stop talking about this Ambrose Bierce tale you brought her, young lady," Cal began. "Giving her nightmares fit to scare a sheep, I expect, although she claims not. I reckoned I would take a look myself, even though I'm not much of a hand at reading. Where'd you get that, anyway?"

"Clara left it behind," Rose answered. "It seemed as if he were telling the truth, Uncle. How could anyone make that kind of thing up?"

"Oh, he was telling it true, all right," Cal answered with a frown. "Saw those arms and legs stacked up myself, heard the screams coming from the doctor tents, saw the bloody bandages over whatever stumps the boys had left ..."

"Stop," Rose cried. "I read it. It's hard enough when it's words on a page, but it's even worse when it's words aloud."

"Need to see the reality, Rose," he said gruffly. "None who warn't there sees the reality. They gabble about slaves and freedom and the blasted wonder of winning the war. But down there in Virginia and Pennsylvania, it was hell, sheer hell. I'd ask your pardon for saying the word, Rose, but that reverend of yours who's forever yellin' about fire and brimstone has no idea what being under fire is like, or looking at the slaughter afterward."

"Is that why you came home?" Rose asked softly.

"And why I went back," he growled. "Couldn't stand it. Then couldn't stand not being there where every man was needed to get it over with. War, Rose, is prob'bly never a good thing. It's a sorry business when you have to kill and maim hundreds of people to set some others free and give 'em a chance to draw a pay every week or two if they've a mind to work."

Rose could not speak. She knew Cal Chandler had left the army without permission and that everyone had shied away from asking him why he was home. And they were just as reluctant to ask why he had gone back. And now she knew. He was very brave, she thought, and shivered at the picture he had created of severed legs and arms. Until now she had harbored a shred of hope that Mr. Bierce was making it all up. She wondered how anyone would teach a horror like that in a classroom. Be of some benefit, she reckoned, if a body could get through it.

"Anyone care for a cup of tea?" Jane Hibbard asked as she returned to the kitchen. She started to say something else but stopped when she saw the expressions on Cal and Rose's faces.

"What in heaven's name are you two talking about, or not talking, I should say?" she asked.

"Civil War," Rose said abruptly.

"That Ambrose man's book," Jane said, nodding. "Cal says he's telling the truth in that book, and knowing it's true doesn't make my mind any easier."

"That's how I felt, Grandmother, and now I know Uncle Cal is a true hero because he went back, even though he already knew what was there." She turned to her uncle and added, "I am so grateful that you came home with all your arms and legs."

"I'll put the kettle on the fire," Jane said, "and perhaps we can find a more cheerful topic. Not that I am sorry you exposed me to that book, Rose. The whole town should read it. Prob'bly the whole country." And with that, she set out a moustache mug for Cal and cups and saucers for herself and Rose and busied herself heating the teapot and filling a tea ball. "Just bought these leaves from Henry," she said. "He guarantees they're as fresh as anything could be after traveling thousands of miles." She dropped the metal ball into the teapot and set the pot on the table. Then the three sat down around the table, ready to talk about most anything other than Ambrose Bierce.

CHAPTER THIRTEEN
Hope from the Past

Abby was ready to dish up supper by the time Rose reached the house, so they sat down almost immediately. As they were finishing the floating island pudding Rose had made the day before, they heard wagon wheels in the yard and in a few minutes, Jason Harris walked into the kitchen.

"Sorry to interrupt," he said, pulling out a chair at the dining room table and sitting down. "I'll have a bite of that pudding, though, seeing as I'm here. And providing Charles hasn't eaten all of it already."

Charles started to protest that he'd barely dug into his first serving and realized he was being teased. Abby just nodded and went to the kitchen to get her uncle a helping of dessert.

"What brings you here after dark, Jason, and with the wagon?" Silas asked. "Not that you aren't welcome any time."

Jason grinned. "I heard Miss Rose is actually deciding to get married come late spring, so I've brought her some encouragement. When we've finished the pudding -- this remarkable pudding, by the by – I'll need a hand, Silas, to get it in the house. Your muscle might add a little something, Charles."

Charles wasn't taking the bait, and Rose looked puzzled but made no comment. She could not imagine what her uncle could be bringing that would get her to the altar (or wherever, she thought, smiling a little) sooner or better. Minutes later, while she and Abby cleared, Charles and the two men went down the back stairs to Jason's wagon.

The next think Rose heard was voices on the stairs. "Set it down easy," Jason was saying. "Now, Silas, let Charles take the upper end. His knees should be right smart about backing up a staircase. Mine don't take to it well anymore."

"Best let me ahead of you, Charles," she heard her father say. "Someone has to get the door." And then they were in the kitchen, Charles and Jason carefully setting down a shiny new wooden chest with brass hinges and a brass latch.

"Oh, my," Abby said. "That's real pretty."

But it was Rose who gasped because she saw the delicate letter R that had been carved into the lid just above the latch. She had been thinking about the hope chest she didn't have, and Uncle had made her just such. She felt her eyes start to water and hoped she wasn't going to be a silly goose and cry over a chest.

"Pretty nice, I'd say," Charles said. "Unaccountably heavy, but pretty nice."

Jason realized that Rose had seen her initial, but she looked as if her feet were frozen to the floor. He reached out a hand and she came over to him and the chest, still unable to speak.

"It is for you, of course, Rose. I've had it finished for some time, but you ..." He paused and then, a little worried about shedding a tear himself, said as lightly as he could, "...you kept dawdling around to the point where I was thinking of filling it with my own extra quilts."

At that, they all laughed and Rose slid her hand along the top of the chest. "It's cherry, isn't it," she said.

"A-yuh," Jason said. "Nell thought that would be your favorite."

At that, a tear rolled down Rose's left cheek. "So she saw it?" Rose asked, choking out the words.

"Didn't just see it, Rose." He flipped up the lid, and the whole room took a quick breath. "Filled it for you, just as your mother would have done if she had lived to do it."

Through the tears that were now rushing down her face, Rose could see lace and quilting and all kinds of white fabric. She turned to Jason and hugged him, trying to speak and failing completely. Then she bent over the chest and lifted one layer after another – sheets, pillow slips, a blue and white quilt, at least two nightdresses – one flannel and the other a gauzy batiste, all kinds of lace and hemstitching trims – she couldn't believe it even as she looked at it.

"When?" she asked her uncle. "When could she have done this?"

"Right after Sarah was gone, Rose. She knew you'd be in need of these things one day, and when a girl gets to be fourteen or fifteen, she should have a hope chest. That's what Nell said. You will find one or two things in there that your mother made when the two of them were sewing together. I can't rightly say how many items Sarah did, but Nell put a note on those."

"I can't thank you enough," Rose said very solemnly. "And I can't thank Nell at all." She felt a tear slide down her cheek and

136

didn't bother to wipe it away. She couldn't think when she had been at such a loss for words.

"Your friendship was your thank you to Nell, Rose. Not to worry about that. She treasured your friendship."

Silas, feeling a little choked up himself, cleared his throat and asked where they might put the chest while they had enough manpower to move it. Rose said she'd like it in her room if they could manage another flight of stairs, and the two men nodded and looked at Charles.

"I'm superb at doing things backwards," Charles said, "although I might remind all of you that we'll have to take it down again when Rose moves on." Getting no response, he added, "I suppose Newton's aunties have prepared him a chest, too, filled with long underwear, barn boots and a bed for all those linens?"

That made everyone laugh, and the men picked up the chest and moved cautiously through doorways to reach the stairs. Rose followed, still teary, thinking about Nell sewing and tatting and ironing all those beautiful things for her. And Uncle never saying a word until after she had been to the chicken house to tell him they were getting married soon. Was she ever going to be an adult like these people? Thinking of everything so far in advance and then being patient, waiting until the proper time to reveal a secret. She didn't think so. Well, she did keep secrets pretty well. She hoped Newton was doing that, too.

The men set the chest under the south window, and Rose nodded her approval. Jason immediately said she should cover the whole top with a clean sheet so the sun wouldn't fade the wood.

"If you just put a small towel or one of those lace doo-dads on it," he said, "the light will fade the wood around it and leave a darker square. When you're settled, mebbe you would put the chest at the foot of your bed where it wouldn't get the sun."

Rose went right to the bottom drawer of her chest, took out a well-worn sheet and carefully covered the chest. "Nearly dark, Rose," Charles said. "You can stare at it for some time now before the sun comes up. Candles don't fade wood."

"You are such a smart fellow, Charles," Rose said, taking the sheet off the chest again. "And you have my permission to leave the room."

Grinning from ear to ear, Charles went, followed by the two men. Jason closed the door as they left, having a notion that Rose might like a little privacy. Abby looked at the closed door, then back at Rose and decided she'd risk staying. Perhaps her sister would want to look at every single thing in that beautiful box, and she certainly wanted to. Especially the ones made by their mother.

"Let's open it again," Rose whispered to Abby, hoping she wouldn't be overheard by Charles, who might well be lurking outside the door.

"Yes," Abby said, hardly able to contain herself. "Let's."

Rose reached for the clean sheet she had fetched to cover the chest and spread it out on the floor. Then the sisters sat down and carefully began to remove the things Nell and Sarah had made. They exclaimed over each one, examining bits of lace, fine stitches and pretty embroidery, taking so much time that Silas called up the stairs after an hour or so to inquire whether everything was all right.

"Right as rain," Rose called back and then giggled, thinking that was a Grandmother Jane answer.

"We'll be down soon," Abby added. Then she and Rose refolded the tablecloth, napkins, nightdresses, pillow slips and other things and laid them in the chest again. Rose closed the lid, ran her finger through the etched R on the cover and put the sheet in place.

"That," she said to Abby, "is what's called a trousseau, I believe. If I had a dress and a swimming costume, I would be ready to get married."

"Swimming?" Abby said. "Are you going swimming?"

Rose knew she had come close to spilling the beans, but she answered quickly, "Newton is always talking about swimming in the river when we're at my rock, so I am going to need a swimming costume in the near future."

"Trousseau," Abby said. "It's a pretty word, isn't it? But I would call it a treasure chest." She turned away thinking about the swimming idea. She knew Rose was a good swimmer, but she'd taken little interest in it since the days when she hiked up her skirts and waded barefoot across the river with her and Charles. Why, she wondered, would swimming come up now, right along with a whatchamacallit chest full of things and an upcoming wedding. Sometimes she wished she were Charles. He had such a canny way of figuring things out. Mrs. Munson was canny, too, but she knew she shouldn't mention swimming to her, not connected to Rose, at least.

"Father is prob'bly looking for a cup of tea," was all she said aloud. And the sisters headed for the stairs, Rose suddenly feeling teary all over again.

CHAPTER FOURTEEN
The Secret Journey Begins

That spring, Rose felt as if the days disappeared almost before she had gotten each one started. While Newton made arrangements for their wedding, she searched the Hibbard and Harris attics for furniture her father and Jason didn't need or want anymore. Each time Newton came to town, he took one of the new acquisitions back with him. She refinished a spool bed, and when the new mattress she ordered from Mr. Goodnow came in, she asked him if he would take it to the Chittenden place without telling anyone where he was going.

Henry Goodnow managed to hide a smile at this suggestion. He reckoned Rose didn't want the town thinking about her sharing a bed with Newton, but he didn't see it as exactly a secret. They all knew the wedding was going to happen this year, didn't they? He was proud as a peacock to be in on all the plans, which could never have succeeded without him. He was the one who suggested Rose might announce a shopping excursion to Ripton with him and his wife. When she asked how she could do that with a dress box and a valise, he offered to pick both up after dark one night and hide them in the back room of the store.

Henry had to admit that all this intrigue was more fun than he'd had in some time. He told Newton he could board Tommy and his buggy in Ripton so the newlyweds would have transportation back to Eastborough from the train station if that was needed. And he told everyone who came by for flour or buttons that Rose would be in the store the week after school closed because he had never managed inventory well without her. So, when Rose said she and Newton would be married on the Fourth of July, the townspeople put that with Henry's chatter and suspected nothing.

At the eastern end of Massachusetts, Ruthann's parents were taking care of everything else and sent Rose one letter after another as they completed various details. As for Rose, she had taken to reading all her mail in Mr. Goodnow's storage room, simply because every note from the Hartys or Newton was a new thrill for her, and she knew the words turned her face as red as Uncle Cal's winter underwear. She told Mr. Goodnow she wanted to keep every one of the letters but was worried about taking them home.

"Charles, you know," she said. "He sticks his nose into everything, and he'll surely see a new postmark and be moved to snoop."

"I'll lock them in the bottom drawer of my desk," Henry proposed, "if that suits you."

Rose wanted to hug him but held back. He did think of everything, she thought. Aloud, she simply said, "Thank you, Mr. Goodnow. Thank you again and again."

"It's my pleasure, Rose, my pleasure," he answered. "You've made quite a difference here at the store, and I'm grateful. But it's not just all the new business your ideas brought in. It's that you've become part of our lives, me and Mrs. Goodnow, and we have grown fond of you."

"And I of you," Rose answered, rather shakily. "What would I ever do without you?"

"Get along with your life, just as you always do, my dear," he answered and turned quickly back to sorting the rest of the mail. No need for this young lady to see that an old fellow like himself was near tears, now was there? And he'd always thought it was only the ladies who wept at weddings.

After that, time flew so fast that Rose had few moments to think about how much she would miss seeing the children, but as she wrote "Today is June 1, in the year 1891" on the big slate at the front of her room, she felt a sudden pang and knew it was going to be hard to stop teaching. She sensed Newton knew that. He always seemed to know what was in her head, even when she wasn't sure herself. Almost immediately her thoughts shifted to the spool bed she had refinished, and color slowly started to flood her face. Not a bad exchange, she told herself, trading a passel of children for a place in Newton's bed. Our bed, she corrected herself. Our bed. Enough of this, she thought, reaching for the school bell rope.

At the first clang, the children came through the front door noisily and then quieted down as they filed into the classroom and took their places. When they all rose to say, "Good morning, Miss Hibbard," Rose firmly put herself back on the teaching track and pushed away thoughts of her wedding.

142

Seventeen days later, she dismissed them all for the last time and wrote to Newton that night that she had no compunctions about it. Now that was a good word, she reckoned, hoping he knew what a compunction was. She, in fact, wasn't certain you could have one compunction. She sighed. The world had so many words, and she hadn't mastered a third of them.

Home from that last day, she looked around the room she had shared with Abby for most of the years since their mother was killed, studying every detail, just as she had scrutinized every board and desk in the schoolroom that week. The brown stain on the ceiling, probably from a leak in the slate roof, was bigger than when she first slept here, and no one had fixed the window cord that had been broken for five years. She had finally fetched a brick to use as a prop because the window was heavy enough to make a dent in the books she had stuck under there.

"Abby will love having the whole closet," she said to herself. But she knew she couldn't take all her belongings until after the wedding – that was one of the hard things. She couldn't get her dresses and underthings out to Chittendens' now because no one knew she was about to leave. Even her hope chest was still here, right under the window. But they would come for that on their way home. At least Mr. Goodnow had been able to take a few pieces of her clothing out to the house when he delivered the mattress. She sighed. She would miss him more than almost anyone else.

But she did not want to think about losses tonight. She turned her mind to the little house. Home, she thought. A home I can make myself. And Mother prepared me well, some before she went and then, because she went. Rose's lower lip trembled when she thought of those terrible days when she tried to remember everything her mother ever said and learn new things at the same time. Uh-oh. She was getting on thin ice again. Resolutely, she shifted gears once more. She was ready for the little house, for taking care of things in the kitchen and the yard. She wasn't so sure about the spool bed, torn between wanting to sleep in it with Newton and worrying about all the things she and Ruthann had talked about and the things she'd not dared to ask. Still, Emily had survived and seemed to enjoy every part of her relationship with Peter. At least she wouldn't have to think about the rules anymore. All the "no" rules and the "stop" rules. She felt a shiver run down her spine and knew it was more anticipation than fear. She put on her nightdress and crawled in beside Abby, who was fast asleep, unaware that Rose's shopping trip tomorrow was taking her away.

"Goodnight, little sister," Rose whispered as she nestled into her pillow. "Sweet dreams." And for me, too, she thought. No more nightmares, at least not tonight. She thought she might not sleep a wink, but she was so tired that she drifted off and when she woke at first light, she couldn't remember dreaming a single thing.

"Abby," she said, poking her sister gently in the back. "Abby, it's time to get up."

"You're in a terrible hurry for someone who doesn't like to get up," Abby grumbled. "What's – oh, I remember. It's your shopping day. Are you taking money from the sugar bowl?"

"I have some spending money from my teacher pay, silly girl," Rose said, swinging her legs over the side of the bed and starting to get dressed.

"You are wearing Sunday best to go to Ripton?" Abby said as she sat up in the bed.

"I'll be with Mrs. Goodnow," Rose answered. "I thought I should look my best. And my school outfits all need laundering and ironing now that school is out."

"Will you bring me something?" Abby asked.

"I certainly will," Rose promised, thinking that Abby was sometimes a real child again. And wouldn't she be surprised to get a shell from the shore rather than penny candy from Mr. Hawkes' store in Ripton. She buttoned her shirtwaist to the very top and sat on the edge of the bed to put on her shoes. As she plied the silver-handled button hook that she so treasured, she decided she would slip it into her bag and take it with her. It would, after all, be useful, in addition to pleasing her.

"Are they coming by for you?"

"Yes. And I'd better get breakfast on the table before they get here."

"Are they coming for breakfast?"

"No, Abby, but Father and Charles are," Rose said laughing. "And so far you haven't lifted a finger to make it happen."

"Neither have you," Abby answered saucily.

"My finger is in a raised position," Rose said, and she hurried out the door.

No one but Rose, Abby thought, would give an answer like that. She slowly rolled out of bed, realized she had to use the bathroom and, worried that Charles would be shaving in there, pulled out the chamber pot and squatted over it. When she was finished, she pushed it back under the bed with great care and promised herself that she'd remember to empty it once Rose was out of the house. She did wish Charles would just grow a beard. He seemed to spend enormous amounts of time with the shaving brush and razor. Well, he did look nice most all the time, she had to admit.

She pulled on her clothes and skipped down the stairs to help Rose with breakfast. And they had hardly finished eating when the Goodnows' buggy rolled into the yard. Rose jumped up to get her wrap and the satchel that held her money, handkerchief and extra sweater. She touched her father's shoulder as she went past him, gave Abby a hug and kissed Charles on top of the head.

"What did I do to deserve that?" the boy asked.

"Nothing," Rose said. "We are all happiest when you are doing nothing except chores and eating."

Silas Hibbard tilted his chair back from the table and laughed. "Pretty sharp for so early in the day, Rose," he said. "The idea of shopping perks you up no end."

Rose smiled and gave a little wave as she headed for the door. Little do they know, she thought. But she had tucked a note under her father's pillow, telling him she was running off to get married. She still had moments of resenting things he had done in the past, but she knew he had changed his ways because of her and she thought it would be fair to let him be the first to know.

With a light heart, she practically ran down the stairs and quickly climbed into the buggy next to Mrs. Goodnow, who gave her a big smile and squeezed her hand. Henry Goodnow gave the reins a little slap, and they were on their way.

Back at the table, Abby pushed food from one side of her plate to the other and thought about Rose. The swimming costume was a puzzle, and her older sister had seemed a little odd lately, not paying attention the way she usually did. Something was up, Abby thought. She did hope Rose wasn't going to change her mind about marrying Newton.

That idea was far from Rose's thoughts as she bounced a little on the seat next to Mrs. Goodnow. She had peeked into the wagon and seen that her valise and the big box containing her dress were safely stowed there. She leaned back and gave a huge sigh. It was such a relief to be on the way to the train and to Ruthann's parent's house. She would stay there tonight while Newton stayed at the inn by the beach, and they would be married in the morning.

She shivered just thinking about it, and Mrs. Goodnow asked if she were warm enough. They had a large blanket over their legs, and Mr. Goodnow had tucked them in carefully before starting off.

"I am warm as toast just off the stove, thank you," Rose said, smiling.

"Can't get cold feet now," Mrs. Goodnow laughed. "Henry's taken a lot of trouble to make this all work out, and he'd be mighty disappointed if anything went wrong."

"You have both gone so out of your way for me," Rose answered. She turned toward the older woman and added, "I can't ever repay you."

"No need, my dear, no need. We just want you to be happy, and we're quite certain you will be. I do hope we haven't forgotten some silly detail."

Rose shook her head. She was sure they had covered everything under the sun and then some. Mrs. Goodnow had sent her a sealed note three days earlier reminding her that even if she wasn't expecting her monthlies at this time, she would still need to be prepared for some unexpected bleeding on her wedding night. Nothing to worry about, but quite natural, and she was only writing this because Rose didn't have a mother to explain it to her.

Rose had stopped in to talk with Mrs. Goodnow about that, a little frightened once again about the mysteries that seemed to surround wedding nights. And that lady, blushing a little, had sat down at the kitchen table with Rose and explained what might happen. Reassured, Rose had packed what she might need and forgotten all about it until now.

"I'm pretty sure you've remembered everything I haven't and then some," Rose said. She leaned back again and in a few minutes she dozed off, rocked to sleep by the steady sound of the horse's hoofs on the gravel road and the sway of the buggy. Edith Goodnow looked at her and smiled. This had all been such a grand adventure for her and Henry. She did hope Silas Hibbard would take their interference in good grace, but that wasn't something one should wager one's dinner on. She nudged Henry, who was sitting up ahead of them, with her foot and when he turned, she pointed to the sleeping girl beside her, and his face broke into a broad grin.

Then Edith, responding to the rock of the buggy, felt her eyelids drooping and decided to relax and enjoy the ride. In a few minutes, she too was sound asleep. Henry twisted in his seat and shook his head. Two sleeping beauties, he thought, and he wished them both well, the very best. He settled into his seat and put his mind on the horse and the road, a grin again crossing his face. He couldn't remember when he'd had as much downright fun as this.

When the buggy rolled into the train station, both women woke. "Here already?" Rose said, standing quickly and looking first one way and then the other, trying to find Newton.

"Took us quite a bit," Henry Goodnow answered, "but you two were snoring away back there …"

Edith hooted and interrupted, "You know quite well, Mr. Goodnow, that I do NOT snore. And Rose prob'bly doesn't either."

"I just don't know," Rose said. "I hope not," she added, looking a little worried.

"Just pulling your leg, Rose, just pulling your leg."

"All too easy to do, sir," came a familiar voice just behind Rose. "Hardly seems fair." She whirled, jumped down from the buggy and threw her arms around Newton's neck, surprising him so much that she nearly toppled him.

He pulled away, held her at arm's length and said, "Lady, will you marry me?" And when they all laughed, he picked her up, twirled her around and set her down again. "I have our tickets, and the train is due just before the forenoon," he said. "About forty minutes from now. So you're just in time."

"Rose's baggage is in the back of the wagon," Mr. Goodnow said. The two men went around to the rear of the buggy and lifted the wool blanket that covered the box containing Rose's special dress and her valise. Newton took the things out and set them by the door to the station. Rose saw that another piece of luggage was already there.

"Tommy and my buggy are at the stable over there," Newton said, pointing. "And I have paid the owner. He's expecting you."

"But how is that going to work?" Rose asked.

"What?" Newton said.

"Tommy," she answered.

"I was going to board him here, but Mrs. Goodwin has agreed to take him home," Newton said. "After she goes shopping. So our return tickets will take us all the way to Eastborough. And Tommy will be in familiar hands."

"Now stop worrying about us," Edith Goodwin said. "Get along with you. You can wait inside the station, and we'll go on about our town business." She turned to Rose, hugged her, whispered a good luck wish in her ear, and turned to shake hands with Newton.

Rose picked up the box containing her dress, Newton took the two bags, and they said goodbye to Henry Goodwin. As Newton reached for the latch, the door swung open toward him, and out stepped Charles Baldwin, who looked at Rose, Newton and the luggage with considerable surprise and said, "Well, well, well, if it isn't Rose Hibbard. How are you?"

Rose was so taken aback at being caught at the last minute that she could not make any words come out of her mouth. Newton stepped forward and said, "Newton Barnes, Mr. Baldwin, nice to meet you." Mr. Baldwin said, "Hmm," and looked past the couple to where the Goodnows were standing, looking as if they'd just seen a skunk.

"Mornin', Charles," Henry Goodnow finally managed. "On your way to Eastborough soon?"

"Yes, sir. Was looking forward to visiting with you there."

"I'll be back by nightfall," Henry answered, backing away from the door. "And I'll take it kindly if you only saw me and the missus and Rose here today, embarking on a little shopping, should you meet anyone you know between now and then."

"Whatever you say, Henry, whatever you say. But it's hardly fair not to tell a fellow what's going on here. Nothing that will make trouble for you, I trust."

150

"They're getting married," Henry answered, ignoring Rose's gasp. "They're taking the train to friends on the coast, and it's a secret until at least early evening."

"Actually," put in Edith, getting hold of herself, "Rose is supposed to be staying with us overnight tonight, since we'll be a tad late getting home. So your discretion is sorely needed."

"Waal, if you're in charge, Henry, and you too, Edith, I reckon this is all on the up and up, chaperoned and everything. I'll not say more than hello to anyone, including Miss Hattie, and you can bank on that. As for you two, long life and happiness." He reached for Newton's hand, gave it a firm pump and added, "Getting married is the best thing I ever did in my life, past or future." He looked at Rose and added, "Be missing you at the store."

"Thank you, sir," Newton said, just as a train whistle started to blow. "C'mon, Rose, that's our train." And he grabbed her hand and pulled open the station door. Still almost paralyzed, Rose stumbled once when the big box caught on the door and then let Newton pull her into the station. They crossed the big waiting room and went right out to the platform.

"Will he tell?" she asked.

"Not a chance," Newton said. "Henry will take care of that."

"But it was close, Newton, so close. We didn't even think of the fact that we might encounter someone we knew. We didn't even think!"

"No harm done," Newton answered calmly. "Now let's get us a decent seat on the train so I can look at you and talk about what we're up to."

Newton mounted the steps first, the conductor handed up the bags and then put his hand out to steady Rose. They found seats together in a car that was nearly empty, and as soon as Newton had stowed the bags on the seat across the aisle, he took Rose's hand in his and gently stroked her fingers with his other hand. After a couple of minutes, Rose realized her pounding heart had slowed down to nearly normal, and then the train lurched, squealed and started forward.

"We're on our way," she whispered. "And most folks don't know where we are." It was, for her, a delicious thought. For so many years, she thought, she had to be somewhere doing something for somebody, whether it was raising her brother and sister, cooking for her father, helping out at the teacher's house or seeing to the children in her classroom. Today, she was escaping them all – with Newton. She shivered with excitement.

"Chilly?" Newton asked.

"No, sir. Just agog."

"No one but you says agog," he chuckled and added, "but I think I might be agog, too."

That made them laugh, and they settled their heads against the back of the seat and looked out the window, craning their necks when the train crossed a trestle over the river and watching as houses, barns and fields seemed to be moving past them. Newton let go of her hand, mindful that he ought to be looking more like a brother than a suitor, and they rode on, he thinking that he had waited so long for this and she worrying, in the typical Rose way, about whether she could live up to his expectations. She didn't like not knowing exactly what everyone's expectations were, and now she was approaching something mysterious and not a little frightening.

Her thoughts were interrupted when the conductor pushed through the car door and called for tickets, stopping at their seats to make what Rose knew was called "small talk," about the weather and whether they were comfortable. The train rumbled past a number of stations, and Newton said he thought the early morning train would stop at nearly every town, but not this one. Most of the names were unfamiliar to him, but Rose remembered some from her trip with Ruthann. And then, hours later, they arrived at Naumkeag, where the conductor helped Rose down to the platform, and she immediately saw Mr. Harty standing on the platform. Everything, she thought – except for Charles Baldwin's untimely appearance – was working perfectly.

Aware that she was feeling quite jittery again, Rose reached out to shake hands with Mr. Harty. But he pushed her hand aside and pulled her into what she had to admit was a bear hug. If bears actually hug, her two-track mind said. That made her smile, and she hugged Ruthann's father back.

"You are looking mighty fine," he said, letting her go. "And I am pleased to see you again, young man. If Rose has decided to spend her life with you, that's a ticket to acceptance at our house."

"Thank you, sir," Newton said, firmly shaking the proffered hand. "I – we – appreciate all the help you have given us."

"You're a patient man, Mr. Barnes," Mr. Harty said, chuckling a little.

"Worth waiting," Newton said. "A treasure worth waiting for."

Rose felt the dreaded color start rising in her face. Why didn't she outgrow this, she wondered for the thousandth time. Watching her, Mr. Harty picked up the dress box, turned abruptly, said, "This way," and strode into the station.

"He's almost as tall as I am," Newton muttered to Rose, taking the other pieces of luggage and motioning for her to go ahead of him. In one door and out another, they came to a lovely carriage with a young boy holding the horse's head, and Rose recognized the animal as one of the Hartys'. They climbed in, Newton taking the seat opposite Rose and Mr. Harty, and the boy hopped up to take the reins. Off they went, clattering over the cobblestones of the town Rose had become so fond of during her brief stay with Ruthann several years before. Admiring the soft seats and the brass trim, Newton found himself suddenly shy and feeling a little out of place in the presence of Mr. Harty, whose clothes were very fine and whose manners seemed effortlessly correct.

"It's quite wonderful," Newton said, looking at the large, colonial-style houses with black shutters. "Not exactly Eastborough."

Mr. Harty chuckled again. "We had a grand time in Eastborough when we came for Ruthann's wedding. I thought that town was wonderful, too. Always good to see how other people live and work."

They rode on for several minutes in silence and soon reached the Harty house where Mrs. Harty was on the porch waiting for them. The boy hopped down, gave Rose his hand and then waited for the two men to step down. He unloaded the bags and the dress box, placed them on the porch, then took his seat again and guided the horse around the house to the barn.

Rose did not hesitate when she reached Mrs. Harty on the top step. She held out her arms and waited to be wrapped in Mrs. Harty's. The two stood there for what seemed like a whole minute, then parted and smiled at each other.

"Welcome, welcome, welcome," Ida Harty said. "We could not be more delighted." She turned to Newton, reached out both hands and after he responded with his, she said, "You need no introduction here, Newton Barnes. I remember you from Ruthann's wedding, of course, but even more from when Rose was here, talking about you all the time."

It was Newton's turn to blush, and to Rose's delight, he did. Then they all went inside to wash up and sit down for a pleasant late lunch in the Harty dining room. Everything here was so elegant that Newton started thinking about how different Ruthann's life with Joshua was. Even as a teacher in Eastborough, she had been far removed from the way her parents lived in this beautiful house with a boy who drove the carriage and apparently took care of the horse. Or maybe horses, he thought.

"How many horses do you keep?" he asked.

"Two," Mr. Harty answered. "We have a larger buggy that requires two horses and will carry as many as six people if need be. It will also carry a bride quite nicely."

"I don't have one of those big flowing dresses," Rose put in. She had felt rather shy at first, but the Hartys' easy manners were helping her to relax. "I am wearing the same dress I wore for Ruthann's wedding."

"How lovely," Mrs. Harty said. "The color really becomes you."

"Is it acceptable that it is not white?" Rose asked anxiously.

"Of course," Mrs. Harty answered. "You are not going to be in a church. You will be at Town Hall, and it will be quite acceptable."

When they finished eating, Mr. Harty announced that he would be taking Newton to the inn to get settled and that Rose would not see him again until the next day when they would meet at Town Hall. "I'll show him the way, and he can walk there," Mr. Harty said. "And I have made provision for his evening meal." Turning to Newton, he said, "I first planned to get you a small room at the inn for tonight and a larger one for tomorrow, but Mrs. Harty persuaded me that there was no need for you to unpack and pack and move, so you'll be in the larger room today. I trust you can amuse yourself for the rest of the day? I believe the womenfolk have things to do and things to talk about."

Newton was surprised to find that he would not spend the afternoon with Rose, but he nodded. Rose was surprised also, having no idea what she and Mrs. Harty would be doing for the great part of the afternoon and the evening. But she nodded also.

The two men left the room, and Mrs. Harty took Rose to the bedroom she had slept in on her previous visit. They unpacked her things, hung up the wedding dress and decided it probably would not need pressing before the ceremony. Then they returned to the parlor and sat down for an afternoon of talk, with Mrs. Harty reassuring Rose about the wedding ceremony and describing the celebration dinner they would have afterward.

"You are probably," she said at last, "worrying about tomorrow night and at the same time anticipating it."

"Yes," Rose said, hesitating. Then she added, "Mrs. Goodnow has talked to me about it some." She paused again and then went on. "We have been engaged a long time and we are great friends, but we have been very circumspect, Mrs. Harty, and I know it may be a difficult time for me."

156

"Just keep in mind how much you care for him, my dear," Mrs. Harty said. "And don't worry about a thing. I am certain you and Newton will be – soon, if not right now – as compatible in bed as you are sitting on that rock of yours."

That made Rose laugh. "Everyone seems to know about what I thought was my private rock," she said. "And we are good friends as well as people who love each other." She could not believe she was talking like this, but Ruthann's mother made it seem perfectly natural. And she had to admit it was a relief to air some of the things that had been rattling around in her head.

"That's all that matters," Ida Harty said. "When he comes to you tomorrow night, just try to relax. He's going to be unsure, as well, you know. I sense that he has not been with another woman in that way, so he'll be a little anxious, too."

"Ah," said Rose. "I hadn't thought of that."

"It's true in all things, Rose. When you are uneasy or apprehensive, you have to remember that whoever is on the other side of the table – or the bed," she added laughing, "whoever is there is worried, too."

"Thank you," Rose said.

"And now you are to go upstairs and take a nap, my dear."

Rose thought this was madness, but she obeyed, went to her room, removed her dress so it would not get more wrinkled and lay down on the bed. Minutes later she was sound asleep.

CHAPTER FIFTEEN
Happiest Day So Far

"Are you quite certain Newton will get his supper?" Rose asked for the third time. She had come downstairs considerably refreshed from an hour's nap and had dragged out a new bone to worry.

"He's an adult," Mrs. Harty answered for the third time, not a trace of impatience in her pleasant voice. "And Ephraim has made provision for it anyway. He showed Newton a place just along the street from the inn, and he'll get a decent meal there. No need for you to fuss over that."

Rose sighed. She knew she was just pestering herself about Newton's supper because she did not want to set off a worrying streak about all the other things that were far more important. She decided to tell Mrs. Harty about the encounter with the vanilla merchant at the train station, and they were both laughing by the time she was finished.

"He'll never tell, I warrant," Mrs. Harty said firmly. "He sounds like a gem of a man. And I shall have to scold Ruthann for never letting me in on the secret of Baldwin's grand vanilla. Now if you would put on this apron, you could give me a hand with peeling some potatoes for our supper. I know you are accustomed to dinner at the noon hour, but we usually have our main meal in the evening. Except for Sunday, of course."

Rose set to work on the potatoes, happy to have something ordinary to think about. She finished the task so quickly that Mrs. Harty seemed surprised when she brought the pot to the stove.

"I've learned to be quick, Ma'am," Rose said.

"With all the work you had to do at home, plus see to your father and your brother and sister, I reckon you learned quickness quite quickly. I do wish you wouldn't call me ma'am, though. Could you try Ida, please? I consider you a friend, and I don't call you Miss Hibbard."

"Ida," Rose said softly. "I can do that. It will just take a little concentration at first."

"So concentrate on that, and take your mind off tomorrow," Ida Harty counseled. "It is likely to be a beautiful day of sunshine and a breeze off the water, and I want you to enjoy it as much as we are going to."

"I am a little nervous, Ida," Rose confessed. "But it's a day I have waited a long time for. And Newton has waited for me way past what I had a right to expect."

"He is a wonderful young man," Ida said, not looking up from the carrots she was scraping. "Ruthann sets great store by him."

"Me, too," Rose said, her words barely more than a whisper. "Oh, me, too." Then the two women continued to prepare what was called dinner at this house, with Mrs. Harty explaining how she wanted the table set and so forth. Rose decided she would have candles and flowers at her table, at least some of the time, because it all looked so pretty. She hoped Newton would not mind. That made her wonder what he might be doing at that very moment. A little shiver of excitement ran down her spine – tomorrow at this time she would be Mrs. Newton Barnes, no longer Miss Hibbard in a classroom. It was happening, really happening.

A short time later, with the aroma of dinner floating through the house, she sat for a few minutes on the Hartys' back porch, catching a glimpse of the ocean and listening to the "ha-ha-ha" of what she knew were the never-silent laughing gulls. It is so peaceful here, she thought, and it is such a different life. But she didn't want to trade. She liked the farms in her family, and she didn't know how she would deal with being quite so dressed up all the time the way the Hartys were. It surely would require a good deal of ironing. She was not used to so many houses, either. Still, she did like being on the coast, and if Newton liked it half as well, she hoped they would come back here now and then.

"Dinner will be ready in five minutes or so, Rose," Mr. Harty said from the doorway. "Perhaps you'd like to freshen up beforehand?"

Rose knew that was what she called a euphemism. The question was not so much whether she needed to wash her hands before dinner, but whether she needed to relieve herself. She smiled, thanked him and went to the small room off the front hall where the Hartys had installed a sink and toilet. Imagine, she thought, having a toilet upstairs, and downstairs as well. She hadn't lifted the bedskirt upstairs, but she'd warrant no chamber pot was hidden there. When she emerged, she went to the kitchen to see if her help was needed, but everything was on the table, and Mr. Harty was holding her chair. Unaccustomed to

160

that politeness, she sat rather awkwardly and considered that it was a good thing she was going back to the farm. She'd have a lot to learn here.

She felt a little shy at first, but as soon as Mr. Harty asked her about the children in her classroom, she relaxed and told them about some of the special things she had done to make school more fun. They laughed at several of her stories, and Mr. Harty said it was his hope that someday married women would not be expelled from the classroom. "Foolish law," he muttered. "Waste of talent."

"I feel that way, sir," Rose said. "I reckon my ability to get knowledge inside children's head isn't going to fly out the window when I say 'I do' tomorrow."

"Indeed not. But the world is not ready to admit that yet," he said. "Doesn't even admit that womenfolk make the best teachers for the young'uns." Rose smiled at his use of the colloquial for children. Until that moment, she had considered Mr. Harty's speech very elegant, and it was nice to know that ordinary terms were in his vocabulary, too. She relaxed and started to eat her dinner with relish.

When they were finished, she helped Ida clean up in the kitchen, wondering if the family did not serve dessert. Then Mrs. Harty announced that they would have tea and pie in the parlor, and she and Rose served both and took the food and drink there on a tray. As it grew dark, the Hartys lit several kerosene lamps. Ida brought out a pillowcase she was hemstitching, and Rose admired the fine, even needlework.

"Do you know how to do this?" Ida asked.

"No, ma'am – I mean, Ida. I can sew, mend most anything and darn socks, but not fine work. Except for knitting, and most of that isn't fancy."

So Ida Harty moved close to Rose and started to teach her the art of hemstitching, as well as showing her how she did the smooth satin stitches that formed the H monogram. Paying close attention, Rose forgot for the moment that Newton was alone in an unfamiliar inn and that this was the eve of her wedding. After an hour or so, the women put the needlework aside, roused Mr. Harty, who was dozing near the fire, turned down the lamp wicks and, each with a candle, went upstairs to bed.

In minutes, Rose had put on her nightgown – one of her old nightgowns – and poured water from the gold-trimmed pitcher into the bowl so she could wash her face. Then she slipped into the big, comfortable bed and blew out the candle. A minute later, she heard a tap on her door, and Ida opened it a crack to peek in.

"Not asleep yet?" she asked.

"I don't know if I can shut my eyes at all tonight," Rose answered. She looked down at the worn edges of her nightdress and added, not looking up, "This isn't what I'm wearing tomorrow night."

"May I see the other one?" Ida asked. "I would love to see it. Ruthann said your mother and her sister made you some beautiful things."

"Oh, yes," Rose said, quickly getting out of bed, happy to show the nightdress to Ida but feeling her face start to flush at the same time. She went to the wardrobe that stood in the corner of the room and took out the gown that her mother and Aunt Nell had fashioned all those years ago. It was white, long-sleeved with buttons from the lace that rimmed the neck to the waist. The material was cotton batiste, and the ladies had used a shocking amount of fabric to make the gown full and long. Rose swirled it in front of her, suddenly no longer shy about the intimate garment, and said, "Isn't it the grandest?"

Ida Harty thought it was unbelievably lovely. She fingered the material, noted that the long sleeves were open rather than cuffed and said she thought the flat, pearly buttons were perfect.

"I was surprised – I work at the store, you know – at how plain the buttons are, to tell you the truth," Rose answered. "We sell any number of fancier buttons that would have gone with this. Not that I don't admire it – I can barely believe I own such a thing."

"You can sleep on flat buttons, Rose," Ida answered. "Pearls or satin-covered may be pretty, but they're very bumpy."

That made Rose laugh and admit, "I sometimes think it is much too nice to sleep in."

It was Ida Harty's turn to chuckle. "You will be such a beautiful bride tomorrow, Rose, and such a beautiful wife tomorrow night. Perhaps I should not say this, but I'll warrant your time for sleeping in that gown may be quite limited. And now, to bed with you. You must try to sleep, no matter how excited you are."

"I will," Rose said. "Mother always said to imagine a clear blue sky, and it would put you to sleep. It does work. She didn't set much store on counting sheep."

"Goodnight, Rose. I wish you a lifetime of blue skies," Ida said, stepping out of the room and softly closing the door. She shook her head as she walked down the hall, candle in hand, thinking how truly dreadful it was that this lovely girl was to be married without either her father or her mother there. When she reached the bedroom she shared with Mr. Harty, she blew out the candle and slid into bed beside him, starting to talk about her new sadness before she even checked to see if he were asleep.

"Now, now, Ida," Ephraim Harty said. "You promised not to get all in a dither about Rose's hard life. We are doing our best to give her a wonderful day, and whatever is missing is not our concern. She clearly didn't want her father in attendance, and her mother has been gone for years. I think it's too bad the Barnes family won't be here, but they understand. You need to concentrate on that cake you made, the wedding dinner you arranged and the marvel of Newton and Rose finding each other and knowing enough to get married."

"That might be the longest speech I've heard from you in a month of Sundays," Ida answered, starting to laugh in spite of herself. "And it is all true, right on the mark. I will go back to being as pleased as a gardener finding spring's first daffodils." She paused and added, "But I'm quite likely to weep at the wedding."

Mr. Harty took her hand under the covers, stroking it gently, and said, "Goodnight, my dear." And, holding hands, the two fell asleep. Two doors away, Rose conjured a cloudless sky in her mind, lost it when she started to wonder what Ida meant about getting little sleep – would Newton expect her to come to bed wearing nothing at all – she didn't think so. But perhaps. She didn't want to think about that part so she concentrated on her mother's smile and the sweet taste of Newton's lips. Then she put the sky back in place and went to sleep.

The sun had been up for several hours when she woke, puzzled at first by the sight of a strange ceiling and then alarmed that it was really light outside, not dawn light but much later light. Rose almost jumped out of bed and decided to look under the bed for a chamber pot. The Hartys had two bathrooms, but the chamber pot was there as well, white china with gold trim and a pretty cover. Rose giggled and decided she had to use it – she'd never see another as elegant as this.

A few minutes later, wearing the clothes she had traveled in the day before, she crept downstairs and found that Mr. and Mrs. Harty were having coffee at the kitchen table. To her dismay, they were surrounded by empty dishes with crumbs and bits of egg. She was late for breakfast and stood very still, not knowing what to do.

"Good morning, Rose," Ida Harty said. "It's a beautiful day for your wedding, and you've had a marvelous sleep, I think."

"Good morning, Ma'am," Rose mumbled, still unsure.

"Good morning to you," Mr. Harty joined in. "Ready for breakfast? Better eat up. Once you're married to that farmer, you may be reduced to wax beans and parsnips."

That made Rose laugh. "I am ready," she said. "To eat and to get married and to starve." But she wasn't sure her stomach, which seemed to be flopping about, was going to welcom food. She sat down at the place that had been set for her and tried a nibble of dry toast. Ida Harty had bustled over to the stove, ladled a hard-boiled egg out of a small pot and placed it in an egg cup painted with pink roses.

Rose eyed the egg uncertainly. "Just slice the top off with this little tool," Mr. Harty advised, "put a little butter in there and dig in with a spoon. Doubt if you have much time for egg cups at home."

He always makes a person feel at ease when they have no idea what they're doing, Rose thought, managing to use the little egg slicer perfectly. It would be nice to own two egg cups, she thought, digging in as instructed. The egg proved delicious, a bit soft but not running everywhere, and she found she really was hungry, despite the uneasy rumblings in her midsection. She ate a piece of toast and then another and drank almost a whole cup of coffee. She looked up then to find the Hartys watching her and smiling.

"Am I funny?" she asked.

"You are charming, my dear," Mr. Harty said. "And if you are through eating, you had better start packing your things. I'll be glad to run your valise over to the inn this morning and make certain that Newton Barnes hasn't changed his mind during the night."

"What time is it?" Rose asked, ignoring the comment about Newton. "And thank you, sir, for taking care of my clothes. I hadn't given a thought to how my things would be transferred from here to there."

"Getting on toward noon," Ida Harty said. "You'll be hearing the train whistle in a moment or two, unless it's late again." "I'm having breakfast for dinner – I mean lunch," Rose said, giggling. "Perhaps the starvation is setting in already."

"You won't be starving today, young lady," Mr. Harty said. "The meal Ida has arranged at the inn sounds so appetizing that I'm starting to salivate just thinking about it. This is definitely not your day to starve. Now get along upstairs and put your things together." Rose thanked him again and offered to help with the dishes, but Ida waved her away. "He's right," she said. "It's time to pack everything except what you will wear this afternoon. When you start back to Eastborough, you can stop by for what you are wearing now. And for that old nightgown," she added with a smile.

Upstairs, Rose made up the bed and laid out her blue dress, her stockings and her underthings. She took out the pretty satin boots that Ruthann said she must wear for getting married. She had packed them inside an old pillowcase. She'd certainly leave that here, perhaps even discard it. Silly goose, she told herself, you'll need it to wrap the shoes up again. Heaven knows when you'll wear that elegant footwear again. She sat down in the small rocker by the window and was almost surprised by the long sigh that almost immediately came out of her mouth.

Sigh? Why sigh now? Wasn't she embarking on the happiest day of her life? That was another silly goose thing, she thought. Happiest day of her life *so far.* No one her age wanted to think their happiest day had already come and gone. She sighed again, this time because it was a trial sometimes to live with her wandering brain. She was as sure as she was of bluebirds in spring that Emily never had thoughts like this. She did have, she thought suddenly, one thing to sigh about: Emily and Alice weren't here for her happy day. They'd put up with plenty of her unhappy days and done it well. She wished they were here, and she knew Emily would be outraged to find out that Rose and Newton had run off without telling her. Alice, miles away, would have to find out by post.

She heard a light tap at the door and said, "Come in."

"May I?" said a male voice.

"Oh, I'm sorry," Rose said. "Of course, you may. My things are ready, and I am sitting here daydreaming."

Ephraim Harty opened the door. "Nice to meet a young person who knows the difference between 'can' and 'may,' " he said, walking over to pick up the valise. "Not too heavy, this. Trust you have your hairbrush and your clothes for tomorrow and all that?"

"But I need to brush my hair here," Rose answered, frowning.

"You'll borrow Ida's. Put yours in the bag, and I'll be off, if you have everything else in here."

Rose nodded, tucked in the brush, and he was gone, leaving Rose to wonder how she could make another couple of hours go away. She went back to the rocker and rocked back and forth slowly, watching the leaves dance on the trees outside the window and looking down at the sidewalk where men and women were walking along as if this were an ordinary day. She wished she had time to go to the shore and listen to the waves, but she knew that would be foolish.

She heard another knock and Ida's voice this time. "I'm drawing a bath for you, Rose, so I'm leaving a dressing gown on the floor outside the door for you. Put it on, and go enjoy a warm soak – it will calm your nerves."

"Are you sure?" Rose asked.

Ida laughed. "Ah, so you are a bit nervous. Not to worry. All brides get the jitters. Some even decide not to get married at all."

"Thank you, Mrs. Harty, I mean Ida," Rose said, opening the door and reaching out to hug this woman who was being so kind to her. The two embraced for more than a minute, which made

168

Rose a little teary, but she pulled herself together and took the dressing gown from Ida. Minutes later, she was up to her shoulders in warm water in the nicest tub she had ever seen, washing with scented soap and feeling like royalty.

"You should wait a half hour before getting dressed," Ida called from the hallway. "You don't want to put on your wedding outfit when your skin is damp. Just put on the dressing gown again and lie on the bed. You could open the window if you like."

Rose did as she was told and waited more than a half hour before starting to get dressed, one layer after another. She did love the petticoat that went with this dress and made it stay nice and full at the hem. As Ruthann had taught her, she put on her gloves before pulling up the fragile stockings, which attached to the bands dangling from her corset. Then the shoes, buttoned with the precious silver buttonhook and, finally, the dress with its high lace collar and twenty pearl buttons down the front. She wondered if she should have done her hair first and decided it was too late to backtrack. She would do it standing up, and she did, twisting her long locks into a smooth round bun. It would show under her hat brim but not be crushed by the hat, which she planned to wear for as short a time as seemed to be acceptable.

She put away the dressing gown and her clothes and shoes, tucking the buttonhook into one of the shoes so it would not get lost or left behind. Then she walked carefully down the stairs to the parlor where the Hartys gasped in unison as she came through the door.

"Did I get something wrong?" Rose asked anxiously.

"Oh, no, my dear. You have everything exactly right and look so lovely," Ida said quickly, knowing that Rose by now must be as jumpy as a cat being chased toward a pond. "And I trust you will not even think about sitting down, which might cause a crease in the back of your dress."

"Turn around slowly, Rose," Mr. Harty asked. "I want the 360-degree view." She obliged, and he murmured, "Lovely, simply lovely. Newton Barnes is a fortunate young man, and I am certain he knows that."

"I am fortunate, too," Rose answered firmly, wishing they would stop looking at her. She was blushing again, she knew, and she had hoped not to do that today. "What is the hour?"

"We will leave in about thirty minutes," Mr. Harty said. "I fear you'll have to sit in the carriage, creases or no creases. I have no vehicle in which to transport you standing up."

At that, Rose and Ida both started to laugh, and Rose felt her tension slide away. "I could walk," she said. "But I might perspire, and I would have to go barefoot because these shoes" – she kicked out one foot – "were not made for long strolls."

"Your dress will take a short sitting," Ida said. "And come to think of it, no one will be standing behind you anyway. Excuse me for a moment." She left the room and returned with a sizable bouquet of pink peonies and white daisies. "Half cultivated and half wild," she said, handing the flowers to Rose. "Like the best people, it seems to me."

Rose buried her nose in the fragrant peonies and was horrified to realize that a tear was rolling down her cheek and then another. Her shoulders started to shake, and she heard Mr. Harty excuse himself. Ida quickly took the bouquet back and put her arms around Rose.

"I won't crease you," she said in her softest voice. "But I will mop up your face when you're done. It's a happy day, yes, but they most all have a touch of sadness in them, you'll find as you go along. It's all right, Rose. Cry now, smile later."

Rose pulled away, let Ida dry her face with a lacy handkerchief and then managed a weak smile as this new friend tucked the handkerchief into the almost invisible pocket in her dress. "They say a borrowed thing is good luck," Ida said. "So you've earned this one, and now it's time to get ourselves to the inn for the ceremony and the celebration. I have a touch of sadness, too, you know. I would so like to have Ruthann here for this, I would. Some days she seems so far off."

Rose nodded and squeezed Ida's hand. Then she impulsively leaned forward and kissed the older woman's cheek. "She's thinking about it every minute," Rose said, wondering if Reverend Lockhead might be right for once. Perhaps Sarah was somehow seeing this day. She would, Rose was sure, approve of it all, perhaps including the running away. And arm in arm, they joined Mr. Harty in the dining room and went out the porch door to the waiting carriage.

"Oh, look at that," Rose cried as she started down the steps. "The horse is wearing peonies and daisies, too."

"I stuck with the daisies," Mr. Harty said, showing her the small bouquet in his buttonhole. "Thought a peony might make me sneeze about the time you're supposed to be talking."

That made Rose laugh again, and she decided she actually could relax now that the day was here. Her stomach was as settled into place as her hair, the weather was perfect, and she was soon going to realize one of her grandest dreams: to be Mrs. Newton Barnes. She would have new cards made as soon as she was home. Well, not home, but at the new home, she corrected herself. Putting one hand on Mr. Harty's arm and lifting her skirt and petticoats with the other, she climbed into the carriage.

As Mrs. Harty joined her, Rose asked, "Will I see Newton right away?"

"Not until the ceremony, Rose. But soon, quite soon," Ida laughed. She took Rose's hand in hers, two white gloves together, and Mr. Harty called quietly to the horse. The carriage started to roll. Rolling into a new life, Rose thought, a whole new life.

CHAPTER SIXTEEN
Rose Tells the Family

As the sun set in Eastborough Friday evening, Silas Hibbard lit a candle so he could finish reading the newspaper, but he dozed off in his rocking chair in the kitchen before he had even finished the first page. He wasn't in a deep sleep, just a little over the edge. He was aware that Abby was washing up the dishes and heard her whisper to Charles that he had better dry them for her or she'd tell on him. Drowsily, he wondered what Abby knew about Charles. It was usually Charles who had things to hang over people's heads. Quite the bargainer, that one, he thought, a smile forming under his mustache. But where in tarnation was Rose? He knew he had long lost the authority to even think about where Rose was, but this had to be the world's longest shopping trip. He hoped that horse of Henry's hadn't given out on the way home, shed a shoe or plain wore out. Worn, Rose would tell him. More he thought about it, more he had the notion that she might be staying at the Goodnows' tonight. He couldn't quite remember.

But he was more tired than worried, and his doze dropped into a real sleep. Abby and Charles had finished all the after-dinner chores and left the kitchen when he woke to darkness. He reached for the candle and realized his son or daughter had blown it out. Just as well. At least they worried about the house burning down. He heaved himself out of the rocker and headed for the stairs to find out who might be abed and whether it was time to lock the doors. Not that anyone in Eastborough really needed to lock a door. Town was short on thieves.

Neither Charles nor Abby were in their beds, so he decided they must have gone for a walk to the river. Or somewhere. He set the relit candle on the dresser, dropped his suspenders off his shoulders, pulled off his pants and shirt, put on his nightshirt and started to get into bed when he remembered he hadn't been to the bathroom. He had intended to go back down to take care of the doors. Too tired to bother, he pulled out the chamber pot. Might's well spend a penny right here, he thought. Then he turned back the quilt, blew out the candle and crawled into bed. As his head touched the pillow, he felt what seemed to be a piece of paper. He sat up, reached for the matchbox, lit the candle again and read, "Father: Newton and I have gone away to get married. We will return on Monday. I did not want you to worry." The note was not signed.

"Judas priest," he said aloud. And then, louder, "Judas priest! That girl has gone off and gotten married without so much as a by-the-by to the rest of us? She will be the death of me yet."

Father?" came a voice from the hallway. "Who are you talking to, Father?" It was Abigail, and in another minute, she was knocking on his door.

"Give me a minute, daughter," Silas said, trying to digest the note and trying to squelch his impulse to be wildly angry about Rose sneaking off to do such a thing. She was forever running off, he thought, forever doing something brash or unexpected. He took a deep breath and told himself Rose was a grown woman and had a right to do as she pleased. He needed to calm down and talk to Abigail.

"Father?" Abby said again.

"Come in, come in," he said. And both Charles and Abby immediately appeared, their faces creased with concern. "Your sister is still not home from shopping, and I was beginning to worry some until I came to bed and found she had left me a note. She won't return this evening," he finished, holding the paper out to Abby.

She held the paper close to the candle, read the few words and clapped her hand over her mouth. "Oh, Father. Oh, Charles! It's the best news it could be. I should have known, I should have known. Where do you think they are?"

Now Charles was reading the note, and a frown crossed his face. "I can't believe she managed this without my knowing a blamed thing about it," he muttered.

"Nice to know you fail in the nosy parker business now and then," Silas said. "But your dismay is not without merit. How indeed did this get managed without a hint falling anywhere?"

"She's at the shore," Abby said suddenly.

"What?" Silas and Charles said simultaneously.

"She said she needed to purchase a swimming costume," Abby said, jumping up and down. "So they have gone to the shore where she went with Miss Harty, I mean Mrs. Chittenden, and she's going swimming."

175

"Now that," Charles said, "is almost up to my standards of deducing what's happening or about to happen."

"Deducing?" Silas said, still overwhelmed by Rose's note. "What do you know about deducing?"

"I live by deducing, sir," Charles said. "And I also deduce that tomorrow morning we can corner Mr. Goodnow, and he will be able to enlighten us. She did leave in the Goodnow buggy, Father. We know that."

Abby was whirling around now, waving the note and laughing. "It is grand," she said. "Just grand. Rose will come back married to Newton, and he'll be my brother."

"Brother-in-law," Charles corrected. "And, Miss Abby, this means a new life for you because Rose won't be living here anymore. It will be your place to take on the cooking and cleaning and the mending of my socks."

"Mend your own," Abby retorted.

"Now, now," Silas interrupted. "I think you, Charles, will lock the doors downstairs, and we will all go to bed. Charles is right, Abigail. Henry Goodnow holds the key to all this, and we can be grateful that Rose left a note so we wouldn't worry. I say goodnight now to you both." They each nodded and left the room. Once again, Silas blew out the candle, pinched the wick to stop it from smoking and rolled into bed. He pulled up the quilt and tucked one hand and arm under his pillow. He wondered where Rose's pillow was tonight. Wherever they were, he knew Rose was happy. She must have been planning this for some time because she wasn't a girl who jumped into things, and she had certainly kept that young man waiting until Silas had felt he might well move on. That fortunate young man, he thought with a sigh. And then he fell asleep.

Across town, Hattie Munson was awake in her spool bed, puzzled by what she had noticed that day. Along about suppertime, she had seen Henry Goodnow go by in his buggy, and neither Edith nor Rose were with him. She gave a small sigh and told herself they must have taken Edith home first, then Rose – well, that didn't really work out right, either. She couldn't figure it. She would stop in at the store tomorrow and see what she could see. And hear what she could hear. Certainly she could browse the button drawers for several minutes. She smiled with anticipation. If only young Abigail were coming to work tomorrow, but she wasn't. Well, that was pretty much a dead end trail anyway. Abby had proved to be more close-mouthed than a dog with a new bone. A treasure as a worker but an empty bucket when it came to gossip. But Hattie knew both Henry and Edith should have been in that buggy and she would get to the bottom of that. She dozed off, convinced a story was in the making and she would be among the first to hear it.

Miles away at the Chittenden farm, Ruthann and Joshua snuffed out the candles in their bedroom and lay in the dark talking about Rose and Newton. "They will be married tomorrow and spend two nights at the inn," Ruthann said. "It's a beautiful place, and Newton put down a precious amount of money on the best room in the house. It has yellow paint and ruffled curtains and big windows."

"Doubt if the walls and curtains will be their concern," Joshua drawled, reaching for his wife and pulling her close. "Your parents will make the day as perfect as possible, and we can only trust that Newton will manage the rest. I cautioned him to go easy, not to scare her."

"She was quite fearful," Ruthann said, "and eager and excited all at once. But if you had a talk with him, it will turn out all right. I think it will. It is a grand stage of life, but quite fearful," she allowed.

"Were you afraid?" Joshua asked, his mouth close to her ear.

"Yes," she said, putting one arm around him and rubbing his back gently.

"And now?" he persisted.

"No," she said.

It was a half hour or more before either of them thought of Rose and Newton again.

High on Hibbard Hill, Grandmother Jane had Rose in mind, too. She was up past her usual bedtime – sunset or thereabouts, the year 'round – and she wished she had told Rose to send a telegram. No, that wouldn't do, she muttered to herself. The telegraph operator at the train station rarely gossiped, but he might be tempted by the news of a marriage that many in town had predicted would never happen. She would just have to be patient. She knew it wasn't one of her virtues, but she smiled thinking about the day she had suggested that Rose elope with Newton.

Across the room, her brother Cal saw the smile and wanted to know what could be amusing her at the end of a long day. It occurred to Jane Hibbard that no harm could come now of telling Cal all about it and that he would enjoy the story, given his fascination with Rose when she'd come visiting. She had never heard him go on about the war the way he had with Rose, and it was good for him. Since then, he'd had only one of his nightmares, which were accompanied by such screaming that they always woke and frightened her.

178

"This has been a long day," she began, "not just for you and me and the mister but for Rose Hibbard, who spent much of it on a train." She stopped and looked at him for a moment.

"You'd better go on," Cal said, leaning forward. "That girl interests me no end. A good deal of thinking seems to whirl about under those braids."

Jane nodded her agreement and began the story of Newton and Rose and where they were at this very moment, God willing, and how not even Silas knew about the plan. Cal listened without interruption and when she finished said, "Well, I'll be damned. And you are still quite the rascal, Jane, that you are."

She smiled and announced she was going to bed now and he'd better consider that, too. So they went upstairs to their rooms together, with Jane carrying a candle to light their way. As she readied herself for bed, she decided she would get to town tomorrow and find out if any word had come from Rose. She reckoned not, but she was also thinking Rose would have made certain not to worry her father. And, even more, not to worry Abby and Charles. At the very least, she wanted to exchange a wink and a smile with Henry Goodnow. It had never crossed her mind that such a quiet soul would turn out to be such a grand conspirator. She sat gingerly on the edge of the bed and carefully swung her legs under the covers, so as not to disturb her sleeping husband.

CHAPTER SEVENTEEN
A New Flat Rock

"Is your hand all right?" Rose whispered to Newton as they followed the Hartys into the dining room of the inn. She had held it so tight during the brief wedding ceremony that she was sure his fingers must have gone numb. "Did I hurt you?"

"Any time, Rose, any time," Newton said, looking down at her with a grin that spread across his face and into his eyes. "I am a lad who is pleased to have you hanging onto me for dear life." He reached for her hand and held it as they walked on.

"For all life," Rose said softly. Hearing that, Newton stopped in the hallway and pulled her toward the wall where the grandfather clock stood. He bent down, tipped her face toward his and gave her a long kiss. After a moment of worrying about what people might think, Rose put her arms around his neck and kissed him back.

"You may kiss the bride, the man said, and I intend to, many times a day," Newton said.

"And at night," Rose answered.

"Ah," Newton said with a huge sigh, "I keep forgetting that you are a forward maid. But right now you must stop hiding behind time and move on to the feast. The Hartys have noticed that we are no longer following in their footsteps."

Rose peered around the clock, and Ida waved to her. She waved back and blew her new friend a kiss. "No more sharing," Newton growled, taking her hand and setting off again. "I want them all, even the air ones."

"If I am forward, you are greedy," Rose retorted, thinking she had never, ever, felt like this before. Married, committed to a lifetime with this man, and for some reason feeling freer than ever. She supposed she'd still have to worry about Charles and Abby and Father, but they seemed far away and unimportant. Perhaps it was a selfish way to feel, she thought. But she was going to feel that way anyway. At least for now.

"Very greedy," Newton said. "Did you go off somewhere? I said, 'very greedy.' "

"Piggish," Rose said, laughing up at him. And he bent down again and kissed her quickly, just as they caught up with Ephraim and Ida at the entrance to the dining room. The older couple seemed unperturbed by what they were seeing, so Rose decided not to apologize for the delay or the display. Delay or display, she repeated to herself, thinking it was a happy combination. How greedy was Newton going to be, she wondered with no small amount of apprehension, as Mr. Harty pulled out her chair at a small table by the windows.

Ida insisted that Newton take the place near Rose instead of across from her and Rose almost immediately realized that greedy meant his knee was going to seek hers under the table. Even through a skirt and two petticoats, she could feel it and hoped she wasn't going to turn into a beet again. She took a deep breath and then a sip of water from the stemmed glass in front of her. They probably called these goblets, she thought, not tumblers. She would look it up.

What Ida had ordered for them was delicious, and Rose quickly found out that her usual good appetite was in place, that her previously flopping stomach had decided to welcome food instead of jumping about. The clam chowder was milky and sweet with an herb flavor she did not recognize. Tiny salty crackers were served with it, and when the soup cups were cleared, the serving woman brought warm bread and butter, followed by roasted salmon, fresh peas and scalloped potatoes.

They had been very quiet during the soup course, but when the bowls disappeared, they all started talking at once. Newton admitted that he was doubly hungry because he'd been unable to eat breakfast and had eaten only a muffin from the bakery down the street for lunch.

"The day we married," Mr. Harty began, putting his big hand on top of Ida's, "I was so nervous I couldn't get my trousers and shirt buttoned. I called down to my mother, and she did me up properly and never told a soul that I couldn't dress myself to get married."

"And I," Ida Harty said, "was across town dressing myself without a single problem until it was time to put up my hair. It would not go and looked worse with each try, so my sister made braids and twisted them into a lovely figure eight on the back of my head. I was never able to copy that feat, but it was wonderful that day."

Rose glanced at Newton and thought he looked as charmed as she was by these two people who had been married for decades and could still remember details of the day it all began. His knee pressed harder against her skirt, and she pushed back, then reached the toe of her pretty shoes over and poked his ankle.

"Uh," Newton said when the pointed toe of the shoe jabbed him. "Uh, I have never had salmon better than this," he added quickly, hoping his first grunt would be overlooked.

"I've almost never had salmon at all," Rose said. "It is delicious. I would even say scrumptious," she went on, jabbing Newton again while she smiled sweetly at him.

"They're going to be fine, Ephraim," Ida said, laughing. "They have known each other so long that they already speak in code. Is that correct, Rose?"

Rose smiled and allowed as how they did have their private phrases and words that had meaning. She was going to say more, but she saw the server arriving with the exquisite little cake Ida had made and decorated with freshly picked daisies. Ida immediately set about cutting it into generous slices. Once again, the table fell silent. But to Rose's amazement, the surprises were not over. She had barely taken her last mouthful of cake when two fiddlers entered the room playing a tune she did not recognize but one that made toes start tapping around the dining room.

"This is the last surprise," Ida said, reaching over to pat Rose's hand. "But we saw you two dance at Ruthann's wedding, and we thought you should have a chance here. And then," she said gleefully, "we can dance. It's a grand day for us, too."

Newton pushed back his chair and, taking his cue from Mr. Harty's earlier action, put his hand on Rose's chair to move it back. "May I have this dance, Mrs. Barnes?" he asked, Rose felt her face warming, but she stood quickly, gave him her hand and moved onto the floor in the center of the room. As soon as they were on their feet, the fiddlers started a waltz, and Newton and Rose began to dance, quickly joined by the Hartys.

In the midst of the second song, Mr. Harty tapped Newton on the shoulder and gestured toward his wife. The men traded partners, and the dancing went on. But after two more songs, Newton came back to Rose and smiled as the fiddlers slowed the tempo. He pulled her closer, and they moved slowly around the small space, completely unaware that several other people at the inn were watching them with wide smiles.

"You promised to obey, you know," Newton whispered to Rose.

"Did I? I can't remember a thing about the ceremony," Rose said.

"Did."

"And maybe I will."

"But not always?"

"I reckon not always."

"What about now?"

"That might depend on what the orders were," Rose said, enjoying this immensely. "I would not, for instance, kiss you on the dance floor in front of all these people."

"That's not it."

"Then what?"

"When that grandfather clock strikes seven, I want you to excuse yourself, go to our room, number twelve, and remove your cage."

"Cage?" Rose whispered, puzzled. "What cage?"

"Perhaps you call it a corset, I don't know. But it feels like a cage, and it has you trapped."

"And then what?" Rose demanded, looking up at him curiously and realizing that one of his fingers was putting a bit of pressure on one of the bones in the cage.

"You will put everything else back on and return to the dining room and we will say our thank-yous and our farewells, and we will depart."

"Where to?"

"The fiddlers," he said loftily, "were not the last surprise."

Rose thought for a moment and realized she trusted this man totally. So she nodded and said nothing more until they were seated at the table with the Hartys again. A few minutes later, the fiddlers broke into a fast polka, and the newlyweds jumped up to whirl around the floor with the rest of the guests joining in. As they returned to Ephraim and Ida, both of them panting, Rose heard the clock strike seven.

"If you'll excuse me for a moment," she said, "I need something in our room. I will be back in five minutes."

"Our first separation," Newton sighed as he took his seat. "I am bereft."

"Actually, Newton," Ida began, "we need to get back to our house and let you two have the evening to yourselves."

"No rush, Ida," Newton said. "No rush. We have the rest of our lives."

"And this part of your lives is very special, young man, so we old folks will take ourselves elsewhere," Mr. Harty said. "You give our excuses to Rose, and we will hope to see you to the train on Monday morning."

"Very early," Newton sighed. "So early." He stood again while Ida Harty rose and watched her take her husband's arm as they walked across the dining room to the door. They had made this day such a happy one, and he did hope Rose agreed. Running off had been her idea, and the Hartys had made it work. Smooth as a plate glass window.

He sat down, sipped his coffee and grinned to himself as he thought about his plan for the evening. And then Rose was back, slipping into the chair kitty-corner from him and reaching for his hand.

"Where are Ida and Ephraim?" she asked.

"Gone home, my dear, leaving us to our own devices, you might say. Said to give you 'their excuses' and off they went."

"But I didn't get a chance to thank them for all of this," Rose said, a frown starting between her eyebrows.

"They'll next see us Monday for the train," Newton answered. "You are alone with me, Mrs. Barnes, all alone with me. No chaperones, none a-tall."

"And we'll never need them again," Rose said, a grin wiping out the line between her eyes. "I am uncaged and ready for whatever this surprise is. I must admit, when I proposed running off, I had no notion it could be this grand."

"Then wave to the fiddlers, and we will depart."

"Is that another order?" Rose asked mischievously.

Newton laughed. "In fact, yes."

Rose stood, waved to the fiddlers, took Newton's arm and walked toward the door. I am a married woman, she thought, and I thought I knew this man as well as I know the lines on the palm of my hand, but it seems I don't know everything. But I trust him. So we are leaving, and we are apparently not going upstairs, and I feel very funny without my cage. They walked out into a perfect evening, already approaching dusk and getting cool. Rose hung onto Newton's arm so she could look up at the sky, and before they reached the road in front of the inn, she had spied the first star.

"Stop," she said. "I hope you promised to obey now and then, too."

"Didn't." But he stopped.

"We need to make wishes on that star and not tell each other what they are," she said. So she made her wish, and he made his, and neither told the other what the wishes were, although Rose was certain Newton's had to do with haying weather or Jersey cows. She took his arm again and they strolled along the street without talking. When they came to a small fenced alley, he turned in, walked a short distance and then said she must take off her shoes. Seeing that the beach was just ahead, she knew that was a good idea, but he had to help her with the buttons on the pretty boots. They were so pretty, she thought, even in a size nine. It had never occurred to her that her big feet would look nice in a shoe, but she did like these. And she didn't want to soil them in the sand. They went through a little gate and were on the beach. Newton hung each shoe on a picket in the fence and said he reckoned they'd be right there when they came back.

"Not a thieving kind of town," he said, reassuringly.

Rose nodded, put her hand in his, picked up her skirt a little with the other hand and started to enjoy the feel of the soft sand, although she wondered what it would do to her stockings. She needn't have worried. When they were beyond the line of houses, he stopped, knelt down, reached up under her skirt, found the top of her stocking, which she had rolled tight after taking off the corset, and pulled down first one and then the other.

The touch of Newton's hand, calloused though it was, was almost too much for Rose. Fear and desire collided in her head and body as she stood there, and it was good thing she had to think about balancing on first one foot and then the other. The thrill that had run down her spine when his hand touched her thigh was so overwhelming that it was frightening. And then he was standing, rolling up the stockings, shoving them into his pants pocket and looking as calm as if he removed ladies' stockings every day.

For his part, Newton could not believe how much effort it took to look as if nothing were happening except the very ordinary removal of stockings. He had paused a moment with his head down trying to regain his usual calm, but he was shaken, very shaken, by the very act of putting his hands on Rose's legs. Limbs, he thought, which made him grin. They're supposed to be called limbs.

"What's funny?" Rose said, her voice coming out in a bit of a croak. She cleared her throat and asked again, "What's funny?"

"I was thinking I was touching your legs for the first time and had to correct myself. Limbs, not legs. Ladies aren't supposed to have legs."

That made Rose laugh. "Nor chickens," she said. "They can't have legs or breasts. It's unseemly, even though you're eating them."

Breasts, Newton thought with a shiver. He stepped behind Rose so she was facing the ocean and put his arms around her, quite pleased with himself about the lack of a cage. Hesitantly, wondering if he would be rebuffed again, he slid his left hand up from her waist and cupped her left breast. Rose flinched. Then she froze.

188

"It may not be seemly, Mrs. Barnes, but I am reassured that you have both. Not being a chicken, I presume."

Rose twisted quickly, put her arms around his neck and kissed him for a long time, hard at first, then with small tender nips at his lips and then hard again. Pleased that his overtures hadn't sent her running for cover, Newton returned the kiss, holding her first by the shoulders and then sliding his hands down to her bottom, which stiffened under his touch and then became as soft as a loaf of newly risen bread. Chickens prob'ly don't like cages either, he thought, marveling at the feel of her.

He pulled away first, moving his hands to her face and looking at her intently in the dim light. Her eyes were shining, her face blazed with heat so he knew she was blushing, but she returned his look steadily. "You said I was forward," she said, taking his hand and starting to walk again.

"Go easy," Joshua had counseled. "Don't scare her. Don't hurt her any more than you might have to." Newton had never made love to a woman, although he'd certainly heard enough talk about it with some of his rowdier friends and the men folk in the barn. They didn't talk so much about love as about having a woman, and he hadn't really thought about the difference. Tonight he was starting to realize there might well be a big difference. But he would try to go easy, if this passionate girl would let him.

Suddenly she let go of his hand, grabbed her skirt and started to run. "There's a rock, Newton, there's a huge flat rock! I cannot believe it."

"I know," he said. "I found it this morning."

"For me," she said, stopping suddenly, and it wasn't a question.

"Yes."

Rose went on to the rock and saw that some kind of bundle had been rolled up next to it, half hidden from sight. She looked at Newton, and he nodded. She picked up the bundle and found a thick soft blanket, wrapped around several small objects that were also wrapped.

"Clark Bars," Newton said. "They melt in your mouth. I found them this morning when I went to get something to eat. Just came on the market. You'd better tell Mr. Goodnow."

"Chocolate?" Rose cried. "Stars and a rock and chocolate?"

"And chickens," Newton said. "But no cages."

Rose ignored him, although she was secretly pleased that he was being his usual funny self. She busied herself spreading the blanket out, realizing it was big enough to lie on and fold over them. She could not believe this, and she was suddenly overcome with a kind of joy she had never felt before. "Oh, Newton, I do love you so," she cried, throwing her arms around him again and scattering kisses all over his face.

"And I love you so, so and so," he answered, smiling. "Let's sit."

So they sat down and then, as he had done so often at Rose's rock back in Eastborough, he leaned back on one elbow and pulled her down to him. They lay facing each other, and after a long silence Rose whispered, "I don't know what to say or what to do."

Newton sighed and reached for the pins that held her hair. As her long hair fell around her shoulders, he admitted, "Nor do I, Rose. But we've visited big flat rocks before, so let's just lie here and see what happens, just like we do at home."

"I think I know what happens, Newton," Rose said slowly, "and it's not just like we do at home, and you know it. I think I want everything to happen, and nothing to happen. Does that make me a flibbertigibbet?"

That made Newton chuckle, but he said nothing. Instead he pushed her onto her back and lay next to her, staring at the sky, and together they watched the stars come out. He pointed to an especially bright one, which Rose said had to be a planet, and she found the Big Dipper. And then he reached for the first of the dozen or so satin buttons that went from the neck to well below the waist of her dress. He heard her sharp intake of breath as he opened the first and the second, but she did not move, so he went on. With his somewhat clumsy, rough-skinned fingers, it seemed to take forever to pull the small loop over the last button, but she made no move to help him. Finished, he pushed the dress open and found that a lacy chemise lay underneath. He'd seen less fancy garments like this on his mother's clothesline, although she always hung them inside, hidden by sheets and shirts. He knew it was only waist long. He found the lower edge and ran one hand under the lace, his longing to touch her making his hand tremble slightly. Rose lay still, not knowing whether she should be doing something, and if she should, what would it be? Then she remembered Ruthann saying, "He will want to see you, Rose, I mean really see you, all of you." Rose had been shocked by the idea, and Ruthann had admitted she was at first, too. But, she had said, "A word to the wise: Be ready, expect it. He's waited a long time, Rose." Here? Rose asked herself. Here on a rock with the sea and the stars?

Rose made up her mind and sat up suddenly, which made Newton jump. He quickly sat up, too, afraid he had moved too

191

fast and watched in awe as she quickly pulled her arms out of the dress and let the top half fall behind her. She lowered her head, took off the chemise, set it aside and lay back on the blanket without a word. Newton stared at her, astonished by what she had done and by how beautiful she looked in the low light. He had to go easy, Joshua said so, but what did that mean right now? He lay down again, hoping she could not hear his heart pounding and filled with the wonder of actually seeing what had been hidden under all those clothes for all these years. It was more than he had imagined, yet so much simpler.

Lacing her fingers through his hair, Rose rolled toward him. He lifted his face and gently kissed her neck and began stroking the soft skin on her back. As his hands moved, Rose fumbled for the buttons on his shirt and started undoing them. She felt a sudden need to touch his skin, too, but she felt unsure. She looked over his shoulder to make sure they were quite alone on the beach and told herself that this was a time she would never share with anyone, that it was hers and Newton's for the rest of their lives. She ran her hand inside his shirt, felt his heart beating fast and reached around to his back, pulling him closer.

So there, under the stars, they kissed and touched and whispered until Rose suddenly said aloud, "I can't stand it," she cried. "I really can't stand it."

Newton pulled back, shocked by her tone.

"No, no," she said, when he started to sit up, wondering how to make this right again. But she was whispering, "I can't stand it, but I don't want you to stop."

"Worth waiting for, I reckon," Newton said, trying for a lighter moment and instantly feeling foolish.

"I can't stand it either," he muttered, "but I don't want you to stop, either." He threw off his jacket and shirt and sprawled on the rock again, pulling half the blanket over them to fend off the cooling night air. For a long time, they stayed there, relishing their new freedom to forget all those rules Rose had made so long ago while the Atlantic crashed and receded and moved closer and closer to their rock.

"I am greedy, too," Rose said after awhile.

"I can see that," Newton answered. "And you, wanton girl, wanton woman, have made me even greedier now that I can actually feel all this smooth, incredible skin." She shivered as his hands stroked her. Never in her wildest dreams had she imagined that she would turn inside out with a thousand sensations if a man touched her. She buried her face against his chest and wondered if all brides felt like this. She wanted to laugh and to scream.

"Newton," she said, her voice hoarse. "Newton?"

His hands stopped, and he drew back to look at her. She was so beautiful. She had held him off for so long that he had begun to wonder what would happen when they were married. What if the rules were a defense that would stay in place always? Now she had tossed the rules into the sea, making it clear that she was as passionate as he was. It was time to get dressed, take her back to the room and get undressed again. He wondered what she would look like in the light, whether she would let him really see her.

"Newton?"

"We should go back to the inn, Rose," he said, hoping his voice sounded normal. He had come to the time of this day when he must not scare her. Bed her, as he'd heard his friends say, but with care.

She sat up slowly, reached for her chemise and then her dress and without saying a word, stood up and handed him his shirt. He stuffed the collar and tie in his suit coat pocket while she folded the blanket. Then he took her hands in his and told her this had been the greatest day of his life, that her seaside wedding plan was her best idea ever.

"So far," she said.

"So far what?"

"Greatest day of your life so far," she teased.

"Teaching again," he said, cuffing her gently on the arm.

"I made only the original plan after Grandmother Jane suggested it," Rose pointed out. "You created this," she said, gesturing to the rock and the sky.

"And it turned out quite decently, I do believe," Newton answered.

"Perhaps not decent," Rose retorted, "but lovely, quite lovely. I am a little less afraid of this day than I was."

He pulled her close and whispered, "Don't be afraid, Rose. I love you, you love me, and we are no longer sentenced to the front porch. I am taking you to bed, something I've dreamed of for years, and you will make my dreams come true."

A tear slid down Rose's cheek, but he did not see it, and she did not allow a second one. Arms around each other and only a little disheveled, they strolled back to the gate where Newton retrieved her shoes and helped her put them on. She paused and started to twist her hair back into place, but he stopped her.

"Keep it down," he said. "I will only pull it apart again."

Inside the big paneled door of the inn, he took one of the lighted kerosene lamps off the marble-topped table and handed it to her. "Time for more obedience," he said.

"Oh, dear," Rose said, starting to laugh.

"You get on up to the room and do whatever womenfolk do to get ready for bed, and I will follow when the clock strikes nine."

Privacy, Rose thought. What a blessing that would be. How did he know that I couldn't figure out how to get undressed and into my nightgown in privacy? She smiled at him, nodded and was at the first stair when she stopped and came back. Standing on tiptoe, she kissed his right ear, and then she went up the curved staircase to the second floor. He watched until the last of her skirt was out of sight and then seated himself in a big wing chair where he could watch the clock and wait for its chime.

It had been, so far, a grand day, so much more wonderful than he had ever dreamed. His thoughts went back to that first day when he had taken Rose's books away from her and walked her home from school. He was smiling to himself when Mrs. Newcomb, the innkeeper's wife, came bustling into the room.

"Mr. Barnes," she said, smoothing her apron, "I am so glad I have caught up with you." She looked around the parlor and said, "And Mrs. Barnes?"

"She is upstairs," Newton said, hoping nothing was about to go awry.

"I just wanted to say that I sent Cora up earlier to change all the linen on the bed because you had slept in it last night and I thought, well, it seemed, I didn't know ..." She looked very fussed, and Newton tried to rescue her by telling her that was a thoughtful thing to do. She relaxed a little and added, "And Cora filled the ewer with very hot water so it would still be warm when your wife was ready to wash up. I hope everything else is satisfactory, Mr. Barnes?" she asked anxiously, her fingers still smoothing her apron.

"Perfect," Newton said. He heard the clock start its hour song and hoped she would not delay him further.

"Sleep well," she said. And then she blushed, turned to go and over her shoulder added, "Our congratulations!"

Chuckling, Newton took another lamp from the hall table and made his way up the staircase. When he opened the door, he saw that the bed had been turned down, and Rose was sitting in the rocker by the window. She had turned down the wick on her lamp, but candles were burning in sconces around the room, casting a dim but warm light on her face. He could see that she was in her nightgown.

"Good evening, Mrs. Barnes," he said softly. "Is the room satisfactory?"

Rose giggled. It was a slightly nervous sound, but he was pleased he had made her laugh. "It will do," she said, "it will do nicely." Then she giggled again.

Now for it, he thought, starting to remove his clothes. He had never been particularly shy, but he hadn't undressed in front of another person, certainly not a woman, since he was knee-high to a grasshopper as Grandmother Jane would have said. As he hung up his jacket in the armoire, stowed his shoes and unbuttoned his trousers, he was very aware that she had made no attempt at discreetly looking away. She was staring at him, her eyes moving from his hands to his face as he stepped out of the pants, took off his shirt, his undershirt and his socks and his gaiters. He was surprised to find that he was quite rattled from her watchful attention, and he took his nightshirt out of the armoire and put it on before removing his drawers. He heard Rose giggle again and turned to look at her.

She stood up, and he gasped as the long, full, white nightdress swirled around her ankles. The fabric was so fine that her legs were outlined by the candlelight behind her. "You look unbelievable," he said. "Unbelievable."

"And from what I can see, Mr. Barnes, you do as well."

He took her in his arms then, and they held each other, swaying a little and not talking. They could hear the sound of the waves on the rocks through the open window, but the rest of the world seemed very quiet.

"We're still going to just see what happens," he whispered finally. "But I need to know which side of the bed you are going to take."

"On your left," Rose answered immediately. And before she could think, he picked her up and placed her there. Then he washed his hands in the water Cora had left for them, blew out all the candles and slipped into bed beside her.

197

CHAPTER EIGHTEEN
Fooling Miss Hattie

It was pouring pitchforks and hoe handles in Eastborough on Saturday morning when Jane Hibbard set off for town in her small buggy. She told Cal he and the mister would have to fend for themselves, that she was taking a holiday till near suppertime. When she reached the bottom of the hill, she sent her horse straight to Henry Goodnow's store and hitched up at one of the posts out front. The road was already turning to mud, and the rain felt quite cold for the time of year, so she threw a blanket over the horse and entered the store.

Henry was behind the counter and brightened the second he saw her. She glanced around and decided the place was empty, so she walked up and asked if he were enjoying his day. "As much as an aging man can," he answered calmly, rolling his eyes toward the tall glass cabinets on the north side of the store. Jane couldn't see who might be back there, but she took the warning and tried to signal him without words. First she frowned, then she grinned, then she spread her hands by her side and raised her eyebrows as high as she could.

"What can we do for you today, Miss Jane?" Henry asked in his most matter-of-fact voice, at the same time touching the ring on her hand and nodding.

"I wondered if you had received any post for me," Jane Hibbard said, so set up by this signal that she could barely keep from giggling like some adolescent girl. Mischievously tilting her head at the sound of a small drawer closing not quite silently on the other side of the store, she added. "And buttons. I am in need of shirt buttons again."

"No mail, today, Miss Jane. I know you've been expecting to hear from Cal's wife, but she hasn't come through with so much as a penny postcard. Is he doing well?

"He's so improved, Henry, that it is a sight for my sore eyes to see him rocking and reading in my kitchen. His nightmares have calmed considerable. And you know, I think it was his heart-to-heart talk with Silas's Rose that set his path a little straighter?"

"That so?" Henry said with a small frown.

"That girl – I should say young woman – has a way with her, don't you agree?" And without waiting for his answer, Jane continued, "He opened up to her about the war and what he saw and what happened to him, and it was amazing to see his improvement, starting the very next day. Did you know, Henry, that they cut off so many arms and legs that they stacked them outside the surgery?"

Henry ignored this last and inquired, "Rose make it up Hibbard Hill often?"

"Not often enough," Jane Hibbard said, shaking her head. "I haven't seen her in more than a week, it seems."

"She went to town Friday with me and the missus," Henry said, trying not to grin from ear to ear. "I expect you'll see her soon, sashaying around in some new clothes, unless she puts them aside until after the wedding in July." He stopped talking abruptly, afraid that if he uttered another word, he would start to laugh.

"Think she'll go through with it this time?" Jane asked anxiously.

"Not a doubt of it," Henry said, nodding his head emphatically. Hearing footsteps on the bare, oiled floor, he turned and said, "Oh, there you are, Hattie. I thought you had gotten lost in the hooks and eyes."

"Good morning, Jane," Hattie Munson said, holding out several buttons to Mr. Goodnow. "What brings you off the mountain so early in the day?"

"Wanted to catch up on the news, if there was any," Jane answered with a smile. "And I need buttons, too."

"Not much news today, Jane," Mr. Goodnow said. "Edith is still all gigged up about the trip to town, but that's about it for our excitement."

"I saw you coming back quite late," Hattie remarked. "Just you up on the seat. Rose was nowhere to be seen, nor Edith, for that matter."

Uh-oh, Henry thought. "Hm, just me? Oh, yes, I recollect now. We left Rose off, and Edith had a notion she should look in on Addie Warner, so I dropped her off and went on home to see to the chickens while they were visiting."

"Is Addie ill?" Jane Hibbard wanted to know, not realizing that Henry was making up his story as he went along.

"Not as ill as we had heard," Henry said, hoping he wasn't about to break out in a sweat. This was when he wanted the bells on the door to jangle, but no one was coming in to rescue him. "She should be herself in time for church tomorrow, I reckon. Woman trouble, Edith said," adding that last in an effort to keep them from asking anything else about Addie's health. "And now, if you ladies will excuse me, I need to sort out some goods we brought back from town and left in the back." And he quickly walked away and disappeared through the storeroom door.

"Humph," Hattie said. "I must be on my way." Jane nodded and started to follow her out of the store. She stopped in the doorway and said, almost to herself, "But I had better stock up on sugar and flour while I'm here." So she waved to Hattie and went back inside.

"Humph," Hattie muttered. "Something going on there. Don't know as I ever heard Henry Goodnow say that many sentences in ten minutes, especially since he really didn't say a thing. Something is going on, and I'm not in on it. If only Abigail were working today." Then she sighed, remembering that Abigail Hibbard had proved completely unsatisfactory when it came to providing news about anyone.

"Everything went smooth as plate glass," Henry was saying to Jane inside the store, now that he was certain they were alone. "That was a close call just now with her spotting me alone in the buggy. Edith drove Newton's Tommy back from Ripton and sneaked around the back way, so Hattie missed that. Fine little horse, that one. We did meet Mr. Baldwin at the train station, and he swore he'd say nothing about running into Rose and Newton boarding a train for Boston.

"Oh, dear," Jane said. "He might well be coming here today."

"I expect so," Henry agreed. "But his lips are as sealed as a letter from the queen."

"Not that you've received such," Jane Hibbard teased, relaxed again. She did so hope Rose's secret would not come out until it was supposed to. She wondered if Silas had told Charles and Abigail.

"You do know that she left her father a note on his pillow?" Jane asked.

"I did not know," Henry said. "That prob'bly means Silas will come tearing through that door sooner rather than later. He's too smart to figure she could plan this all on her own, and he'll be thinking he should string me up from that beech tree out front."

"I think not, Henry. I think he will be all settled in his head about it by the time he gets here, mark my words. Keep in mind that the best defense is a good offense and keep the counter between you!" And with that, she turned to go, putting her hand on the latch just as Silas Hibbard grasped it from the other side, shoved the door with his shoulder and nearly toppled her into the flour barrels.

"Pardon, Ma," he said, raising his eyebrows in surprise. "I wasn't expecting to see you this morning." Saying no more, he marched to the counter where Henry stood, and Jane made her escape, climbing into her buggy with alacrity and sending the horse quickly down the road.

"What in tarnation is going on?" Silas said, but Henry was relieved to see that his volatile friend wasn't red-faced and shouting, his common demeanor when furious. "And don't tell me you have no idea what I'm talking about."

Henry Goodnow smiled and held out his hand. "Congratulations, Silas," he said. "This is the day you become a father-in-law and Rose becomes a wife."

"Judas priest, Henry," Silas said, taking the hand and shaking it hard. "Never mind the fancy talk. Tell me where she is and when she'll be back. The last time she ran off ..." He stopped as his voice broke.

"Nothing like that this time, Silas, nothing to fear. She's at the town on the coast where Ruthann's parents live, and the answer to your other question is Monday," Henry said, thinking this was going better than he had expected.

"And since when," Silas started, his annoyance returning now that he was certain Rose was safe, "since when have you been stepping into other people's business as if it were yours?"

Henry took a step backward and decided it wasn't going quite as well as he had thought. This was the old Silas coming to life. He pushed his sleeves up, scratched at a scab on his forearm and figured he'd better pay the piper, as Jane Hibbard would say.

"I am Rose's friend," he began. "She came to me to ask for help because she needed a ride to the train station in Ripton. She couldn't take the train here with Newton because that would have put the town in an uproar. So Edith and I set up a shopping trip, and we took Rose to Ripton to catch her train. That's about it," he finished, still looking straight at Silas.

"I s'pose the Hartys down there by Boston were in on it, too," Silas grumbled, a bit calmer than he had been. "And I must say I am grateful that she saw fit to leave me a note telling me what she was doing. Reckon I didn't deserve a whole lot more than that, come to think of it."

"She's a fine young woman, Silas, brought up well, a credit to her classroom and her family. But she didn't want a wedding here in town. For all the things she's done, she's still a shy one, and she was terrified of walking down an aisle with folks staring at her."

To Henry's relief, Silas began to laugh. "What a time Sarah had with that very thing," he said, remembering how she had cried and carried on and protested. "She gave in to her mother, but she said her knees were knocking all day that day, she was that frightened." He paused, looked down at his boots and then back at the storekeeper. "Sorry, Henry. I appreciate your being there when needed. But we may have to raise a rumpus when she gets off that train on Monday, even if it makes her blush for an hour."

Henry Goodnow grinned with relief. "Be happy to help with a rumpus, Silas." The two shook hands, and Silas Hibbard left the store, his mind busy with thoughts of what kind of rumpus could be worked up in two days or less. He reckoned he'd start by asking that Reverend Lockhead announce the event in church. At that thought, he slapped his forehead and began to laugh aloud. That was part of it, wasn't it? Rose had run away from the reverend and his prissy view of life. He shook his head, once again admiring his older daughter's gumption. He heard the church clock strike ten and wondered what time Rose and Newton were getting hitched. For all he knew, they might be married already. He set off for the parson's house, determined to get things under way.

The reverend himself answered Silas's knock and was so startled by the identity of his visitor that he burst out, "What brings you here, Mr. Hibbard?" before he even said "good morning."

"I have an announcement for you to make in church tomorrow, sir," Silas said, while the Reverend Lockhead collected himself, pulled the door wide and invited him in. Stepping into the parsonage, Silas went on, "My daughter Rose is getting married today, and I want that announced at the service tomorrow for the benefit of my friends and neighbors."

The minister was beginning to feel a little shaky. This was too much. First, Silas Hibbard coming here to the house, Silas who was outspoken in his scorn for church doings, and now the daughter married? But where and how? It was supposed to happen right here in July, and he intended to advise the young couple about the bonds and duties of marriage, both before and during the ceremony. Married?

"But, but ..." he began.

"I understand, Calvin, I understand. You are in shock. Rose has run off to get married and will be back in Eastborough Monday with her new husband, Newton Barnes, and we need to get the word out tomorrow."

"Certainly, Silas, certainly," the minister said, trying to get his thoughts together and failing completely. "But what do I say? I am at a loss. I believed I would be performing their ceremony." He was stopped by the scowl on Silas's face and didn't add that he hoped a proper clergyman was officiating. "What is your pleasure?" he said at last, wanting to get the matter settled and get this formidable man out of his house.

"You will announce that Rose Hibbard and Newton Barnes were married yesterday – that's today, but you are saying this tomorrow – and that townspeople are invited to meet their train when they return on Monday and welcome the newly-weds home."

"What time is the train?"

"I don't know yet, but I expect to find out." And with that, Silas turned his back on the minister and went out the door. Calvin Lockhead watched him go down the walk and felt little beads of sweat breaking out on his forehead. He didn't like that man, but worst of all, he was quite afraid of him. He would make the announcement, despite the fact that Rose running off like that was a terrible blow to his position at the Eastborough Congregational Church. What was she thinking? He had never been able, actually, to quite figure out what Rose was thinking about anything, so he supposed her wedding should not be different from all those other times. Still, she had set a date with him for the Fourth of July. That, he decided, feeling stronger and righteous again, was probably a lie, told to mislead him and everyone else. But he would make the announcement. One thing he would avoid at all costs – short of sinning – was Silas Hibbard's wrath.

As for Silas, he began to chuckle before he reached the end of the minister's gravel walk. Rose's running away had given him a most pleasant morning, as it turned out, watching Calvin Lockhead cower in the front hall of the parsonage and then bob up and down in agreement with everything he had proposed. Unlike Rose, Calvin was a cipher when it came to gumption, and Silas felt no shame at all in realizing he had just frightened the minister out of his wits for a second or two. He smiled most of the way home and did not notice Hattie Munson's front curtains moving slightly as she watched his quick step and knew, even from a distance, that something was tickling the often taciturn Silas Hibbard. She twitched the curtain back into place, her annoyance over this whole business, whatever it was, growing by the minute.

CHAPTER NINETEEN
The Honeymoon Day

The ruffled curtains in the hotel room were tinted gold by the morning sun, and when Rose opened her eyes, it took her a minute to identify the circular design on the plaster ceiling. She closed her eyes and cautiously moved her hand toward the right side of the bed, but there was nothing there. She opened them again and saw that Newton was sitting in a chair by the window watching her.

"Good morning, Mrs. Barnes," he said, grinning. "You slept well?"

Rose could feel the hot color starting on her neck and moving quickly up to her cheeks. Was she never going to get over this? Aware that it happened all the time and did not seem to be curable, she pulled the covers up to her chin and smiled back at him.

"Good morning, Mr. Barnes. Why is it that my name changes and yours does not?"

"Questions even at dawn?" he asked. "I can't answer questions at dawn. But since you are awake, I will tell you I am half-starved, having been up for an hour more or less, so I will go to the dining room and find us a table. If you are planning to join me, that is."

Rose laughed. "Yes, sir. As soon as I have washed my face and repaired my hair."

"And put your clothes on," he said.

The color that had just started to fade enveloped her face again, and she merely nodded. She had taken clothes off, she remembered suddenly, on the beach last night. Of all places. *Taken them off.* Had the full moon bewitched her? She turned so he couldn't see her face, but he came over to the bed, lifted her hair and kissed her on the back of the neck. Then he quietly opened the door to the hall and left.

He was leaving her there to get dressed in privacy, she realized. And last night, she had been able to undress and get into her nightdress without his being in the room. She had been so worried about his seeing her, and he must have known that. But who was that person who threw off her dress on the beach? He had certainly seen her then. Or at least part of her. Rose decided she wouldn't think about it anymore, but immediately found she could not stop thinking about it. No evening at her rock at home had ever been like that. She shivered, remembering his hands again, feeling that surge of desire that had made her almost speechless out there on the beach.

She told herself that her face would remain a raw beet if she didn't stop remembering such things. She pulled off her nightdress, noticing that the buttons were already undone, and quickly dressed in the skirt and shirtwaist she had brought for this first day of what people called a honeymoon. It had been, she giggled, a honey of a moon all right. Giving in to remembering, she thought about their whole beach walk and the rock and the walk back and … she took out her buttonhook and fastened her shoes and put her mind on the weather and the possibility of going swimming. She brushed her hair, wound it into a soft bun in the back and headed for the door. She would have to stop at the bathroom in the hall. She had tucked one of her homemade period cloths in her pocket and knew she should check on whether she was still bleeding. Thank heavens Ruthann and Ida had both warned her about that. And about the pain. Oh, dear, she thought, everyone in the dining room will be looking at me as the bride emerging from the wedding night. This is worse than facing all those little faces on the first day of teaching. She headed for the stairs, feeling as shy as a six-year-old at her first spelling bee.

But it was quite simple after all. Once again, Newton was a step ahead of her. Mrs. Newcomb heard Rose on the stairs and was waiting for her in the hall, saying, "Good morning, Mrs. Barnes. I have a special table for you and Mr. Barnes in the alcove by the front window. This way, please."

He's done it again, Rose thought, gratefully following the innkeeper past the door to the main dining room and down a little hallway to a small table where Newton was waiting. He had a steaming cup of coffee in front of him and immediately stood to hold her chair as he had seen Ruthann's father do.

"Are you going to hold my chair at home?" Rose said saucily.

"Not likely, but we won't have anyone serving breakfast to us there, either. Nor," he added mischievously, "will we be frolicking on your rock every evening."

Rose felt herself starting to blush again and wondered if this bride thing was going to mean she glowed all the time. What a confounded nuisance that would be. Then she sat in the high-backed chair and looked up to see that he was laughing at her. He bent and kissed her on the lips, and she realized that being married had taken none of the thrill of that away. No one was in sight, so she kissed him back and pulled away when she heard the kitchen door creak open.

Newton sat opposite her. He still had trouble believing this had all really happened. She was his wife, finally, and so far, all he could think about was how last night was worth waiting for, even though he couldn't quite stop wishing they hadn't waited so long. Around town, she was always friendly but reserved, but in private she was more passionate than even he had suspected. He'd had a few hints in the past, always ending with Rose talking about "Miss Harty's rules." He'd wager Joshua had hated those rules as much as he had. But now – he looked at her and mouthed "I love you," and she whispered, "Me too, you."

Mrs. Newcomb's serving girl appeared with coffee for Rose and asked if they would have oatmeal and fruit or whether they would prefer eggs and toast for breakfast. Rose asked for the eggs and toast, Newton for the cereal. The girl nodded and said she would also bring a plate of crisp bacon.

Alone again, Newton and Rose stared at each other, both a little overwhelmed by all that had happened in the last twenty-four hours. She was the first to speak. "I left a note for Father," she said, "to tell him we were getting married. I didn't want the town in an uproar looking for me."

Newton laughed. "If you hadn't gone off to your mother's grave that day, I might never have rescued you, and you might never …"

She interrupted, "Oh, yes I would. From the day you carried my books, I knew I wanted to be with you."

211

He was incredulous. "So why did we wait so long? Last night, Rose, last night was ..." His voice faltered, then steadied and he went on, "Last night was more than any man could wish for, from sunset to dawn."

"I just can't believe you found a rock, Newton. *You found a rock.*"

"And it turned out to be an even better rock than your real rock, Rose. Much better."

She felt herself starting to blush again and said, "I also can't believe I acted so unladylike out there, Newton. I don't know what came over me."

"Whatever it was, I hope it strikes again," he said. "Something you ate, perhaps? Or the salt air?"

"Don't tease, Newton," she answered. "I think it was most unladylike."

"Delightful, I call it," Newton said. "Remember, we have no rules now." And then, anxiously, "Are you all right?"

She knew immediately what he meant, and she nodded and touched his foot under the table with hers. It had been a difficult moment when he was at last making love to her in their room upstairs. It was all new to her, but as the women had warned her, she had winced with pain and then, minutes later, had felt a flood of overwhelming sensations. They had collapsed afterward, silent for several minutes.

She looked across the table at this man who had made her feel something she had certainly never felt before and would like to feel again, and she smiled. "Quite all right, Newton, so very all right."

Not knowing what else to say, they were both grateful for the arrival of the serving girl with their breakfasts, including the crisp bacon and a small dish of whole fresh strawberries. Each reached for a strawberry and their fingers touched briefly over the dish. Rose shook her head, a little dazed by her reaction to even that contact, and popped her strawberry into her mouth. Then they turned their attention to their breakfasts.

After several mouthfuls of oatmeal, Newton asked, "And what shall we do today, Mrs. Barnes?"

"The beach?"

"The rock again?" he suggested eagerly.

"Swimming," she said, shaking her head. "No rock. Except for sitting demurely."

"This is not your demure time," he retorted. "I have found that out, and I intend to find out more."

"Swimming," she said again. "I have a new bathing dress."

"Then swimming it is," Newton said, wondering if he could get really close to her in the water or whether that was 'demure' territory. He could only hope. He had hungered for her for so long, and yesterday's tastings had made him long for more. He had been startled to wake up beside her and realize the previous day was not a dream.

They finished their breakfasts and went upstairs to change for the beach. Even more shy in daylight than at night, Rose took her swimming costume to the shared bathroom down the hall and quickly shed her skirt, petticoats and underthings. She couldn't remember two days when she had changed her clothes this many times, and there was more to come. She checked the cloth she wore for periods, and it was clean, so she discarded it in the rubbish bin. Dressed to swim, she pulled on a full-length robe, gathered her clothes and returned to the room to find Newton in a dark blue swimming suit she had not seen before.

From mid-forearm to shoulder, his skin was so white, she thought, remembering that he wore long sleeves for haying and rolled them partway. His legs were as pale as hers, and she knew they must take care in the sun. It surprised her that her next thought was how a sunburn would put a crimp in their evening. He's right, she thought, you are a forward girl. Perhaps even a wench, she considered. She'd always loved that word in Shakespeare's plays.

With that, she walked straight toward him, put her arms around him and kissed the tanned V above the neckline of his bathing costume. He pulled her close, and she tried to move away, but he held her tight with one strong arm and lifted her chin so he could kiss her. This was not the dining room morning kiss. This was long and deep. And then he was walking her backwards toward the bed. Finding that she was not resisting, he pushed her onto the bed, opened her robe and pulled off the long skirt of her swim costume. When he stood to take off his suit, she flipped the robe over so he could not see her and thought, feeling absurd, that she'd already miscalculated the number of clothing changes.

"No, Rose. No covers."

She just stared at him, not speaking but not moving, and they made love in the morning. In a few minutes, Newton rolled off the bed, turned his back on her and started to pull on his bathing costume when he felt a hand pat his bare rear end. He turned to find Rose laughing at him.

"What are you up to?" he asked.

"The question, sir, might be what are you up to?" she said. And then she giggled.

"Is this swimming?" he countered.

She giggled again. "Very deep water, I'd say, sir. I keep feeling as if I'm drowning."

He moved away, finished dressing and kept his back turned so she could get dressed without his watching. When he looked again, she was back in her long robe and was making a single braid in her hair. Then she looped the braid around her head and fastened it in place. She took her beach hat off the coat tree by the door and announced that she was ready for swimming.

"But not drowning," Newton said, grinning.

"Not now," she said, giving him a mischievous smile that made his heart give a little jump. She started to pull the bedclothes together, but he stopped her. "They'll be taking care of that," he said. "Part of the price."

So, hand in hand, they headed for the beach. As they went out the door, Mrs. Newcomb called for Cora and together the two women went up the stairs to make up their room. The innkeeper's wife had high hopes that these two would come back, so she quickly snatched off the sheets and handed them to Cora for laundering. She remade the bed, replaced the towels and put a bar of rose-scented soap next to the wash basin. She couldn't imagine how she had forgotten that yesterday, but it had been some time since a honeymoon couple had stayed her. And been married right in her parlor! It had been a treat.

At the long, sandy beach near the inn, Newton gave a young man a fifty-cent piece to set up chairs for them, and they took their places, facing the sun and the sea. Rose sighed with happiness, watching the gulls and the waves and the other people. Next to her, Newton had a brief moment of wondering if Eastborough was having this kind of good haying weather and then dismissed the thought. The hay would wait. It would have to. He would enjoy Rose's profile while she watched the water and the birds. And then he'd get her into the water where he expected even she would shriek at the coldness of it. He had stuck his hand in to test it before the wedding, and the water had seemed colder than something from a deep well. That might send her into his arms again, he thought. He could not stop thinking about feeling her and seeing her, even so briefly. And he was embarrassed to admit, even to himself, that he was already anticipating the hour when they would go to bed again. He wanted the clock to move quickly. Then he felt guilty for having the thought, especially when she was so enjoying her day.

He watched out of the corner of his eye as she pulled her wide straw hat a little lower to keep the sun off her face, ever mindful of Aunt Nell's constant preaching about the sun being wonderful and also the creator of leathery skin. She leaned back, closed her eyes and listened to the murmur of voices around her, the occasional shriek of a gull and the increasing crash of the waves on the sand. She did not want to go to sleep. That would waste this precious day, their last before returning to Eastborough. But she had slept only a few hours on her wedding night, and in a few minutes, she dozed off, soothed by the sounds of the incoming tide and the chattering people.

Newton smiled when her hand fell out of his. He did not feel like sleeping, and he had no intention of letting Rose nap all day. But he gave her a half hour, contenting himself with thoughts of the little house where they would sleep the next night and for thousands of nights after that. He had been aware for several years that Joshua Chittenden cherished his marriage and his home in a way that he had not really understood. Now it was coming to him. This was forever. It was way more than a flat rock. He grinned, pleased all over again with finding a rock here on the beach. He wondered if any such existed in the woods near their house. They could search together. Together. He liked it. For a long time, he had thought of him and Rose as together, but he had no idea until yesterday how limited that together was. Now he had a bigger and better idea of "together." He chuckled out loud, and Rose stirred.

"What's funny?" she mumbled, trying to open her eyes.

" Oh, I've been together with you so long that my brain has gotten together with yours and the two of them are making mine into a muddle that's something like the totally confused way yours works," he said.

"I had better wake up. You are speaking gibberish."

"Yes. And I am very warm and ready to go in the water." He jumped up, reached a hand to her and pulled her out of the beach chair. "Let's go. This, I wager, will wake you quickly." Still holding her hand, he half ran toward the water with Rose protesting and laughing beside him. She was in halfway to her knees when she gave the shriek he was expecting.

"It's cold!" she said in a near yell and immediately looked around to see if other people had heard her, but the only reaction was from a woman standing in the water nearby.

"It's very refreshing once you get in," she said, smiling at Rose. "Still freezing, but refreshing."

Rose moved gingerly into deeper water, getting the hem of her costume wet and still muttering about the cold. Newton announced that he was going in, ran out a bit farther and dove in headfirst. When he came up, Rose was dipping her wrists in the water.

"No splashing," she said in her best schoolmarm manner. "I'm cooling all of my blood first."

"Does the wrist blood take a long time to get all the way around?" Newton wanted to know.

"I don't know," she said. "But my ankles are now as cold as the ice in the ice house."

Ankles, Newton thought. Haven't seen enough of her ankles yet. Then he chided himself for being obsessed with Rose's body and stood up, reaching a hand to her. "Come on, bride," he said. "We'll walk out a little and see if you like it."

A few minutes later, Rose was swimming, the salt water taste sharp on her lips. It's so much easier to swim in the ocean, she thought, and it really isn't that much colder than the mountain brook on Hibbard Hill. Hibbard Hill. She wished she could tell Grandmother Jane what a grand time they were having, but it would have to wait. She felt for the bottom with her feet and found she could still stand, so she did and then jumped when Newton's face suddenly popped up right in front of her. As he came up, he dropped a quick kiss at her waistline and then put his wet hands on her shoulders and kissed her on the nose.

"Not here, Newton," Rose protested.

"Here, Rose, here. The rules are gone, and I can kiss you on the nose anywhere except in church where it would be too much of an interruption."

That made her laugh, and she looked up at him with mischief in her eyes. "How about on the mouth?" she asked. "Since we're not in church."

"The forward girl again," he sighed. But he bent down and gave her what he reckoned would be a small peck. But before he could think, she had her hands on both sides of his head and was

218

holding him in place, kissing him back and then licking the salt off his lips with her tongue.

"You are outrageous," he said, backing off and splashing her lightly.

"But you are not outraged," she said, splashing him back.

"True."

"And I've always been partial to salt."

"And I am partial to you and your surprising self," he answered, suddenly serious. "Quite partial."

This was too much for Rose, and she turned away, plunged into the water and swam off. She was quite a good swimmer, and it took Newton a minute to catch up with her. When she stopped and turned on her back to float, Newton did the same, and Rose, feeling self-conscious about the emotions that were overwhelming her, started to talk about the inn and where they would have lunch or dinner, or whatever they were going to call it here.

Buoyed by the salt and occasionally turning over to tread water, they went on to talk about their little house. Rose had not seen all the things Newton had done, but she knew the kitchen had at least two or three pots and pans and a spider, and the spool bed had long since been set up in the bedroom. They moved toward shore where they could sit in the water and continue to talk about the house, what it had and what it needed. Rose knew Newton was very proud of the work he had done there, and she was anxious to see the cupboards he had built, even though they were quite bare.

But he surprised her again. He had already put in an order at Mr. Goodnow's for supplies they would need right away, and Henry had helped him with quantities of flour, sugar and oats.

"Will you have a few chickens?" he asked eagerly. "I am partial to eggs, too."

"Plain chickens," she said. "Ones that don't peck." She looked at her fingers and said she thought it was high time they left the water. "My hands are as wrinkled as prunes, and I fear my neck may be as pink as my face when someone looks at me," Rose said. "This sun will go right through fabric."

"I reckon I'll be looking at you a good deal in the next fifty years, Miss Rose, so you'd better get the pink face under control. As for the back, you are right as rain, whatever that means. Our white parts are getting fried."

They returned to their chairs and settled back, covering themselves with towels. The conversation turned to what their days would be like, and Rose said she wanted one day a week at least when she did not get up before the sun.

"No reason for you to get up before the sun, my love, no reason a-tall."

"Oh, Newton," Rose said, her voice high and excited. "Oh, Newton."

"Is it that important?"

"No, no. It was what you called me. I came all over goose bumps," Rose said, hugging her robe and the damp towels.

Newton backtracked in his mind and wished he had Rose's ability to go in any direction with her brain. Ah, it was "my love." Had he never said that before? He looked at her and said, "Aren't you?"

"I am," she said, not smiling. "And you are mine. And I am ready for tea and crumpets, or whatever they serve midday here."

"Crumpets? What are crumpets? It's Sunday, so it will be dinner about two, I believe," Newton answered, adding with his eyebrows raised, "but you will need to get undressed and dressed again, and it's likely to take you awhile."

"Oh, no," Rose said, getting up immediately. "I am going back now to get ready for dinner, and I will be waiting in the parlor for you when you are ready." She started to move away and said, over her shoulder, "They're delicious. They eat them in England."

Newton watched her go, frowning. What did that last mean? Ah, the crumpets. She had read so many more books than he had. He sighed. Apparently she was still looking for privacy when it came to dressing and undressing, and she was taking care not to be alone with him in the room before dinner. He grinned as he sat down again and stared at the water. The Reverend Lockhead would certainly not approve of the way they had spent the early part of Sunday morning. Lust is what the minister would call it, Newton thought, sinful lust. Whatever it was, he was looking forward to more. Likely the preacher wouldn't accept swimming in place of hymn singing either.

CHAPTER TWENTY
A Sabbath Opening

When people spilled out of the Eastborough Congregational Church that Sunday, they quickly gathered around Silas Hibbard and his children. True to his word, Calvin Lockhead had reluctantly announced the marriage of Rose Hibbard and Newton Barnes, and the eighty or so folks in the pews had gasped almost in unison. Taken aback at first, Silas quickly realized that he could see rows and rows of teeth on the folks swarming toward him. All smiling, he thought, thanking his lucky stars that at least some of the congregation had turned instead to Eliva and Elmer Barnes. Lucky stars? He wondered if he had any.

Hattie Munson couldn't make up her mind which group to join, so she followed Jason Harris and slipped into place beside him when he stopped not far from his brother-in-law. "Did you know?" she asked, speaking quite loudly so he could hear her above the hubbub.

"Not a whisper," Rose's uncle said. Then he could not resist adding, "Did you?"

"No!" Hattie said. "Why in heaven's name would she tell me?" As soon as the words were out of her mouth, she realized he was ribbing her, and she made an effort to smile, still dismayed to be so far behind on this choice piece of gossip.

"Why," she ventured, "would they run off like that?" Secretly, she was wondering if the seemingly sainted Rose had become less than sainted and perhaps was even now with child. But she had better not hint of that to this handsome uncle who seemed to prize Rose even more than his Chinese chickens.

"She's shy," Jason speculated, knowing full well that Hattie's imagination was running off with her. "I reckon she wanted a quiet wedding, something she couldn't get here." Then, trying to shift Hattie's thinking in a new direction, he added, "The reverend didn't like it a whit, did he?"

Hattie laughed. "I thought he would choke on every word," she answered. "Who could blame Rose for not wanting that ranting preacher to perform a marriage ceremony? I remember all his imprecations to the bride at the last one, and it was enough to make a girl turn tail and run."

They both laughed, then Jason put his finger to his lips and nodded toward Silas. "They will be here tomorrow," Rose's father was saying, his voice rising so more folks could hear him, "and we're going to have us a time when the train rolls in. I reckon the best place for the party will be right at the station when they get off."

"A party!" one woman exclaimed, and Sabbath or no Sabbath, the group began to applaud. A little embarrassed, Silas looked around to see where Charles had gotten to but couldn't find him. "Yes," he said, "a wedding reception of sorts."

"What time you expect them, Silas?"

"They'll be in on the three o'clock," he said, "if Henry Goodnow knows what he's talking about. We'll have lemonade and cake and …"

"And a gauntlet, Silas, a gauntlet," hollered Bob Chandler. "We won't beat them with a stick, but we'll make them march through and greet us all. Ought to be some torment connected to spoiling a wedding day hereabouts." The gathering whooped at that, paying no attention to the minister, who was trying to shush everyone into a seemly Sabbath silence.

"Presents," Mr. Chandler's wife chimed in. "We must give them what they need for their new house. Henry should know what they have and don't have. Henry," she called out, "can you open the store today so we can find things for Rose?"

"Can," Henry said. "If it's acceptable to the sheriff."

"No store can be opened on the Sabbath," came the voice of Calvin Lockhead, the minister seizing on something he thought he could enforce. As one, the crowd groaned. "It's the law," he added. "It's state law and God's law, and heaven help the man who answers to neither." They groaned louder.

Edith Goodnow waved her hands over her head, and everyone quieted down. "We cannot sell anything on the Sabbath," she said, "but we can unlock the door, give things away and collect the money tomorrow." The crowd cheered, and Calvin Lockhead realized this was not his day. He pushed his way out of the group and started for the parsonage, his wife by his side, his eyes on the ground. Confound the Hibbards, he muttered, and this time it was his turn to be shushed.

"They'll hear you, Calvin," his wife said, taking his arm and smiling at him. "And you are cussing on the Sabbath, I declare. Sometimes you amaze me." The two moved silently away, the minister feeling gloomier by the minute. He would not watch while Henry Goodnow unlocked his store, no sireee. On occasion, he felt the Catholics were right about making sinners confess to the clergy, not that he told anyone about that thinking. This was one of those times. He'd like to have Henry on his knees declaring himself a sinner.

In the meantime, Charles was moving quietly through the group, his ever curious self hoping to overhear something that would give him a hint about why Rose had done what she had done. He was secretly appalled – said the very word to himself rather proudly – that he had missed this one entirely. But as he well knew, Rose could keep a secret better than anyone in Eastborough, mebbe even the world. He paused behind his uncle and Hattie Munson and grinned when he heard them saying bad things about the preacher, but that didn't help him. He reckoned he might as well get on home, feed his cow and possibly sneak a little frosting off the cake Abby had made for Sunday dinner. He'd discovered a sharp knife would skin a layer and leave little evidence, especially if he warmed the knife a trifle.

On the church lawn, the crowd was moving toward the store. Henry had his key out, wondering if the sheriff was going to stop all this. Probably about the time they are all in the place, he thought, he'll come along with a warrant or something that looks like one. But he could see no other way, so he put on a smile and lifted the latch. He reckoned they wouldn't all fit in the store, and he hoped he'd be able to recall what Rose already owned and what she didn't have. Mostly didn't have, he figured. Mebbe he could get a few of them to join forces and get the bride something she would really want. But what would that be? And then it struck him: A sewing machine. He had one, and Rose

225

always dusted it so carefully that he knew she coveted it. Well, not coveted. The reverend wouldn't like coveted. Desired, perhaps. Come to think of it, that prissy preacher prob'bly wouldn't like desired either. Wasn't he the one, trying to throw a wet blanket over a good day? He hoped Newton and Rose, married now, were having such, enjoying their brief time away. Day and night, he hoped, still a little apprehensive about the night part.

As the shoppers entered, he pulled Bob Chandler aside and suggested some folks might get together on a precious item like a sewing machine. He'd put a reasonable price on it. Mr. Chandler, who had gone regularly to Rose's class when she first started teaching, was quite taken with the idea. It had been his job as a school committee member to make sure the very young Rose Hibbard wasn't in over her head in that school. He'd ended up so fascinated with her introduction of the new author Mark Twain that he had stolen away from his farm several afternoons a week to hear more about that rascal Tom Sawyer. And he'd learned a good deal about Miss Rose Hibbard at the same time.

He nodded to Henry and hoisted himself onto the counter. "Hear ye, hear ye," he shouted, and the crowd quieted. "A passel of us could join up and get Rose a sewing machine. It's pricey, but together we could manage. Henry says Rose has been dusting that machine as if it were fine china, so he thinks she wishes it were hers. Anyone who wants in on it, come forward and write down what you'll contribute. Remember, no money on the counter today. We want our clergyman to enjoy his Sunday roast chicken without palpitations." The group laughed and cheered, and he jumped down to get paper and pencil from

Henry. A line formed in front of him, and Bob gave the pencil tip a quick lick and began to write.

Elsewhere in the store, Hattie Munson was doing her own shopping. She knew how clever Rose was with her sewing, so she had decided to give her an assortment of buttons, six or so of each kind and perhaps three kinds. She didn't know why buttons had so much appeal to her, but she rarely came into the store without spending time puttering through the button drawers. She drifted toward the big cabinet that held all the sewing notions and began her little collection. She tended toward the pearly ones and the ones shaped like daisies. Perhaps, she thought, it's all those Shaker years of plain, plain, plain.

She was absorbed in her task and started when a voice from behind her said, "What's that you're doing on the Sabbath?"

"Jason Harris, you must not sneak up on a lady like that," she scolded, smiling up at him.

"Hattie Munson, you can't be buying buttons now," he scolded back.

"I have decided to get Rose's button box under way, since I am certain she won't feel easy about taking Sarah's along with her. And every seamstress needs a nearly endless supply of buttons, so that's going to be my gift to her. Come to think of it, you, down there in your woodworking cellar, you might consider creating her a button box."

Jason lit up at the idea. "That's a piece of advice I might accept right now," he said, giving her a little bow and moving away. "And pardon me for startling you." W'aal, he thought to himself, perhaps a button box. Or, mebbe, just mebbe, a table like Miss Hattie's. He chuckled at the idea of Rose having such – and Hattie not knowing about it.

He really is a handsome specimen, Hattie decided, glancing over her shoulder as Jason moved off. Setting one's cap for him would be a capital idea. Then she smiled at her own thought. That day when he brought her table she'd certainly had her cap in place, hadn't she? And she still hoped he hadn't noticed it, though she was certain as rain in April that he had. No one in Eastborough, where ladies' hats were numerous, wore anything like her neat.

While she gathered a dozen or so buttons, Henry Goodnow was totting up the promised contributions for a sewing machine and soon announced that he had enough. People started to leave the store and those who had not been needed for the machine lined up for his other suggestions. He thought of bobbins, a length of fabric, a spider and a stove-top toaster. He found he could not stop smiling as he thought about how surprised Rose would be with all this bounty. She never seemed to expect much from people and was always so grateful when something nice happened.

Then, suddenly, the store was empty as everyone hurried home for their delayed Sunday dinner. Hattie Munson was the last one at the counter, where she spread out the various buttons. "That's a grand idea, Hattie," Henry commented, getting out a small envelope for the buttons.

"She's a seamstress in her own right, Henry. Sarah taught her well, and the little one has learned a fair amount from Rose. But I reckon the new housewife will not be spending money on buttons in the near future. Is that young man making a decent living out there?"

Henry smiled inwardly, thinking that Hattie never could get away from asking questions, even if she was buying a wedding present. "I expect so," was all he said, as he bid her good day. He watched as she went out the door, on her way home to a solitary meal.

CHAPTER TWENTY-ONE
The Town Turns Out

Rose slipped out of bed and stole across the room to the table where Newton had placed his pocket watch. The room seemed very bright, so she was not surprised to read that she had slept until seven o'clock. Their train would be leaving at 11, so they had plenty of time, but she could not remember ever sleeping that late. She looked over at the bed where Newton was still asleep. Starting tomorrow, she thought with a sigh, he'll be out of the house by five, heading for the barn to feed his cows and milk the two that had been separated from the calves shortly before they left town. Then she scolded herself. What was she thinking? They would be together and, to her surprise, the very thought made her stomach do that flip-flop thing that had so often made her feel strange in the past. Even way back when he sat behind her at school, she thought with a smile.

She crossed the room and ran the back of her hand down Newton's cheek. He opened his eyes and immediately reached up to pull her face toward him. "This," he said, "makes waking up a worthwhile thing to do." He gave another tug, and she lost her balance, falling on top of him as he moved to make a space on the edge of the bed. They lay there for several minutes, savoring the newness of it all, and then he kissed her quickly and said they had little time to spare.

"How do you know?" she teased.

"I can see where the sun is. Must be nigh onto seven."

"That's about right," she answered. "And we're expected at breakfast shortly." She sat up, put on her dressing gown and left the room to use the bathroom down the hall, hoping she wouldn't meet any of the other inn guests. She was back before he had finished washing his face in the basin on the washstand, and he noticed that while she turned her back to him, she was planning to get dressed right there in the room without his leaving. He grinned as he gathered his shaving equipment and made his way to the community bathroom where he would find hot water. No point in pressing his luck. He would give her time to get her clothes on. No one was in the men's bath, and he set up in front of the mirror, still thinking about Rose getting dressed back there in the room. Take it easy, Joshua had said more than once. But Newton could not stop thinking about the possibility that she might let him undress her that very night. As he dipped the shaving brush into the warm soap and lathered his face, he pushed the thought aside. It was the kind of distraction that could lead to a razor cut and blood trickling down his face half the day. Finished, he went back to the room where Rose was folding clothes and putting them into their two valises. He sighed – she was completely clothed. And lovely, he added to himself.

Downstairs, Mrs. Newcomb showed them to their small alcove once again, and they ordered the same breakfast they had eaten the previous morning. Watching Rose eat, Newton saw a shadow cross her face, so quickly that at first he doubted it had come and gone. Then he saw it again.

"What are you thinking?" he asked, holding up a piece of toast and slathering it with the soft butter.

"Whether Father will be angry when we get home," she answered, so softly that he barely heard the words. Her expression now was, well, he thought, not childlike, but not wife-like, either. "Not truly worried, are you?" he asked, realizing that she certainly was in one of her worrying moods.

"A little," she confessed.

"If he is," Newton said gently, "it doesn't matter a whit. It's less important than whether the blueberries have gone by, less than whether we have sheets for our bed, less than ..." Now Rose was laughing, and she finished for him, "Less than whether Hattie cares."

"Precisely," he said. "I have a notion he's going to be pleased, not angry."

"He's not often pleased," Rose said. "Even now." But her brow was smooth again, and she smiled up at the serving girl who had appeared with her silver coffee pot. "Yes, please," she said. "It is quite delicious."

Before she had finished her second cup, Mr. Harty appeared in the door and said, "Good morning to you both." Newton sprang up, returned the greeting and pulled out a chair for him. Before seating himself, Ruthann's father gave Rose a pat on the back and a kiss on the forehead.

"How are you, dear girl?" he asked.

"Never any better than today, sir," Rose said, smiling up at him and thinking that he was a Harty and had a hearty voice.

Only you, Rose, she told herself, still smiling, would come up with an idea like that.

"Ida and I are so happy for you both," he went on. "But time's a-wasting. She's outside in the carriage, and we must get you to the station and say our goodbyes."

"We can never thank you enough for all you did for us," Newton began. But Mr. Harty was having none of it. "Haven't enjoyed a project that much since my last day at the company," he said. "Delighted that it worked out."

"I will see to the bill and the valises, sir, if you will keep Rose company for a moment," Newton said. "Everything is packed and ready to go." Rose nodded agreement, and Newton headed for the stairs.

"He's a fine young man, Rose," Mr. Harty said, "and we are looking forward to visiting Ruthann and Joshua soon, so it won't be long before we're with you again."

"That's a happy thought," Rose said. She hesitated and added, "It has been all happy thoughts since we arrived here. You have done so much for us, and we will be very pleased to repay your hospitality at least a little when you come to Chittenden Farm."

"No repayments necessary," he answered gruffly. "We are friends. Friends just get together without thinking about who owes what to whom." Like me with Alice and Emily, she thought. She owed them so much, ever since her mother's death, but they didn't recognize any debt. Mr. Harty stood then, hearing Newton's voice in the hall, and held her chair. As they went out, Mrs. Newcomb bobbed her head at Mr. Harty and wished Newton and Rose a grand life together. Then the three of them joined Ida in the carriage, the driver spoke a word to the horses, and they moved off. At the station, Rose felt the tears welling up as Ida Harty hugged her and whispered that she hoped everything was fine with her and would be for years to come.

"It's all too wonderful to believe," Rose said softly, pulling away and looking at Ida. "You were so good to me, and all my worries have disappeared without a trace. I am even ready to face all of Eastborough at once." She laughed and added, giving Newton a special look, "Especially now that I know I don't have to."

Ida Harty handed her a small parcel and said she hoped it would fit in Rose's handbag, a little memento of their time together. Mr. Harty hugged her then, the train rolled in, and the conductor dropped a small stool by the open door, then reached his white-gloved hand for hers. She stepped up to the platform between the cars, turning to wave to the Hartys before she and Newton went on to the first car on their left and found two seats together. He was carrying the light blanket he had hidden at the rock and he quickly dropped it over her lap. When she started to protest that she was quite warm enough and ask if it was a little sandy, he shook his head, put his left hand under the blanket and waited while she pulled off her right glove and slid her hand under the blanket to find his.

"I still can't stand it," she whispered to him. "You make me think unseemly thoughts."

"Mine are worse than yours," he answered in little more than a whisper. "But if you protest, I am afraid my hand will get to wandering."

She blushed then, and he chuckled. "I can't stand it either, Mrs. Barnes, but we have taken our vows and must put up with each other, now and for always."

"I like always," Rose said aloud and, hearing her voice, looked around to see if anyone else had. No one seemed to be paying any attention to them, so she leaned her head against the velvet fabric of the seat and let her hand relax in his while his calloused thumb stroked her index finger end to end, over and over. His gentle touch sent a thrill up her arm, and she thought again, with wonder, about their wedding eve on the rock and their nights in the inn. She had not dreamed anything could be like this.

The combination of his stroking and the rhythmic chuck-a-chuck-a of the train wheels made her very drowsy, and she let herself drift off into a half-sleep where she heard the conductor ask for their tickets and heard the whistle blow as they went through one station after another. But her eyelids did not lift, so Newton looked past her profile and watched the countryside roll past. When they reached the town of Orange, he roused her, so she would be really awake when they reached Eastborough.

"I've missed the whole ride," she exclaimed when she saw the Ripton sign on the station platform and realized they were almost home.

"Same scenery we saw on the way down," Newton said. "Hardly changed a-tall except for some new mowing."

"You'll be back to that by tomorrow, won't you," she said. "And I will be preparing a noon meal, bringing you ginger milk to drink at mid-afternoon and doing the washing."

"It doesn't sound much like a roomful of noisy youngsters," he said, glancing sideways at her. "And you are right about me. The weather smells good to me right now."

"I will miss them," she answered. "But this way I get to scrub your clothes." That made them both laugh. Then Newton

235

squeezed her hand under the blanket and said, "I want to be a fair trade for that classroom, Rose. I hope I can be."

He looked so serious that she swallowed her smile, leaned toward him and planted a small kiss on his cheek. "You already are," she said. Her eyes filled with tears then, and she added, "I should have traded them in long ago, but I kept thinking I needed a little time to be me."

"I reckon those are tears of sheer joy, not some new form of grief," he answered. And, saved from the serious moment, they both laughed again and settled back for the rest of the ride. Now it was Newton's turn to feel drowsy, and when Rose was certain he was really asleep, she pulled her hand carefully away from his and reached into her satchel to get the parcel Ida had given her.

She was delighted and touched when she pulled out a small linen napkin with just the beginnings of hemstitching along one side. The package included thread, the smallest scissors Rose had ever seen and a delicate needle. A note was tucked inside the napkin, and Rose read, "If you decide to finish this, I will send on more fabric. Please enjoy it if you've a mind to, and set it aside if it doesn't appeal." How lovely, Rose thought, hoping she'd have time for such handwork, and how beautiful Ida's writing was, straight across the paper as if it had lines. She smiled to herself, wondering if only a schoolteacher would think about the penmanship. But it was quite beautiful. She put the parcel back in her bag and stared out the window as the train left pastures and cows and church steeples behind. It was hard to imagine she'd have time for hemstitching, what with blueberries to pick and preserve, three meals a day to cook, a garden to take care of and all those sweaty haying clothes to wash. Ugh, she thought, as she remembered the chaff stuck in pants pockets and the grubby handkerchiefs the men pulled out to wipe their foreheads out in the hot fields. At this time of year, she'd need evenings to put the bread together and then store it overnight in the ice box. Hemstitching would have to wait. But it did appeal to her. It was such fine work, not like knitting socks. The train was slowing, and she glanced at the station platform and realized they were only one stop from Eastborough. She touched Newton's shoulder lightly, and he jumped a little.

"What's the matter?" he asked.

"One more stop," she said, and suddenly her heart sank. She hoped they would find the station empty – except for Henry, who'd be there to transport them to where he had stabled Tommy. Otherwise she'd be face to face with someone she knew, someone who would know she was married and that she had shared a bed with Newton. They would *know*, she fretted silently. She glanced at Newton and saw that he was watching her.

"Reckon you'd like to keep going to California," he drawled.

"Do you live inside my head?" she demanded in return.

"Be happy to live inside you anywhere," he said, speaking much more quickly.

"Newton!" she said and felt the hot color start rising from her neck to her face.

"Blushing bride," he said. "Apparently it's a common affliction."

"I am *not* afflicted," Rose began and then saw that his mouth was starting to curl up. "And you," she finished, a smile starting to flicker across her face, "are as rascally as any of the older boys in school."

"Do they try to make you blush?"

"I believe so," Rose answered. "And I try not to, and it mostly doesn't work. But I made them behave anyway."

"I have no intention of behaving," Newton said, reaching under the blanket and hoping he could distract her from thinking about not going back to her classroom. She extended her hand toward his, but he didn't take it, reaching for her leg instead, and she felt the familiar shiver. "Even with all that fabric," he remarked, and then wished he'd pretended he hadn't noticed her reaction. She might be embarrassed again. But instead, she turned toward him, kissed him on the cheek and said she thought he might be overstepping the bounds of train rules.

That brought a laugh loud enough to make two of the passengers turn around. He immediately withdrew the hand and said it must be time for the engineer to blow the whistle for Eastborough. It sounded almost immediately, and Newton quickly folded the blanket and leaned toward her.

"Don't fret about who we might run into at the station," he whispered. "No one will be interested in us anymore. We're an old, married couple. Even Hattie will be on to something new."

"I pray you are correct, Mr. Barnes," she said in her primmest voice. "I pray for that."

But it was not to be. Rose was paying attention to her feet as she moved from the train car to the less steady platform between the cars, so she didn't see the dozens of familiar faces outside the windows. But Newton did. "Lordy, lordy," he muttered to himself. "Has Henry betrayed us? Or the vanilla man? Surely it wasn't Silas?"

He heard the conductor say, "Wait here, Madam," as Rose reached the door. Dropping a small stool to the platform, the conductor jumped down and held his hand up for Rose's gloved one. She took it, holding up her long skirt with her other hand, still looking at her feet and hoping she would not slip on the metal step or catch her heel. And then she nearly tumbled into the arms of the conductor anyway because a loud cheer went up the second her face came into view. Catching herself, she stepped down and looked around in amazement. Dozens of people were on the platform, waving their arms above their heads and shouting.

Down the track, the engineer, who knew full well he'd never seen more than a handful of folks at this stop before, reckoned it was time to take part in whatever was going on. He pulled the whistle rope three times, which quieted the crowd just long enough for Henry Goodnow to call out, "Welcome home, Mr. and Mrs. Barnes." And then Newton was taking Rose's arm, surrendering the valises to the porter who had come out of the station. Uncertain and worried about Rose, he stopped for a second and saw that the crowd was providing an answer for him. They had formed an aisle, creating a double line that looped around the station, and he and Rose would be required to walk through it. So much for eloping, he muttered to himself and started forward, his hand firm under Rose's elbow.

"Nothing for it but to keep going," Newton whispered.

Rose looked up at him, tears in her eyes, and said, "I don't know if my feet will go."

He grinned and slid his arm around her. "Side by side," he said. "I'll give you a kick if your parts don't work."

That made her smile, and they moved onto the space the townspeople had made, with Newton shaking hands with the men and Rose getting an occasional hug from both men and women. They came to a section that was mostly the youngsters from her school, and she nearly choked up again but hid her blushing face by bending down and speaking right to the smallest ones, one by one. There was Delbert, all dressed up in his best bib and tucker and as she said hello and called him by name, he said, "But what do I call you, ma'am? You're not Miss Hibbard anymore."

"How right you are," Rose answered, relaxing in the thought of it. "Mrs. Barnes," she said, liking the sound of it. Then she straightened, smiled at Newton and whispered, "I am fine, as fine as the day," and without answering, he pulled her so close that her skirt swirled around his leg, and he had to take care not to trip on the hem.

The lines snaked around the station to the entrance at the front of the building where she found her father, Uncle Jason, Charles and Abby and Newton's parents waiting for her. She hugged Charles and Jason while Newton swung Abby right off the floor. When he set her down, Abby threw her arms around Rose, with Newton's mother embracing her new daughter-in-law as soon as Abby let go. "Welcome, dear Rose," Mrs. Barnes whispered. "Welcome to our family."

Once she was free, Rose looked at her father. "Thank you for coming," she said in a voice just a half octave above a whisper. "Am I to gather that this is your doing?"

"Daughters don't get married every day," he said, still a tad worried about how she was going to react to all this. "Aren't you the one, though?" he added. "Always another surprise."

She looked over her shoulder at the group that had filled in behind her, now nearly silent and watching this meeting with great interest. "Not bad at surprises yourself, apparently," she said. And when he reached out both arms, she walked into them, laid her face on his shoulder and hugged him. "Welcome, Rose Barnes," he said. And the crowd started to chatter again.

"In here," he said, gesturing to the station door. So she took Newton's hand, entered the station and gasped. On a long table at the end of the waiting room was a cake and three punch bowls and coming toward her, bowing and smiling, was Thaddeus Clapp, fiddle in hand. He started to play a waltz, and as if it had been rehearsed, she turned to Newton and they began to circle the floor while the townspeople crowded into the station.

"Did you know?" Rose asked Newton as they danced.

"Not a-tall," he said. "Are you ready to bolt?"

"Not me," she said. "This is amazing – I want to dance the rest of the day."

"That's my bride," he said, pulling her a little closer and, to her astonishment, kissing her on the mouth. The crowd roared its approval and then roared again minutes later when Silas Hibbard stepped forward and tapped Newton on the shoulder.

"My turn, young man," he said, signaling to Thaddeus that he needed to change the rhythm. "Don't do the waltz thing well, Rose," he apologized.

"It seems you do a party quite well," she said, smiling, "but can't they watch someone else?"

"A shindig for the most beautiful girl in the room," he answered. "Congratulations, Rose. I am mighty pleased for you."

Unable to speak, she squeezed his arm and concentrated on the somewhat erratic movements of his feet. And then Charles was there, tapping on his father's shoulder. "I reckon I can do this cutting in thing, too," he said. He took Rose's hand, twirled her around, and muttered, "Have to grab any chance to tell him what to do."

"You are a piece of work, Charles," Rose said, totally relaxed now. "But I can tell *you* what to do, still. So dance me over to that table where the punch and cake are. It's going to be all gone before we get there, and I'm starving. Not a bite since breakfast."

"Are you going to get fat now that you're married?"

"No, silly. But I'm still going to make you mind your manners," Rose answered, giving him a not so gentle cuff on the arm. "We'll begin with my taking your arm, you escorting me to that table, and you offering me refreshment."

"Same old Rose," Charles said with a sigh. "Why did I think three days of billing and cooing or whatever you people do after 'I do' would change anything?"

That made Rose laugh, although she had a second of wondering just how much Charles knew about "billing and cooing or whatever." Everything, prob'bly, she admitted to herself with a little sigh.

"Sighing already," Charles remarked as he rushed her across the floor to the table. "And I had the idea that bliss took away sighs as well. I am a disillusioned boy, just plain disillusioned. And that after being turned down on my shivaree idea."

"It's grand to be with you, Charles," his sister answered. "I can't imagine how I survived three days without your advice and your elegant thoughts about parties." She released him and watched with satisfaction while he placed a piece of cake on a plate for her, delivered it and then went for a cup of punch.

"No spirits in this," he said as he handed her the cup. "You, of course, are now unable to eat your cake because both of your hands are occupied. So you can have it and not eat it, too, as they say. But I have done my duty and must be off to find young ladies to dance around the hall. And feed, if they are so inclined." And with that, he left Rose standing at the refreshment table, wondering what to do next but amused by the fact that Charles, once again, had turned the tables on her. Who, she wondered, came up with that one – no one ever turned their tables. You could turn over a train table to read the other side, but dining tables and kitchen tables stayed put. You are off track, Rose, she told herself, again wondering what she should do besides stand there with her hands full.

She did not wonder long. A familiar voice made her turn, and there was Jane Hibbard, her smile wide and both hands stretched out in front of her. Rose set down her cake and punch and hugged her, and Jane whispered, "I have not told Silas that I knew all along about this because I thought he would sever my head from my body."

"Not to worry," Rose said. "He's quite the mellow fellow today." And they both grinned at the very idea of Silas Hibbard being termed a mellow fellow. She was about to go on when she realized Jane's attention was on something behind her, and then she felt Newton's hand on her back.

"Afternoon, Missus Hibbard," he said. "From now on I will come to you for advice on all serious matters."

"You may call me Grandmother Jane from now on, young man," the old woman said, "but I reckon you'll not listen to most of my advice, even if I am right as rain."

"Right as rain is right," Newton said, nodding. "I am now in favor of running away to get married."

"Just this once, you hear me?" she answered tartly. "Once in a lifetime."

"It is all I will need," he said, putting his arm around Rose's waist. As Jane Hibbard moved away, she said over her shoulder,

"And I perceive that the cat is quite satisfied, the canary no longer in its cage." Rose was still laughing, but a mite embarrassed to think she might look like the successful cat, when she felt Newton's warm breath on her neck and heard him whisper in her ear, "How long do we have to stay here? I am ready for bed."

Startled, she nearly spilled her punch. "You are very bad, Mr. Barnes. The sun, as they say aboard ship, is not yet over the yardarm, I have hardly talked with your father and mother, and you are thinking the day's work is done and you can now rest."

"No rest for a bridegroom," he answered, turning her around toward him. He took her punch cup and cake, set them on a windowsill and bowed low before gathering her in his arms for another dance. Thaddeus Clapp, who often made mischief with his music, shifted from the slow cadence of a waltz into a polka. Rose threw back her head, linked her hands behind Newton's neck so she wouldn't fall, and they went into a mad whirl around the room, soon joined by other dancers – including Charles, who had pulled Abby onto the floor, knowing that she was good at this dance the whole family loved.

When the music stopped, Henry Goodnow tapped on a table for attention and announced, "A goodly number of townspeople, Rose, have gathered their resources together to give you a wedding gift. If you will join me in the far corner of the room, I will make the presentation."

Rose didn't enjoy walking across the room with all eyes on her and all hands clapping, but she held Newton's hand firmly and hoped she wasn't going to blush or cry. When she reached Mr. Goodnow, he flipped away a white linen cloth with the flourish of a magician, and then Rose did start to weep. She was looking at a sewing machine, its cabinet a warm oak and its black treadle gleaming. She could not believe it. "For me," she said softly. "A new machine for me."

With tears streaming down her face, she hugged Henry Goodnow and then turned toward the townspeople. "There's no way to thank you for this," she said. She held out her arms in a big circle and added, "I embrace you all. I will treasure this always and use it more often than you can imagine."

While the crowd cheered, she turned to Newton and asked, "Will it fit in the buggy tonight?"

"It will fit in the buggy tomorrow," he answered. "It is too late for us to travel tonight."

"So we cannot go to our little house now?" she asked, disappointment clouding her face.

Without answering, Newton pointed to the station door, which had just reopened, letting Ruthann, Joshua and their two youngsters in. Leaving the children with Joshua, Ruthann almost ran across the room to throw her arms around both Newton and Rose, who gathered her in, all three of them dancing around without a care about what the neighbors might think. In another minute, Joshua and the children had joined them, everyone laughing and talking at once.

"I want a minute by minute description of the wedding," Ruthann said, breaking her hold on the couple.

"We will be home too late for that tonight," Rose said. "But can we find an hour or two tomorrow?"

"Not going 'home' tonight, Mrs. Barnes," Joshua cut in. "Our first gift to you is an extra honeymoon night in Ruthann's little house, right here in Eastborough. Then you can set out fresh, bright and early tomorrow."

"Oh, Ruthann! That's just the loveliest idea," Rose said. "But what have you done with your tenants?"

"They are away for the summer, so Joshua and I use the house when need be, and today it's yours."

"And I," said Newton with a grin, "will at last get to see that upstairs bedroom that has been off limits since before I started to shave my face."

At that point, Thaddeus Clapp decided that this little reunion might spoil the party, so he skipped into the center of the railroad waiting room and launched into a Virginia reel. As lines for three groups started to form, he paused and then began again as soon as they were ready. Newton and Joshua lined up opposite Rose and Ruthann, and all four watched as Hattie Munson maneuvered her way to a place opposite Jason Harris, while Silas Hibbard was pulled into the dance by daughter Abby.

"He's not going to get hooked by that gossip, is he?" Joshua muttered to Newton.

"Unlikely. But you cannot fault a widow for setting her cap for a good thing."

"I reckon you're right," Joshua said. "I gather you didn't tell Rose about the plan for staying in Eastborough tonight."

"Didn't. For the first time in her life, she hasn't thought much past the moment we are in, and it's quite something." He looked over at Rose, who was still talking to Ruthann, and said quietly, "All is well, Joshua. All, and I mean all, is more than well. Now, Virginia reel or not, I must get my bride out of here," Newton said. "I am quite tired of sharing her with so many people."

Joshua grinned. "We are going to stop at the house to see that everything is ready," he said, "so you'll have to put up with extra people a bit longer, and then we'll be off to the farm." And then the dance began, with more people than they ever had at the monthly square dances. Just for me, Rose thought, it is so lovely that it's just for me. Us, she corrected herself. Just for us.

After the first round, the two couples tried to slip away, but once again, with the fiddle jumping, everyone lined up to make a path, and with much laughter and shouting, the four made it to the door and the Chittenden buggy. Ruthann climbed up beside Joshua, and the newlyweds sat behind them, a child on either lap. Somewhere along the way, Newton noticed, their valises had been stowed in the back. He shook his head, marveling at the day's events.

"Henry has Tommy stabled at his place," Joshua explained. "And he'll bring horse and buggy here in the morning. Has quite a few things stowed in it already." Then he grinned over his shoulder at Rose and added, "We didn't want to burden Newton with any chores tonight. He needs time to explore that mysterious bedroom." And the two men turned toward each other at the same time and shared an extra firm handshake.

Rose's face was in full bloom at that, but she was determined to answer in any case. "Joshua," she began, "you must not tell stories like that about married women. And I am a married woman."

"So I may infer," he answered, suddenly sounding more like a lawyer than she ever remembered, "that it will be acceptable for me to speak thusly about *unmarried* ladies?"

"Objection," Ruthann called out, falling in with his lawyerly tone.

"Sustained," Rose said, surprising them with her knowledge of courtroom talk. And then they were all silent, with Newton

247

putting one arm around his bride and holding one of her hands with the other. He heard her sigh and pulled her closer.

"Is everything satisfactory?" he whispered.

"More than," she whispered back, leaning her head against his shoulder. "Can you believe that Father arranged all that? And that I have a beautiful sewing machine?"

"The better to turn my collars, my dear," he said, growling like a wolf.

"Only when the need is dire, my dear," she replied. And they both laughed. "We have laughed so much today," Rose said, "and yesterday, too. I hope the inventory of laughs is large enough to last as long as we do."

"Laughs breed like rabbits," Newton said solemnly. "No way to stop them."

"You are sometimes the strangest man," Rose said.

"Recently married to the strangest woman," he said. "And mighty proud of it."

CHAPTER TWENTY-TWO
Hattie Remembers the Shaker Days

To Rose's delight, the little house where she had lived with Miss Harty all those years ago hadn't changed much. The teacher had left some of her furniture for the new tenant, and in a matter of minutes, the friends were standing around the familiar kitchen table, its surface slightly more worn now that two young children had lived in the house.

"What is that smell?" Newton asked, thinking that his stomach would soon growl from hunger. Cake at a party was not his idea of a meal.

"Aroma," Rose said without thinking.

Joshua chuckled. "Some day, Newton," he said wryly, "you will learn the right words from the teacher. I thought I had 'em all pretty straight, but I get 'em wrong as regular as a Jersey moos for her hay."

"My pleasure," Newton answered, grinning at him. "In a matter of weeks, I will be an educated man."

"Them," Ruthann said. Rose smiled, raised one eyebrow and said nothing. Miss Harty turned her back, picked up a potholder and pulled open the door of the oven. A rush of warmth came out, along with a considerable increase in the aroma. She drew out a somewhat battered baking pan and set it on the wrought iron trivet in the middle of the table. In the meantime, Rose was opening cupboard doors in search of six plates and, not finding any, went to the dining room and fetched the good china.

"Fancy tonight," Joshua commented. "Do you think the teacher always dines on porcelain?"

"I will eat on a square of burlap as long as it's aroma food," Newton said, pulling out a chair for Rose and then seating himself.

"Good to know," Rose said. "Last I looked, we hadn't much in the way of plates at the little house."

Joshua and Ruthann exchanged a look, but neither said anything. Instead, Ruthann dished up the casserole, a mixture of chicken, potatoes and carrots. She apologized for serving what amounted to chicken pie without a crust but said she couldn't figure a way to be sure it wouldn't overcook while they were at the train station. It was quickly apparent that no one cared. They were all silent for several minutes while they dug their forks into the food, stopping only when Joshua lifted his tumbler of cider and proposed a toast to the newlyweds, telling his children to do the same with their milk.

"Oh, oh," Rose said after Newton had returned the toast. "I haven't even delivered greetings from your parents, nor have I told you how splendid they were with every detail of our wedding day."

"And the day after," Newton said with a grin.

"We did not see them on the day after," Rose began. Then her face flushed, she looked down at her plate, and they heard her mutter a small, "Oh." And then, knowing what good friends these were, she looked up, gave a tiny smile and said, "Well, I reckon it was the day after that."

"Did you swim?" Ruthann asked, hoping to get past the moment.

"We did, we did!" Rose exclaimed. "And the salt water lets you float. It was delicious."

"I would like to float like that," John Chittenden said in a small voice.

"And you will," his mother answered. "When we visit Grandfather and Grandmother in September."

"And your mother arranged a wonderful lunch for us," Rose went on, "and she taught me to hemstitch – well, she began to teach me – and your father was elegant, elegant all the time."

"Whew!" Joshua said, wiping his forehead in an exaggerated motion.

"Stop it, Mr. Chittenden," Ruthann laughed. "They *are* the best hosts in the world, you know." She offered seconds to Newton and Joshua and a few minutes later, she cleared the plates and set down a tray of oatmeal cookies.

Within the hour, they had finished eating, washed and put away the dishes and the Chittendens were saying their goodbyes at the door. Newton and Rose watched the four of them to their buggy, and then he pulled her into his arms.

"I have been apart from you quite long enough," he whispered into her ear.

"We haven't been apart for more than a dance or two," Rose protested. But she knew what he meant, and she knew what that meant. She tilted her face up, kissed him gently on the lips, all the while tracing his face and ears with her finger, a gentle teasing that he almost couldn't stand. But he also hoped she wouldn't stop. This love thing, he thought, is not so simple. In response, he pulled her close and mumbled, while her kiss continued, "I reckon it's unseemly to go to bed before the sun sets."

She stopped kissing him abruptly. "I am a married woman, sir," she said. "I no longer have to be seemly, at least in certain aspects."

"I've a notion that aspects agree with me," he said. And with that, he scooped her up and carried her up the stairs to the bedroom where he had so many times imagined her slipping into a nightgown and crawling under the covers alone while he and Tommy headed home with the buggy. Inside the door, he dropped her on the bed and, starting with her shoes and stockings, began to undress her. Her body seemed tense, so when he flipped up her skirt and petticoat to reach the fasteners on her stockings, he kissed both her knees while he pulled the stockings off. Her legs suddenly relaxed, and she giggled.

He began to move faster, deftly pulling off her petticoat, unbuttoning her skirt and then undoing the tiny buttons on her shirtwaist. She did not stir, so he went on, a little uncertain, but not stopping. And then, to his surprise, she reached up to undo the buttons on his shirt and then his trousers. To his astonishment, she pulled off his boots, stockings and garters and dropped his drawers to the floor.

"No obstructions," he muttered.

"And no chaperones," she said, giving that now familiar giggle again.

The sun was low and shining into the eyebrow windows of this tiny bedroom. He lifted her onto the bed and thought how

252

beautiful she was, lying there in the sun. Ruthann said he'd want to look at me, Rose recalled again, but she felt frozen in place and wished he would stop. She wondered if he'd be wanting this every day. She wanted to interrupt this look that made her as jittery as drops of water on a hot skillet.

"Come," she said. He nodded and joined her, a little in awe of what was happening to him. He had never dreamed he would be so, so, what was that word Joshua had used once? Besotted. That was it. He gathered her into his arms, still without a word. The sun was down and the moon high before they finally lit a lamp and made their way downstairs for a cup of tea.

They were too absorbed in each other to even think about what was going on in the world beyond what had been Miss Harty's little house. But quite a crowd had lingered at the train station, taking advantage of the rare occurrence of a Silas Hibbard party, and Thaddeus Clapp had played on, happy to make his fiddle sing as long as smiling folks wished to dance. So the sun had been gone an hour or so when Silas made his way up the street toward his house. He was almost to the teacher's place and saw no lights there. In bed already, he muttered to himself. Well, they were young and new at it. Then he chuckled at the sight of a lamp being lit upstairs and then reappearing at the bottom of the stairs. Those little rascals, he thought. They were in bed before sundown, I'll warrant. And you, Silas, he told himself, have better things to do than be staring at your married daughter's bedroom window. He picked up his pace on the gravel road and was moving quickly when he heard a horse and buggy coming up behind him. He stepped to the grassy strip next to the ditch and was surprised to hear the hoof beats slow and then stop. It was dark, but it looked like Hattie Munson's horse and then, sure enough, she called out to him.

"Be pleased to drop you off, Silas," she said.

"I'm fine on foot," he answered.

"Of course you are," she said with a laugh. "But you'll be fine riding, I reckon."

He wasn't of a mind to carry on a conversation like this in the middle of the road, so he climbed up, took a seat beside the widow and waited for her first question. He hadn't a doubt that she would be trying to worm some information about Rose and Newton out of him. Worm, indeed, he thought. He pictured her wriggling her way through the dirt like a night crawler. The idea made him smile. Rose had them all thinking odd things about words.

"Amused?" Hattie said, giving him a sideways glance.

"Jest thinkin' what a fine day it has been," he said, drawling out his words.

"Rose looks very happy," she said.

"Hmm," was his only answer. And they rode on in silence, to his surprise. When they reached the end of his driveway, she pulled up on the reins and the buggy stopped. Silas climbed down immediately, tipped his hat to her and said, "Good night, Hattie." She wished him a good evening, watched him start down the path and then gave the reins a small snap and went on her way.

Somewhat relieved, Silas felt his way into the kitchen, fumbling for the kerosene lamp and for the matchbox he kept beside it. Once the wick was lit and the glass chimney replaced, the room opened up around him. Damned empty, he said to himself, as he drew the teakettle forward on the stove. Should have invited Hattie in for tea. He added a stick to the fire in the stove and filled the small metal tea ball. He always jammed it full of tea leaves, even though he knew it wasn't the proper way to make a single cup of tea. It made the water darken faster, that's what he also knew.

Sitting in the kitchen rocker, sipping the hot tea, he was suddenly overwhelmed by clear memories of the day he and Sarah had tied the knot. What a day it had been, she so lovely and so anxious and he trying to be gentle when all he wanted to do was undress her and make her his own. Make her his own? What an idea that was for a brash young man, he thought. He'd learned soon enough that she didn't *belong* to him. They spent that first night in each other's arms, and after awhile, he had felt her relax and realized she had fallen asleep, still in her frilly nightgown with every button buttoned, right up to her chin. He chuckled, remembering how she apologized the next morning for spoiling his wedding night, and he had reassured her that they had years to make up for it.

"We'll start tonight," she said, her face suddenly pink. "I was very tired last night." Then she had paused and added, so softly he hardly heard it, "And scared to death." Right there by this very stove, he had put his arms around her and kissed her on the mouth for such a long time that they nearly ran out of breath. And when he tried to pull away, she had put her face on his chest and gently stroked his back. Oh, how he missed her, still. In so many ways.

Arriving at her own cozy house, Hattie Munson was struck by the fact that for the first time in a month of Sundays she was feeling a bit lonely. It's what weddings do, she thought. Make you think of yours. The trouble was that such memories always

255

seemed to float along on a calm sea, the rough parts gone, only the smell of roses and the laughter remembered. She forced herself to think about the years after that ceremony, how Caleb Munson's charm had turned sour, how she had worked her fingers to the bone trying to please him and finally learned that she could not. If she made a perfect apple pie, he wished it was blueberry. If she killed and roasted a chicken from their coop, he berated her for cutting into the egg supply. If she served him stew and fresh bread for supper, he had been thinking all day about chicken. And those were just the little things.

She sighed as she added a couple of sticks to the dying fire in her stove and filled the blue and white enamel teakettle halfway. At least she'd had the sense to get out when he first raised his hand against her, cursing the five years they'd been married and accusing her of trapping him into marrying her. He had gone off to the barn to finish his chores that morning, and she had packed a small bag and taken herself down the dirt road that led to town. Once there, she went right to the railroad station and asked the station master where the next train would be headed. Pittsfield, he'd said. She bought a ticket and turned away before he could ask any questions.

Pittsfield would be fine, she had thought. She knew the Shakers were there somewhere, and she'd heard they welcomed anyone who came. When she descended the steps to the Pittsfield platform, she had asked a man by the pushcarts where the Shakers lived. He had given her precise directions and as she started to walk away, had asked if she would like a lift. It was quite a distance for walking, he said. She had accepted, knowing that her mother would have been scandalized about her daughter taking a ride from a stranger. But he had merely driven her there and left her off.

As she had heard, the Shakers welcomed her. In a corner of their big kitchen, the sisters served her a plateful of food left from their midday meal and then asked if she would like to rest before telling them her story. She had only been able to nod. Tears were running down her cheeks, and she had started to tremble uncontrollably. They took her to a bright, clean room with a single bed and placed her satchel on the floor. She lay down and was immediately covered with a soft quilt. She closed her eyes, listening to the sisters murmur around her and then feeling a warm wet cloth on her forehead and a warmed soapstone snugged under the quilt next to her body. Minutes later, she was asleep.

Hattie rocked and sipped her tea, remembering how Mr. Munson had tracked her down same as he went after rabbits and deer. She must have been a sight to behold because everyone on her flight route remembered her. And so, six or seven weeks later, he had appeared at the Shaker village kitchen, an angry man in search of his wife. The sisters had tried to calm him down at first, not admitting that she was there. But when he snatched a skillet from the wall and started to brandish it, Sister Nettie crept quietly away toward the storage rooms and out through a back door. She ran for the Round Barn and alerted the brethren who were unloading their hay wagons into the open silo in the center of the barn.

That ended that, she recalled, smiling a little. They had sat him down, asked questions and decided they would not let her go with him unless she wanted to. She didn't. She had been so grateful for their protection, which was really all she had expected from them. The surprise was that they were so practical about all this. They insisted he come back another day when Mrs. Munson was feeling more like herself and that he bring both goods and money to pay for the cost of her room and board whilst she had been with them. Once Caleb had calmed down, he agreed to return in three weeks, and it was decided how many chickens and how much hard cash he would bring to wipe away his debt to them.

He had carried out his end of the bargain, to Hattie's dismay. But she had underestimated the brethren, who then informed him that Hattie Munson had no wish to live with him again. He protested – from an adjacent room, she heard him say, "But she is mine, she is mine, and I will see her now!" But the brethren had stood fast. Within an hour it was over. Caleb headed home, his debt to the Shakers paid, and his wife lost to him. It took another year for her to be divorced, but she had managed it. And she had found considerable peace working side by side with the Shakers. That was when she became enamored of their designs and their cooking. But after one more year, she had to tell them that their gentle insistence that she join them spiritually was to no avail. They had not taken offense. Instead, it turned out they had put Caleb's money aside for her, and in payment for her diligence over the months she had been there, they provided her with a horse and buggy and all sorts of household things, plus a box of precious garden seeds. When she said she had no wish to take any of the chickens, they added a little more cash to the small oval box they had for her.

They were so kind, she thought, that they had even stopped by to see her during the two months she lived in Pittsfield. Once she had found this house in Eastborough, she had moved on and now saw them only once every two or three years when she would go back to New Lebanon and enjoy the Shakers' seemingly unending outpouring of tranquility. It was enough, she thought wryly, to make a body wonder if perhaps celibacy was the key. It was an idea she had often discarded in the past but lately it had been on her mind a good deal. And in her present mood, she was hoping she might figure on a happy future without the burden of celibacy.

She was beginning to think Jason Harris was a lost cause and after that companionable ride with Silas Hibbard this very night, she was tempted to explore that path further. He certainly was a handsome man, too, and perhaps she needed to look a little deeper, try to discover what it was that Sarah saw. She saw something, Hattie knew, and Sarah Hibbard had been a remarkable woman. Even Hattie had been unable to find fault with her.

That was another thing. The Shakers didn't seem to find fault. They didn't pry into her business, and every time she visited them, she was aware all over again that when she was with them, her own perpetually prying mind went into some kind of cocoon. In Eastborough, she always felt compelled to know what everyone was doing and to pass the word along, sometimes, she knew, embroidering it a little.

At the Shakers' isolated village, smaller even than Eastborough, she felt a peaceful disinterest in gossip. That, she knew, had nothing to do with celibacy. She'd been celibate enough for seven sisters in the past few years. She shook her head, wondering how she had gotten into this state of mind. Weddings, that was it. She finished her tea, washed her cup, rattled the grate on the stove to send some of the ashes into the lower level, lit a candle and put out her lamp. Candle in hand, she mounted the stairs to her bedroom, still a little startled to find herself wishing her house were not so empty. At least Miss Abby would be coming by tomorrow.

CHAPTER TWENTY-THREE
Heading for Home

By the time the sun was hitting kitchens all over Eastborough, Newton and Rose were well on their way to their new home. Eliva Barnes had been anxious to give them breakfast and had promised it would be ready anytime from six o'clock on, so they rose at five and it wasn't long before Henry Goodnow pulled up with Newton's horse and buggy. To Rose's delight, Mr. Goodnow had somehow squeezed in the sewing machine, wrapped in a new quilt that Edith Goodnow had made for her in the log cabin design. He had pinned a note on the quilt to let her know her other gifts were safely put away at the store, and a second note from Edith said a wedding ring quilt would follow, but she hadn't had enough notice to get that fancy one done on time.

After they left Henry off at his home and stopped to savor Eliva Barnes' blueberry muffins, they set Tommy on the road he knew so well to the Chittenden place. Rose began to think how different this morning had been. Not very romantic, a-tall. She had wakened when Newton kissed her, and then he had jumped out of bed as if he'd been stung by a bee. "Time's a-wasting," he had said, pulling on his shirt and trousers, and heading downstairs with his razor in hand. "Honeymoon's over," she muttered to herself, feeling a tad grumpy. But once she was out of bed and starting to get dressed, she looked in the glass over the chest of drawers and laughed at herself. The honeymoon, after all, hadn't been the least bit real. They had been out of place and separated from time. Now their real lives would begin. She would cook and clean and feed chickens and know all day long that when darkness started to creep in, she and Newton would get into bed together. A shiver of anticipation ran down her spine.

She was a little mortified about how much she had enjoyed their lovemaking, at least partly because the Rev. Lockhead had made it clear that lust was dreadfully sinful, and she was pretty certain her reaction to Newton had a fair dab of lust in the love. The problem was she could not seem to locate an iota of guilt in her heart. Surely she had tried. She did hope she wasn't going to hell because of liking to go to bed. It had once seemed like the right place for a tired body to be. Well, she wasn't about to die, so she'd put off worrying about hell. Perhaps she should put her mind on what they might have for supper.

And then the little house came into view, and the wheels had barely stopped turning when Rose jumped down, picked up her skirts and ran to the door as if she were a child arriving for Thanksgiving dinner. He dropped the reins over Tommy's head so the horse would stand still and followed her. She glanced at the kitchen, poked her head into the tiny pantry, admired the cupboards with their bead-board doors and was off to the living room where Newton had set up a Franklin stove since the last time she had visited. While he trailed behind, she practically flew up the stairs to see the two little bedrooms and the larger one and was sitting on the edge of the bed by the time he reached her.

"Better not get near that, dear wife," he muttered. "Been several hours."

She jumped up, hugged him and said, "It is so lovely, so cozy, so perfect. And we are *not* going to bed right now." And then she was off again, back down the stairs and out to the buggy to begin unloading their things. Newton followed, a smile on his face. He could not figure out how he had known this girl, this woman, so long and, apparently, hadn't known much about her a-tall. Each hour was more satisfying than getting his price for a Jersey heifer, or watching a newborn calf stagger to its feet, or getting all the hay in just as the first lightning zigzagged across the sky. He reckoned he wouldn't mention any of that to Rose. For some reason she didn't like to be compared to Jerseys or haystacks. He would just enjoy watching her unfold.

One thing he did know. She would need a few more minutes before he mentioned that he ought to see to the livestock. For some reason he didn't quite understand, she bridled a little whenever his prized Jerseys came up. Or haying, for that matter. And tomorrow morning, if the wind and the clouds were right – and it seemed to his practiced eye that they might be – he'd be mowing as much as he could. Getting married in the summer wasn't something a farmer oughta do. He grinned, thinking it certainly had its merits, hay or no hay.

And then she flew by again, her arms full of their belongings. "I'd be grateful if you could bring in that beautiful sewing machine," she said. "I reckon it's too heavy for me." Newton nodded and went after the prized object. He wondered if she'd set it up in one of the spare bedrooms for the time being and sure enough, as he went through the kitchen door, Rose said, "In the smallest bedroom, I think. That will keep my sewing paraphernalia out of sight, and I so dislike putting away and getting out again just for appearances."

Paraphernalia, he thought, as he climbed the stairs. He might need a dictionary at his bedside. Most womenfolk would just say "mess" or "clutter" when talking about something they didn't want the neighbors to see. His mother had a sewing nook upstairs because she said no good seamstress would waste time putting every last scrap away every time. She said you would just lose your place and never get a task finished. It occurred to him that it was something of a relief to find Rose didn't always care about order. He tended toward the clutter side himself.

"Perfect," Rose said from behind him. She threw her arms around him and gently kissed the back of his neck between the hairline and his collar and felt a shiver run down his body. "Sorry," she said, letting him go.

"Never apologize for surprises like that," Newton laughed, whirling around and grabbing her before she could run off. He pulled her against him and then whispered in her ear, "You just make me want to unbutton your buttons and toss your stays aside."

"Not now, sir," Rose said, giving him a little push. "You must get to the barn, sir, and I to the kitchen. It will be suppertime before we know it."

With a sigh that mixed regret and thankfulness that she, not he, had mentioned cows first, Newton dropped his arms to his side. "You are right," he said. "I'll get my barn clothes on and see to the cows and chickens. I expect Ruthann and Joshua have put some foodstuffs in the ice box, and Henry tucked in sacks of flour and sugar and some eggs."

"And your mother made a dessert."

"And your father packed up part of the cake from the party."

"We will not starve. Not today at least," Rose said. "Now be off before I give you another shiver."

By the time Newton returned from his chores, Rose had unpacked most of the things they had brought from Eastborough and had started to sort through some boxes that Henry Goodnow and Joshua had brought along ahead of time. She had a fire going in the wood stove, and a delicious aroma greeted Newton's nose as he came in.

"What's that?" he asked, sniffing.

"Just biscuits and soup, I fear," Rose said. "You must be hungry, and I was trying to fix something quickly. Ruthann and Joshua did leave a few things in the ice box, and it turns out we have a stack of new plates and bowls." She turned and grinned, "And we can always eat cake."

"Marie Antoinette, I presume," he answered, bowing. "I did some listening in that classroom, you know, besides admiring your hair and trying to keep you awake."

In a few minutes, a somewhat late noon meal was on the table, and they sat down for the first time in the new house. Rose wondered if it meant as much to Newton as it did to her. This was a place that was just theirs, and she was thinking her cup was very full today. She looked at him and discovered he was staring at her, his spoon halfway to his mouth.

"I like having a house that's ours," he explained. "It just came over me like a big, soft blanket."

"Me, too," Rose said, her voice barely above a whisper. She did hope she wasn't going to get all teary now, but her eyes felt very watery. When Newton put down his spoon and reached over to take her hand, the eyes betrayed her. The first tear didn't quietly roll down her cheek – it fell right into the soup in front of her. He squeezed her hand and nodded at her.

"I feel like that, too," he said. "But watch out. The soup has enough salt in it."

She laughed then, and the teary moment was gone. "Thank you," she said.

"No need to thank me. That was a happy tear, am I right?"

"Indeed."

"Now, what else do we need to do to get settled?"

"Find the towels, unpack the rest of the things Ruthann and Joshua left in the back room and make the bed." With this last, she raised an eyebrow at him and quickly added, "I'll take care of that last chore myself. Men are not adept at beds."

"I am very adept, I believe, with bed," Newton answered in a teasing voice.

"Bed, but not beds," Rose retorted, getting up to clear the table.

"On to the boxes and barrels, then," Newton said. "I have two or three hours before the animals need me again. But first, I need to get this fire really going and get us some hot water. You can't do many dishes in what's there now."

Rose had realized it would take time to get water heated up, so she had the teakettle almost at a boil for washing the dishes. She poured it into the dishpan and added a little cold. Then she quickly washed the dishes and set them in the drainer. As soon as Newton went out to get firewood, she ran upstairs to make the bed. She wanted to get that done before he reappeared – it seemed to be a problem for him to be near beds without getting in them. She giggled and admitted to herself that she no longer thought only of sleeping when she saw a bed. Was Emily like this, too, she wondered. And what about Alice? She would like to see Alice, but she and Ethan were a hundred miles away and hadn't been at the station when she and Newton walked into that grand party.

She quickly took the thin mattress off the bed, stretched the ropes as tight as she could, put the mattress back and added the sheets Aunt Nell had put in the chest. She ran her fingers over the satin-stitched B's on the pillow slips and stuffed the feather pillows into them. Then she added a heavy quilt and a plain coverlet and looked at the result with satisfaction. As she turned toward the door, she took one more look at the bed and felt her stomach flip-flop in a familiar way. She had to confess, at least to herself, that she could hardly wait for dark to fall. Stop it, she scolded herself, as she hurried down the narrow stairs. She would get Newton to take the beautiful chest upstairs and put it at the foot of the bed. But she needed to empty it, or he'd never manage it alone.

CHAPTER TWENTY-FOUR
Summertime Begins

Abby would be getting up about now, Rose thought the next morning as she added a stick to her new wood stove and drew water for coffee. She was quite right. As the sun rose over the Hibbard barn, Abby slowly crawled out of the bed she had shared with Rose for years. Barely paying attention to what she was doing, she quickly put on the clothes she had laid out the night before and ran downstairs to the bathroom. Her face washed, she fetched two sticks from the wood box and added them to the stove. Father, she could see, had already coaxed a morning fire out of the overnight coals. It was still cool enough in the evenings for them to keep the fire going until bedtime, but pretty soon she would have to get up a little earlier and get a fire going from cold ashes. She would not mind. Summer was upon them, school was out, and the wash would dry outside, no spring fog, no ice on the lines. Abby admitted only to herself that she hated doing the wash, and she hated hanging out wet clothes in winter, freezing her hands and, in a few minutes, freezing the sheets and shirts, too.

She filled a pot with water for coffee and set it on the stove. She wondered if Rose was making coffee in her new house at the Chittendens'. She did miss her so. Must not be thinking about that, she told herself sternly. No flowing water today, except from the faucets. She had cried herself to sleep for two nights after she found out that Rose wasn't ever coming home to Eastborough again and, each time, she scolded herself for crying over something that was making Rose happier than she had ever seen her.

The two things had nothing to do with each other, she decided. She was so pleased for Rose, and she loved having Newton for a brother-in-law. But she wanted Rose right there, too, in charge and sleeping beside her and telling her what to do next when she sort of lost her sense of direction about tasks. Now she sleeps next to Newton, Abby thought suddenly. She hadn't really thought about that. How strange would it be to have a man in the bed next to you instead of your sister. Did they get undressed at the same time without looking at each other, the way she and Rose always did? Abby measured out the coffee and decided she had better keep her mind on breakfast. But she was curious about how these things worked.

She heard her father's heavy steps on the stairs and quickly turned her attention to his oatmeal, which was bubbling on the back of the stove. She had a warm bowl on the stove shelf for that, and the bread Mehitabel had made yesterday was in the toasting rack, ready to set on the stove.

"Mornin', Abby," Silas Hibbard said as he came through the door in his stocking feet. "Fine day for haying. 'Spect Newton is grateful to be home in time for this weather."

"Will the weather be the same at their place?" Abby asked.

"Certain sure. It's only down the road a piece, Abby. Rose hasn't moved to China or Africa."

"I knew *that*," Abby said, frowning. "But it does sometimes rain up on the mountain and not down here."

"Right you are," Silas agreed. "But this is going to be a grand June day. Wind's right. Grass is at its peak. Breakfast about ready?"

"Sit right down," she answered, and watched as her father rolled up his sleeves to the elbows and went to his place at the dining room table. She put his oatmeal in front of him, along with a small pitcher of maple syrup and a larger one of milk. She knew he always washed up when he came in from chores, but he still smelled a bit like a barn. She'd have to get after him to put on a clean set of clothes.

"I'll take a little top milk for my coffee today if you have it," he said. He reached to the spoon holder on the table and took out a tablespoon. Abby saw that it was the one with an S inscribed on the handle. Mother's special one, she thought. She had noticed that he most always used that one if it was there. He must still think of her, even after all this time, she decided. She finished fixing his toast and then ran upstairs to make her bed and put on her work shoes. Father might be relishing the hayfield, but she was happier to be going back to the school for clean-up day. Classes were over, but all children not needed for haying were expected to help put the entire place into perfect order. Abby thought it was grand fun. Besides, when she helped with haying, they always put her on the wagon to stomp down each forkful as they loaded it on. The higher the load, the more her stomach churned. If it wasn't loaded and stomped just right, it could sway and tip off, and everyone would blame her, even if it was their fault. She hated it. If it tipped off, more than likely she'd fall off, too, and be under all that newly dried grass. I could even be dead, she thought. She smoothed her skirt and hurried back to the kitchen.

"I'll see to clearing up," her father said as she reappeared. "Charles can't catch up with himself this morning, never mind get any extras in. But he's bound to want to be at the school cleaning. Could use him with the haying, but I don't need Rose here to tell me *that* won't do."

Abby laughed. "I miss her already, Father. But she does keep getting inside my head to tell me what to do."

"Powerful girl," Silas said, nodding. "Woman, now, I reckon." He paused and stared out the window at the bright, clear sky. "Truth told, been a woman inside these walls for a considerable time."

Abby felt her eyes filling up and barely managed to choke out, "Yes," and "Thank you, sir," before she picked up her lunch box and went out the door. She couldn't wait for Charles. Who knew when he'd get in from the barn. And then he would take a piece of bread and tear down the road as if bobcats were after him. Probably run right by her. Rose had been gone only a few days, and Charles was already out of kilter. What is kilter, anyway, she wondered and smiled to herself. She liked it when her mind took a Rose track. But she could not think what kilter might be. Not related, certainly, to a Scotsman's skirt, was it?

She heard thudding feet behind her and reckoned Charles was about to overtake her. If he stayed on the path, their shortcut to school, she could reach out a foot and trip him. The thought was barely into her head when he whizzed by, and she wondered if she had to apologize to him for something that had never been more than an idea. She thought not. She would just forget it. She looked ahead and saw Addie and Flora were on the corner where she would rejoin the road. She quickened her step, using her free hand to raise her skirt a little. The road was so rutted that small puddles seemed to last for days. She glanced at the sky and figured all the puddles would be gone overnight. It was indeed a grand day for haying.

"Are you working for that old biddy today?" Addie wanted to know, as soon as Abby was within earshot.

"Addie," Abby scolded. "You must use her name. Old biddy is reserved for hens we are on the brink of eating."

"Brink, *brink?*" Flora chimed in. "What in heaven's name is a brink?"

"No need to get all church-y about it," Abby replied in her calmest voice.

"Ooooh, when you talk like that, I want to stamp my foot and yours, too," Flora said.

"Must of gotten out of the wrong side of the bed today," Abby said, still maddenly calm.

Flora stopped walking abruptly. The other two each took several more steps and then they stopped and turned to look at her. Tears were streaming down her face, and she was using the corner of her apron to dab at them. Addie and Abby hurried back to her, and each put an arm around her.

"I was only teasing," Abby began, blaming herself for the downpour.

"It's not you," Flora sobbed. "It's my house, it's all the yelling and it goes on at night and I can't sleep and I did, in fact, get out of the wrong side of the bed because my sister was on the side where I usually get out."

"It's just a saying," Addie said. "Which side doesn't really matter."

"I know that," Flora said, and stopped crying. "But Abby said it, and it was true, and everything was so wrong."

"Why do they yell?" Abby wanted to know. "Do you want to tell?"

"Ma and Pa, I think," Flora said slowly, "don't like each other. And Pa says terrible things to Leonard – that's Ma's brother – whenever he's staying with us. And he always stays for several days because Ma feels sorry for him. He doesn't have any work right now, so she always says he should come and get a good feed for a few days, get his backbone back, whatever that means."

"We need to move on," Abby said, "but keep telling."

The three girls picked up their pace, and Flora said, "That is really all. It's the whole story. And I am sorry I fell apart."

"Rose says friends can always fall apart when it's just them," Abby said reassuringly. "Otherwise, she says, you have to hold up. And she says holding up is very important to grownups. Grownups ain't allowed to cry in front of people."

"Aren't," Abby said, instantly thinking Rose and her corrections had just pushed into her head again.

"Except their friends?" Addie asked.

Ignoring Abby's correction, Flora said, "Not even then, I reckon. I always hold up when grownups are around, unless one of them is giving me a spanking."

The other two giggled, and Addie commented, "That's a good time to howl. If you don't howl, they keep whacking you. I yell at the first blow."

"I never get spanked or whipped," Abby said and then, seeing the surprise on her friends' faces, wished she hadn't spoken. So she went on, "Mother died when I was pretty little – but I remember her swatting me with that little wooden paddle she used to make butter."

"So you did get spanked," Addie said.

"Only when I was really small," Abby said. "Nothing I would have howled at. And Rose didn't think it was proper to hit anyone, so she didn't do it."

"I would've traded places with you quicker than the reverend can say amen," Flora said.

Abby sighed. "And been without a mother, too?"

Her friends stopped walking. "No, no, no," Flora said. "Some days I am so stupid that I can't believe how stupid I am."

"Me either," Addie said in little more than a whisper. "Oh, Abby."

Abby wiped a tear off her cheek and said, "It's a long time ago, so let's think of something cheerful. Unless you want to cry now, Addie. It's how Flora and I are starting the day."

"No, ma'am," Addie answered. "This is what my mother is talking about when she says the brain must stay in front of the mouth." She moved between her two friends and linked her arms through theirs, and the three went on to school where they would dust and scrub and get every vestige of chalk off the blackboards. And then Mr. Chandler would come with his two ice cream makers, plenty of ice and salt, and they would take turns cranking until the ice cream was ready.

Out at her new house, Rose could not possibly have imagined what an odd start Abby's day was having. Hers was already quite routine, not all that different from being at the farm

274

in Eastborough. She had made breakfast, made up the bed and fed the chickens after she and Newton agreed that he would kill them if she would take care of the feeding and collect the eggs.

"And dress them," Rose said, a bit of question in her voice.

"Women's work," Newton had said.

"Not my mother," Rose said. "She didn't clean chickens and she didn't clean fish, and I don't want to either. Please. And why do they call it dressing when all their parts inside and out are getting removed?"

Newton had thrown back his head and laughed. "I just thought you wanted to vote," he had answered. And she had laughed, too. It was so grand to share several laughs a day with someone who seemed to care, she thought. Now she must set her mind to doing the wash. She reckoned their bathing outfits should get an extra soaking to get out all that salt. Next time they went swimming it would be in the cold fresh water of the river. That made her smile again, remembering how Newton wanted to swim at night all those months ago, promising not to look at her or touch her when she left her clothing on the riverbank. She had been so tempted, but her mother's voice in her head was clear as a bell, and she had refused to go. It would be less exciting now, she thought – unless they went to the rock at night and left their clothes on the bank. She liked that idea. She wondered if Newton would consider her a wicked woman for wanting to do it. She would ask him anyway. Come to think of it, the days here were a long way from her old routine.

She decided to start with the bathing suits, so she filled the set tub part way and held the garments under water until the heavy fabric had absorbed enough to keep them there. She closed the cover on the set tub, admiring Newton's idea of having a cover and making it with wood instead of a sheet of metal. This way the soaking clothes were out of sight, and she could use the cover as a shelf.

Abby would be scrubbing away by now, Rose knew. She hoped Father had let Charles go, too, even though the haying would be the day's work. Charles ought to go to college, but even these days, she'd hardly dared bring up the subject with her father. She needed her mother's support – again. She couldn't believe how often she felt that, even after all these years. And time was running out. He was nearly done with the high school. School, school, school – they were at the school and she wasn't. She hoped her room wouldn't take the longest – she had tried to leave it tidy, but she had been in a bit of a rush. She wouldn't say a word to Newton, but she was missing those children mightily this morning. She didn't want to leave where she was, but she wanted to be there. Father would say that was plain contrary, she told herself. She pushed school thoughts out of her mind and turned to the task of the noon meal.

Running the mowing machine most of the morning would make Newton hungry as a horse, as Grandmother Jane would say. She whisked together some flour, butter, milk and baking powder and popped the dropped biscuits into the oven. Newton usually ate those right along with his meal, but today she would slice up some of the wild strawberries Ruthann had left for her and surprise him with a shortcake. She was certain some of the top milk was thick enough to whip, and her egg beater soon proved her right. Dessert first, she smiled to herself, as she pulled leftover chicken – Ruthann and Joshua had even provided a few leftovers – from the ice box, chopped up two cooked potatoes into a spider with butter and then turned to the dandelion greens.

She'd dug them first thing, before Newton came in for breakfast, and they'd been soaking ever since. It was near impossible to get all the grit out, but she'd do the best she could. She also tweaked out three flower buds. She wondered if the buds somehow sucked nectar from the leaves and then gave it up to the bees. Anyway, buds made them bitter. When the greens were clean, she put them in a saucepan, covered them with water and put them on to boil. Everything began to smell good as the chicken reheated in its gravy, and the potatoes started to fry. She knew Newton would stop pretty much when the noon train whistle sounded because he liked to eat the midday meal right about the middle of midday. She was learning quickly that he was very calm about many things, but he wanted to eat when he thought it was time to eat.

Rose put the vinegar cruet on the table. She would add butter to the greens in the kitchen, but Newton would put a drop or two of vinegar on the dandelions. Hmm. Taking bitter out and sour going back in. When she heard his footsteps outside, she untied her apron strings and pulled the apron off before she pulled the door open. Newton was kicking off his heavy shoes and was surprised to straighten up and find her right there. He put his arms around her, kissed her hard on the mouth, pulled away and said, "I apologize for being damp. It's a hot sun out there."

"No need," Rose said, eagerly reaching out to put her arms around his neck and return the kiss. His hands slid down her back and pressed her to him. He found himself wishing that the mowing was done for the day, but he knew it wasn't. Farmers didn't take their wives to bed in the noon hour, he told himself. They just didn't. He kissed her neck and released her.

"Needed a little something to get me through to suppertime," he said with a grin.

"The meal is ready," Rose said with a straight face. Sometimes when she heard him approaching she remembered how she and Alice had talked about bulls and cows running all over the place and jumping on each other, that day when Miss Harty had explained how babies were made. They'd thought the whole idea disgusting and told Miss Harty that. Rose still worried that making love had to be sinful since it involved nakedness and seemed to have a devilish hold on her. Still, at this very minute, desire was welling up inside her. She shook her head.

"Then I will take my place," he said, wondering why Rose had such an odd look on her face.

Rose gave a long sigh, thinking that she had already made the bed but could do it again. Instead, she turned to the stove to dish up the food. This was no time to be thinking about lovemaking, but one word from him, and she'd undo the buttons on his sweaty shirt and lead him to the stairs. The problem was that she knew he was thinking the same thing about her buttons. The reverend would be bound to blush like a girl if he could see inside her head. She put a mound of dandelion greens on Newton's plate, along with a thick slice of roast chicken and a potato. She carried the plate to the table and set it down in front of him.

"Not quite what I needed to get me through to suppertime," he said, "but it will certainly be a start."

A little flustered by that comment, Rose silently went back to the stove for her dinner and sat down across from him. He took a long drink of water, refilled his glass from the pitcher on the table and began to eat.

"It would be mighty helpful to a man's work day if you set all this out and then disappeared," he said in a mischievous tone. "It's hard enough to be thinking about you while the blades on the cutter bar are chattering away beside me, but it's downright impossible when you are in plain sight."

"You must learn not to be distracted from your work," Rose said in her best schoolmarm voice. "Good work requires concentration on the task at hand."

"Had in mind I might change the task," Newton said. "The greens, by the by, are excellent. When did you pick them?"

"Before breakfast," Rose answered, happy to have a slight change of direction in the conversation. "I do hope all the grit washed out."

Sprinkling a bit of vinegar atop the dandelions, Newton commented that he hadn't run into an iota of dirt. "They are delicious," he added. He finished his food quickly and broke into a smile when Rose presented the strawberry shortcake.

"You are full of surprises today," he said. "Is this going to be the standard fare here? If so, I'll be staying on."

"One hopes," Rose said with a hint of sarcasm, "that other inducements besides wild greens would persuade you to stay."

"No question, no question. And before I am further induced, or deduced or whatever it is, I am going back to the mowing."

"Seduced," Rose said softly.

"You are the vocabulary teacher," he said. "But I'll be deuced if I don't get back out there while the sun shines." That made them both laugh. They finished their shortcakes, and Rose remained in her chair while Newton pushed his back, ready to leave. He bent over to kiss her upturned face, whispered "I love you" in her ear and was gone. Then she stood, cleared the table and did up the dishes. That done, she retrieved the soaked bathing costumes, rinsed them and laid them in the sink. To get rid of some of the excess water, she pushed and pulled them until the water stopped running out. Kneading cloth instead of bread, she thought. Her mind veered off to Newton's last words, and she wondered if Silas Hibbard had ever done that before heading back to the haying. Perhaps she should ask him. The very idea made her chuckle, and she turned back to her wash, scooping the bathing costumes into a large pan. In the clothes yard, she pinned the suits to the lines, glad no one could see them. She looked at her swimming bloomers and started to laugh. Water was dripping to the ground and the legs of the outfit started to dance in the breeze. She didn't think Abby had a bathing costume and resolved that she would try to make her one for Christmas, even though she'd have to wait to wear it.

Back in the kitchen, she felt beads of sweat breaking out on her forehead. She decided to make ginger milk and take it to Newton. Sometimes the heat and humidity made his stomach a little queasy. She prepared the drink, scraped a little of her precious cinnamon stick into the bottle, put on her large straw hat and headed out to the field. He was at the far end, Joshua's mare pulling the mowing machine steadily toward her, so she stood in the sun and waited. She loved the way the grass fell before the knives on the cutter bar, such a perfect pattern. But she hoped the meadowlarks were off their nests by now. She knew Newton tried to look out for them, but they disguised their places so well that it was hard to see them from his perch on the metal seat. He came closer, sleeves rolled up to his elbows, shirt collar open, his straw hat shading his face. Oh, my, how she loved him. She had not dreamed she could love him more, and each day something he said, or his touch on her arm, made her stomach flop just the way it had when he touched her hand that very first time. He waved, breaking into her thoughts and she waved back. Then he was close, reining in the horse and jumping down.

"Just what I needed," he said, taking a long drink from the bottle. "And cool, too."

"It mustn't be too cold," she said.

"I know. This is 'bout perfect. And so are you, standing there in the sun with the sweat running down your face. We had better jump into the farm pond or walk down to the river after supper tonight and get cooled off."

"A fine idea," Rose said, "but our bathing suits are dripping on the line."

"River, then," he answered immediately, a mischievous grin crossing his face. "No need for costumes there."

Rose felt her face start to get even warmer and knew she was turning red. It would never stop, she had decided, even when she was old and gray. The right words would just make her into a beet every time.

"No need to blush, either. I've waited a long time for this."

"Indeed," Rose said. She reached for the bottle, which was now empty. "And I will have supper ready when you are finished mowing. Shall we picnic by the river?"

"Indeed," he said, mimicking her tone, and he quickly climbed back on the mowing machine and turned the horse without another word. Rose went back to the house, considering what might make a decent picnic. For a not-so-decent outing, she thought. And she smiled. Despite the humidity, her step was quick as she went back to the house. She even thought of running and had to remind herself that she was supposed to be past that stage of her life. Actually, she did hope not. Perhaps she would go out after dark and just run.

By the time Newton washed up and changed his shirt, it was getting on toward half after five, and Rose had the picnic carefully packed in a small basket and covered with a tea towel. She had brewed strong tea, added sugar and diluted it with ice. She added the juice of a lemon, tasted a spoonful and decided it would do. It occurred to her that she had no idea whether Newton even liked iced tea.

"We'll need a blanket," Newton said as he appeared in the kitchen.

"And towels," Rose added.

"Indeed," he said, imitating her again. "Indeed."

They set off, walking toward Joshua's big barn and the river beyond it. Peeling potatoes at the sink in her kitchen, Ruthann looked out the window and saw them. It was a picnic, she realized, and wished she and Joshua were going, too. She started toward the door and stopped suddenly. What was she thinking? They were here only a few days, married less than a month, and they didn't need anyone tagging along on their outing.

Rose and Newton reached the river, and he pointed toward a tangle of alders along the bank, several of them reduced to sharp stumps by the colony of beavers that lived in the nearby pond.

When they reached the spot, she dropped the blanket and clapped her hands. A large rock jutted out toward the river behind the alders. It was not her rock, but it looked very satisfactory. She retrieved the blanket, spread it and looked up to find Newton grinning at her.

"I just keep bumping into rocks, Mrs. Barnes," he said. She threw her arms around his neck and kissed him, first on the lips and then on his neck. She drew back and said, "You're still a little sweaty from your day."

"Yes, Ma'am, and I intend to take care of that right now," he said.

"But the iced tea will get warm," Rose protested, watching him unbuckle his belt and step out of his pants.

"And I will be cool," he answered, stripping off the rest of his clothes. "Before you are," he challenged.

Rose sighed and realized it was no use. The tea would be warm, but they were going swimming now, and it wasn't dark, wouldn't be for another hour or so. She sighed again while she took off her shoes and stockings and started unbuttoning her dress, peering into the woods around her in fear of seeing another person. Newton watched her for a minute and then scrambled down the riverbank and plunged into the water. Grateful that he apparently wasn't going to watch her, she carefully folded the dress, then turned her back to the river and took off her chemise and drawers. It had been so hot that she hadn't worn a corset or a petticoat and had felt guilty about her improper dress on her way to the hayfield that afternoon. Taking the towels, she saw that Newton was still swimming away from her, so she quickly slipped down the bank, dropped the towels and practically fell into the water, which was cold enough to make her shriek.

Newton was swimming in the middle of the stream where the water was deep. He held his nose and ducked under several times, feeling cool for the first time that day. He swam to a flat rock on the far side, leaned against it and kicked his feet, his body only half out of the water. Then he beckoned for Rose to swim to him.

"It's so cold," she said.

"And feels great. A sight better than the hot metal of that mower seat."

Rose easily made it through the current and grabbed the rock with one hand, suddenly discovering that she liked the feel of the cold water on her skin, without the wool bathing costume she had worn on their wedding weekend. She backed up to the rock, put her elbows on it and kicked her feet out beside Newton's. She did hope no one would happen by. The Reverend Lockhead would be scandalized at the sight of them. She pictured his sharp-featured face appearing through the perpetually twisting alder leaves and giggled. When Newton raised an eyebrow, she explained what she'd been thinking.

"You are the forward girl," Newton said. "I have maintained that for years. I would have to tell the reverend how you tempted me with food and then took your clothes off before I could stop you. And I had to rescue you when you found you could not swim in fresh water. Then I would plead with him to forgive you and forget the whole thing."

Rose was laughing now, and he flipped over on his stomach, putting a hand on either side of her elbows. His face was lifted toward hers, and without giving it a thought, she kissed his forehead and then his nose. Pushing off quickly, she slid right under him into the water and was swimming to shore and wrapping herself in a towel before he knew what had happened.

"Now," she said sternly, as he arrived dripping wet, "we will dress, drink cool tea, eat stuffed eggs and other things." Seeing the scowl on Newton's face, she added quickly in her more ordinary tone, "And when we are finished, we'll swim again."

"Indeed," he said, his smile back in place. "I sometimes like your thinking." Then he noticed that Rose had left her underthings folded in a neat pile, which made him smile even wider. "Sometimes," he added, "I even understand it." She had meant what she said. He pulled on his pants.

"Is a shirt required in this dining room?" he asked.

"Not in July," she answered, pouring him a tin cup of tea. She had packed more of the cold chicken, several stuffed eggs, half a loaf of bread, butter in a jar and the sliced strawberries left from the noon meal. Despite the heat of the late afternoon sun, the chicken was still cool.

"Delicious," Newton said, his mouth half full. After that, they ate without talking, watching the river as it rippled over the smooth stones. The alder leaves danced, the sun dropped lower, and the heavy air lifted a bit. It wouldn't be long before the pesky mosquitoes appeared, but in the meantime, Rose thought, she considered it about perfect. Newton set his plate aside and lay back on the rock.

"Newton?" Rose said.

"Right here," he answered without opening his eyes.

"Does this river go to Eastborough?"

"Not exactly. But it runs into the Green River, so it gets there eventually."

"So when will the water we just swam in get to our river in Eastborough?" she wanted to know.

Newton sat up. "You do wonder about the darndest things," he said, laughing. "If you were of a mind to swim in that water we just sent on its way, we'd have to get on horseback right now and ride hell for leather to Eastborough and plunge into the river below your rock and we still wouldn't know if we'd made it in time."

Now Rose was laughing. "I reckon I don't need to see that particular water again," she said.

"I am grateful," he said, lying back and closing his eyes again. Rose put all the leavings back in the basket and sat, her arms around her knees, listening to the birds singing day's end songs and watching the water go by, each ripple topped with a ruffle. She did love this time of day. She glanced sideways at Newton and saw that his eyes were closed. Moving quietly, she pushed her skirt up under her and slipped her dress over her head. In the fading light, she went down the bank and into the river, swimming a short distance and then turning to watch him.

She saw his hand reach across the blanket to find her, and she giggled. His eyes were taking more than a few winks. Actually, if his eyes were sleeping, they couldn't wink at all, Rose told herself, wondering if people blink during the night. When the idea made her snicker out loud, Newton sat up and looked around. Then he saw her, pulled off his pants, ran down the bank and joined her where she was sitting in shallow water. Pink and orange streaks climbed higher and higher as the hot sun disappeared. But Newton saw only how beautiful Rose looked in the softening light. She had resisted the river swim for years, so he felt a little uncertain now. But he sat behind her and put his arms around her. He heard her catch her breath and then caught his as she turned and stretched toward him. Dusk crept over them as they lay in the water, their bodies cool and joined once more.

It was dark by the time they made their way to their house and Ruthann, cleaning up supper dishes in her kitchen, smiled as she saw their lantern bobbing along in the darkness. She'd have had no place joining that picnic, she thought, delighted all over again that Rose had finally been able to walk away from the classroom and marry her young man.

CHAPTER TWENTY-FIVE
Men and Their Wives

Back in Eastborough, Abby drew her arm across her forehead and wished summer would be over. She knew that was silly, but she was so hot, and she knew she and Mehitabel should have figured out a cool meal and let the fire go out. Rose would have been so much smarter about it. She missed her so, especially after Flora telling her and Addie that the Carpenters didn't like each other. Even when Father had been at the drink, she hadn't disliked him. She knew, although the memory was fading, that her mother liked him. And Rose said so, too. She believed what Rose said, that things would get better. Except, now that she was older, Abby knew that Rose didn't really believe that herself. And then, like a miracle, things did get better. Father was a different person now. But the Carpenters. She reckoned it wasn't going to get better. At least Flora had been able to laugh on the way home from the school, telling how she'd used up all her anger washing the seats in the outhouse. "Ugh," was Addie's response, but Abby knew how often she'd pulled weeds furiously or scrubbed dirty clothes to get rid of bad thoughts.

She heard Father's footsteps on the stairs and started to dish up the food. He still liked to walk in and find something on the table. She took the macaroni and cheese out of the oven, putting a sizable helping on his plate, along with the wax beans she had picked that morning before breakfast. They had come in early this year, and few things tasted better to her.

"Evening, Abby," Silas Hibbard said as he entered the kitchen. "Something smells worth eating."

"I hope so," Abby smiled. Next thing, she knew, he'd take a bite and say, "Not bad." How Rose hated that upside down compliment. She put the plate in front of him, watched him take his first bite and then waited.

"Not bad, little one," he said.

"Not so little anymore."

"That's true. A working schoolgirl, as it happens. And what were you and Miss Hattie up to today?"

"She wanted ironing done," Abby said with a sigh. "And I nearly dripped sweat all over her tablecloth, it was so hot."

"Have to damp it with something," he said with a chuckle. "But she's good to you?"

"She's always very nice," Abby said. "She's very particular about everything, but she's never cross. And, Father, you don't put salt water on ironing."

"S'pose that's true. Can she cook?"

"Yes, she makes delicious cornbread, and she says she makes good corn chowder. I hope to try that when the corn is ripe." Abby did not remember her father asking so many questions about Mrs. Munson before, but she decided he was just interested in how things were going there. "And she paid me today," Abby added. "I went to the store and bought some fabric for a new square dancing skirt."

"Square dancing in this weather will be something," Silas said. "But I reckon you'll have your heart set on going Saturday night. Is Miss Hattie planning to be there?"

That last made Abby start to wonder what her father was up to. She had more than a dim memory of the last time he had taken up with a woman, that Miss Jenny from the hotel, and she had no hankering to deal with anything like that again. Still, she'd seen, at the cemetery, that so many men had two wives. She and Rose and Charles had read the inscriptions and studied the dates. Often as not, they'd figured out, the men remarried within a year after the first wife went to heaven. They'd also noticed that women whose husbands died tended to stay unmarried. Abby could remember Rose's words exactly: "They need us more than we need them, and they never say so." She hadn't understood at the time, but she knew Father would have had a sight more trouble getting on if his son and daughters hadn't tried to fill their mother's shoes. All three of us in those shoes at once, Abby thought, and again, she laughed at herself for thinking like Rose.

"Abby?" she heard her father say.

"What is it, sir?"

"I asked if Miss Hattie would be at the square dance."

"She didn't exactly say, but she had me iron a square dance skirt and two petticoats today," Abby answered with a grin. "And if I am not supposed to talk about us when I am there, sir, why should I talk about there when I am here?" Oh, my, she thought, seeing the frown on her father's face, I am beginning to talk like Rose, too.

"Fair enough," Silas said, "fair enough. You are on the way to being a lawyer when you grow up." But he smiled as he said it, and Abby heaved a sigh of relief.

"Are you ready for dessert?" she asked.

"Every day," he answered. "And I would take it kindly if you could find time to iron my best Sunday shirt. If you can face up to an iron again. I'll need it for the dancing."

"Yes, Father," Abby said. She really didn't talk about their family when she was at Mrs. Munson's, but she might have to find a way to mention that Father would be at the square dance, just to see what Miss Hattie might say. She sighed. It would be so nice to be able to tell Rose about this. She wasn't far away, but she might as well have been in Australia.

Abby saw that Silas was dozing off at the table, so she cleared quietly. She put the macaroni and cheese baking pan on the back of the stove where it would keep warm for Charles. He had gone off somewhere, she didn't know where, and was home late to do his chores. Father apparently wasn't angry about that, but she hadn't chanced mentioning it. She knew Charles liked to go fishing, but if he'd gone that day, he hadn't had a bit of luck. No fish had appeared in the kitchen.

Abby quickly washed the dishes, dried them and put them away. She was nearly done when she heard Charles run up the stairs from the milk room. He burst into the kitchen and was about to shout something when he saw Abby's finger over her mouth. He stopped, teetered a second and then whispered, "I think my heifer is with child."

"With calf, you mean," Abby said, laughing out loud in spite of herself.

"Have it your way," Charles said loftily. "But she was springing, and I took her to Mr. Chandler's bull, and it was love at first sight."

"Cows don't love each other," Abby said. "They don't kiss or hold hoofs or anything."

"What do you know about the love life of a cow?" Charles demanded. Then he turned, saw the pan on the stove and said, "I am burning starving."

"Another ridiculous remark," Abby scoffed, but she took a warm plate from the shelf above the stove and dished up a huge helping of the macaroni and cheese. She handed him the plate, and he took his place at the dining room table, glancing at his father and deciding he was indeed asleep.

"Clear your dishes, please," Abby said, taking off her apron and heading for the stairs.

"Where are you off to," Charles demanded, whispering as loudly as he dared.

"To sew my new square dance skirt," she said and disappeared.

Square dance, Charles thought. He'd had his eye on more than one of the girls at the school and now wondered whether they would be at the dance. He'd better clear things up well here because he'd need Abby to iron a shirt. He never could get the hang of making the cuffs and the cloth around the buttonholes as smooth as she did. He sighed. He hoped she hadn't taken offense when he scoffed at her about her cow knowledge. You just never knew with girls. You teased them one minute and made them mad as wet hens, and the next minute you needed them for something. He wondered if it was like that for grownup men, too. Prob'bly.

Since nobody was watching, he took his plate to the kitchen and picked up the macaroni pan, scraping every bit of crust off the sides and bottom without bothering to put it on his plate. Would save considerable time, he thought, if they all just ate from the pan instead of dirtying all these dishes. But he scrubbed the pan and his plate and fork and then settled into the kitchen rocker to think about the coming calf.

At the table, Silas stirred and sneezed loudly. He stood, pulled his sleeves down and buttoned the cuffs. Entering the kitchen, he said, "Evening, Charles. What made you so late today?"

"I tried my hand at a bit of fishing," Charles said without hesitation. "But no luck. I think it's too hot for the trout to come up from the deep pools."

"Mebbe. Or mebbe you make too much racket thrashing around in the brush."

"Quieter than a cricket, sir," Charles said with a grin.

"I'll be out for a spell," Silas said, reaching for his hat with one hand and the doorknob with the other.

"Yes, sir," Charles said, having no idea how to respond to this. Father never went out after supper, especially when he was haying. That was a season when his custom was to be in bed before the lanterns were lit. But his father was not about to enlighten him. He left the house quickly, and Charles went to the window expecting he must be seeing to something at the barn. But no, he was walking up the driveway and had turned south on the road. No telling what that was about, Charles decided, but he hoped it had nothing to do with the drink. It had been years since he had found his father lying in the rose bushes outside the back door with the empty cider keg next to him, and it wasn't a day he wanted to live again. He settled back in his chair, figuring he'd better think like Rose and assume the best, not the worst. Sometimes she was wrong, though.

Silas, it seemed, didn't have cider on his mind. He had decided to walk on past Miss Hattie's house and see if she was out weeding her flower bed, something he knew she often did in the evening. If he could muster the courage, he was going to ask her if she planned to be at the square dance. Mebbe, he thought, I'll take her there in our buggy. That would set the town on its ear, now wouldn't it? He chuckled, walked over a little rise in the road and saw that, indeed, Miss Hattie was out working on her posies.

He cleared his throat as he approached, not wanting to startle her. Not many people were apt to be out walking around at this time of day in Eastborough. She looked up, straightened and greeted him with a smile.

"What brings you out walking, Silas Hibbard?" she said. "A day of haying wasn't enough for you?"

"It's a nice evening," Silas answered, "and the young ones had laid out a jigsaw puzzle, so I left them at it." You're an old fool, he told himself. You've no idea what the "young ones" are up to. But he went on, "I reckon they don't need to ask my help on any of that kind of thing."

"Perhaps you'd like a short rest before you head home again? There is fresh lemonade in my ice box and an extra chair on the porch," Hattie offered, having an idea that he might have been strolling around to see if she was in her yard.

"I've a mind to accept," Silas said. "A man gets thirsty after a day of haying."

"Hmm," she answered, picking up her trowel and starting toward her small house. Silas followed and took a seat on the porch while Hattie, smiling to herself, poured two tumblers of lemonade and brought them out. She took a seat across from him, sipped her lemonade and waited.

"Abby working out all right?" Silas asked.

"She is a capable and pleasant girl," Hattie answered, thinking she might have had the wrong idea about this visit. "I have become quite fond of her and her work is good."

"Nice to hear. She tells me she bought cloth for a new square dance skirt with her pay this week, so I have a notion she may be sewing right now."

"She hasn't much time, Silas," Hattie said, noting that the jigsaw puzzle had just disappeared. "The next dance is Saturday."

"I know. Been thinking about it myself. It occurred to me, well, it crossed my mind . . ." He hesitated and started again. "I reckoned it would be neighborly of me to give you a ride to the dance and home again so you wouldn't be out on the road in the dark with your horse and buggy."

"Very neighborly," Hattie said, smiling again and hoping her inner excitement didn't show. "I am not afraid of the dark, but that would be very neighborly."

Now Silas wasn't quite sure whether she had accepted or rejected his offer, but he didn't see any way to retreat, so he asked, "What time should we come by?"

"Who's we?" Hattie asked.

"Just a manner of speaking," he said, hoping he wouldn't stammer. "Me and the horse, I reckon. Abby and Charles will find their own way as they usually do these days." He hadn't really thought that through, but he certainly hoped they wouldn't be aboard.

"I would think half after six," Hattie said. "I appreciate your being such a good neighbor, Silas." She stood, reached for his empty glass and waited for him to get up. He pulled himself slowly out of the chair, feeling he had been dismissed, nodded to her and left the porch.

"Have I been a damn fool?" he asked himself as he walked quickly home. "Why did I get into being 'neighborly' when I just wanted to ask her to go to the dance with me? Sarah would laugh her head off."

But as daylight faded into dusk and the fireflies began to appear, he lengthened his stride and smiled. It had been a long time since he had thought about a woman. This one might be the town gossip, but she was respectable -- and with a mind of her own, that was certain. He feared he'd never told Sarah about admiring her mind, but he had admired it mightily. And he admired Rose's independence, too, although it had been quite a trial for him at times.

CHAPTER TWENTY-SIX
Miscarriage

At breakfast the next day, Newton announced that he'd be getting hay into the barn that day if the weather held, and Rose could hardly believe how relieved she was. Only a few months ago, her mind was focused on getting children to read without moving their lips or pointing to each word with a finger, and now she constantly had an eye on the sky and the clouds. When he left the house, she decided to walk over to Ruthann's and see if they had any parsnips to spare. Next year she'd have her own, but right now she wanted a new vegetable for the noon meal. For supper, she was looking forward to bowls of peas, surrounded by buttery cooking water, and fresh bread. Food and hay. It was about all she considered these days. Well, just food really. Come to think of it, Newton was making Jersey food.

Cross lots, it took only a few minutes to get to Ruthann's, but it was already hot, and she wiped droplets of sweat off her nose before she tapped lightly on the back door. She was startled when Ruthann opened it almost immediately, her face very pale and frowning.

"What's wrong?" Rose said, forgetting her errand entirely.

Ruthann glanced over her shoulder at John and Adelaide, who were playing on the kitchen floor with some alphabet blocks. She shook her head, asked Rose to come in, then took a used envelope and, wetting the pencil with her tongue, wrote "bleeding" on the paper.

"From what?" Rose said, starting to frown herself. Surely Ruthann wouldn't bother to tell her about her monthly bleeding, and she could see no sign of an accident anywhere.

"Losing the baby," Ruthann wrote, her hand shaking a bit.

"I didn't know ..." Rose began.

"It was too soon to tell you," Ruthann said. "But it's quite bad, so I'm glad you came in just now."

"Shall I fetch the doctor?" Rose asked. "Tell me what to do. I have not an idea in the world about these things." She heard a little tremble in her voice and silently scolded herself. She must be calm.

"If you could go to the barn or the field or wherever Joshua is and fetch him," Ruthann said, "that would be the first thing. And if you take John and Adelaide with you, I will lie down until you are back."

Relieved that Ruthann at least seemed calm, Rose invited the two youngsters to go on a father hunt with her, and they immediately latched onto the idea. She settled Ruthann on the sofa and gave her a glass of cold water from the bottle in the ice box. Then she made an effort to erase the worry from her own face and set off after the children.

"Not in the barn!" John yelled, running ahead to have a look. "Not in the barn!"

Gratefully, Rose saw that Joshua was just coming out of the henhouse, which meant they wouldn't be looking for him all over the farm. The children saw him a minute later and started to run toward him.

"Welcome, all," Joshua said, setting down a basket of eggs and lifting up a child with each arm. Then he looked at Rose and raised an eyebrow. "What's going on?" he asked.

"Ruthann is lying down," Rose said, trying to get a message across without saying anything.

"Come on, you two. Race you back to the house," Joshua said. They took off, Adelaide trying desperately to keep up with her brother, and Rose quickly told Joshua what was happening.

"Shall I go for Dr. Potter?" she asked. "She's feeling very poorly, I think, although we couldn't really talk with the children there."

"She had some pain last night," Joshua said, his pace at a near trot. "If you keep the children in the kitchen, I will see what we should do next. It might be better to take her to Eastborough and not waste time getting the word to Seth and then his coming out here."

Worried that her voice would break if she said anything, Rose just nodded and took the children in hand as soon as they reached the house. Instead of taking them inside, she reminded them that their father had forgotten the eggs, so the three of them went back to get the basket. Then they stopped to pick dandelions and found two that had gone to seed, so she sat them down on the steps and showed them how to blow away all the fluff on the stem.

"Where do they go?" John wanted to know.

"They fly off and land in a field, and after the rain gives them water, they grow a new dandelion plant," Rose said, suddenly feeling like a teacher again. Sometimes her two-track mind was a burden, but right now she could worry about Ruthann with one track and distract these two with the other one. Then, from the corner of her eye, she saw Joshua at the door again.

"What's next?" Rose said, keeping her tone even.

"We will go," Joshua said. "Where is Newton, do you know?"

"He's prob'ly in the barn by now with the first load of hay," Rose said. "Working alone, he could not be much farther along than that."

"If you could harness the horse, Rose – will the children be in your way?"

"Heavens, no. I'll just set them down to watch."

"I'm grateful," he said and disappeared into the house again.

"Come on, you two," Rose said. "We need to say hello to Billy and get his harness on. You can sit in his manger while I do that."

"In the manger?" John said, his eyes wide. "We've never done that."

"Horsy eat me?" Adelaide asked fearfully.

"No, silly. Billy doesn't eat people, only hay and grain. And we will get him ready to take your mother to town today."

"Are you going, too?" John asked, skipping along next to her.

"Me, too," Adelaide said, taking Rose's hand.

"No," Rose said firmly. "We are the harnessers. We are not the shoppers today." And she led them into the barn, backed Billy part way out of his stall and hitched him to a ring on the

300

side wall, then boosted the children into his manger where she could keep track of them. Billy was easy to harness, she knew, a steady old horse with lots of endurance. He didn't shy away from children or adults, and Rose quickly had the harness in place and tightened.

"Don't either of you move an inch," she warned, hoping they would take her seriously. "I have to take Billy to the buggy, and I need you to sit perfectly still. If you are still, I will find you a cookie in the kitchen."

They grinned at her, and John took Adelaide's hand. "I'll make sure she doesn't move," he said solemnly, and Rose led the horse around the corner to the shed where the buggy was kept. She worked quickly, calling back to the children the whole time, and in a few minutes, all was ready. She put the youngsters on the buggy seat, climbed up and flicked the reins. Billy moved forward, and she guided him toward the house, where Joshua and Ruthann were just coming out the door.

"You are a treasure," Ruthann said to Rose, who lifted the children down so Joshua could get Ruthann into the buggy. "No way, really, for you to lie down," he said, his eyebrows closing in on a frown.

"I will be all right," Ruthann answered. "What about the children?"

"I'll see to them," Rose answered quickly. "We will find Newton and have some lunch and look for more dandelions, right?"

"And make them fly away," John said. "Are we going to your house?"

"Aunt Rose?" John prompted when she didn't answer. Rose was watching the buggy as it moved quickly down the dirt road, a small cloud of dust rising behind each wheel. Oh, dear, she thought to herself. And then she turned to John, realizing he had spoken, and said, "Again, please, John."

"Are we going to your house?" he asked patiently, holding onto her hand tightly.

"That is a grand idea," Rose said. "We will find Newton, and then we will see about cooking something for his noon meal."

"And mine?" John asked anxiously.

"And yours."

"Addie cook, too" she chimed in.

This, Rose decided, was going to be an interesting morning, and she would have to get her concentration back, put Ruthann and Joshua out of her mind, or at least below the surface. She will be all right, she will be. She's strong and healthy, and I didn't even know she was with child again. She will be all right. Both of Ruthann's children were looking at her rather strangely, and she wondered if she'd been talking out loud. She was quite certain not, but sometimes words came out. She held out her left hand to Adelaide, while John continued to hold her right, and they set off for her house.

They hadn't gone even half way when she saw Newton running toward them through the field. He had seen the buggy go by, and Joshua had called out to him that they were going to the doctor. Rose quickly explained what was happening, spelling some of the words so the children would not ask more questions than she wanted to answer.

"Mother is sick," John offered, after a minute of silence. "She needs the doctor. He came here when I was sick last winter."

"Sick people can go out in the summer," Newton said quickly. "So they can go to the doctor instead of him coming here."

"Mommy sick?" Adelaide said, looking as if she were about to cry.

"She will be fine," Rose told the little girl. "That's what doctors do. They make you all better."

"The doctor came when Father's calf was sick," John said, "and the calf died."

"Calves, young man, are not the same as people, and animal doctors are not the same as people doctors," Rose said, thinking that possibly the hardest questions in the world were the ones from children.

"Let's go," Newton said, taking John's hand and starting to trot toward the Barnes house. So he and John raced off, Rose picked Adelaide up and followed as quickly as she could. She had started a loaf of bread this morning, so the children could begin cooking by punching it down. She knew they'd like that. It might not be good for the loaf, but she prob'bly could let them knead the dough as well. She wondered how far Joshua and Ruthann had gotten. She knew he would be pushing Billy as fast as he could without rocking the buggy too much.

She learned later that they had stopped after the first mile because Ruthann felt she needed to go to the bathroom. They were nowhere near a house, so Joshua helped her down and held her skirt while she went near the buggy. When she straightened up and stepped away from the spot, he was shocked to see a pool of blood on the ground. Ruthann saw it, too, and shook her head.

"We'd better get on," she said. "This baby does not seem content to stay and grow."

Joshua flicked the reins with one hand and took Ruthann's in his other. "You are the very bravest," he said. "And whatever happens with the baby, we need to make sure you are all right."

Ruthann nodded, her eyes filling with tears. "It hurts, Joshua. It really hurts."

"Should we go slower so it won't be so bumpy?"

"No," she said. She laid her head on his shoulder, and he flicked the reins again. The horse was trotting fast now, and Joshua felt his own stomach contract. His heart was racing, and he told himself to breathe slowly and not panic. But it was hard. His whole body was tight with fear and when he glanced down at Ruthann, he was not reassured by her white face. Her eyes were closed now, but he knew she wasn't asleep. She was just concentrating on getting to Dr. Potter.

And then they were there, pulling up to the hitching posts in front of Seth Potter's small office. Joshua jumped down and had hardly gotten the horse hitched when the door opened and Seth himself stepped out. He did not speak but went right to Ruthann and helped her down from the buggy. With one of them on either side, she stumbled into the doctor's small office, and the two men took her right into the examining room.

"There's a lot of blood," Joshua blurted out. "We stopped on the way and ..."

"She's with child?" Seth asked.

"Yes."

"I think only six or seven weeks," Ruthann said weakly. "Am I going to lose it?"

"I have no nurse here today, Joshua, so I hope you can assist me if need be. I'm sorry to ask," Seth said, avoiding her question.

"Whatever I can do," Joshua answered, hoping he wouldn't faint. He was already feeling a little queasy, so he excused himself and went into the kitchen to get a glass of water. When he came back, Ruthann was stretched out on the table, and the doctor was placing a large wad of toweling between her legs. Almost immediately, a blood stain appeared.

"You understand that I cannot stop what's happening, Ruthann?" he asked.

"Yes."

"We will wait a few minutes now and see if the bleeding stops. I want you to close your eyes, breathe as slowly as you can and try to relax the muscles in your legs and arms."

"Mmm," Ruthann answered. "I'm sure I can relax now – this is very relaxing."

The two men, both worried about her, could not help smiling at this. She was a wonder, the doctor thought, still envious of Joshua Chittenden for marrying this woman he had admired from afar for so long. Speak for yourself, Seth, or someone else will speak for himself. He'd learnt the hard way and was still alone. He knew Joshua and Ruthann had two children already, but that didn't making losing one any easier. He wondered why some of these babies just couldn't seem to settle in and float about for nine months. He reckoned he'd never know. He saw a look of real pain cross Ruthann's face, and he fetched the chloroform bottle, dampened a piece of gauze with the liquid and passed it quickly under her nose.

"Don't put me out," Ruthann mumbled, instantly having a reaction to the chloroform. "I will be all right. Will our baby be all right?"

"Hard to say, Ruthann, hard to say. It's a time for waiting, I fear. That's hard, too."

"You tell me true, Seth Potter. I have no need for pampering," Ruthann said, sounding as if she were scolding a small pupil.

"Sorry, Ruthann. The truth is that the chances are not good. You have lost a great deal of blood, which may mean you have already lost tissue." He pulled away the wadded towel and replaced it with another, and Joshua watched as the doctor crossed the room to a bright light, spread the towel out and proceeded to examine it with a small magnifying glass. He looked up, saw Joshua watching and shook his head. Then he came back, took away the new towel and replaced it.

"The good news is that the bleeding has slowed," he said.

"Is there bad news?" Ruthann said impatiently. "You have to say."

"I believe I perceived signs of tissue on that towel," Seth Potter said. "I am right sorry to say so."

A tear rolled down Ruthann's cheek, and Joshua wiped it away with his handkerchief, wondering if there was any right thing to say at a time like this. They had two at home, true, but she had wanted this one, too. So that wouldn't do. Besides, she knew she had two at home. Saying he was sorry was absurd. She knew that also. So he leaned over her, put one hand on her right cheek and laid his face against her left one. He felt her shudder, then she began to shake with her crying. He could not remember when he had last seen her cry.

CHAPTER TWENTY-SEVEN
Punching the Bread

At the farm, John and Adelaide were having a grand time with Rose who was trying to distract herself as well as the children. She had sent Newton back to the field, figuring at least the hay could be gotten under cover before the storm, and not everything would be lost on this day. She hadn't said as much, but she was quite certain that Ruthann would lose the baby, a baby Rose hadn't even known about. In the meantime, John and Adelaide had each given the puffy bread a good punch, and then she had let them start the kneading.

"When does it cook?" John wanted to know.

"After the next rising," Rose answered, tucking the round shape back into a buttered bowl.

"What is rising?" Adelaide asked.

"When it gets all puffy again," Rose said.

"Adelaide punch," the little girl said. "Please."

"Yes, you can, but only once."

"Me, too?" John said.

"Yes." Rose put a tea towel over the bowl and announced that while the bread puffed up, they would hunt for dandelion blossoms and forget-me-nots for a bouquet for the dinner table. She knew the dandelions would droop almost immediately, but she, at least, needed something to do. And the children would be bored with waiting for bread to rise.

Somehow they made their way through the morning, and Rose left extra time for preparing the noon meal. She figured six hands would make every task harder than it was with two. But the youngsters were excited and helpful, and she had years of experience with patiently shepherding children through tasks that were a little too hard for them. They had just finished setting the table when she heard a clatter of feet on the stairs – not Newton's feet, surely, so who could it be, she wondered as she went to the door. It opened before she could get there, and Charles burst into the kitchen, a little out of breath.

"Charles?" Rose said. "Where did you come from?"

"My mother's womb," Charles answered as he flopped into the kitchen rocker.

"This is no time for your tomfoolery," Rose said sternly. But she softened her tone when Charles shook his head and waggled a finger at her. "Remember the young-uns, Rosie," he chided.

She hated it when he called her that, and he knew it. But she drew a deep breath and said, "How did you get here, short of sprouting wings?" She realized he was pulling her into his kind of talk and added quickly, "And what news do you bring?"

"Not much of anything," he said. "I took the train and then a kind soul at the station let me share the seat on his buggy. He went a bit out of his way, but he knew where Chittendens' farm was, and I told him I was needed there in a hurry."

"Did you ..." Rose started, but Charles interrupted to assure her that he had told the man nothing. "Name was Warner," he said. "He didn't ask any questions, just picked up the pace a trifle. I didn't stop at Mrs. M's to tell Abby I was leaving town. Was that all right?"

"Excellent thinking, Charles," Rose said with a sigh of relief. She had no wish to get Eastborough's tongues wagging before anyone knew anything. "This, John and Adelaide, is my brother Charles. He often pops through doors or windows when no one is expecting him, and you are to believe nothing he says until you ask me about it."

Charles was frowning at her, but John and Adelaide were moving toward him, eyes wide. "How do you pop through windows?" John wanted to know. "And what do I do if you tell me, and I'm not supposed to believe you."

Charles started to laugh. "I will show you later about the windows, young sir," he said. "In the meantime, can you feed me? Popping about leaves the stomach feeling very empty."

Rose let out a sigh of relief. Charles would be a blessing this day. His nonsense could go on for hours, she well knew, and these little ones would eat it up. In the meantime, she'd better find something he could eat because he probably did feel hungry. Charles was never *not* hungry. It was just that sometimes he was hungrier than usual.

"Bread," Adelaide said, smiling up at Charles. "Punch bread."

"We're making bread, but it's not ready," John explained. "We punched it. Now it's rising for the second time."

"Cruel, so cruel," Charles began and stopped in mid sentence when Rose kicked his ankle. He wagged his finger at the two children and said, "And when it goes in the oven, the air will be filled with little bread bubbles, and we will all hear our stomachs rumbling with hunger."

"Bubbles?" John asked.

"Remember what I said, John," Rose interrupted. "Don't believe his tales until you are sure they are true."

"But we do smell something when bread bakes," John said. "Is it invisible bubbles?"

"Certainly invisible," Rose said. "Now set another place at the table for Charles, and we'll offer him a biscuit to tide him over until Newton gets here for the noon meal." John and Adelaide trotted quickly into the dining room and set out another fork and knife and tumbler for Charles. They fetched a napkin from the drawer and placed it beside the fork, just as Rose had told them.

"In training already, I see," Charles said. "You do whip the troops into shape quickly."

"No whipping, Charles," Rose chided. "Did you really not bring any news?"

"Little hope, I'd wager," Charles said. "Sorry. But I saw Joshua less than a minute, and he looked …" He paused and glanced toward the youngsters, who had looked up at mention of their father's name. "His visage was diametrically opposed to cheerful," he finished, making a small bow in Rose's direction.

"Thank you," she said, her face crumpling a little. "And even at this time, you manage to be quite remarkable, I must admit. Are you sitting or standing for your biscuit?"

"Standing, ma'am. Standing and standing by." Charles took the proffered biscuit and held a plate under it while he took a bite. "No crumbs on this clean floor, ma'am."

"And then we will have a dandelion hunt," Rose said.

"Dandy, just dandy," he said, reaching out to tickle Adelaide under her arm. She giggled and said, "Addie want lion. No dandy." Rose watched the two youngsters watching Charles's every move. What was it about him that makes everyone pay attention, she wondered. She smiled and thought, including me. She picked up a knife and a metal colander and beckoned John and Adelaide to follow her.

When they reached the door, Charles asked, "Rose, please, what can I do? I came to do, and I have nothing to do."

"Oh, dear," Rose said. "Of course. You might find Newton, somewhere in the haying process and tell him what little you know."

"I follow you to the outside," Charles said in a grand tone, adding, "You must take care of the lion." When both children turned to look at him, wide-eyed, he shooed them toward Rose and loped off toward the barn.

Rose sighed. Here they were, at wit's end over Ruthann and Joshua, and Charles had burst in ready to seriously help and be ridiculous at the same time. Well, she had to confess, the ridiculous part was good, too. The children were quite taken with him, and the distraction was welcome. How was it that Charles managed to be a thorn, as Newton had frequently called him, and a person you needed to hug at the same moment. He so often made life possible. Two of him, she thought with a small smile, would, however, make life quite impossible. She hoped Ruthann was all right. She had a dark feeling that the baby was not to be, but nothing could happen to Ruthann, nothing.

She felt a tugging at her skirt and looked down at Adelaide's upturned face. "Go to barn?" the little girl asked, still fixed on Charles.

"After we find the dandelions," Rose said firmly. "And they are plants, Adelaide, not real lions." They set off, John carrying the colander and Adelaide trotting to keep up with her brother and Rose.

At Dr. Potter's office, Ruthann had dozed off, and Joshua was still standing by her bed holding her hand. He knew how much she wanted this third child, but right now he was grateful that Seth Potter had assured him Ruthann would be fine in a few days. He had felt very queasy while the doctor worked quickly to stop the bleeding but knew he had to hang on because no one else was there if Seth needed help. He had seen extra concern in the doctor's eyes and knew, suddenly, that he'd been right all those years ago at the box social. Seth Potter had loved Ruthann and failed to tell her so. Joshua had a feeling the man still loved her but would not let that distract him from concentrating on his medical skills. And he was skilled, Joshua realized, not only in doing what was needed but also in calming Ruthann's nerves, which were raw with anxiety.

He turned as the doctor came back into the room. Seth had exchanged his stained jacket and pants for clean clothes and stepped quickly to the bedside, reaching for Ruthann's wrist to take her pulse. He bent over her with his stethoscope and listened to her heart, then straightened and nodded at Joshua.

"Everything was racing pretty fast there when you came in, but she's slowed down now. I'll get you a chair if you insist on staying right there, but I think she's going to sleep for an hour or two. I'm sorry, Joshua, that the baby could not be saved ..."

"You saved Ruthann, I think," Joshua said. "I have never seen anything like this, but I know it was skilled and quick and needed. I thank you and am in your debt."

"No need to thank me," Seth said quickly. "I feel, you know, although there's no science on it, that these miscarriages often take place when the baby wasn't meant to be. I'm not talking about God or religion or anything like that. I'm talking about some physical problem that triggers something and does not allow the baby to go full term. I'd call it a blessing, but again, I don't happen to believe it's a heavenly matter a-tall." He paused, a little embarrassed at saying so much, but he needn't have worried.

"Thank you again for that. Ruthann will need some time, but she will understand the logic. I don't happen to cotton to the idea that these things are legislated by some ethereal being I can neither see nor hear, but I know a good deal about what can go wrong when an animal is about to give birth."

"Just don't let her blame herself, Joshua. It has nothing to do with carrying a heavy pail of milk from the barn or turning a mattress or running after those two youngsters of yours," the doctor said. He stretched out his hand to Joshua, and they shook, holding an extra second beyond the usual. "She ought to stay here another day or two if that's possible. I don't want her back on her feet just now. If you feel comfortable leaving her, I'd like you to fetch my nurse and tell her she'll be staying overnight."

Joshua felt his eyes burn and hoped he wasn't about to break down. He allowed as how he could leave if the doctor was staying, and he set off to get the Chandlers' daughter, who wasn't really a nurse but was being trained by Dr. Potter to work in the clinic. He found the girl and on his way back took an extra minute to stop at Henry Goodnow's store. He needed to get word back to Rose and Newton somehow.

313

"Be glad to take a run out there," Henry said as soon as he heard the story. "Young Charles is already there, I reckon. I saw him heading into the train station awhile ago, and he's not much of a traveler on the ordinary day. He'll be able to help out, and I can let Newton and Rose know what's happened." He paused, looked down at the counter and then back at Joshua's strained face. "I'm right sorry, Joshua. But I'm glad Ruthann is going to be all right." He paused again. "I trust you will right yourself, too."

"Yes, sir," Joshua said, feeling better already. "But I'll take a couple of chunks of that crystallized ginger and hope my stomach gets back in its regular place soon. No need for you to go, Henry. I'll be heading home by nightfall, I trust."

"No charge," Henry said, when Joshua started to fish in his pocket for change. So he tucked one piece in his pocket and the other in his mouth, nodded his thanks and headed back to the doctor's office.

Hours later, in bed but wide awake, Rose heard the sound of buggy wheels on the road. Newton was asleep, as were John, Adelaide and Charles, so she slipped cautiously out of bed and hurried down the stairs barefoot. And there in the yard was Joshua's buggy, and he was swinging down from the seat. She opened the door, half hiding behind it. She'd been in such a hurry she had no dressing gown on. But Joshua didn't even notice. He pushed the door back and came into the kitchen and put his arms around her.

"She will be all right in a few days, Rose, but we lost the baby." Rose felt his shoulders shake and then heard Newton on the stairs. He went straight to Joshua and pulled him close in what Rose decided was a bear hug. Rose could not think when

314

she had last seen two men hug like that. It sent a warm feeling through her and brought tears to her eyes. The men held each other for what seemed like a long time, and when they separated, Rose could see that they, too, were teary.

"Ruthann will mend soon," she said, thinking the good news should come first. Newton nodded. He had figured the small fetus would not survive and had only been worried about Ruthann. "Your youngsters are here, fast asleep," Newton said, "and you are welcome to the sofa if you want to stay."

"I'll go on home," Joshua said. "The chores will be closer that way."

"Henry and Charles and I took care of things today," Newton said. "Don't trouble yourself with even a peek at the barn tonight. It's in grand order. He may be a storekeeper now, but he ain't forgot his upbringing."

"Hasn't," Rose said to herself, managing for once not to correct a mistake aloud. "And forgotten."

"Thought I left it with Henry that he needn't trouble himself with a trip," Joshua said, his voice cracking before he reached the end of the sentence. An awkward silence followed, the friends unable to think of anything more to say and not ready for trivial chat. In a minute or two, Joshua thanked them and quickly left the house. They heard the buggy start to roll and realized he was being as quiet about it as possible, but when they headed for the stairs, they saw Charles looking down at them, his nightshirt flaring in the breeze from the hall window.

"Joshua's home," Rose said. "Ruthann will be on the mend soon, but the baby was – the baby is lost. Are the children asleep?"

315

"As if they hadn't a care in the world," Charles said. "I must rest now." And he vanished. Rose shook her head and found she couldn't help smiling, despite the day's events. "He is a thorn, Newton, yes. And a rose."

"Joshua looks as if he's crossed a desert and back again," her husband replied.

"How could he not?" Rose asked. "Mr. Goodnow said he had to be Dr. Potter's nurse through the whole ordeal. I cannot begin to imagine …"

"You mustn't. You must come to bed with me," Newton said, putting his arm around her and moving toward the stairs. She carried the lamp and in the bedroom, set it on the dresser and then climbed willingly into bed. Those children were likely to wake at dawn, and Newton would be off to the barn well before the sun appeared.

CHAPTER TWENTY-EIGHT
The Family Visits

A few days later, most things were back to normal, Rose thought as she stirred oats into the pot of water she had placed on the stove. Mr. Goodnow, who apparently never forgot anything, had taken the time to pack up some supplies for her, and she now had more to choose from when she set about making the noon meal and the supper. He was a wonder, a treasure. But so was Charles, who had pitched in on chores here and at Chittendens' and had chased those children over what seemed like forty acres, keeping them busy and making them so tired they could hardly keep their eyes open to eat. And Ruthann was home, looking peaked and not smiling a whole lot, but home. John and Adelaide were bursting with excitement the day Joshua fetched her, and they wanted to sleep in their own beds that night, so they did. But during the day they were here, and Rose had moments of thinking it was easier to see to youngsters when you sent them home at three in the afternoon.

Charles would be going back to Eastborough today and had already begun to talk about the square dance, which was just one day off. Small wonder Father hadn't figured out some way to send for him before this, but she knew Mr. Goodnow would have explained the need for him to stay. She sighed. They had all been so busy taking care of things that she and Newton had hardly talked in four days. He was out of bed before she was and asleep, some nights, by the time she went upstairs to bed. She smiled to herself, thinking how she tried to slip into bed without disturbing him. But he always roused enough to pull her close and then go back to sleep instantly. When it was time for him to rise, he tried to disentangle himself without waking her, but it never worked. So he would kiss the back of her neck and quietly get ready for his long day.

She decided to ask if she could take the buggy and give Charles a ride to the train. Two days ago, that Warner man who had given Charles a ride had dropped by, introduced himself and asked if he could help out in any way. Rose had frowned, wondering if Charles had been untruthful about not telling the stranger anything.

"Jes' figured that young man was in some kind of anxious state, ma'am, although he didn't let on what he was rushing out here for. I'm not a near neighbor, but I'm about as near as a neighbor gets in these parts, so I thought I'd intrude on you folks a bit."

"Thank you so much," Rose said, smiling at him. "I didn't mean to seem inhospitable."

"That young fellow your brother?"

"Indeed."

"Some resemblance there. Now, how can I be of service?"

So Rose told him about the crisis at the Chittenden house and that they'd all been out straight, what with the regular work plus the haying and Joshua spending much of his time at

318

Ruthann's side in Eastborough. "And the worrying," she added. "That takes its toll, too."

"Reckon it does," Hiram Warner said. "P'raps I'll just get on out to the hayfield and see if two extra hands might lighten the load a tad."

So Rose told him she thought Newton and Charles were unloading hay in the barn and then would be going to Chittendens' to help with the haying there. Mr. Warner had stayed all day, taken dinner with them at noon and at four o'clock announced he would be off to milk his herd. "Good feed here," he had said to Rose, who almost instantly felt a blush heating her cheeks. "I may turn up on your doorstep again."

"You are always welcome," Newton had told him. "You helped with the work, and you gave our spirits a lift. A godsend on both counts." Hiram Warner had merely nodded, and then he was gone.

The oatmeal was about ready when Rose heard Newton's footsteps on the stairs. He's as dependable as the clock, she thought, but never needs winding. He came in the door and when she did not turn around, he crossed quickly to the stove and twirled her around, pulling her close and kissing her on the mouth. Surprised and holding the sticky oatmeal spoon high above his head, Rose responded. It was a long kiss, something she'd been missing ever since Ruthann had taken sick. He broke away first and grinned at her.

"Been going without," he said.

"Hmm," Rose said, managing to get the spoon back in the saucepan without dripping oatmeal on his shirt. "Thought I'd give Charles a buggy ride to the train after breakfast if you can spare him that early. The children will be staying at their house today."

"I can, and the buggy is a good idea as long as you come straight home. I should have another load of hay by then and could use your help in the barn."

Rose nodded, dished up his oatmeal, poured his coffee and found herself thinking it would be quite fine if Charles was already gone. She had been unable to get being in bed with Newton out of her mind for the past two days, even though it made her feel selfish and guilty. But she knew Charles would be in soon. He had crossed the field to Ruthann's early to get the children's day under way. She sighed. Apparently haying still came first, at least in daylight.

An hour later, Newton was back in the field and Charles was next to her on the buggy seat, his small sack of clothes stowed under his feet. He told her Father and Abby had been wanting to visit but had stayed away because of Ruthann. Should he tell them they could come on Sunday if they were of a mind to? Father, he ventured, might be tuckered out by the square dance and unable to travel.

"Father worn out dancing?" Rose said, laughing. "That will be the day. Tell them to come ahead – I do so miss Abby."

"And me?"

"Can't miss you when you're here, Charles. I'll think on it when you are not here."

"Pleasant of you," he said. "Nothing like sisterhood." And they both laughed. He was good for her, never letting her serious moods last too long. And he was thinking how sorely he missed her and how he envied Newton for being with her every day of the week. But he'd never tell her. It wasn't rewarding to have people know how much you liked them. He'd stick with confiding in cows. He knew they loved him. Or would, as long as he fed them.

"I have letters for you to post," Rose said, as they rolled along on the hard dirt road. She handed them to him, and Charles said, "With stamps? Couldn't Old Goodnow just tuck them into a box without your spending all those pennies for stamps?"

Now she was annoyed with him again. "Old Goodnow? Mr. Goodnow, nearly my best friend in the world? He has a conscience, young man, and we all hope that somewhere inside your hairy chest you are developing one, too. He's not about to cheat the United States of America, nor am I."

"I am your penitent companion," Charles said solemnly.

That made Rose laugh. "And an engaging rascal. Penitent, indeed. Have you begun to keep company with an intelligent young lady?" She did not look at him, but she had a feeling he was close to blushing, so perhaps a girl had entered the picture.

"Why do you ask?" was all he said.

"Your vocabulary has increased exponentially, which means you've made a new friend or that you knew all these words from birth and have decided only now to bring them forth."

Charles heaved an exaggerated sigh and said, "You are stabbing me in the solar plexus. How's that?"

"Or the heart," Rose said, now starting to believe Charles was courting someone.

"Grace Van Buren," he said, so softly that Rose nearly missed it. She was so overwhelmed by having stumbled on this amazing turn of events that all she could do was pat his knee and mumble something about luck.

"What's that?" he shouted. "What's that?"

"All the luck in the world to you, Charles. It may not last past next Tuesday, but I set my cap for Newton when I still had braids, so you never know." At that point, they arrived at the station, and Rose pulled up toward the door. Charles swung down, grinned at her, grabbed his sack and left without another word.

Now who, thought Rose, as she pulled on the left rein and turned the horse, is Grace Van Buren? Charles, of course, could be making her up, just to tease her, but this time she doubted it. She would ask Abby, first thing. Oh, dear, her mind reminded her – Abby is miles away. But perhaps she will visit on Sunday, and she'll have the story on Grace Van Buren.

Rose dozed a little once they were within a mile or so of the house, and Tommy, quite accustomed to making his own way home, trotted along the dirt road at a good pace. When he stopped near Rose and Newton's house, she woke up and could not believe she'd allowed herself to nap. She reckoned the wakeful nights of worrying about Ruthann had taken their toll. She flicked the reins, and Tommy moved on toward the barn, a trifle worried about backing the buggy into the shed. But Tommy pretty much took care of the problem. Then she unhitched him, walked him to his stall, took off the harness and hung it up. She brought him a fresh pail of water, closed his stall door and went back to the house.

In less than an hour, she had changed into a house dress, prepared the fixings for the noon meal and was ready to find Newton and see how she could help. She did hope he wouldn't put her on the wagon to pack the hay. It always gave her a stomach ache, teetering around up there as the load went higher and higher. She never could understand why the proper way to load a hay wagon was to stack forkfuls of hay a couple of feet wider than the wagon bed. They'd always shout for her to fix the corners, and she was never sure whether her feet were on thin air or solid wood.

But when she went out the back door, Newton was already coming up the slope to the barn with his first load. She waved, and he pointed toward the open barn door. He'd need her to mow the hay away, she reckoned, while he threw pitchforks full up to her. Well, it would make her nose itch, and the sharp ends would pick at her stockings, but at least she wouldn't fall off. She picked up her skirts, ran to the barn and was halfway up the ladder when he backed the wagon in. In no time at all, he was tossing hay to her, and she was pushing it back as far as she could. The only hazard here was the open space in the floor that allowed for dropping hay down to the cows. She wondered what it was called. Not a trap door because that had a door. This was a hole. In any case, she kept well away from it and smiled as she looked down on what seemed to be a mound of hay with legs coming toward her.

"That's it," Newton called as he tossed that forkful, and before she could get to the ladder, he was on the second rung, coming up to her.

"Did I get it wrong?" she asked, glancing around at the newly stored hay.

"Not a-tall," Newton said, taking the pitchfork away from her and tossing it aside. "You are as right as a haymaker could possibly be, except for one thing."

"What's that?" she asked, wondering if he had gone a little daft in the sun.

"I need some kissing from my new wife, need it right now," he answered with a wide smile. And with that, he pushed her down gently into the sweet-smelling new hay and dropped next to her, his mouth finding hers before she could speak. And then they were both laughing and kissing and hugging, shedding the tension of the week.

"We are alone again," Newton said. "Charles is gone, and no one knows where we are."

"I'd think," Rose said, holding his face in her hands, "that the two horses just outside the barn door might give us away."

"Then we'll get a move on," Newton said, starting to unbutton her shirtwaist.

"Here?" Rose exclaimed. "In the hay mow?"

"On a rock, in a river, in a bed, in the hay – anywhere, my love, anywhere that you are."

Without another word, Rose kissed Newton on the mouth, trying to push away the idea that this was certainly nice enough to be sinful. "Is this bad?" she asked suddenly.

"Bad? Does it feel bad? I know my hands are very rough."

"Bad to like this so much," she mumbled. "Bad as in sinful."

"Not bad," he said. He chuckled. "Know how you hate that phrase, but it works here. Not bad."

"You're sure?" she asked.

"Hmm," he said. "We need to recover from the week we had. This is the medicine, and you must take it."

"Yes, doctor," Rose said. The sun had moved another hour toward noon before they descended the ladder.

"I love you, Rose," Newton said and jumped onto the wagon seat and was gone before she could answer. "And I love you even more," she muttered to herself, hurrying to the house for fear someone would see her disheveled state. Once inside, she glanced at the glass and saw pieces of hay stuck in her hair, which was half out of its bun. She undid it, wound it up again and then took off her stockings and shook them out the window to get rid of the hay seeds. In a few minutes, as she started a loaf of bread and considered food for the noon meal, no one would have guessed she'd already been to the train and stowed the hay. And been kissed, she thought, smiling. Perhaps she was a sinner in the eyes of the Reverend Lockhead. He never did approve much of a person enjoying anything. But she enjoyed enjoying.

Rose hummed as she scrubbed the kitchen sink, kneaded the bread that she would share with Ruthann and Joshua, put Newton's filthy haying clothes into the set tub to soak awhile and thought about what else she might contribute to the Chittenden table. Chocolate cake, she decided. Ruthann would be taking care of the necessities, but she might not have the strength to tackle a dessert. And those two children so often had a bit of chocolate smeared on their faces – she knew that was a favorite. She wished she knew whether the fish peddler might come by this day or the next and whether Charles, Abby and Silas were going to appear for Sunday dinner. She sighed. Even Indian smoke signals couldn't be seen in Eastborough. She wondered again if a person on horseback could beat that river water as it sped off toward Eastborough from their new swimming place. They'd be square dancing tonight down there, Charles trying to get in a square with someone named Grace Van Buren. Was he going to marry her? She shook her head. If she shook it real hard, would it put away all her unconnected thoughts? She reckoned not. She sloshed Newton's grimy trousers and shirt around, dropped them in the sink and changed the brown water for clean. Hard scrubbing and rubbing was called for and might keep her mind from wandering. She'd take care of that and then make the cake.

The morning flew by, and Rose was surprised when the train whistled through and Newton's footsteps were on the stairs. She began to dish up the food, but when he came in the door, he grabbed her at the waist with his two hands and whirled her around, ducking to avoid the spoon she seemed to be waving. He kissed her, then let her go and went to the bathroom to wash up.

"You are the forward one," she called. "I am just a haymaker, washerwoman, cook and sweeper."

"And you think only of me while you are doing those things," Newton teased, as he came back to the kitchen. "If your ferocious father actually comes here tomorrow, I hope you will keep your hands off me."

"Why?" Rose said mischievously.

"I don't know," he answered, and they both laughed. He took his dinner plate from her hand and went to the dining room.

That afternoon Rose put together a cold supper, divided it in half and took one part to Ruthann and Joshua. She stayed only long enough to take down Ruthann's wash and chided her for hanging it out in the first place.

"Needed to do something useful, Rose," Ruthann protested. "And I must confess, I find it very soothing to string clean clothes across the line in a neat formation, clipping each with two clothespins. I hope that doesn't sound so absurd that you will just laugh at me."

326

"On the contrary, it's one of the tasks that always pleases me, and I was sorry to give it up to Mehitabel when she came to work for Father."

"Do you think your father will marry her some day?" Ruthann said suddenly.

Rose was startled by the very idea. "It had never crossed my mind," she said. "Mehitabel is so uneasy around men, including the fish peddler and the ice man, that I have worried about whether she could have even a man friend again."

"Hmm," was all Ruthann said. "And is it true your family might be coming tomorrow for Sunday dinner?"

"I wish I knew. Then I would know whether I need to make a dinner for two or five, or four."

"You can always rustle up potatoes, applesauce and scrambled eggs," Ruthann said, trying not to smile.

"You are well on the road to recovery, I can tell," Rose said. "You are no help at all, and you think the dilemma is amusing. So I will leave you this supper for today and go home to worry about tomorrow." But she also smiled as she said it and gave Ruthann a quick kiss on the cheek before she headed for the door.

Back at the house she barely had the table set for supper when she heard Newton's footsteps. She opened the door for him and was startled to see that he was carrying a freshly killed chicken in one hand and one of her bowls in the other.

"Whatever …?" Rose stopped with just one word out of her mouth.

"Off chance that a passel of Hibbards show up tomorrow, I selected a dinner, and here she is," Newton said with a smile. "I reckon we'll manage to use it if they don't appear."

Rose took the chicken from him. She peered into the bowl and discovered the giblets were there, already washed. She threw her arms around Newton, and he hugged her back.

"I've been fretting half the afternoon about what to do about company that might come or might not," Rose said. "If you keep reading my mind like this, I will be afraid to have another thought."

"That'll be the day," Newton growled. "But it'd be a sight more quiet here then."

"You are changing the subject," she said, following his lead and using her schoolroom voice. She paused and added, "And I love the chicken. Was it one of the ones that hasn't been laying much?"

"Not a-tall, far as I can see. She sits on an empty nest all day and makes that egg-laying cluck as if she were producing."

"A girl can sing, can't she, without a reason?"

"Certainly *you* can. But I have never known what goes through a chicken's mind. If she has a mind."

"Mind of her own, Grandmother Jane would say," Rose said, laughing. "It's a good thing no one is hearing this talk, or they'd be shutting us in the attic. Right now, I'd better wash that biddy and get her in the ice box."

"And our supper?"

"It's ready. We are sharing it with Joshua and Ruthann. She is so much better today." Rose put the chicken away and took out the plates she had already made up for Newton and herself. At the table, they ate without talking, cleared everything away and then took their usual places in the kitchen rocking chairs where they read the three-day-old newspaper that had come in their mailbox.

The next morning Rose rubbed the inside of the chicken with fresh sage leaves from the tiny herb garden Newton had started in the spring. Then she tore up three slices of bread that was getting stale, added an egg, water, salt and pepper and stuffed the cavity. She scooped up a little soft butter and rubbed it over the breast and legs of the chicken and then put the bird back in the ice box. She peeled potatoes, carefully removing every eye so she could mash them perfectly, and then went to the garden to see about string beans. The yellow pods were hanging thick, so she picked them off, wondering what she would do with all this food if Abby and Father didn't come. But she wasn't even out of the garden when she heard a buggy rattling into the yard of her little house, and she picked up her colander of beans and ran up the slope to the back door.

Abby was out of the buggy before the wheels stopped rolling and nearly knocked her down with a giant hug. Holding her sister, she saw that Charles had come, too, and Father, of course. Weren't they all in their Sunday best, she thought, Father there in his starched white shirt, his mustache trimmed tightly, Abby wearing little black boots and a long skirt she didn't recognize. She suddenly felt weak in the knees and overwhelmed. She clung to Abby, then turned to her father and embraced him. When she approached Charles, he backed off, his hands in front of him to keep her away.

"We met only hours ago, Rosie," he said, delighting in the sudden look of irritation that crossed her face. "No need to carry on with me."

"Right, as usual," Rose said. "No doubt you've had better hugging than mine since last we met." Then it was her turn to enjoy the sight of Charles' face getting a little red. Aha, she thought, he at least danced with Miss Grace.

"Perhaps," Silas Hibbard interrupted in his mildest voice, "you would invite us in to see your new home?"

Now Rose was truly flustered, but she turned quickly and led Abby and her father to the house while Charles took care of the horse. Once inside, Abby asked permission to look at every room, and Rose nodded. Her sister was off immediately, quickly perusing the parlor and heading for the stairs. Silas grinned, glanced around the kitchen and nodded what Rose took to be approval.

A minute later he said, "You have once again created a real home, Rose." Despite her best efforts, Rose could not stop a tear from escaping her left eye, followed by another on the right. She wiped them away and managed a smile.

"Do your eyes commonly leak separately?" Silas asked, hoping to ease the situation.

"Always," Rose answered, starting to laugh. She crossed quickly to where he was standing, hugged his arm and said she would show him the house herself. First, she pulled the chicken out of the ice box, wanting it to be closer to room temperature before she put it in the oven. Then they set off, Rose explaining and Silas making very brief comments.

When they nearly collided with Abby on the stairs, she announced, "It is so perfect, Rose, so perfect, and you even have a room where I can sleep when I come to visit."

"Thank you, Abby. Come anytime." Abby grinned and whisked past them on her way to see the downstairs.

"Me, too?" asked Charles from behind them.

"I fear, Rose," Silas said, "that they are leaving me in short order. That, however, will entail your feeding them and cutting their hair."

"As long as it doesn't involve dirty clothing," Rose answered. She and her father continued up the stairs where Silas looked into each room and felt a surge of pride in his daughter. He suddenly had a sharp memory of how Sarah had so loved to make curtains and arrange rooms so they were warm and welcoming. She took the time at summer's end to dry a few flowers from her garden and put them on the wash stands in each room to break the gloom of winter. He hoped his eyes, which felt a little wet, would not betray him, but he was uncertain, so he crossed Rose and Newton's bedroom to look out the window at the recently mown meadow.

"Pleasant view," he said, his voice a bit gruff.

"Yes," Rose said, realizing that her father – her *father* – was having some kind of struggle with his emotions. She tried to remember the last time his voice had failed him, but couldn't. Somehow this visit was triggering unexpected feelings. "I had better get to the kitchen and see to the biddy," she said.

While she and Abby worked on dinner, Charles took Silas to the barn where Newton was finishing up his regular chores. Here, too, Silas could not help admiring how orderly everything was. Harnesses were neatly hung, grain pails were out of reach of hungry rats, clean straw looked shiny and yellow in the pens and through the stanchion area. He knew all this was being maintained while Newton did the haying, and they all helped out at the Chittendens' because of Ruthann's loss. He had been certain young Barnes was getting a treasure in marrying his daughter, but he now knew Rose had done well, too, very well.

How proud her mother would be. And he knew, not for the first time, that this girl, this woman, was truly Sarah's daughter.

When they all gathered at Rose and Newton's table, Silas announced that he would say grace, and they all, quite surprised, bowed their heads while he gave thanks for family and a good life. Rose lifted her head enough to peek at everyone in considerable wonder – her family under her roof and all seemingly happy. She closed her eyes quickly when she realized that Charles was peeping also and would catch her. They said "Amen" in unison, and Newton began to carve the chicken.

CHAPTER TWENTY-NINE
Wishing on a Planet

"This is quite a feed," Silas said, dabbing at his mustache with his napkin. "'Specially for unannounced company. It is a pleasure to be eating your cooking again, Rose."

Rose glanced at Newton and smiled. Whatever would she have done if he had not shown up in the kitchen with that killed and dressed biddy. The very sight had unknotted all the worry she had about her family appearing on the doorstep. And here they all were at her table, hers and Newton's, happy to see each other. It had been a long road, sometimes so dreadful that she tried not to remember it – but never could wipe out the memory of some of the bad days and the bad things that had been said and done. But now is now, she told herself. And it is all good. She wondered if she could ask Charles about Miss Grace whatever her name was. Hmm. That might turn a good moment into a sour one, so instead she asked Charles if he would like more potatoes.

"Can I see Mrs. Chittenden today?" Abby asked suddenly.

"May I," Rose answered.

"Well, may I?"

"We'll all walk over there after the dishes are done. She is doing well, and you will love seeing John and Adelaide," Rose said. "By the by, did you all go to the square dance last night?"

"Father did," Charles said, a note of mischief in his voice.

"Charles did," Abby said, matching his tone.

"And you, Abby?" Rose asked.

"I," Abby said in a superior tone, "was lacking for partners."

Charles and Silas both gave her a look, but she was not to be silenced. She had learned long ago that the Sunday dinner table was a safe place to say things because it was unlikely anyone would make a fuss.

"Some people," she said, "had no time to dance with me."

"And who were they dancing with, Abby?" Newton said, finally entering the conversation.

"Mrs. Munson and Grace," Abby answered with alacrity.

"Why would you dance with Hattie Munson, Charles?" Newton asked, his eyes doing the dancing now.

"Please, Newton," Charles said. "Oh, please."

Rose couldn't contain herself any longer. She began to giggle, and in half a second, Silas joined her. Then the whole table was laughing, even Charles, whose face was nearly as red as Rose's oftentimes was.

Taking pity on him, Rose said, "If you will clear, Charles, I will fetch the pie."

"Is it custard?" Abby cried.

"Indeed," Newton said. "I gazed upon its splendor first thing this morning. Rose stayed up and made it by candlelight last night. It was so late when she took it out that the stove still had a spark when the sun came up."

By that time, Charles had a stack of plates in his hands and was fleeing to the safety of the kitchen. He returned quickly, head down, and picked up another pile. Silas heaved a sigh of relief. He had escaped handily from any comments about his evening with Hattie Munson, which had proved more than satisfactory. He had stopped by for her, a little taken aback when he saw what he knew was a new square dancing skirt and a long-sleeved shirtwaist with pearl buttons and a lace-trimmed collar. He had hopped down to assist her into the buggy, startled when a wave of desire swept through him the minute he touched her arm.

They had danced nearly every dance, and he became more and more aware that it had been a long time since he had even really looked at a woman as a woman. He enjoyed putting his arm around her in answer to every command to "promenade your partner" and he felt no resistance when he gradually held her tighter as the evening went on. They had ridden home in companionable silence, and when they reached her door, he once again leaped down to assist her. Had she deliberately stumbled, he wondered. In any case, he caught her, their eyes met, and he had quickly kissed her cheek. When she did not pull away, he reached down and lightly brushed her lips with his. Then he stood back and offered her his arm. They walked to the door where she turned once again, tilted her head at him and said, "You are a remarkable dancer, Silas Hibbard." And with that, she whirled into the house, closing the door behind her. Back in the buggy, he had been surprised to realize how much he had enjoyed himself. And Hattie had not burdened him with a speck of gossip. Mighty certain they had given the rest of the village a little to talk about. It had been a pleasant evening. With the exception of Rose and Newton's train station party, he hadn't had much of that. Hadn't wanted it.

But he had relaxed too soon. He emerged from his reverie to hear Abby saying, "No, Rose, I didn't dance as much as Father or Charles. Mrs. Munson was with Father the whole time, and Charles danced even the waltz with Grace – but not very well."

Coming back for the chicken platter, Charles scowled at her but said nothing. Remembering all the times he and Abby had teased her about Newton or spied on her, Rose kept her thoughts to herself with more than a little effort. She was quite shocked to hear that her father had actually arranged an evening with Hattie Munson in advance and then paid court to her in front of the whole town. She broke into a smile when she realized that Hattie might be gossiped about instead of spreading stories about others.

"You may bring in the pie now, Charles," she said. "And you, Abby, can get plates from the sideboard behind your chair, the small white ones with the roses on." Attention turned to the pie, which looked perfect. Rose started to cut it, using the pierced silver knife with the "S" on the handle. It made her think of that awful day, also a Sunday, when Father had announced she would have to leave school and Ruthann had argued with him. She had nearly dripped tears on the pie that day. She took out the first piece without breaking it and looked around the table. What a long way they had all come.

When dinner was over, they started out for the Chittenden house, taking a shortcut across the newly mown field. They hadn't gone far when Silas stopped and put a hand on Newton's arm.

"Sir?" Newton asked.

"I've a mind to take a better look at your heifers first," he said.

"And I would be proud to introduce you to each one," Newton said, grinning. "A barn visit will keep us from all barging in on Ruthann at the same time." Seeing a shadow cross his father-in-law's face, he added quickly, "She's doing well, sir." Silas grunted, and the two men veered off toward the barn. Charles, after hesitating a second, followed them. A half hour later, they had moved on to Joshua's barn.

"You are mighty neat farmers," Silas said. "It pleases me to see such kempt stables." But when he paused by the iron bars that enclosed Lord Coopersmith, he frowned. The bull was pacing back and forth. They watched him go to a corner, turn, paw the straw under his hooves and move to the opposite corner. When he made his second turn, he saw them, lowered his large, mostly black head and charged toward them, sliding to a stop just short of the bars. Silas jumped back, startled, and Joshua, who had come up behind them, spoke quietly to the bull, who almost immediately became very still.

"He's shy about strangers," Joshua said.

"I am wary of all bulls, especially Jerseys," Silas answered. "But I would judge this one to be somewhat mean-spirited."

"He does his work well," Joshua said.

"And you must not turn your back on him," Silas counseled. Joshua nodded.

"We should get on up to the house," Newton said, hoping to interrupt this conversation. He himself was more than wary of Lord Coopersmith and felt the animal seemed enraged more often than not. The bull had never hurt a heifer, however, and he had to admit that his own experience with bulls was quite limited. At the Barnes place, they had always walked their cows to a nearby farm when they were springing. They had never owned any bull larger than a newborn calf.

At the Chittenden house, the men found everyone in the parlor, including John and Adelaide. The room was buzzing with conversation, and Ruthann was smiling and talking in her usual way.

Not wanting to rush over to her, Silas turned back to Joshua, a little worried that he had offended him about the bull. He said, "Nice farm you have here. I am not inclined to spend much time with your bull, but my understanding is that Jersey bulls tend to be crotchety. You two," he said, nodding toward Newton, "may be the neatest farmers in the county. It's a pleasure to see."

Joshua nodded his thanks, thinking for an instant about much less cordial moments in the past with this man who had given Rose such a hard time about so many things. But if she could forgive and possibly even forget, then he would join her. Silas went to Ruthann and whispered something in her ear, then patted her on the back, and she smiled up at him.

"I am doing well," she said. "Quite well."

Rose looked at her friend and realized that it was true. Ruthann looked almost herself and had already told Rose and Abby that she was doing all the kitchen work again, with the usual help from John and Adelaide.

"We'll be in the kitchen," Joshua said, motioning to Charles to join them. And the men moved off, leaving the women and children to their own conversation. A half hour later, the visitors were back at Rose and Newton's house, getting ready for their return trip to Eastborough. Rose stood in the yard and watched the dust roiling up from the buggy wheels until her family was out of sight.

At that moment, Newton's arms came around her, and he said, "Do you miss them? Is this too far away?"

She twisted around to face him, putting her arms under his and clasping her hands behind his back. "I do miss them," she said. "And this might just be the perfect distance. They can come for dinner, and they have to head home early so's to beat the sunset."

Newton threw back his head and laughed. "You're staying then, I gather," he said, lifting her up and swinging her around. "Even though you missed the chance to see Charles making up to a girl and your father dancing with Miss Hattie?"

"Staying," Rose said. "Put me down, sir."

"When I'm ready," he answered. And he carried her into the kitchen and straight upstairs to the bedroom. "There," he said, dropping her onto the quilt.

"Don't you have chores to do?" she asked, surprised but trying to look as innocent as possible.

"Indeed," he said, "if you are already considering this a chore." And he leaned over to reach the buttons on her shirtwaist.

"Some chores are tolerable," she said, starting to laugh and reaching for his belt buckle. "Practicing makes all chores more tolerable," he answered, and for the next hour, few words were spoken in that room. As the afternoon turned to dusk, Newton roused himself from a half sleep and announced that his other chores were still undone. He dressed in his barn clothes, kissed Rose and said, "I trust some supper will be your next chore?"

A little drowsy herself, Rose nodded. Once he had left, she got up, carefully put away her Sunday clothes and dressed. She had many dishes to do, and she hadn't given a thought to what they might eat that evening. She paused at the bedroom window and looked out at the western sky where Venus had suddenly appeared between two long lines of dark clouds. The sun had not totally let go of its hold on the day so the planet was not at full brilliance yet. The day, Rose thought. It had been quite a day. She stared at Venus, made a silent wish and went down the stairs to poke up the fire and put a meal together. Another grand day. Sometimes she figured a great day meant the other kind was coming. But not today.

CHAPTER THIRTY
A Dizzying Idea

The summer rolled on, the first crop of hay in, the wax beans canned and the cranberry beans laid out to dry on a sheet on the parlor floor. Rose had spent hours filling the shelves in the dark corner of the cellar where Newton had made a space for storing preserves and winter vegetables. She had put up apple jelly and wild blackberry jam, along with a few jars of tomatoes. On the lower shelves, she would store all the extra beets and carrots in a basket of sand, and she had space for onions, potatoes and winter squash. It wasn't much, she knew, but she loved lining up the jelly jars and the tomatoes. Ruthann had raised a few hills of popcorn, and Rose planned to dry the ears, then strip off the kernels by rubbing the ears together. Last time she'd done it, she learned that popcorn kernels were a little prickly and made her hands hurt. But she smiled remembering popping corn on a cold winter evening.

She had saved a space on the lowest shelf for pumpkins, which were always a latecomer. She liked to keep them off the damp floor but in as dark a place as possible so they would keep. She leaned down to sweep some dust off that shelf and when she

341

straightened, the rows of glass jelly jars blurred and she grabbed an edge of wood to steady herself. In a second or two, everything came right again, but she did not move.

"Judas priest," she muttered to herself. "What was that?" Feeling steady again, she made her way to the kitchen, filled a tumbler with cool water and drank it down. A little uneasy, she sat down in one of the kitchen rockers for a minute, hoping she wasn't coming down with the grippe. Pushing back and forth, toe-heel-toe-heel, she realized she had been a little queasy when she was melting butter for Newton's fried eggs.

"Oh, dear," she said aloud. "No laundry for – how long? I reckon I'm expecting. And I'm a nincompoop." She grinned at the very word while she tried to remember the last time she had secretly washed out the soft cloths she used for her menstruation, but she kept losing count. Was it before Father and Abby and Charles had come? She did not know. But it had been awhile. Well, she thought, chuckling a little, with all the "chores" they'd been doing, this was more than possible. If that was what made her dizzy, she would get on with her day and hope it didn't come back.

But her stomach flip-flopped in a not-nice way when she started to make the noon meal. She knew from talks with Ruthann that what they called "morning sickness" was common and unpleasant. She also knew some women never had it at all. Rose sighed. This was yet another time when she wished her mother were alive. Sarah had never talked to Rose about what happened when girls turned into women, but at least she had explained about menstruation. If she hadn't, Rose thought, I would have worried that my life was about to end by bleeding. As the milk for the white sauce started to heat, her stomach flopped again, and she told it to be still. Why did warm milk suddenly have an objectionable smell. Not an aroma, a smell. She went on stirring the pot of white sauce, hoping she could fix dinner without being truly ill.

She added chopped chicken to the sauce and fetched two biscuits from the pantry. She flicked away a tiny speck of green from one of the biscuits. She couldn't throw them away just for that bit of what might be the beginning of mold. Heated in the oven for a few minutes, they would be tender enough not to seem like leftovers. She pulled the simmering pan of carrots onto a hotter part of the stove and took a deep breath. Perhaps, she thought, a cracker would make her stomach stop talking. She opened the canister of oyster crackers and tried one, then another and another. Her insides seemed to settle down. The wonder of Westminster, she told herself. Westminster crackers had always been the perfect thing when she was a child with a misbehaving tummy. She remembered that her mother told her about visiting the place where they were made, not all that far from Eastborough. Well, as the crow flies, Rose thought. We who take a buggy have to snake around a good deal no matter where we go. Was that town named for the London church? She had no idea.

She sighed – her mind was running off the face of the earth again. She needed to think about whether she should tell Newton or wait until she was sure. Would he be pleased? She didn't know. She started to count on her fingers – September, October, November, December, January, February, March, April, May – oh, it took such a long time, she thought. But at least she wouldn't have to worry about having a baby in a blizzard. She didn't know whether it was April or May, but she was quite certain it wouldn't be March. How silly not to keep track of such things, she told herself.

It was getting on toward dinner time, and she stirred the sauce once again, turning the chunks of chicken so they were well covered. She heard Newton's firm step on the stairs and resolved to be herself for the meal and not let on that she'd as soon eat a piece of paper as tackle a dinner plate.

He came up behind her, put his hands on her shoulders and said, "You're the best Rose, the very best." And as she started to turn, he chuckled and added, "Better even than Jerseys."

"Newton!" she cried out. "That's not fair."

"You are fair, my lady, very fair. Fairest of them all," he said, chuckling again.

"And you have spent too much time with Charles since our wedding," she said. "One has to feel a little sorry for Miss Grace Van Buren."

"If she can catch him at this young age and hang on," Newton answered quickly, "she'll be the second luckiest girl in the county."

"I suppose I'm first?" Rose countered, starting to enjoy this conversation immensely.

"Oh, no," he said. "Hattie Munson is in the running for first, I reckon."

Rose put her hands on his shoulders, her face suddenly serious. "Do you think Father is falling in love with her? Has she set her cap for him?"

"Mebbe yes on both counts. Time will tell. But it wouldn't be a tragedy for either side, would it?"

"He'd not be lonely anymore," Rose conceded, thinking that her news had certainly been thrust aside by the bent of this conversation. It was her turn to chuckle, and Newton raised an eyebrow.

"Well now," Rose said, "I've had my grievances with Miss Hattie over the years, and if she weds my father, that will bring my favorite fairy tale straight into real life. I will only have to worry about whether we have enough white mice."

"Whatever are you talking about?" Newton said, grabbing her around the waist and pulling her close. "Are the fumes from the stove shattering your mind?"

"Cinderella," Rose mumbled. "Wicked stepmother. I'll need mice to pull my carriage, only they'll be horses when they do that."

"Lordy, lordy," Newton said. "Your mind jumps around so that I sometimes feel I am lost in a bramble." He paused and looked down at her. "But I like it." He kissed her then, and Rose felt herself melting into his shirt, returning the kiss and running her hands down his back. He pulled away but not before she felt the familiar shiver run down her spine.

"We need to have dinner now," she gasped, her breathing heavy.

"Indeed," he said. "My apologies. My appetite went off in a different direction."

That made her smile. She shrugged his hands off and returned to the pot of chicken on the stove, her face burning. Sometimes she'd give up three meals for an afternoon of lovemaking, and she hoped that didn't make her a harlot. Especially since it appeared she was about to become a mother. She would have to tell Newton soon because she was dying to talk to Emily about it, and it would hardly be proper to tell an outsider first.

So it was that after a cold supper, she asked Newton if he had the strength left to walk down to the pasture gate and see the moon come up. She knew it was plain foolishness to do anything besides just tell him straight out, but she wanted to make it special. He raised an eyebrow but said he was willing. "Can certainly get down the slope, not certain of the strength to get back to the house," he said.

"Come on, old fellow," she said, grabbing his hand. And they set off past the barn to the pasture gate where Newton boosted her up to the top bar and then joined her. Something out of the way was going on, he was certain, but he knew better than to ask even a single question. It was enough to hold her hand and enjoy a silence broken only by an occasional m-m-maht sound from one of the cows or the monotonous chirp of a cricket. M-m-maht, he thought, smiling at himself. Since Rose had come into his life, he'd learned cows actually don't moo. They m-m-maht.

He turned toward her and ventured, "I've lost track of the moon, Rose. What size will it be when it shows up?"

"Tiny," she answered quickly. "Just a sliver of light, balancing there, looking as if a breeze could set it rocking."

"Silver then," he said, knowing much more about moons now than he ever had before he started courting Rose.

"Silver," she agreed. "Silver sliver. Anagram."

"Oh, that," Newton said and stopped when he realized Rose had merely paused, her face serious in the dusky light. When she went on, her voice sounded strange, a little croaky, as she said, "I have reason to believe we have created a sliver that will grow to full size, just like the moon."

346

"Whaat?" Newton said. "You have lost me – again." And then, as he managed to get his head around what seemed like a riddle, he nearly toppled off the gate. "Rose!" he shouted. "A sliver of a thing that we created? You mean it?"

"I think so."

"Our own baby? When? How do you know?"

"Are you shocked or pleased, sir?" Rose demanded.

Newton jumped down, put his arms around her waist and buried his head in her skirt, about where he figured the sliver of life might be. "Excited," he said in a muffled voice. "Overwhelmed, happy, oh, and a little bit scared, too. What about you? Is it too soon?"

He was always so in tune with her, Rose thought, pleased that he would have been satisfied to be two for a while longer. "It's soon," she said, "but we've been so busy with chores ..."

"Ahh," Newton said, looking up at her. "So many chores, so well done. But too soon, my lovely Rose, too soon?"

"Not too soon."

"And when?"

"The when," she said, recovering the teasing voice she often used with him, "is not as simple with humans as with Jerseys. I am uncertain. But surely not until early spring."

Newton, who actually had been thinking of the gestation period of cows, quickly denied having any bovine thoughts. He knew how Rose hated to be compared to the four-legged creatures he cherished, so he tried to be on his guard when it came to comparing people with cows, especially Rose with cows.

"It did cross your mind, didn't it?" she persisted.

"Hmm. I can't imagine why you would accuse me of such a thing. My mind was occupied with a sliver rocking."

347

Then she laughed, bent down to drop a quick kiss on his nose, put her hands on his shoulders and jumped off the gate.

"Easy there," Newton started, wondering if she were now a fragile person. But Rose had her arms around his neck and her face tilted up. He pulled her tight and kissed her so long and hard that she was gasping when he pulled away. Then they kissed again, this time so gently that Rose felt tears in her eyes. How she loved this man.

"I gather," Newton tried again. "I gather the sliver doesn't mind about jumping off gates and kissing a boy for five minutes at a time."

"Not a-tall," Rose said. Then she looked over his shoulder and squealed, "The moon, it's coming now."

Sure enough, just above the trees at the edge of the pasture a tiny point of light was coming. They watched in silence as the crescent came into full view with a bright planet appearing just outside its curve. Rose sighed and put her head on Newton's shoulder and they stood there in the warm evening, neither of them wanting to say another word.

CHAPTER THIRTY-ONE
Charles Learns About Spooning

In Eastborough, Charles was waiting for the moon to come up, too, and began to wonder if he should meander about and find Miss Grace Van Buren. He wouldn't admit it to a soul – barely to himself – but she was beginning to wedge herself into his thinking, pushing aside even his beloved heifer that he had capriciously named for Ruthann.

Hands in his pockets, he set off along the road toward Grace's house, already anticipating even the possibility of seeing her. Not courting her, he told himself. She's just a decent partner for the square dances, and I have a need to stay in her good graces – ha! Grace's good graces. That's something. He grinned and broke into a trot.

He was just shy of her house when he realized she was sitting on the front steps reading a book in the fading light. To his surprise, he felt a little tingle somewhere behind the buttons on his pants, but he slowed to a saunter and kept his eyes on the road, not appearing to notice that she was there.

"Mr. Charles," she called out. "Whither?"

"Or whether," he returned, jumping a bit as if she'd startled him.

"Or weather," she said. And they both laughed. "Come sit, you foolish boy."

"Whenever," he said and plunked down one step below her, his long legs reaching across two slates of the narrow path leading away from the house.

"If I say salt," Grace went on, "what do you say?"

"Pepper," he answered immediately. "How about you with 'sun'?"

"Moon," she said. "Black."

"White."

"Man," he said.

"Woman." She frowned. "These are all too easy."

" How about fork?"

"Spoon," she said quickly.

"Knife?"

"Spoon," she said again and bent down quickly to plant a kiss right on his mouth.

"Whatever?" he gulped, leaning back enough to end the kiss.

"Don't you spoon?' she wanted to know. "Or am I just a person who promenades the Town Hall with the best of them?"

"Ah," he muttered. "Spooning. Heard of that. Thought it had to do with eating." And before she could think of a retort, he pulled her face toward him, kissed her neck and nose softly and, with a hand on each of her cheeks, gave her a long kiss on the mouth.

When he let her go, she looked at him in astonishment. "You promenade well yourself," she said.

"You've been spooned," he answered and stood up to leave. Grace didn't want him to go, but she didn't want to beg him to stay, either. So she stood up to say good night.

"Will you join me on my stroll?" Charles then asked. She put her hand in his, said not a word, and the two walked off down the road together, each privately wondering what this might mean or whether it meant nothing at all. After they had gone a short way, Charles found himself thinking about Newton and Rose and how he had plagued them when he could see quite plainly that Newton was trying to get Rose alone. He was beginning to understand why and was wondering if he could risk another kiss this very evening when he realized they were catching up with another pair of walkers. He put his hand on Grace's arm to slow her down and a finger on his lips so she would not speak. They stopped, and Charles realized that his first thought was on the mark: Just ahead of him, his very own father was walking along with a woman beside him. What, whither and whether, indeed.

He nudged Grace's shoulder and indicated a small lane off to the right, and they moved on without speaking. As soon as they turned the corner, she said, "What's going on? You aren't the only one who can stroll."

"That's my father," he said with a groan.

Her eyes popped wide open. "With Mrs. Munson?"

"Judas priest. Excuse me. Is it?"

"Without a doubt," Grace replied. "Is he courting her, or is there a problem with Abby?"

"Judas priest," Charles said again. "Um, excuse me again. Abby works for her, and it's never been a problem. But I'd like that. I'd like it as a reason for them walking and talking."

"Not the courting?" And as she saw Charles' mouth open, she said, "And no more Judas priest. Profanity is never part of strolling."

351

That made him laugh, and they went down the narrow lane toward the Chandler farm hand in hand. After a few minutes, Charles crossed in front of her, turning her back toward the main road. "They must be out of sight by now," he said.

"And I must get on home," she answered. "It's very dark tonight, and that moon may be pretty up there, but it gives less light than a melted candle." Charles put his hand under her elbow, thinking that was gentlemanly on rough ground but nowhere near the same as holding her hand. But she jerked her elbow back and suddenly her small hand was in his again, and he felt something run through his slender frame, once again a very new sensation. From a hand? he thought in wonder. Just from a hand. He would have to ponder this in daylight.

On her part, Grace was smiling to herself, thinking it had taken her a long time to get his brown, rough-skinned hand in hers. She gave a little sigh, hoping it wasn't going to be the last time. Or even the last thing, she thought, smiling again. They came back to the road where they once again admired the moon, and then Charles walked her home. On her doorstep, he let go of her hand, gave a little bow and said in his usual casual tone, "Sleep well, miss. Don't let the moon keep you up." And he was gone. She heard his footsteps on the gravel road and knew he had broken into a run.

If they had looked back when they emerged from the lane, they would have seen Hattie Munson and Silas Hibbard coming toward them. But they didn't. Hattie recognized them both instantly and then Silas said, "Well, well, who is that with Charles?"

"Grace Van Buren, I believe," Hattie answered with considerable satisfaction. This was a whole new tidbit for her to chew on overnight and then spread about in the morning.

"Didn't know they were stepping out," Silas said.

"They certainly were stepping at the square dance," Hattie said, still delighting in this new chapter. She had taken note at the dance that Charles had never been far from the Van Buren girl's side the whole evening. But she had not dreamed that the pretty girl would be enamored of the young man she considered rather brash. She also had to admit she was a little in awe of him as well. Charles was polite enough, but he had a way of saying things that made a body wonder sometimes.

"And you'll not be telling this at the store tomorrow?" Silas asked in a tone so lazy that anyone but Hattie would think he couldn't care less what she did.

She paused. Say nothing? That's what the Shakers would have counseled. She was silent so long that Silas stopped walking and turned toward her. "Hattie?" he asked.

"Not a word," she said, her heart sinking a little at the very idea of this promise but wary of saying no to this rather fierce man. "Not a single word, Silas," she said. She took his arm, turned him toward home again, and they strolled on in silence. At her door, Silas turned toward her again, put his arms around her and kissed her on the mouth, as gently as a butterfly landing on a flower. It was a short kiss, and when he pulled away, he looked down at her and said, "Thank you, Hattie. I do know how you love a story." And then he, as suddenly as Charles had left Grace, was gone.

Hattie pushed her door open, walked into the kitchen and sank into her rocking chair. He kissed me on the mouth, she said aloud. She touched her lips with her forefinger, leaned back in her chair and closed her eyes. It had been a long time since she had liked anything as much as that kiss. If that was pay for ignoring Charles' budding romance, she'd put her mind on earning another.

Miles away, under the same moon, Ruthann was kneeling between John and Adelaide at Adelaide's bedroom window, watching the crescent rise over the gable of the barn. The window was open, and they could hear the murmuring of the cows in the barn and the occasional snort from the bull pen. But the night was pretty quiet, and so were they.

Joshua came up the stairs as quietly as he could manage with his bum leg and saw them there, a picture so perfect that he felt a sudden salty sting in his eyes. They were so dear to him, these three, and he knew the little ones were puzzled in their own childlike ways about the moments when their mother looked very sad. He had to give her credit for hiding her grief most of the time, but he ached for her. And part of his ache was for the future. She'd want to try again, and he feared that, feared it enough to make his belly hurt. He hoped she'd listen to his reluctance, but he knew her. She had a mind of her own. He grinned then. Hadn't he and Newton attached themselves to a grand pair. They'd never scrape their boots on those two.

Ruthann moved then and spoke softly to the children. They stood, Adelaide in her long nightgown and John in a nightshirt that was too big for him. "Off to bed now," Ruthann said, and then they saw him in the doorway. Both ran, each grabbing his sound leg, and he reached down to boost them up, one on each arm. He dropped Adelaide on her bed and did the same with

John in his bedroom. Ruthann kissed each of them on the forehead and joined him in the hall with her lighted candle.

"Shall we slip outside and have a better look at the moon?" he asked. "If you're not tired to the point of exhaustion?"

"Never too tired to look at a moon," she said. And they went out into the warm night air, hand in hand.

Jason, meanwhile, perched on the frame of his grindstone, was having a look at the moon, too. Mooning, he told himself, shaking his shoulders and making an effort to get rid of his gloomy mood. Moping was more like it. Nell never would put up with his occasional doldrums. "Shake it off," she'd say, "life is short." Well, hers had been far too short to suit him, and he missed her every waking minute. Some of the sleeping ones, too, if his dreams were any indication. He sighed, then stood and shook himself again. He knew she didn't mean actually shaking, but it did seem to get some of the kinks out.

He decided to take one more look at his chickens before turning in. Inside the chicken house, most of the birds were already roosting, each head tucked under a wing. Sort of like putting the pillow over your head when the moonlight makes it too bright in the bedroom, he thought. He glanced up at the small windows in the chicken house and chuckled. That bit of moon wasn't going to keep anyone up. Pretty, though. As he turned to the door to leave, he was startled to find himself considering that Mehitabel was pretty, too. Now where had that come from? He must be more of a lonely old fool than he'd known. Or he had spent so much time with Rose that his mind had started jumping about the way hers did. Thinking about Rose made him smile in spite of himself. Mehitabel. He wondered if Silas had considered Mehitabel as a wife. We menfolk aren't very good at taking care of things by ourselves, he knew. He too often found spoiled leftovers in the ice box and even more frequently left soiled dishes in the sink. Spoiled and soiled. And fearful of appearing weak if we admit how much we need our wives.

Inside his house, Jason lit a candle and looked around at the comfortable home Nell had created, starting the very first day of their marriage. When Clara was born, she added caring for the baby to her already full day. He was a hard worker, but he had come to realize that Nell and the other farm women worked as hard as anyone in the village, their fingers knitting or mending or sewing in the evening when his work was done. He reckoned most husbands, himself included, were having a little snooze while their wives worked on.

He sighed again and mounted the stairs to the bedroom. He undressed, blew out the candle and crawled into bed, chuckling again as he put the pillow over his head. He had, indeed, nearly shaken off the doldrums.

CHAPTER THIRTY-TWO
Queasy at Dawn

Newton woke early the next morning to the sound of Rose retching. He sat up and realized she had her head over the chamber pot on her side of the bed. He jumped up and went to her, but she waved him off. "It's all right," she gasped. "The sliver ..." and then she heaved again. He fetched a washcloth, dipped it in the bowl on the washstand and laid it on the back of her neck. Then he hustled into his clothes, figuring he was pretty useless wandering around in a nightshirt. To his relief, the miserable sounds had stopped, and Rose was sitting on the floor, using the cloth to wipe her face and trying to smile at him.

"Been feeling queasy every morning," she said. "But this was the worst."

"And it lasts for weeks?" he answered, trying to keep his tone even and hoping he sounded as if this were an ordinary way to wake up in the morning.

"Might," she allowed. "We can only hope the sliver settles in and leaves my stomach alone soon."

"Slivers do hurt," Newton said. "Sneaky. Troublesome. I'll think on it," Newton promised, reaching out a hand to pull her up. He kissed her on the cheek and announced that he'd save her lips for a time when they were more appealing. That made her smile again, and she told him to leave her be so she could get dressed.

"Can do that while I'm here," he teased.

"No, siree. You will surely get in the way," she said.

"Part of my plan," he said.

"Go." Her tone won out, and he went.

As soon as she heard his stocking feet padding down the stairs, Rose regretted being so short with him. But she needed to concentrate on making her stomach behave if that was possible. She'd have to ask Ruthann. No, couldn't ask Ruthann, whose eyes were so sad sometimes that Rose knew she was a far cry from being over the loss of that baby. Many cries, in fact. She could ask Emily. Whenever she could get there. Far cry, far piece. She sighed and dressed quickly, startled to feel her head go into a spin when she bent to button her shoes. She sat down on the floor abruptly and pulled her knees up to make a resting place for her head. Her belly, her head – what was next? She knew her feet would be hurting a few months from now, but she hoped no other body parts were going to protest this new presence. She rolled onto her knees and stood, holding very still for a long minute. All was right for now. She headed down to the kitchen.

Newton had already gone to the barn, and Rose felt better as she busied herself with coffee grounds, water, oats, water and the little toaster. She knew he'd be in for breakfast soon, cutting his chores short out of worry for her condition. Sure enough, she barely had enough time to set things out on the table and give the oats a good stir when she heard him whistling on the stairs. At least he wasn't sneaking up on her to find out if she was favoring herself in some way. She didn't want to be babied. Oh, my – babied. Well, she didn't.

"Going to sit up and take nourishment?" he inquired as he opened the door.

"Good morning, Grandmother Jane," she said, laughing. "Reckon the sliver needs nourishment even if I'm not so certain."

"You sit. I'll serve," he said, pushing her toward the table. So she sat and laughed again as he flourished her bowl of oatmeal on high as if he were a waiter with a tray. Putting the dish in front of her, he bowed and asked, "Would madam prefer top milk or plain today? Sugar or maple syrup?"

She pointed to the top milk and reached for the sugar bowl. He poured, spilling a little as he tried to simultaneously plant a kiss on the top of her head. "Service satisfactory?"

"I am signing up for nine months of same," she said, trying to look stern. "It's the least you can do while I carry this burden."

He grinned at her, took his place at the table and concentrated on his food. When his bowl was half empty he looked up and asked, "Shall we call it 'burden'?"

"Newton!"

"I have firmly in mind, my dear, that I am married to the sister of a person who named his calf Ruthann, the given name of his teacher. So how am I to know how to proceed with identifying this new entry?"

"Sliver will be fine, I think. No one will know what that means. I can say, 'come to the kitchen, I have a sliver,' and you'll appear immediately.

"Obeying," he said, trying to frown. "Sliver it is." He pushed back his chair, stretched his arms high above his head and added, "Time to get to work. I'll spare you the henhouse today, if you like, but not tomorrow."

The very thought of the henhouse smell, dusty and intense, made Rose's nose and stomach contract simultaneously. She took a sip of coffee rather tentatively, then relaxed and nodded. When Newton was out the door, she stayed still for a minute, then set about the cleaning up and found the oatmeal was not wriggling in her stomach. She hurried through her morning routine and went to the garden to see what would be best for the noon meal. She wondered when they could tell Joshua and Ruthann – if Ruthann didn't just guess all on her own. She had a way of seeing right into your brain, especially when you were hoping to hide something.

The black caps finally looked dark enough to pick, and Rose rolled down the sleeves of her shirtwaist before approaching the berry patch. These weren't as wicked as blackberries, but the thorns were long and seemed alive to her, always ready to attack. She had a clean lard pail with her and in no time it was half full. A few biscuits, and dessert will be a grand surprise. She set the pail down in the shade of a tall sunflower and went on to the beans, knowing she should have picked them two days ago. Slim beans, as yellow as bananas, were hanging from the plants, surrounded by the pink flowers that promised a continuing crop. She reckoned she'd have to put some up or they'd go to waste. Mother always put a little cream on beans, she remembered, but she preferred them with a chunk of butter melting through them. In no time, she had enough for the noon meal and an afternoon of preserving. If Ruthann came over, they could sit on the steps to cut beans and talk. Why did everyone make it seem like a sin to talk without your hands busying themselves with some kind of work? She smiled, thinking women had certainly found some ways to get in their conversations – in the kitchen at church suppers, at the quilting frame, even cutting beans. But Sarah, she thought, would have liked more than that.

She pulled a few pigweeds, thinking they were quite un-hoglike. Maybe they were what pigs liked to eat. Grandmother Jane called this other large plant the smart weed, but it seemed no more intelligent than the others, unless figuring out how to grow fast was a sign of a brain. She retrieved her berry pail and headed toward the house, leaving the beans and berries by the back door. Then she half ran, half walked to the Chittenden house, wondering if Sliver was going to mind that kind of jostling. She did so love to run.

A little breathless but no longer queasy, she dropped down on Ruthann's back steps and called out to her. John and Adelaide appeared instantly, slamming the door and surrounding her with hugs. By the time Ruthann appeared at the door, the children were on Rose's lap, begging for a story. The teacher didn't touch the door, waiting to hear what Rose was going to do.

"Once upon a time," Rose began, "a small boy and a small girl went for a walk through a cornfield in August. The corn was very tall. When the small boy raised his hand above his head, he could not reach the highest leaf of the cornstalks."

"What was his name?" John wanted to know.

"Duck," Rose answered.

"That's not a name," John protested.

"Everything can be a name," Rose answered. "Shall I tell more?'

"Yes'm," Adelaide said in her squeaky voice. "And girl name."

"Ida. So, Duck started to run through the corn with leaves swiping his face and his bare feet stumbling on the stones between the rows. Suddenly he tripped on a large rock and went calarupp onto the dirt."

"Calarupp?" said a voice from the doorway.

"Calarupp," Rose said, wondering if this story could end soon. "Calarupp is a perfectly fine, made-up English word, which all words must have been at one time." John, impatient with this interruption, jabbed her with his elbow. Rose went on, "So, Duck sat up and looked around. He could see nothing. It was very cool in the shade of the corn, but the only sound was when the breeze rattled the leaves. He looked back and did not see his sister on the path. He didn't like the rattle sound.

"He called Ida's name and no answer came, so he got up and started back the way he had come. He reached the end of the row without finding her. Now he had a funny feeling in his belly. He was supposed to know where Ida was – at all times."

"I have to keep an eye on Adelaide," John offered.

"Right," Rose said. "Duck called again, and Ida answered. He started toward the place where her voice had come from and called again. This time her answer came from a different spot. Duck decided Ida was playing a new game, so he stopped calling and carefully worked his way through the cornfield. Then he heard another voice, his mother's. She was calling 'Duck, Ida, Duck, Ida,' and he headed for her voice. He was almost at the edge of the field when Ida jumped out from behind a thick corn plant and yelled, 'Boo!' which scared him so that he screamed and then saw his sister, rolling on the ground, laughing at him.

"He tried to pounce on her, but she jumped up and ran faster than a rabbit for the house, reaching the kitchen way ahead of him. Duck stopped at the trough in the yard to rinse off his hands and decided he wasn't going to say a word. He could only hope Ida would keep still. But the first words he heard when he reached the kitchen were, "And then I jumped out and yelled ..." Rose paused and jiggled the children on her lap.

"BOO!" John and Adelaide shouted together and then burst out laughing.

At that, Ruthann joined them on the steps, noticing right away that Rose had unusual circles under her eyes. Hmm, she thought. I wonder. But all she said was, "Please don't ever, ever get lost in the cornfield. But if you do, how would you get out, John?"

"Follow any row to the end," he said promptly.

"That's my boy," she said. "And not lose sight of Miss Adelaide, here."

"No, ma'am."

"I came," Rose said, "to see if you would like to cut yellow beans this afternoon. I was of a mind to put some up but would be glad to share with you instead. Newton and I can make a meal of fresh beans with bread and butter."

"Can't think of anything I'd rather do than sit on your little porch, have a long chat and get some beans cut. I trust we can all do that?"

"Yes," John shouted, jumping off Rose's lap and tearing across the lawn. When he heard Adelaide behind him, he ducked behind the sheets on the clothesline, but she quickly spotted his ankles and shoes and tried to tackle him. With a rush of big brotherhood, he collapsed so she could dance around and chant, "Me won, me won."

Rose and Ruthann exchanged a smile. "You miss those schoolchildren, don't you," Ruthann said.

"No question," Rose said promptly but added, "No one has everything all at once. I had that, now I have this." She glanced up at Ruthann and decided to plunge ahead. "And this, too," she added, stroking her belly.

"Oh, Rose," Ruthann said, jumping down to where Rose was sitting and hugging her. "I am so happy for you. I did notice you were wearing new circles under your eyes, but I didn't want to ask."

"No one knows," Rose said.

"My lips are sealed. Except for Joshua, of course. Any idea when?"

"Not exactly. But not in the winter." Rose hesitated and then said, her voice cracking a bit, "I didn't want to tell you ... we could have been having babies almost together."

"It's all right, Rose," Ruthann said. "I won't ever forget the one we lost, but perhaps we'll have another. We have to see what Seth says about that."

The two friends sat on the steps in the sun with no need to say more. John and Adelaide were running in and out of the wash on the line, banging the sheets with their fists. Suddenly, the two women jumped up when they heard a yell from the barn.

"Sit on the steps and stay there," Ruthann told the children, and she and Rose ran toward the barn. It was Joshua shouting, shrieking with pain. As they ran, they saw Newton coming at a near gallop from the field. He reached the barn before they did, shocked to find that Lord Coopersmith had Joshua pinned in a corner of the iron-barred pen. He immediately reached for the rifle Joshua kept on the wall.

Quickly, he fired into the air, the bullet ripping a chunk of wood out of the rafter over the bull's head. Startled, the animal jumped back, and Newton, cradling the rifle, ran toward the corner, hoping to pull Joshua out. Behind him, he heard Rose and Ruthann come in, and he shouted that they should somehow divert the bull, which was roaring in a fury such as they had never heard before.

Rose unfastened her skirt, let it drop to the floor, grabbed it and climbed onto one of the bars on the pen, not far from the bull. She whirled the skirt around her head and let go, sending it to the far corner of the pen.

"Give me yours," she cried, reaching toward Ruthann, who seemed to be frozen in place, a dazed look on her face. She saw Ruthann snap out of it and tear off her skirt. She handed it to Rose, who was watching the bull catch the first skirt on his horns and toss it in the air. She threw the second one, further away, and heaved a sigh of relief when she saw that Newton had somehow yanked Joshua through the bars. Lord Coopersmith had gone after the second heap of fabric and was pushing it about with his horns, still bellowing but no longer paying any attention to the two men.

"Go," she told Ruthann. "See to him."

Ruthann felt as if her feet were stuck to the barn floor, but with an effort, she began to move and then, hearing Joshua's agonized voice, started to run. Newton had his shirt off, she saw, and had twisted it into a rope-like shape that he was binding around Joshua's leg. She saw blood, lots of blood, on the straw inside the pen and on the floor where her husband was writhing in pain, his upper lip biting down on the lower one. Holding the shirt, Newton straddled Joshua in an attempt to keep him still.

"Need a stick," Newton said grimly. "Strong stick."

Ruthann found a short handle that had broken off a shovel. She handed it to Newton, who quickly thrust it under the knot on the improvised rope and twisted it tight. She dropped to her knees by Joshua's head and lifted it off the floor, resting it on her petticoat, stroking his forehead and squeezing one of his hands every time his moans were punctuated with loud cries of pain. When Rose joined the trio, she looked to Newton for direction. Her stomach churned at the sight of Joshua's blood, and she willed it to behave. She had seen how the blood was pulsing out, but Newton's shirt had stopped that. She knew that was good, but she had no idea what came next.

"Can you ride?" Newton asked anxiously, glancing up at her.

"Yes."

"Then head for the Warner place, send Hiram here and ride on to the train station where you can send a telegram to Eastborough. Send it to Henry. He'll get the message to Seth."

Before she could answer, the bull charged the fence near them, his horns clanging against the metal.

"What about him?" Rose asked, her voice filled with fear.

"Not now, my love. It's just Joshua now."

Rose turned to go, ready to saddle one of the horses and be on her way. As she moved off, Lord Coopersmith pawed the ground and followed her along the rail. She shivered and walked faster, afraid that if she ran, he would go on another rampage. No one needed that.

"He should have a blanket," Ruthann told Newton. She was emerging from the shock of what had happened and was struggling to think and be calm. "And you have to loosen that shirt every now and then or he'll lose his leg." Her voice broke on the last three words, and she looked down at Joshua, who seemed to be calming down.

"Horse blanket," Newton said with a nod. "Then keep him awake," Newton said still astride his friend. "Eyes open. Talk to him."

Ruthann snagged a thick blanket from a nearby hook, covered Joshua's upper body and began to talk, telling Joshua she was going to cut beans with Rose that afternoon, that Rose had told the children a grand story, that John and Adelaide had been playing tag between the sheets on the clothesline. Oh, John and Adelaide, she thought – what about them? They were supposed to sit on the steps and wait, but would they?

"Newton, the children."

"Rose will check as she leaves," Newton replied as calmly as if he were buttoning a shirt, not making one into a tourniquet. "But if they appear here, you'll have to leave Joshua and see to them."

"No sleeping, Joshua," Ruthann said in her calmest teacher voice. "No sleeping on the barn floor. It just isn't done, and we are always so proper that you must not do it now."

Joshua's mouth twitched in a near smile before he cried out in a new spasm of pain. His fingers wrapped around hers, and he squeezed so hard that she wondered if her hand would ever be normally shaped again.

"No cat-napping either," she said. "You seem unable to speak, so I will take this opportunity to talk endlessly, and you will have to listen because Newton is sitting on you."

Newton remembered how the animal doctor had loosened the tight band on the horse's leg every now and then, back when he was eight or nine years old, and the cut on the animal's leg had sent blood out in spurts. The doc said the leg would die without a little blood. He knew Ruthann was right about that. So he loosened his grip on the stick slightly and thought about Rose, whose stomach had been upside down only a few hours earlier. He shook his head in wonder. These two women were amazing. They had to know, he thought, that Joshua was in danger of bleeding to death, and their voices were as even as if they were explaining long division to Peter Granger. Ruthann was even being a little comical. He tightened his grip again and hoped that Rose would ride well and that the journey would not harm the sliver. He wished he knew of something he ought to do besides what he was doing, but he didn't. He remembered that, without knowing much, he had saved Rose's life. Could he be lucky twice? Should he have put the bullet in Lord Coopersmith's brain instead of the rafter? Was Rose almost to Warner's place?

A few minutes after he had that thought Rose galloped into Hiram Warner's yard, gave a couple of breathless hoo-hoos, dismounted and as Mr. Warner came out of the barn, vomited on the ground beside the sweating horse. He grabbed her by the shoulders and held her as she retched again.

She straightened and choked out, "Bull, Joshua, bleeding."

"I'll go," he said quickly. "But you need a glass of water."

"I'll be all right," Rose said. But he saw how pale her face was, so he guided her to the steps and made her sit down. He threw the horse reins over the post and hurried to the kitchen for a tumbler of water. When he returned, he saw that her color was better, and she quickly explained the situation to him.

"I will be better in a short time," she said, "and I'll ride back when the horse has cooled down."

"He will need to go to the hospital," Mr. Warner said. "Shall I take the wagon?"

"No. Go quickly. He could die. Newton was trying to work out a way to get him into the wagon, but they were still in the barn when I left."

Running toward the barn door, Mr. Warner called back, "Is the bull loose?"

"No," Rose said. Then she leaned back against the porch railing post and closed her eyes. She was still in that position when Mr. Warner emerged from the barn, and he dismounted quickly to make sure she was conscious. When she felt his hand on her forehead, she mumbled, "Expecting. That's all."

He sighed his relief, gripped her shoulder, remounted and galloped toward the road. Rose closed her eyes again and in a rare moment mouthed a silent prayer, even as she wondered where it might go. She had never thought God would have time to listen to the Rev. Lockhead's long, fiery prayers, especially if the world had hundreds of Reverend Lockheads in it. But maybe, just maybe, a short prayer for Joshua. Then she closed her eyes again and, with her hands on her belly, let the sun warm her face. After a few minutes, she sat up straight, finished the water in the tumbler and stood, ready to water the horse and head for home.

Still numb from the scene at the Chittenden barn, she was moving along on the road when she remembered she was supposed to send a telegram to Henry. She took a turn on a road she was certain led to town and noticed a plume of smoke from a train not too far off. She put the horse into a gentle canter and was soon at the railroad station where she quickly found the telegraph operator. She was already at his window when she realized she had no money. She would have to impose on his good will, she reckoned, if he would believe her.

"Good morning," she said to the gray-haired man at the window. "I need to send an emergency telegram."

"The message?" he asked without expression.

"Joshua gored. Tell Seth. Wagon on way."

"Ye gods," the operator cried. "That is dreadful. Where do I send?"

"Henry Goodwin, Eastborough."

His fingers quickly clicked out the message and sent it, his expression shocked. He's forgotten I have to pay, and the message is already on its way, Rose realized. She wondered what he would do.

"Ten cents a word," he said, peering at her over his glasses. "Why, child alive, is that blood on your skirt?" He paused, took another look and said, "Or is that your petticoat?"

"My skirt, sir, distracted the bull while my husband pulled Joshua out of the pen."

"No charge, madam," the operator said, instantly admiring the fortitude of this young woman. "No charge. Is it your husband?"

"No," Rose said. "It's Joshua, Joshua Chittenden," and turned her back to leave. As she mounted her horse again, the telegraph operator ran to her and said, "Can I help?"

"Mr. Hiram Warner is on his way there," she answered. "I must hurry back now."

"Godspeed, young lady, godspeed." The kindness that now shone in his face brought tears to Rose's eyes, and she could only nod to him. He patted her arm with one hand and the horse's neck with the other, and she clicked her tongue so the horse would set out. Behind her the operator shook his head in wonderment. Ethel would never believe his latest customer had arrived wearing a bloody petticoat. He wondered who her husband was.

Now I can go home, she was thinking. But it made her shiver to think what she might find there. As she rode off, the telegraph operator hurried back into the station and sat down at his place. "Dear God," he muttered to himself, "ain't that the Chittendens who lost a baby around planting time? Or maybe even more recently." A few taps later, Caleb Hall had sent emergency messages to every train stop anywhere near the route they'd use to get Joshua Chittenden to Eastborough. On foot and on horseback, they'd turn out, he knew, with water for the horses and wagon driver and whatever else they could do. He hoped some would see to the missus, who must be nearly beside herself. "We're on our own out here, but sometimes that plain ain't enough," he thought.

On the narrow dirt road that would take her back to the Chittenden farm, Rose pulled up on the reins and checked the horse's breathing. Hearing no rasping and seeing no foam around the bit, she started again, holding Mollie to a walk. But the mare was having none of that. She soon tossed her head and broke into a canter, apparently anxious to get back where she belonged. Rose let her go.

CHAPTER THIRTY-THREE
The Neighbors Gather

By the time Mollie reached the Chittenden place, Rose was exhausted. It wasn't just the long ride. Her always busy mind had been running on so many tracks at once that she felt as if the world were upside down. Well, it is, she told herself, thinking about Newton's face as he held his bloody shirt in place with a stick, Joshua's agonized screams and attempts to stifle them, Ruthann having to leave to see to John and Adelaide – and tell them everything was fine? She had thoroughly jostled her tiny baby and anxiously waited to see if it would kick, if it could still kick. It was only a few hours since she'd worried only about retching at the stove and getting the yellow beans picked. Her head drooped as Mollie made her way toward the hitching post near the back door.

"Rose!" someone shouted, and she looked up to find that several strangers were running toward her, helping her down from the horse. Her legs buckled, but strong hands kept her from falling and led her inside. A tall thin woman immediately put a quilt over her, and even at this moment, Rose felt her face flush. She was in front of all these people in her petticoat.

"What, where ..." she began, her voice hoarse. Then someone thrust a tumbler of icy water into her hand and helped her get it to her lips. "Your Mr. Hall sent out the word," a young woman said, "and of course we came."

"Newton? Joshua?" Rose asked, trying to catch her breath and wondering if she knew anyone named Hall.

"Ruthann left in our wagon as soon as we arrived," said the woman who had given her the water. "John and Adelaide are down by the brook with my Jacob, who is teaching them to fish."

"Fiddling while Rome burns," Rose thought. But then she smiled. John and Adelaide needed to be off somewhere, not here where the foul smell of fear was in the air, despite the kind expressions on these faces. "And who is Mr. Hall?"

"Telegraph operator," a man said gruffly. "Sent the word to all the nearby train stations."

"And the church bells rang," Rose said softly, remembering Newton telling her about the boys sending out the alarm when she was freezing to death in the cemetery all those years ago. It was a signal not only for church, but for jubilation and disaster.

"Indeed," he said. "Perhaps I should tell you about it now? If you are feeling a little stronger?"

"Please," Rose said, leaning her head against the chair back and closing her eyes.

"She's not ready," one of the women protested.

"I am, I am," Rose said weakly, thinking she really should change her clothes. "Will he live?"

The air seemed to leave the room for a second and then the man went on, "It appears he has a good chance, Rose. Your friend Mr. Warner and Newton made it as comfortable as possible for Joshua and then Newton and Mr. Warner's friend

373

left for Dr. Potter's. As soon as some of us arrived here, Ruthann followed in a buggy. Newton saved Joshua's life by binding the leg to control the bleeding, and we all pray the doctor can take care of the wound."

"Mr. Warner's friend?" Rose asked, her face puzzled.

"Some neighbor of his that he stopped for on his way here."

"So Hiram Warner is still here?"

"Indeed," the man said hesitantly. As he spoke, everyone in the room jumped as a shot rang out from the direction of the barn. It was quickly followed by a second.

"What is that?" Rose cried. "What is that?"

The man who had been explaining things to her was halfway out the door as she spoke. His wife put a hand on Rose's shoulder and whispered, "Hiram's seeing to the bull."

"Shooting him?" Rose nearly screamed the words, then heard her voice and said more quietly, "Did he kill Lord Coopersmith?"

"You can't keep a bull that's smelled blood, Mrs. Barnes. It's not safe."

Rose heaved a sigh and hoped the salty feeling in her eyes didn't mean she was going to cry. She knew a farmer couldn't keep a bull that went wild, but she also knew how Joshua treasured that magnificent animal. She stood and went to the window, just as Hiram Walker emerged from the barn. His usually brown and smiling face looked pale and grim, and his strong shoulders seemed to sag. She watched as he fetched two buckets of water from the trough near the well and went back to the barn. Behind her, she was conscious of a murmur of voices but could not make out what they were saying. Then one of the women approached and said, "Ruthann said to."

"Ruthann?" Rose asked.

"She said the bull must go," the woman said, her voice shaking a little. "She said it more than once."

"I understand," Rose answered, her voice even shakier than the woman's. "But Lord Coopersmith was the pride of the farm, so I must mourn him." The woman nodded and went back to her chair at the table. And a primary source of whatever cash the Chittendens kept in their sugar bowl, she thought. Neighbors had brought their heifers here and paid Joshua for breeding with a distinguished Jersey bull. A tear ran unchecked down her cheek. Who would tell Joshua, she wondered, thinking they should tell him nothing until he was out of danger himself. She turned back to the room and asked, "And the heifer? What about the heifer?" In her mind's eye she could see the young animal cowering in a corner of the bull pen. She knew that had to be why Joshua was there – he had brought in a heifer for breeding. She snuffled a little and turned back to the women. "Would they be there yet?" she asked.

"I don't have a timepiece, but I reckon so," one of the women said. "They left at a pretty decent pace." Then Charles will come soon, Rose told herself, suddenly realizing that she longed for one of her own, despite the kindness of these strangers. Certainly she should not let them be strangers any longer – she moved toward them, her hand out, and asked them to introduce themselves.

"She didn't take the children," Rose said quietly, wondering what those two observant little people had been told. She didn't take them because she's afraid Joshua is going to die, Rose thought, realizing she knew more than she had ever known why adults insisted on "holding up." It was not the day, nor the hour, to collapse, weeping and wailing and carrying on. She nodded to herself and asked, "Shall I see about something to eat?"

That stirred the three women in the room into action. Two of them bustled off to the kitchen, and the third insisted Rose go upstairs and change her clothes. When she reappeared in the kitchen, she found one of the women had snatched up a loaf of bread, still warm, before she left her house, and another had pulled a pot of beans out of her oven and put them into Ruthann's. Rose could hardly believe that the makings of a belated noon meal were already under way.

As she took down plates from the cupboard, she saw that the men had hitched up Joshua's oxen. They'd have their work cut out for them, she knew, when they were called upon to drag the carcass to a grave that was probably being dug even now. Another tear dropped, and she wiped it off the table with her sleeve. Hold up, she said, hold up.

An hour later the women saw their men washing up at the outside trough. They might not want to talk now, but they'd need to eat, and the wives started to put the hot food on the table. One of them had run across to Newton and Rose's house to get the yellow beans she had picked that morning. They had cut them, cooked them and now a generous slab of butter was melting into the bowl. When that offering went to the table, Rose turned away and let tears run down her face. So much for a pleasant afternoon sharing the bean-cutting.

CHAPTER THIRTY-FOUR
Sticks for Walking

Rose was reading a story to John and Adelaide, paying no more attention than necessary to the words. Her mind was on Joshua and Ruthann, making their way home from the hospital, and as John turned each page, she looked out the window to the road where she hoped they were coming into view. But the road was empty. Newton was in the barn, seeing to the Chittendens' cows and chickens. Rose had brought over a cold supper for Ruthann and Joshua and would make some hot tea for them as soon as they arrived. And she was prepared to get the children into the kitchen, out of the way, as soon as the buggy appeared.

Newton would have to help Joshua into the house, and she didn't want John and Adelaide to see their father until he was comfortably settled in a chair. She was prepared to explain his bandaged leg, but she didn't want them to see him struggle with the walking. Tears sprang into her eyes along with clear pictures, one after another, of John playing hide-and-seek with the children, striding off to the barn, trotting back to the field after the noon meal. She wiped her eyes quickly and turned back to the alphabet book. "G," she said as clearly as she could manage and paused.

"For Goose," John piped up.

"For Goosey, Goosey Grandma," Adelaide said.

"Not Grandma, Addie," John said, a little scornfully. "It's the boy goose, it's not Grandma."

"And?" Rose said, looking sternly at him.

"Gander," he said.

"Gander," Adelaide echoed.

"Silly geese you are," Rose said. And they all began to laugh, interrupted when John shouted, "They're here"and jumped off the couch so fast that he stumbled to his knees. He stood quickly and ran to the door. "They're here!"

So much for my plans, Rose thought. Grandma Jane would say, "The best laid plans ..." Scottish wasn't it? Robert Burns. Oh, drat, her inner voice went on. How can your bumptious brain be wandering off at a time like this. She quickly moved past John and put her hand against the door. His small one was on the latch, and he looked up at her in protest when he found he could not open it.

"We'll watch from here," Rose said gently. "Your father has a wound on his leg and we should let him come in before we greet him."

"What's a wound?" John wanted to know.

"He hurt his leg, John. A wound is when your skin is damaged in an accident, like when you cut your finger and we had to bandage it."

"Oh. Can I see it?"

"We'll see."

"That always means 'no,'" the little boy said, shaking his head. "Always." But he took his hand off the latch and went to the window where Adelaide was holding the sill and jumping up and down, trying to see better.

Outside, Joshua was standing in the wagon, with Ruthann's hand on his shoulder. Newton had heard the wheels crunch on the driveway and was racing toward the wagon, shouting, "Hold on there. Wait for me."

Joshua leaned heavily on his crutches, and he took a step forward toward Newton. He looked very pale and weak, Rose thought, and she wondered if he could even make it up the path to the house.

"Stay right here and see to Adelaide," Rose said suddenly. "Do not come outside, John, do you understand?"

"Yes, ma'am," he answered, startled by her severe tone.

Rose grabbed a straight-backed dining room chair and ran out to meet the trio, thinking Joshua would need to sit and rest as soon as he stepped down from the wagon. She saw Newton nod his approval as she plunked the chair down by the wagon step.

"Put it right behind me, Rose," he said. "And hold onto it. When he comes down, I may sit right on it myself." She did as she was asked, trying to steady her shaking hands.

"And push toward me, Rose. I don't want that chair to hit the sliver."

She took a step back and leaned into the chair with her shoulders, hoping she was strong enough to catch not one but two men. Newton told Joshua he was ready, that it was time to move.

"No, no, Newton," Ruthann said. "First, he needs to sit on the wagon floor. That will help distribute the weight when he moves."

"Indeed," Newton said. Gritting his teeth, Joshua slowly lowered himself onto the wagon floor, keeping one leg stiffly raised in front of him. Tears spilling onto her face, Ruthann kissed the top of his head and whispered something that brought a tiny smile to his face.

"Ready, Rose?" Newton asked.

"Ready."

Newton reached up, carefully staying away from the injured leg, grabbed Joshua under the arms and pulled him forward. Newton's full weight hit the chair, but Rose held fast, Joshua had his crutches at the ready, and suddenly he was on the ground, standing between Newton's outstretched legs. In unison, the four exhaled so loudly that Newton couldn't help chuckling. But he wasted no time getting out of the chair. Before he could speak, Rose had moved the seat so Newton could turn the injured man and set him on it.

Joshua looked up at them and forced a grin. "You are a remarkable group," he said.

"Welcome home," Ruthann answered.

"You get the remarkable prize, Joshua," Newton commented. "The doctors wrote you off quite some time ago, but you paid them no mind."

"I am ready to start the journey to the door," Joshua said. "But I reckon I'll be needing that trusty chair along the way."

"Rest another minute while I greet the children," Ruthann said. "Rose must have tethered them to a table leg in there."

"Just threatened," Rose said. "But they are near to bursting."

380

Ruthann ran up the path, opened the door and was nearly bowled over when both children attacked her. She hugged them close, whispered that they needed to watch from the window and came running back to the wagon, as Rose ran into the house.

As she approached, Joshua stood, adjusted his crutches and started to swing slowly along the path. He went about 10 feet and called for the chair. "Could've made this path level if I'd thought about it," he said, breathing hard.

"Or downhill," Newton said, the tense lines on his face easing a little. "On your feet, sir," he said. "Or your sticks, I reckon I should say."

Joshua looked up at Newton and tried to smile. "Reckon I'm a little winded from lying down in a wagon."

Newton grinned. "Reckon you are. Also reckon Rose is setting right on those young-uns of yours to keep 'em from knocking the rest of the wind out of you. Now, let's get on with this traveling."

Joshua took a deep breath, adjusted his crutches and, with Newton's hand on his elbow, hoisted himself upright again. "Going to make it to the steps," he said, "but you'd better drag that chair with your other hand."

They were an odd pair, there on the walk, Rose thought as she watched from the window. Newton so brown and strong and Joshua, once brown and strong, now pale and so thin. She felt tears start to poke their way into her eyes again, and she shook her head hard. Ruthann was outside again, right behind Joshua, ready to catch him if he stumbled. She wasn't crying. This, it occurred to her, once again, was when all that "holding up" mattered. Her relatives had nattered on and on about it when Sarah died. What really mattered, she decided, was holding up, not when people were dead, but when they were alive and in need. She would not cry. She tightened her hold on John's shoulder and, when he looked up, gave him a small smile. He moved a little closer and on her other side, Adelaide leaned forward to peek at him.

"What are those sticks for?" the little girl wanted to know.

"They help Father stand," John answered solemnly.

Newton and Joshua came through the door, and once again Rose had a straight chair ready, bracing herself so that when Joshua nearly fell into it, she kept her balance. She saw Newton's worried glance and then saw his face relax. He reached out to squeeze her arm, and the warmth of his touch steadied her. She looked out the window at the green meadows, the pink phlox growing near the porch steps, the bright, calm day. We can do this, she thought. We will do it.

Newton's voice interrupted her train of thought. "Ready?" he asked.

"Ready," Joshua said.

"Ready," Ruthann said.

"Ready," Rose said. "Ready for anything."

"And anything is what you might get," Joshua said, almost managing a smile. "Right now, just get me to that sofa."

So they did, propping up his leg with pillows on a footstool. The children immediately pulled up their small stools and fixed their eyes on the heavily bandaged leg. Ruthann managed her most reassuring voice as she explained that the bull had hurt their father, but he would be on his feet as soon as the wound was healed. She reminded them of cuts and bruises they had suffered and how she had bandaged them and made them rest.

John nodded solemnly, and Rose knew he was much too aware that this was not a skinned knee. He'd never been sent off lying in a wagon. But he said nothing. Adelaide was too young for big worries. She leaned forward to look closely at the leg and then looked up at her father and asked, "Me see? Adelaide see ouch?"

"Another day, Adelaide," Ruthann said. "Your father needs to rest now."

Hiram Walker appeared on the porch then, tapped on the window glass and came in to shake Joshua's hand. Joshua's voice was weak with fatigue as he thanked this new friend. "You'd do the same for me," came the answer. And then Hiram Walker allowed himself to grin as he added, "but I'm going to try like hell not to create the need."

"Had to put Lord Coopersmith to rest, I understand," Joshua said.

"No real choice, neighbor. And Ruthann here gave the final word."

"No choice at all," Joshua said. "No choice at all. We'd be pleased for you to stay out of trouble, but we owe you."

CHAPTER THIRTY-FIVE
Hanging a Shingle

Hours later, Rose sat in her parlor with John and Adelaide snuggled against her. She hardly needed the warmth of their very warm bodies, but she didn't move. In a near drone, she was telling yet another story and hoping they would give in to a nap. They were tuckered out from weeding her garden – which involved John efficiently uprooting what he called the "bad boys," and Adelaide failing to see the difference between a carrot and a pig weed. Their father's homecoming had been almost too much for them, so she'd brought them to her house and would keep them overnight.

Seconds later, she realized their breathing had slowed and they had both fallen asleep. Fortunately, each had slumped away from her, so she carefully inched to the edge of the sofa and stood, smoothing her skirt, and tiptoed off to the kitchen. She quickly put together a cold supper of Dutch cheese, egg salad and floating island pudding and then poked up the fire so she could make hot biscuits. She divided everything in two, popped half the biscuits into the oven and put together a basket to take to Ruthann. She had a feeling Newton would be eating there as well, but she didn't think Joshua was up to any more commotion today, even from his children.

Children, she thought. She hadn't considered the sliver for hours. She rubbed her belly and wondered when the tiny thing would stretch its muscles and give her a kick. She'd get a kick out of that, wouldn't she? That made a smile sweep across her face, and it felt so strange that she realized she had not stretched her lip muscles much in that direction of late. Remembering her wild ride to get help for Newton and Joshua, she decided the sliver must already have a strong constitution. And she'd even managed to tell a near stranger about her condition. Newton was right. She was a forward girl, likely too outspoken for her own good.

Lemonade. She had lemonade in the ice box. She poured some into two small glasses and took them to the parlor. "Time to go visiting," she announced softly, noticing that John was already awake. But he did not move. His little sister was sound asleep and had toppled over onto his leg.

"I'm not asleep, but my leg is," he whispered. "Can I move it?"

"May I," Rose responded automatically.

"May I?"

"Yes, you may," she answered, and they grinned at each other. "But gently." With great care, John inched his leg to one side, and after a minute Adelaide opened her eyes and sat up abruptly, her face bewildered. "At Auntie Rose's, Addie," John said, instantly knowing why her face was about to dissolve into crying. He was just in time, and Adelaide took a long look around her before reaching her arms to be picked up. Thinking about the little mite growing inside her, Rose reached out and took the little girl's hands, pulling her off the sofa.

"We are taking supper to your father and mother," Rose announced, "soon as the biscuits are ready. And we'll get your nightshirts so you can sleep here tonight while your father gets better."

John was up quickly, anxious to be off. He trotted to the kitchen, carefully opened the oven door and cried, "They're done, they're done!"

"Have biscuit," Adelaide said decidedly, as she peeked under his arm to see the puffed up biscuits.

"Later," Rose said. "These are for your parents." She added the hot biscuits to the supper basket and the three set off, Rose wishing with all her heart and mind that this day would end soon, and she could crawl into bed beside Newton and sleep until the sun was ready for a new day. Still, she wasn't surprised when he whispered that he'd be staying overnight, and he hoped she'd put enough food in that basket for him, too. He reported that Joshua had slept most of the afternoon but was now ready for supper, another of Dr. Potter's pain pills and a night's sleep, if it was to be had.

Within minutes, Rose and the children were back at the Barnes house. A wisp of steam popped out as Rose opened each of the second batch of biscuits and dabbed on a bit of butter. She let the children pour a little honey over the melting butter and then sighed with pleasure as she tasted her biscuit. Supper over, she scrubbed their faces and hands and even their feet, which were dirty from the gardening. Then she put them into her big bed, heard their prayers and managed not to laugh when

Adelaide recited, "If I die before I bake." Perhaps there was some virtue in that thought – at least it would eliminate one chore. She went to the spare room, tugged a coverlet out of the drawer, put on her nightdress and lay down on the bare mattress, too tired to think about sheets. What would Sarah think about this, she wondered, instantly remembering her mother 's advice about imagining a clear blue sky instead of counting sheep. Could she keep the clouds out? Before she could think another thought, sleep latched onto her brain and didn't let go until she heard a small voice at her bedside.

It was John, wanting to see his mother and father. Once again, as soon as the children were washed, dressed and fed, they set off for the Chittenden house with a loaf of oatmeal bread and three hard-boiled eggs in Rose's basket. As they walked, she heard voices and pounding and could see three men working away at the end of Ruthann and Joshua's driveway. What on earth? She did hope nothing was broken. Aunt Nell believed things, both good and bad, came in threes, and she was of a mind to believe that, too. But Ruthann and Joshua had had enough, hadn't they? And then someone was running toward her, flying toward her -- this was certainly not bad news. This was Abigail, and the men were Father and Uncle Jason and, it looked like, Mr. Goodnow. Henry. He wanted her to call him Henry, she remembered, as she held out her arms for Abby.

"Hug Addie," came a small voice after Rose and Abby had hung onto each other for what the little girl thought was entirely long enough. Abby scooped her up with one hand, took John's with the other and smiled at Rose. "Need help?" she asked.

"Heavens, yes," Rose said. But her heart was the lightest it had been in several days. "First tell me what they're digging up."

387

"Not digging up, digging down" Abigail said with a giggle. "It's Joshua's new sign. He told them when he was first hurt that if he ever got back here, he'd be hanging out his shingle. It turned out that meant he was going to be a lawyer again, if he lived to see the day. And he did," she finished, her smile gone and a little hoarseness creeping into her voice.

"Oh, Abby, what they've been through," Rose said, putting her hand on Abby's arm. "Hanging out his shingle. Well, I'll be …" She paused, thinking about all those phrases men were allowed to use. "I'll be the reverend's daughter." Then they both laughed and were still laughing when they reached the house and found Ruthann and Joshua on the porch watching the shingle go up. Rose saw the skin under Joshua's eyes, dark as Concord grapes in October, but she also noticed that his fingers were relaxed on the arm of the wicker love seat. Ruthann moved toward Joshua, leaving room for John and Adelaide on her other side, but Adelaide instantly clambered onto her lap and reached toward Joshua.

"One moment there," Ruthann said, holding her back. "New rule: Anytime you are near your father, you must not make his leg move. It has to be stiller than you are in church, much stiller. And no forgetting. It will hurt him if you forget." Even for Adelaide, likely to wriggle like an unearthed earthworm, this seemed dire. She leaned back on her mother and stared at her father's inert and bandaged leg.

"Pants broke," she said, making Joshua chuckle and explain, "They had to cut the cloth off, Addie, so they could change the bandage easily. One day I'll have long pants on both legs again." She nodded solemnly and turned her attention to the men lowering a fencepost into the ground. She squirmed off and said,

"Addie dig. Addie see." And she was off down the driveway where the three men straightened up to show her the hole.

"The world stops for Addie," Ruthann said. "And I haven't even said good morning nor thanked you for our lovely supper."

"What did you have?" came a voice from just inside the house, and Rose was astonished to see Charles opening the screened door. She tried to give him a hug, but he kept both arms hanging down, so it was more like putting arms around a fence post than a person. "What are you doing here?" she asked, backing off and hoping she hadn't embarrassed him.

"As usual, I am delegated to keep people's spirits above water," he said, "and I spent the journey working out how to do that."

"Somehow you are not involved in digging a hole," Rose said. But she could not help but smile at his clowning. It seemed possible Charles could make a stone chuckle. And she had to admit, he'd pulled her out of the doldrums many times, almost as many as the times he had been a real pest. "Dutch cheese, egg salad, biscuits and floating island," she added. Mock dismay crossed Charles's face, instantly gone when Ruthann pointed toward the kitchen and said she thought a tad of pudding was left. He went back into the house right away, and Rose started to ask Ruthann what she needed done. But she was interrupted by the approach of the hole diggers.

"The law office is open, Joshua," Silas Hibbard announced. "If I were a drinking man, I'd order a tot for everyone." Despite his constant pain, Joshua laughed. "Reckon all I require now is a few clients," he said. "Hope some folks out there are desperate enough to travel a good way to get my help."

"They'll come," Jason said. "What you need to do, if you have the strength, is tell us where you want the shelves for your law books. Better take advantage of all this talented help while you have it handy."

"We talked about it in the middle of the night when we couldn't sleep," Ruthann said. "Rose, please stay with Joshua while I get our rough sketches and show the way." With a bowl of pudding in one hand and a spoon in the other, Charles reappeared, and Silas pointed a calloused finger at his son.

"Don't want to question your ideas, Ruthann, but Charles is the fellow with drawings and an eye for how to put a place together. Better hire him now that he's gained a little strength from the pudding," Silas said. Ruthann couldn't decide who looked more astonished, Rose or Charles, but she just smiled and nodded and beckoned Jason and Charles to follow her.

She and Joshua had decided to turn her small sewing room into his law office. She had already dragged out the boxes of law books, and Charles took note of how handsome the volumes were. "Work table here," he said, "his back to the window. He'll get full advantage of natural light that way, and he isn't supposed to be looking at the meadow." Despite her fatigue, Ruthann started to smile. "Shelves here behind him, reachable – plank thickness – the books are heavy. He'll need a chair with wheels. Couple of chairs for clients in front of desk. Light from the window on their faces, showing up guilt or innocence. No carpet. Curtains for window if the sun is ever too bright, with space to pull them all the way back. Winter is gloomy. Table sizeable enough for work space plus a stack of shelves for current cases and other documents. Table should be elegant, nicely finished. Gives client confidence. For today, a couple of sawhorses and wide boards will do until Uncle Jason can fashion the right thing. Cherry or oak," he finished, glancing at Jason.

Ruthann felt as if her mouth were hanging open or should be. "Yes, Charles," was all she could manage. She glanced at Jason and saw that his grin was literally ear to ear, all his teeth showing. Jason reached out to shake hands with Charles and said, "If that's approval, Ruthann, we'll get at it." She nodded, still stunned by Charles' performance. Jason hustled out of the house to talk with Henry Goodnow and his brother-in-law. As Jason roughed out the plan, Joshua shifted in his chair, grimaced and then, worried that his frown of pain might be construed as disapproval, nodded his head.

"Going to be an architect, your boy is, Silas," Jason said when he had finished detailing the plan for Joshua's office. "Didn't even need a pencil or a rule. Just rattled it off, and it's all just right."

"You never know, Jason, you just never know," Silas answered. "Must have been some value to spend cash money on those old alphabet blocks for him. Not to mention pencils and paper. Sarah insisted on pencils and paper. I nearly wore out my good jack knife sharpening and resharpening that army of pencils. Reckon he was putting them to use." He glanced toward the kitchen and allowed as how they could gather up some materials but would have to accommodate the womenfolk by having the noon meal a bit before noon. "Been busy in there," he said, "for some time, and the smells are making my stomach rumble."

"Aromas," Newton Barnes said, coming up to the group. He'd been doing barn chores at both houses since early morning and had no idea what this bunch was up to. One look told him it wasn't an emergency involving Joshua, who set as still as a cat at a mouse hole but otherwise seemed to be coming along.

Jason pointed to the roadside where a sizable sign swung gently in the hot breeze. Carefully whittled letters spelled out Joshua Chittenden, Attorney at Law on a highly polished cherry board. "Ain't that somethin'?" Newton said, "and beautiful, too."

"Isn't," Rose commented, coming out from the kitchen. He grinned at her and shook his head. "Teacher, teacher," he said.

"Your belly must be growling, too," Jason said. "Give us a hand with boards and nails for Joshua's office, then we'll set down to eat, and we'll still have time to fix up the new office before we head home."

All these taskmasters in one room, Rose thought, and not an argument from a one of them. Joshua's disaster had created something so special among these men – and for Charles as well – that she felt the tears welling up. She turned quickly hoping to find refuge in the kitchen but heard heavy footsteps coming behind her. She wondered if she could make it to the pantry and then Newton's arms were spinning her around, pulling her tight. She buried her face on his work shirt shoulder and sobbed. One of his hands smoothed her back while the other held her close. Rose tried to stop, nearly choking with the effort, and Newton muttered, "Better let it out. It's bad for the sliver to keep that kind of stuff inside." She didn't even notice that the kitchen door had opened, but Newton quickly shook his head and glowered at Charles. Uncharacteristically, Charles backed off with alacrity.

Rose's sobs began to subside, and she raised her head to look at Newton. "For better or for worse," she said haltingly.

"We've had a goodly share of better, Rose. And you have been better than best today. You're plumb wore out, that's all.

My mother said a good cry gets rid of a flood of salt water. She'd say you need a tumbler of sweet water now or your face will dry up."

Rose began to laugh, and Newton loosened his grip on her. "Able to stand on your own now?" he asked.

"Yes. But you're a satisfactory thing to lean on when a body needs such," she answered.

"Thing? Thing? I am not a thing, Miss Teacher."

That really made her laugh, and he stepped back, holding her forearms as if he still thought she might keel over. But she was steady and a bit disheveled. "Better get some cold water on the outside, too," he said."Your eyes are swelled near shut."

Rose hurried to the sink and splashed water over her face, then took a tumbler from the cupboard and filled it with the cool well water that supplied Ruthann and Joshua's house. She drank, sighed and said, "I don't know what came over me." Newton just smiled and went to open the door that led to the dining room so people would feel free to enter the kitchen again.

CHAPTER THIRTY-SIX
Life is Short

Exhausted, Joshua and Ruthann slept through all the hammering and sawing, and in a couple of hours, Jason and Henry Goodnow announced that it was about time for them to head home to finish up their chores in Eastborough. The shelves were up and shellacked, the makeshift desk was in place, Charles had stacked Joshua's law books in a corner, and shavings and sawdust had been swept away. Rose had spread a blanket under the maple tree in the Chittendens' yard, and the children were asleep between her and Abby. They had protested mightily when asked to lie down, but Abby had stretched out and started telling stories about the clouds that were drifting overhead. To Rose's surprise, her little sister's voice was dull, her speech slow. And then she saw that the children were losing the struggle to stay awake. They dozed off, but Abby didn't stir. She watched the sky, lowered her voice and talked more and more slowly until her words were far apart and down to a whisper. Rose's own eyelids felt as if a heavy cloth had been placed over them, and she, too, fell into a light sleep, still aware of bees buzzing and the occasional whistle of a bobwhite.

Abby looked at the three, smiled and closed her eyes. An hour or more later, Newton found them and asked very softly if anyone wanted a drink of lemonade. Four pairs of eyes snapped open, with John and Adelaide shouting "Yes, sirree, sir!" in such perfect unison that Newton wondered if children practiced things like this. He grinned and offered a hand to each.

"You ladies will have to scramble yourselves up," he said. "I'd be afraid your delicate arms might not stand the strain."

"Delicate, indeed," Rose said, her voice a little grumpy and her mind on armloads of wood carried and hay pitched into the mow. She stretched her strong arms over her head and instantly put them down again to stop the intense ache that had run from her wrists to her shoulders. For a minute she couldn't think, but then it came back to her. The horse ride. Her gallop to Hiram Warner's with the reins held so tensely it was a wonder the horse didn't rebel. She tried to smile at Newton, and he grinned back.

"Never a good idea to wake you quickly," he said softly. "Hope the sliver doesn't inherit that."

Rose scowled at him, then gave a little laugh and started toward the house. Adelaide ran after her and tucked her hand into Rose's. Watching them, Newton was astonished to realize he was tearing up. He turned away from Abby quickly and dragged his sleeve across his face, hoping it would appear that he was wiping sweat off his forehead. Behind him, Abby nodded to herself. She suddenly had a feeling that her sister was going to have a baby. Why else would a man like Newton get all weepy over Rose and Adelaide? She hoped with all her heart that she was right and also that maybe, just once, she knew something before Charles did. Or maybe anyone. Well, except for Ruthann, who always knew everything. With a tiny smile on her face, she started toward the house with John and saw that her father was gesturing for her to come to him.

He had already hollered to Charles, and the two looked questioningly at him. "Reckon extra hands would be welcome here for a day or two," he said, "so you two will be staying on with your sister and doing whatever is needed. Soon's we're loaded, we'll be on our way to Eastborough."

Minutes later, the wagon rolled down the Chittenden driveway and onto the road, quickly lost in the cloud of dust that boiled up behind the wheels. Abby watched them go and sighed. She rather liked working for Mrs. Munson, and she realized she was going to miss her days there – and the pay.

"Out from under the iron thumb," Charles said with a trace of excitement. "Our chance to be on the outside."

"Working hard," Abby said. "I'm going to find out right now what can be done for Rose or Ruthann. I am an experienced household employee."

Charles hooted. "And I am a breeder of Jersey cows. You should probably start with all those dishes in the kitchen. I'll be taking a look in the barn to see what needs to be done." And he stalked off.

Abby sighed again. She couldn't ask him about Rose because he'd pretend he knew, and she was just positive he could not know. She decided to find Rose and ask her. And she'd go by way of the kitchen because all those people had made stacks of dirty dishes.

In the wagon, Silas muttered something that neither of the others could quite get. What's that?" Jason asked. And Silas said, a trifle louder, "Life is short, shorter than a newborn calf's horns. Need to use it better."

396

"Got something in mind, Silas?" his brother-in-law asked, immediately suspicious. He certainly wasn't accustomed to his crusty brother-in-law revealing his inner thoughts, never mind anything profound.

"Setting there with Joshua's leg in front of me started me thinking. What could I do? Can't move out here to take care of his cows, can I?"

"Worse yet," Jason chimed in. "If it happened to you, you'd be in that Morris chair in the living room starving to death. You don't know how to do anything bookish. Joshua will pull this off."

"If the gangrene doesn't set in," Henry said with a frown, instantly upset with himself for letting the word out of his mouth.

"Seth Potter is taking care of all that. And he even consulted with a veterinarian in the city to find out what treatments were used on animals with a mashed leg," Jason countered. "He's taken it all very seriously."

"For years he had his eye on Ruthann Harty," Silas said. "Months ago, he saved her for him and now he's saved him for her. Gotta give the man credit."

The men stopped talking, Jason concentrating on the horses and Henry Goodnow wondering if he'd heard Silas right. The man had come a far piece in the years since Rose had stood up to him and delivered her declaration of independence. Right in his store. He still thought of that afternoon with a certain wonderment. And now Silas Hibbard had opened up to share inner thoughts. Henry thought he might never again be surprised by anyone or anything. He would have much to tell Edith tonight.

Back at the Chittenden farm, Rose and Ruthann were calmly establishing a routine that would include Abby and Charles and keep the household on an even keel. The kitchen had been put in order, Newton and Charles had finished the barn chores at this place, and now they were at the other house to get things straight there. All had agreed that the noon meal would be shared every day to save time. It would be wise, Ruthann felt, to create a space when they could share and give everyone a chance to say what was going right and what wasn't.

"You'll have to speak up," Ruthann said in her best schoolmarm voice, "when you hit a bump in the road. That's not complaining. We'll have no complaining, but we need to smooth out the bumps." She went on to assign times of day when each would check on Joshua. These were essential and not to be missed, she said. No one mentioned out loud all the things that might go wrong with him. But visions of fever, infection or falling were uppermost in the adults' minds.

Rose smiled, remembering when that voice had made her sit a little straighter in her seat at school. Abby and Charles's shoulders had twitched a bit as they listened, but she had never seen them more serious. She heard herself sigh and wished she hadn't, but only Ruthann noticed. Rose knew, at that moment, that they would all make this work. It was what they did, as Grandmother Jane would say, when the chips were down, whatever that meant. She didn't think it had anything to do with the wood chips that made it easier to start a fire. But she could not let her mind wander off on some word trail now. Ruthann was still talking.

"If you don't have a time piece, best to check in early rather than late. And call for help if you need it."

"Especially," Joshua said wryly, "if I've tipped over. Or can no longer feel my toes. Seth said, above all, I must mind my toes, right along with my P's and Q's. Are they capitalized, Ruthann, the P's and Q's?"

That made everyone laugh, and it was as if a wisp of late summer air had slipped through the room. Yes, Rose told herself again, they'd do it, whatever it turned out to be.

CHAPTER THIRTY-SEVEN
Moon Watching

Well before dusk, Abby cornered Rose in the Chittendens' small pantry and said, in a pleading tone, "I think you have a secret, and I hope I'm right, and I want you to tell me."

Rose put down the flour sack she was holding and put her arms around her sister. Her words came so fast that Abby felt her own mind speed up to keep up. "It's the best secret, and you need to keep it for a little while, and I don't know how you knew but, yes, we're having a baby and it's so exciting and sometimes I feel I will burst with not telling and sometimes I don't want to share with anyone." She paused, laughed, and said, "Except Ruthann, who guessed anyway, just like you."

"I am so glad," Abby said, pulling away and clapping her hands like an excited child. And then, because she sometimes still felt like a little sister, added, "And Charles don't know."

"Doesn't," Rose said, smiling as she realized it was such a treat for Abby to know something her brother hadn't tumbled to. "You can let on to Newton that you know, if you like."

That will be as delicious as a cherry pie, Abby thought. My sharing such a secret with Rose and Newton, and Charles not knowing yet. Perhaps they'll let me tell him, she thought, and wondered if that was a streak of meanness popping up. She decided not to ask about that. It was such a grand secret. So she hugged Rose again and gave her belly a little pat. "Sleep well in there," she said and opened the door to go, leaving Rose wiping her eyes and thinking she really had to get past crying, whether it was for either joy or sadness. No one needed a weepy wife, sister or friend right now.

When it was nearly dark, Rose took a lantern from Ruthann's pantry shelf and made her way across the field toward her own house. John, Adelaide and Abby were sound asleep in their own house, and Charles had hauled a mattress downstairs for Joshua and Ruthann. It was too soon to take that leg upstairs. Then Charles made himself as comfortable as possible on the floor of the Chittendens' bedroom, determined to keep an ear out if anyone called for help. With a shoulder against a hard floorboard, it occurred to him that his cow had better bedding.

After tossing about for an hour, he sat up and quietly crawled over to the east window. A slim edge of the moon curved over the cornstalks near Joshua's barn, and he sat back on his heels to watch. He wondered what Grace was doing. Perhaps she was looking out, too. He stretched the fingers on his right hand, remembering how hers had felt when they went walking. He would kiss her next time. He would. He might even take her to Rose's rock and kiss her there, right where he'd seen Newton kiss Rose. He hoped no one would spy on him.

Downstairs, Joshua asked Ruthann if they could sit on the porch. She was tired, but she immediately went to help him off the sofa, saw to it that his crutches were properly in place and lit one of the big lanterns. They settled in rocking chairs with a stool for his leg and simultaneously reached out to each other.

Holding hands, they did not speak while the moon rose. It wasn't full, but it was very bright in a cloudless sky and in unison they sighed.

"Synchronicity," Ruthann said. "I hope yours wasn't sad."

"Contented," Joshua said. "Surprisingly."

"We will be all right," she answered. "But I wish I knew whether those men were safely home."

In Eastborough, all three men were not only home but nearly finished with their evening chores. When Jason had given feed and fresh water to his Pekin chickens, he hooked the door to their coop, then pulled the big barn door shut, dropped the wooden bar in place and stood on the old stone step for a minute to watch the moon rise. It must truly create madness, he thought. I'm here like a youngster thinking about Mehitabel and whether she'd marry an old fool like me – for company and for the sake of her child. He grinned then and said aloud, "Reckon I'd better admit the selfish part, my sweet Nell. Make my life easier, too." And for the first time, it came to him that Nell would have agreed.

Silas had hurried through his chores, promising himself he'd neaten up extra in the morning. He drew a pail of water from the barn faucet, and a picture of Sarah flashed through his mind. She'd so wanted running water in the kitchen, and he'd been a stubborn fool about it, waiting until she was gone and then tapping into the town supply anyway. He spilled out the water in the chicken coop and refilled the trough. He added grain to their feeder, then reached a hand under a nesting hen and fetched a warm egg. He went up the path toward the house, thinking about Joshua and Newton and Rose. He wondered if she was with child. Sarah always said you could tell by the circles under the eyes, but he reckoned the fatigue of recent weeks could have done that, too. He hoped troubles were over for the Chittenden farm group, but he knew something else would come. He decided he'd call on Hattie as soon as he washed up. He quickened his step and came around the corner to find Hattie Munson walking down his driveway.

"Fancy meeting you here," he started to say. But she interrupted him by saying she'd seen the wagon go by and was anxious to know how he'd found things at the Chittenden house. While he was telling her, she took the egg, put it on the back step, linked her arm in his and turned him around, heading back toward the barn.

"What are you up to?" he asked. "I've pretty much finished the chores for now."

"Moon-watching," she said with a smile. They reached the big pasture gate, and when she put her foot on the first rail, he boosted her up to the top and joined her there, just as the moon appeared. Hesitantly, Silas put his arm around her and was relieved when she inched a little closer to him. Life was indeed damnably short, and he'd already wasted quite a chunk of it, he thought again. He leaned over, pushed her hat up and kissed her, feeling shy as a boy who'd just started to shave. But she put her hand on the back of his neck and kissed him back, her mouth soft as a horse's nose. When she pulled away, he looked at her with surprise and reckoned he wouldn't mention the horse's nose part. They went back to watching the moon push its way into the dark sky.

Meanwhile, Rose had reached her house and found Newton sprawled in the Morris chair, sound asleep. She shook his shoulder and said, "Better do that upstairs, sir."

"Nope," he answered, sitting up straight. "Going to take the sliver out to see tonight's moon. It's not full, but it's thinking about it."

"The moon doesn't think," Rose answered, nodding eagerly in spite of her fatigue.

"You're sure of that, I suppose?" he countered. And out they went, past the barn to a flat section of the stone wall Newton had built. When he picked her up and set her down on the wall, she was surprised to find the stones quite soft. He had already been here. She was sitting on a thick blanket.

Rose threw her arms around his neck while he was still on the ground and she was face to face with him. They kissed softly, then intensely, paused to look at each other and kissed again. Then Newton hopped onto the wall, and they swung around to find the moon looking down on them.

"Not full," Rose agreed, teetering back and forth to straighten her skirt. "It's more like an egg than a circle. Something not there on the left side." She stared at the moon, the same moon everyone else on the planet would see, but not Sarah. Not Nell. She felt tears coming and willed them to stop.

Sensing her sudden change of mood, Newton put one arm around her and laid the other hand across her belly. "Is everything all right in there?" he asked, a tinge of anxiety in his voice. "We haven't given that child much rest these past few weeks."

"The sliver," she said recovering quickly, "apparently enjoys a ripping good horse ride and a dramatic homecoming. My only problem is kerosene. It seems to bring on the sickness. The sliver is more content with candles or darkness."

"Rather like the darkness myself," Newton said. "It will be good for you to go to bed every day as soon as the sun sets, and I will keep you company."

Rose shot him a quick look, but his face in the waning light was bland, not teasing. Then she moved his hand toward her left side, and he jumped, startled.

"What was that?"

"The sliver," she answered. "And Abby's guessed, so you can tell anyone you want, as long as I don't have to hide in the kitchen for the next few months."

He leaped off the wall, lifted her down and turned her toward the moon. He pulled her close, his arms crossed over her belly and said, "When will it move again?" He put one hand inside her pocket, hoping to have another meeting with this wonder. Rose leaned back against him and said, "I can't tell it to move; it has a mind of its own already." And then he felt it, just a ripple under the fabric of her skirt, and a shiver went down his spine.

"No hiding," he said, his voice cracking a little. She twisted her head to look up at him, and he whispered, "Go wherever you want, as long as you don't run away." She nodded and said, "Only if you come, too." And leaned back to kiss him while the moon turned from pale peach to silver.

About the Author

As a newspaper reporter and columnist, Ruth Bass has been telling the stories of real people for a long time. A descendant of generations of New Englanders, she has also listened all her life to people like the characters in *Sarah's Daughter, Rose* and *A Silver Moon for Rose*. She is also author of eight herbal cookbooks and continues to write her weekly column for The Berkshire Eagle in Pittsfield, Massachusetts.

A resident of the Berkshires for more than 50 years, she has won many awards for writing and editing and has been inducted into the New England Press Association's Hall of Fame. She is a graduate of Bates College and Columbia Graduate School of Journalism and has an honorary doctorate of humane letters from Westfield State University. She and her late husband, novelist Milton Bass, have three adult children and six grandchildren. In addition to writing and reading, she enjoys gardening, knitting, cooking, photography, travel and golf. Her web site is www.ruthbass.com.